Outlier

ALSO BY SUSIE TATE

Daydreamer

Gold Digger

Outlier

SUSIE TATE

Arndell

OUTLIER

This edition has been published by Arndell,
an imprint of Keeperton, in 2025.
1527 New Hampshire Ave. NW
Washington, D.C. 20036

10 9 8 7 6 5 4 3 2 1

ISBN: 978-1-923232-16-7 (Paperback)

Library of Congress Control Number: 2025932705

Printed in the United States of America

Edited by Joanna Edwards
Proofread by Gwendylan Quinn
Formatted by Kirby Jones
Cover design by Arndell
Cover image by Vitalii Arkhypenko, Unsplash

Sydney | Washington D.C. | London
www.keeperton.com/arndell

For all the outliers.

CONTENT WARNING

This novel contains descriptions of assault, domestic violence and past childhood neglect and abuse. Please read at your own discretion.

Author's Note

It was very important to me to portray Vicky in a sensitive and respectful way. I have been a doctor in the NHS for the last 20 years and have looked after many neurodivergent patients during this time, whether this was for physical, mental health or social issues. Some of these patients were on the severe end of the spectrum, and some had much milder forms; all were very different to each other, and all had their own challenges. There are also wonderful Autistic people in my personal life.

So, whilst I do have some experience with neurodiversity, I am not Autistic myself. This did cause me to hesitate before writing a story from an Autistic person's perspective. So before I embarked on the book, I did extensive research on neurodiversity to expand my knowledge base and hopefully enable me to give Vicky an authentic voice. I have also been helped significantly by wonderful sensitivity readers and very kind readers from my ARC team with lived experience of Autism. Their feedback was invaluable, and I really hope that Vicky's story resonates with readers.

However, Vicky is an individual with an additional background of complex childhood trauma, and I do not in any way mean to generalise about other Autistic people whose experiences may be very different.

Thank you so so much to all the wonderful readers who have helped with Vicky's story.

I hope you enjoy it!

CHAPTER 1

Six minutes and forty-five seconds

Vicky

I glanced at the large digital clock next to my front door and frowned. He was three minutes and forty-eight seconds late. Maybe he wasn't coming? I shook my head in short jerks—that was an illogical assumption. Of course he was coming. The man needed to make money – I'd looked into his company accounts and verified that this was the case – and I was paying him *a lot* of money.

The fact that he still did his own deliveries made absolutely no sense. This was something he needed to contract out. His time would be much better spent creating the beautiful furniture he made.

My mind flashed to the glimpse I'd had of him in his workshop a couple of months ago, and my mouth went dry.

I'd been with Lucy, Lottie and Hayley in Little Buckingham looking for a small, runaway pony (a bizarre but actually not uncommon occurrence in Little Buckingham). Lucy had thought that Legolas might have made a beeline for her brother's workshop to "piss him right off". The pony wasn't there, but Mike was, and as always, he looked incredible. His flannel shirt was wrapped around his waist, and he had a tight thermal covering his upper body as he sanded down a large table, his muscles rippling under the material with each pass. He'd smiled at Lucy, Lottie and Hayley, but also as always, when he looked at me, his smile dropped. Mike didn't really like me. To be honest, not a lot of people did. But I was hoping maybe I could change that. Lucy and Lottie had bolstered my confidence enough over the last few months to start believing it was possible at least.

When I brought my hand up to smooth my hair, I noticed it was shaking. I clenched my jaw in frustration. I could not have a meltdown. Not now. Not with him four minutes and twenty-two seconds late.

So I did the breathing exercises Abdul had taught me and balled my hands into fists to stop the tremors. When I shifted on my feet, I felt my muscles protest. I'd been standing in this same spot facing my front door for the last forty-nine minutes, so still and tense, that now, everything had stiffened. I was aware that standing still in one's corridor for nearly an hour, staring at a door, was not normal behaviour, but normal behaviour was not exactly my forte.

When I became hyperfocused on something, my quirks slipped into downright weird territory. And it was fair to say that when it came to Mike, I was *extremely* hyperfocused. I was almost more obsessed with Mike Mayweather than I was with hedgehogs.

Almost.

The problem was that the more hyperfocused I became, the more my behaviour deteriorated into the less-than-normal zone. I did not want Mike to think I was less than normal when he already didn't like me.

My throat tightened as I went over one of the causes for his aversion to me. My memory can be very useful. I can recall events, conversations, and everything I've ever read or seen with perfect clarity. Academically, this is a huge advantage.

However, when you've done something so awful and incorrect that you'd rather forget it completely, the ability to replay it entirely, down to the tiniest detail is not useful; it's a curse.

I could still picture Lucy Mayweather's face the day we threw all those awful accusations at her and then threw *her* out of the office. I could also picture the surveillance footage we recovered of Lucy being assaulted only seconds before. My brain tended to dwell on upsetting things despite how illogical that might be. As a consequence, I'd replayed Will Brent throwing Lucy against the office wall, and her head bouncing against the plaster too many times to count.

So no, Mike did not like me, not after that. When he'd later stormed into the office, stomping through the carefully controlled environment in his steel-capped work boots, all six-foot-four inches of him vibrating with fury over what we'd allowed to happen to Lucy, I'd never seen anything as magnificent in my entire life. I thought I was defective in that area. Well, I was defective in a lot of areas, truth be told, but with men, particularly so.

Until I saw Mike Mayweather that day, I couldn't imagine ever voluntarily letting someone put their mouth on mine, let alone all the *other stuff*. But when it came to Mike, all I could think about was what his lips would feel like, whether his beard was scratchy or soft, and how his large body would feel on top of mine.

After years of believing that I was dead when it came to attraction, my attraction to Mike had become all I could think about. Hence, my standing stock still in the corridor, staring at my front door.

For fifty-two minutes.

I closed my eyes to focus on my breathing again, but they snapped open when the door suddenly shook with two loud pounding knocks. Without thinking, I instantly pulled it open to stare at a huge, flannel-covered chest.

He was right there. So close, I could smell him.

Now, I was very sensitive to scent in general and quite intolerant of most, especially when related to other human beings. But Mike's clean, woodsy, manly scent was so good, it made me feel light-headed for a moment. That, combined with the outline of his muscular chest in another tight thermal under said flannel shirt, worked together to short-circuit my brain. All I could do was stare at his chest. Which was weird, and I so, *so* wanted *not* to be weird in front of this man.

He cleared his throat, and my gaze shot from his chest to his angry brown eyes with their thick eyelashes. The eyelashes were incongruous with the rest of his extremely rugged appearance—thick beard, which was in no way sculpted like the other men of my acquaintance, messy brown hair a few days past needing a cut, tanned skin weathered from all the time he spent outdoors.

I'd never seen anything so beautiful.

"You going to stand there staring at me all day, princess?" he asked in his growly voice. He didn't say *princess* in a nice way, but he did at least leave off the "ice" part.

I hated that nickname. *Ice princess*. I knew what it implied—that I was stuck-up, aloof, and I thought I was better than everyone else. I knew that was Mike's opinion of me too. But this encounter was supposed to change all that. I was wearing actual jeans, for God's sake. Granted, Lottie had had to trial dozens of pairs for me until she found one soft enough for me to tolerate, and even then, I was still really uncomfortable and desperate to be back in my fleece-lined tights, or even better, my buttery soft leggings. But the idea of these jeans was to make me look normal.

In fact, my entire carefully crafted appearance was trying to achieve that aim, from my "messy bun" which had taken me the best part of an hour and involved processing no fewer than five hours of YouTube videos, to my "natural look" make-up, to the relaxed cream jumper, which was just on the wrong side of itchy – itchiness was a real problem for me but I decided that if could put up with the jeans, then I could tolerate the jumper as well. I'd even debated whether I needed to wear sexy underwear. There was no way I would have been able to tolerate lace or any underwiring, but I could maybe, *maybe* have dealt with satin if push came to shove. Instead, I decided to stay with my normal seamless cotton super-soft bra and knickers for now.

I didn't think Mike would accept my proposal initially. He'd likely have a period of consideration, and I could then work up to tolerating uncomfortable underwear so that I'd be ready to wear it at a predetermined place and time.

"You're six minutes and forty-five seconds late."

Yes, that is what I said to him. I am a socially incompetent person, but that was bad, even for me. The trouble was I had a terrible habit of stating facts as they popped into my head. And in my experience, people didn't want to have the unabridged truth foisted on them regularly. It was just one of the various ways I lacked social skills. I did not have the ability to lie, not even white lies.

Now, if everyone functioned like me, that would be fine. With white lies and half-truths eliminated, we could all live in honest harmony, being completely straight with each other at all times, and not taking offence to other people simply stating facts.

But the world was not full of Vickys. We were a rarity. And we were considered rude.

Mike crossed his impressive arms over his chest, his muscles bunching under his shirt as he did it, and his expression darkened.

"Christ, can we just get this over with then?" he snapped. "I wouldn't want to waste any more of your precious seconds than strictly necessary."

I stared up at him and blinked. "I have cleared my entire day for this delivery," I said, yet again, blindly stating the truth without thinking through the consequences.

His eyebrows shot up. "For fuck's sake, why?"

I opened my mouth to speak but then closed it again, just catching myself in time before I could blurt out that I'd spent the entire morning making myself look "normal," and that I was hoping he would be willing to negotiate terms with me this afternoon.

"You say the f-word a lot." This observation is what popped out of my mouth instead, and from his eye roll, it wasn't a lot better than the other options. It's not that I minded swearing; I didn't. But for me, it was too difficult a minefield to negotiate. If you incorporated swear words into your regular vocabulary, you had to have the social awareness and emotional intelligence to know when it was appropriate and when it was not. I had neither social awareness nor emotional intelligence, so I chose to simply avoid swearing altogether.

"Sorry if I've offended your delicate sensibilities, Lady Harding. But if we could move this along, my sweary uncouth carcass will be out of your hair a lot sooner."

He said *Lady Harding* the same way he'd said princess—with undisguised contempt. I wasn't sure if it was just contempt for me or for the peerage system as a whole. I mean, he was friends with my half-brother Ollie, who was the Duke of Buckingham, so I doubted it was only the peerage he objected to. No, Mike Mayweather simply didn't like me.

I doubt he remembered, but he'd never liked me. It had been obvious even on the handful of occasions I was around him as a child. And, back then I had been far less objectionable. I didn't go around stating obvious truths as a child. In fact, I did not speak at all. It was one of the many ways in which I was a disappointment to my mother.

After I stopped speaking, she decided she'd had enough of my constant silent presence in her new family and started dropping me off at my biological father's house for part of the summer holidays.

The trouble with that was that my biological father, the previous Duke of Buckingham, wasn't that keen on me either—

and he also wasn't home a lot. This meant that I became his wife Margot's problem, which seemed supremely unfair, seeing as I was the product of the affair Margot's husband had while still married to her. But she couldn't very well put a six-year-old child out on the street, so I was welcomed, however grudgingly, into the family home for a maximum of two weeks every summer.

The first time I saw Mike Mayweather was at Buckingham Manor, and he was carrying a hedgehog in his bare hands.

"Sorry, Lady Harding," he'd muttered to my stepmother, when blood dripped from his hands onto her rug. "It's just, I found it out in the daytime, and that can mean it's sick." The sight of that large, rough boy gently cradling a tiny creature and not caring that the spikes were ripping his hands to shreds has stayed imprinted on my brain ever since.

The handful of times I followed Ollie to the Mayweather cottage, Mike scowled at me from across the small kitchen, clearly unhappy that I was invading his space. Mike's mum was an extremely kind woman and didn't seem to mind that I didn't talk, or that I only ate the tops of the Jaffa Cakes and would only drink tea out of one specific mug. She also gave the type of hugs I could tolerate—brief, tight side hugs.

I really, *really* liked Hetty Mayweather.

Despite Mike's obvious dislike of me, even back then, he still fascinated me. And unfortunately, I hadn't fully mastered my habit of staring at things I found fascinating as a child. In fact, I hadn't really been able to mask at all—my only saving grace being the mutism.

"I'm not a Lady," I told Mike as he continued to stare down at me.

He shook his head once. "What are you—?"

"I'm not Lady Harding," I explained. "My father didn't pass his title onto me because I'm illegitimate."

His scowl dropped slightly, and he shifted on his feet. "Oh," he said as his arms uncrossed, before he reached back to grip the back of his neck, revealing that glorious chest even more, as his flannel shirt pulled to the side. He cleared his throat. "Right, sorry, love. Didn't think."

At the use of the word love, my gaze shot from its fixation on his chest, to his eyes. There was a softness about them now as he looked down at me, which hadn't been there before. That, combined with his use of an actual endearment, short-circuited my brain again. I could feel my pulse beating in my ears as a wave of light-headedness swept through me. Seconds ticked by until eventually, Mike had enough.

"Okay, if you could move back a little, then I'll..."

It happened when he put his large hands on my shoulders in order to manoeuvre me out of the doorway, as I'd clearly lost the ability to do this myself. He didn't grab me; his touch was gentle, and there was nothing threatening about it. But I wasn't prepared. I *have* to be prepared when people touch me. So, despite how much I'd been dreaming about Mike putting his hands on me, when it actually happened, I yelped and wrenched away from him.

My hands went up, and it took all of my effort and training to stop them from flapping and pressing onto my ears. When I finally got my breathing under control and was sure I wasn't going into a meltdown, I looked up at Mike to see he'd backed away from me with his hands up, a horrified expression on his face.

I swallowed and tried to speak, but as was often the case when I was stressed, no words would actually make it past my tight throat.

"Bloody hell," he snapped. His horror now bleeding into anger. "Chill the fuck out. I wasn't going to attack you. You're the last woman I'd—" He broke off then, but I knew what he was going to say.

I desperately wanted to explain my reaction to him, but aside from the fact I physically couldn't speak at that moment, even if I could, what would I have told him? That I wanted him to touch me more than I've ever wanted anything in my life, but that I needed warning because I was so unbelievably weird? The whole point of today was to try to convince him I *wasn't* weird so he'd agree to my terms. Admitting to all my ridiculously complicated quirks would hardly be working towards that aim.

CHAPTER 2

Empty inside

Mike

"Look, *Miss* Harding," I said through gritted teeth. "If you wouldn't mind standing back from the doorway, then I can actually do what I came here to do and then get gone and leave you in peace."

There it was—that beautiful, blank stare again. I tamped down my irritation and decided to just get the fuck on with it whether she was cooperating or not. Once I'd delivered the bloody coffee table, I could bugger off and hopefully go back to avoiding Victoria Harding again.

I turned away from her, jogged down the stone steps of her fancy bloody townhouse, and picked up the bespoke coffee table that I'd poured countless hours into building, then shaping, sanding and varnishing, only to have it wasted on this ice-cold woman.

"I can help you carry it."

I looked back up the steps at her standing in the doorway. What a bloody waste. The woman was absolutely stunning. Her beauty was almost otherworldly. And today, wearing those fitted jeans with her hair not in its usual severe, scraped-back style, the blonde tendrils framing her face, and her tiny bare feet visible with perfect bright pink nails, she was a knockout.

But it was still a waste because the woman's personality was, well, non-existent. Her nickname was dead-on accurate; she was the absolute *definition* of an ice princess. Not my style at all.

Unfortunately, for whatever fucked-up reason, she had gotten it into her head that I *was* her style. Even that day when I'd stormed into Felix's office to bollock them all for what they'd done to my sister, even then, distracted as I was by my anger, I'd noticed her staring at me. Christ, the woman could stare. It was seriously creepy if you asked me.

At least, that's what I told myself.

And I could just about manage it if I forced my brain to forget the dreams of her that plagued me at night.

In my dreams, she was anything but cold.

"She's just a little fixated on you."

Lucy's explanation floated back to me. Er, okay. I'm not the kind of guy you develop a fixation with. I'm not like Felix or Ollie—sophisticated, three-piece-suit-wearing pretty boys. I'm rough and ready, with an overgrown beard and questionable dress sense.

Girls like Vicky fixated on men like me for one thing—they wanted a walk on the wild side with a bit of rough. *That's* why she was fixated on me. And now she'd ordered one of my favourite pieces simply to mess with me. There was no way I could have anyone else deliver this, not after I'd spent hours and hours perfecting it. Even if it was going to an automaton who wouldn't appreciate art if it slapped her in the face, I still didn't want it to be damaged.

"No offence," I shouted back up to her, well aware that I was fully intending to cause offence. "But you'd be about as much help as a chocolate teapot. This table would crush you. I'll carry it in if you could do me a favour and move out of the bloody way."

Thankfully she did move back in time for me to make it into her fancy fucking house, but then gave no further indication of where she wanted the table to go.

Now, this thing was solid; all my pieces were solid and bloody heavy. It was uncomfortable to stand in the middle of someone's hallway, holding one up in the air, not knowing where to set it down. But this goddamn ice princess just carried on staring at me.

I opened my mouth to say something, then snapped it shut as I noticed the little cracks in the icy persona showing through. Her pupils dilated, and very briefly, she bit her full, pink bottom lip as her eyes traced the muscles bunched and straining on my chest and arms as I kept this bloody table suspended in midair.

"Eyes up here, princess," I said, my voice rougher than it should be, but who could blame me? She was a beautiful woman, and she was blatantly checking me out. And the memories of Dream Vicky were increasingly tricky to suppress.

Immediately, her eyes snapped to mine, and then another more human sign peeped through as pink stained her cheeks.

"If you're quite finished, do you think you could tell me where this is going to go?"

She cleared her throat. "Oh, you can put it down here."

I frowned. "You're going to have a massive bloody coffee table sitting in the middle of your hallway?"

She shrugged. "I hadn't really thought where it would go."

I grunted with the effort of holding up the table, shifting it slightly in my arms. "I'm no expert on interior design, but most people have coffee tables in their sitting rooms."

"I already have a coffee table in there."

"Right." I drew the word out. We weren't getting anywhere here, and I needed to set this thing down. "So why the fuck did you order another one?"

"I wanted to see you."

Bloody hell, she was bold. No pretence. No trying to make any excuses. Just a straight out, fucked-up admission. I had to admire the woman's balls, at least.

Seeing as we were going to get nowhere with the entire *where's the table going* debate, and given I couldn't think straight whilst my arms were screaming at me, I decided to put it down between us. Then I shook out my arms and cracked my neck before focusing back on the small woman in front of me.

She was still staring, but closer up, her expression didn't look so blank anymore. No, closer up, I could see all sorts of things working behind her crystal blue eyes, and I could feel the intensity of her focus.

The coffee table was separating us, but I was near enough to make out just a hint of her lavender scent, not overpowering like some perfumes, but very subtle, and for some reason, it made the hairs on the back of my neck stand up.

"Let me get this straight," I said slowly. "You ordered a two-thousand-pound coffee table just so that you could see *me*?"

"I also admired the table, very much. But yes, my main motivation was to have a private discussion with you."

My eyebrows shot up. "What the fuck have you got to talk to *me* about in a *private discussion*?"

She bit her lip again, and I had the sudden and unexpected urge to reach over and pull her bottom lip free of her teeth. What the hell was wrong with me?

"I find you extremely attractive."

There it was again—absolutely no filter on this woman. She didn't say it in a low, breathy, needy voice. She stated it as an absolute, with no distinguishable emotion behind the statement at all. Almost as though she were approaching some sort of business transaction, which pissed me off when all I could think about was dragging her onto the stupid bloody table I'd made for her and stripping her out of her jeans.

"This has not gone unnoticed, princess," I said in a low voice. Her cheeks stained even pinker at that, and I had to clench my hands into fists to stop myself from reaching for her. "But, for the love of God, why does that mean you order furniture you don't need?"

"My attempts to approach you have so far been unsuccessful," she said, still in that odd business-like tone. "This appeared to be the most expedient option."

My eyebrows went up. "Ordering a fucking expensive one-of-a-kind coffee table was the only way you could think of to talk to me?"

"Yes." She gave a firm nod. "Especially given that we are never alone, and we have never had a direct conversation before. My half-brother is extremely protective. He does not really approve of my… fixation with you."

I smirked at that. "I bet he doesn't. Not surprised he doesn't approve of the likes of me."

"The likes of you?" she asked.

I chuckled.

"Princess, I'm about as rough as they come. There's no way the Duke of Fuckingham would want me anywhere *near* his sister."

"Half-sister."

I shrugged. What was with all the half-sister, half-brother bollocks? Who cared? Clearly Ollie didn't see her as any less than a sister. It seemed cold. But then, this chick's personality was positively Arctic.

"Okay," I said, losing patience with this entire aggravating conversation. "Here I am then. What did you want to say to me?"

She cleared her throat and then swallowed before speaking again. The only indication that she was nervous was the slight shake to her hand as she pushed her hair behind her ear.

"C-can we sit down? Maybe you could come to the kitchen? I could make you a cup of tea as per social protocol."

As per social protocol? What the hell was wrong with her?

"Just spit it out, princess," I said. "I've had a long day, and you're not my only delivery."

"Oh." She stared at me again, and I didn't bother suppressing my sigh. "Okay. Well, as I was saying—I find you very attractive, and as such, I was wondering if you might be open to… to progressing things on a physical level and—"

"Is that a fancy way of saying you want to fuck me?"

Vicky blinked. It was the only indication that what I said got to her at all. "Well, yes that would be part of the—"

I felt my temper spike. I'd always had a bit of a temper, and if I was honest, a slight chip on my shoulder about people born with silver spoons in their mouths. This woman thought that because she could probably buy and sell me and my entire family, that gave her leave to do and say whatever she wanted. Rich people were entitled: she found me attractive, so she felt entitled to snap her fingers and bang me.

"Let me get this straight," I said through gritted teeth. "You get me here on false pretences when you don't even *need* a goddamn coffee table. Then you proceed to make some sort of fucked-up pass at me because you're bored with your rich pretty boys, and you fancy a bit of rough?"

Her eyes went wide, and I was gratified that I was cracking that icy persona and extracting even more of a reaction.

"N-no," she said.

I would never have called her tone hesitant, but compared to the way she spoke before, I could just about make out that quality.

"You misunderstand me. It's actually quite common when someone like you interacts with someone like me. You see I—"

"Someone like me?" I said in a low, furious voice. "What the fuck is that supposed to mean?"

"W-well you and I, we're very different, and it might be hard for you to fully understand what I—"

"Just because I do a manual job does not mean that I'm stupid, princess."

"Of course not. If you would just listen, you would understand—"

"I understand perfectly. You want some fun with a bit of rough, and I'm not interested."

"But… but you *are* interested in me physically."

Oh, wow. This bitch certainly had a high opinion of herself.

I crossed my arms over my chest. "Is that right?"

She blinked at me. "Yes, the evidence would point to the fact that you find me physically attractive."

"Evidence?" How had she gathered any evidence? I'd barely ever spoken to the woman.

"Yes. When I was at the pool in Little Buckingham in a bikini, you spent a large percentage of your time looking at me, and you had to use one of Margot's outdoor throw cushions to cover your groin area after I got out of the pool."

It was my turn to blink at her now. Words stuck in my throat as a vision of Vicky in that barely there bikini floated through my mind. I was ashamed to say that Vicky emerging from the pool, soaking wet in that bikini, had been my go-to when I was on my own late at night, for quite some time. And it annoyed me. It annoyed me even more that she had noticed.

I felt my face heat up and thanked God for my thick beard. It was rare that I got embarrassed, but this woman had managed it. And, fuck my life, she wasn't even finished.

"Your gaze will often shift to me in a group. Your pupils dilate when I look at you directly. And you have been observed 'staring at my arse,' as Lottie put it, which I understand is a surefire way of distinguishing sexual interest. Also, I'm aware that I am, in general, physically attractive to men. I have been aware of this fact since I went through puberty at around fourteen years old."

"Wow, you've got a pretty high opinion of yourself."

She frowned. "On the contrary, I don't—"

"Well, I've got news for you, princess," I said, my tone now full of the anger she'd stirred up for being so beautiful but so unbelievably cold.

Anger at all the bloody rich people I'd known who thought they could walk all over me and treat me like shit. But most of all, anger at the promise of her being nothing but a lie.

"I wouldn't touch you with a barge pole. You're beautiful, and yes, maybe my body *did* react when I saw you half-naked, but just because I had a physiological response to you doesn't mean I would be tempted to ever touch you. I like my women warm, cute, kind, able to express actual emotion and equipped with a personality. You… you're like a beautiful vase—great to look at but empty inside. I'm not so hard up that I'd fall into bed with someone like you just because you made my dick hard once when you wore a bikini. So you can stop with this bullshit staring at me all the time. Stop fantasising about roughing it and go back to the pretty boys you *should* be fucking."

Nothing about her expression changed as I spoke to her. Not one flicker of emotion. So maybe I *had* let my anger get the best of me, but it wasn't like anything I said affected her. I slapped the delivery receipt down on the coffee table, which she did react to with a brief flinch.

"It's been real, princess," I muttered as I turned and stalked out of her house.

I didn't look back, but I should have.

I should have bloody well looked back.

CHAPTER 3

Is Vicky okay?

Vicky

The doorbell was going again. I registered it in the back of my mind, but, just like the last few times, I simply couldn't get up.

I wasn't sure how long I'd been curled up there, but I knew it must have been a good few hours. In fact, thinking about it, it had been dark earlier, and it was light now. Had I been there overnight?

There was pounding on my door and some shouting from behind the thick wood, but it all sounded muffled to me, just like the sound of the doorbell had been.

When I got like this, I tended to shut down my senses to give my overactive brain a rest. It was like I zoned out of the real world for a while to keep out any pain. I wasn't good with pain.

I felt a rush of cold air and heard the door slam, registering that someone was in my house.

"Vics?" Ollie's voice filtered into my brain, but I still couldn't move. "Where the bloody hell... argh!" The table I was under jerked in a sudden movement, making me flinch. "What the fuck is this thing doing in the hallway?"

"Ollie," I heard Lottie say cautiously. "Look underneath."

I kept staring straight ahead, with my arms wrapped around my knees.

"Hey, Vics." Ollie's deep voice was close now. "What's going on?"

"We've been worried, sweetie," Lottie said from my other side. It was good Lottie and Ollie were finally together. They made each other happy. Anyone could see that. Just because that kind of happiness wasn't for me didn't mean I couldn't wish it for the people I loved. "I popped in this morning when you didn't show at work to check you were okay, but nobody was here... At least I *thought* nobody was here."

"Victoria Harding," Ollie said, using that bossy big brother tone he reserved for times he wanted Claire or me to listen to him. "How long have you been lying here under this thing? And why is one of Mike's coffee tables slap-bang in the middle of your hallway? I nearly broke my leg tripping over it."

Lottie cleared her throat. "Vicky, I really think you need to come out of there now. Have you eaten today?"

I could hear the worry in her tone. I didn't want Lottie to worry about me. I wanted to be able to reassure her that I was fine. To tell both of them that they could go. Just go and enjoy their happiness together. I didn't want to hold them back.

I was well aware of how much of a burden I was to Ollie. In fact, Mike's words really brought into sharp relief how much of a burden I must be to everyone. I started to feel a little panicky again when a vision of his face telling me how I was *empty inside* swam back into my consciousness.

His eyes, his beautiful eyes, were so full of disgust. He was disgusted... by me.

What on earth had I been thinking, asking him here? Of course, he wouldn't want to have anything to do with me. Of course, I wasn't good enough for him. The irony was, he didn't even know how much of a freak I actually could be. He seemed to think I was making some sort of sexual proposal to him, and that he'd been the next in a long line of men that I had worked my way through.

He had no idea that I'd never even kissed a man before. I was relieved that I hadn't told him anything more, as clearly the idea of being with me, even for some sort of physical-only affair was totally abhorrent to him. If I'd managed to articulate how I wanted to spend some time with him, then maybe, *maybe*, try physical intimacy. Maybe just a kiss.

He'd have laughed in my face.

At least I managed to salvage some pride from the entire horrendous situation.

"Vicky." Ollie's tone was still set at bossy. "I'm going to put my hand on your shoulder, darling. Okay?"

I wanted to shake my head, but I still couldn't get my body to cooperate with me. I needed to stay here and be very, very still. I didn't want anyone to pull me back into the real world. Not yet.

Ollie sighed.

"I can't leave you here, Vics," he said as his large hand settled on my shoulder.

My body did react to that, though. Even though he'd warned me, I still flinched away from him, jerking to the side to shake off his hand. My whole body screamed at me with that movement as my muscles had all seized up from being held still in one place for so long.

"You're okay, Vicky," Ollie continued in that bossy, determined tone. "You're going to be *fine*. We just need to get you out from under here."

"Ollie," Lottie said in a soft, concerned voice. "I'm not sure that's a good idea. Should we—?"

"No!" I shouted. Or at least, I tried to shout, but it came out as more of a weak, hoarse cry—my throat had seized up, and my mouth was dry from lack of fluids.

Ollie's arms were around me now, and he was dragging me out from under the table.

I fought him as much as I could with my seized-up muscles and weak protests, but Ollie was strong, and he easily pulled me out and up into his arms. I kept struggling against him as he carried me into the sitting room and sat down on one of my white sofas with me in his lap.

For a few minutes I carried on fighting, but his arms stayed tight around me, and eventually, I just simply didn't have the energy anymore. I closed my eyes and went limp in his hold, and he gathered me up closer to him, tight in his strong arms.

I wasn't good with light touch, couldn't ever hold hands with anyone, and needed warning before physical contact, but tight hugs like the one Ollie was giving me could unlock something inside me. Tight hugs from someone I trusted had the power to calm me down, even at the height of one of my meltdowns.

I hadn't cried all day. I'd just curled up under that table and stared into space, but now, with my half-brother's arms tight around me, and the feel of Lottie's hand on my back, I let the tears fall. I let myself soak Ollie's shirt as he swore softly and gathered me closer. There were no sobs or really, any sound. It was rare that I cried, but when I did, it was always silent.

My meltdowns when I was younger used to be quite loud. Until I was about six years old, if I became distressed and something triggered me, everyone knew about it—screaming, hands flapping, all sorts. But Mum made it very, very clear to me how unacceptable that was. So clear, that by the time I turned six, I was silent all the time, not just when I was having a meltdown.

Silence had seemed to be the best option for me. Anything I said was usually met with irritation or outright hostility, so I just gave up trying. I wasn't mute anymore, but if I did melt down, it was very rare for me to scream like I had when I was little.

The last time was when my half-sister from my mum's side of the family tricked me into coming out with her and her friends, telling me we were going to a quiet bar. The quiet bar had been a nightclub where you could actually feel the beat through the floor it was so loud.

Rebecca dragged me to the middle of the dance floor and then left me there with my hands over my ears in a crush of people. I couldn't move through the bodies around me, and it was so loud that I totally lost it. Luckily, a couple of girls, one of whom had an Autistic brother, noticed me on my knees with my hands over my ears, and helped me get out. By the time they put me in a taxi outside the club, I'd screamed myself so hoarse that I could barely say my home address. That was the only time in the last decade that I'd had an obvious meltdown, but that didn't mean I hadn't had them. It was just that now they were of the silent variety, exactly as it had happened this time.

I'm not sure how long Ollie held me on that sofa. I barely noticed when Lottie left to go and get her eight-year-old sister, Hayley, from school. Eventually I calmed down enough to let Ollie get me a cup of tea and some Jaffa cakes. I had to revert to my preferred method of just eating the tops off them, but I needed food, and it was better that than nothing.

Unfortunately by the time Lottie returned with Hayley, the silent tears had started up again, and Ollie had to pull me back into his side on the sofa.

"Is Vicky okay?" Hayley's little voice came from the doorway.

"She's fine, lovebug," Lottie said quietly.

"I don't think she's fine," Hayley said. She sounded closer now, and there was a thread of real worry in her tone.

The last thing I wanted was for Hayley to worry about me. Hayley was struggling herself. She'd only just partly recovered from her own long stint of mutism. Hayley and Lottie had enough problems without adding me into the mix.

"Vicky?" her hesitant little voice was right next to me now, and I felt her small hand join her sister's on my back.

I heard a sniffle behind me and realised that Lottie was crying too.

I swallowed and tried to slow my breathing like I'd been taught in therapy.

"S-sorry," I forced out through my tears, turning my head slightly so I could look at Lottie and Hayley. I tried to speak again, but my tight throat just wouldn't let me.

"Vics, we got a message on Hogwatch," Lottie finally said after a few more minutes of my silent crying.

I blinked a couple of times as my brain slowly shifted gears. As my thoughts moved to hedgehogs, the vice-like grip on my throat began to loosen. My hands unclenched from the fists they'd formed, releasing the handfuls of Ollie's shirt I'd been clutching, and I swiped away the tears from my face.

"What did it say?" I asked as I pushed up from my position buried in my half-brother's chest.

"I think there's a mum and babies in Dulwich out in the open. They're not sure whether to leave them or secure them for tonight."

I bit my lip.

"Did they send photos?"

"They did, but they don't show the hedgerow very clearly," Hayley told me.

Hayley was my little hedgehog protégée. I was training her up to be able to answer Hogwatch queries when I couldn't.

"Let me see," I said, my voice steady now, the tears drying on my face and neck.

Ollie's arms loosened sufficiently so I could move to sit next to him instead of on top of him, and I felt him let out a relieved exhale. Ollie worried about me. I tried to hide my worst meltdowns from him normally because I really didn't want Ollie to worry. It was years since he'd caught me like this. My chest still felt tight, but as I started to read the hog enquiry, my breathing evened out, and I began to feel calmer.

It wasn't until later, on my way to Dulwich with a cardboard box filled with straw on my lap, wearing my soft leggings instead of those horrid jeans, that I thought of Mike again, and I even managed a very small smile.

Which was worse: a stuck-up, upper-class, cold, rich woman who "wanted a bit of rough," as he put it, and felt nothing, or a weird, hedgehog-obsessed, neuro-diverse one who felt *everything* and fell in love with a man who hates her?

Neither were ideal, but for my pride's sake, I thought sticking with the first would be safer.

CHAPTER 4

If we knew the trigger

Mike

"Why are we in another one of your swanky places?" I grumbled, and Felix rolled his eyes.

"Mike, this is hardly *swanky*."

My eyebrows went up. "Maybe not by your standards, but you don't get bloody foliage on the tables at greasy spoons." I prodded the plant in front of me. "Certainly not real stuff, anyway."

"This area is not exactly teeming with greasy spoons, Mike. And there's nothing you could get at one of those that you can't order here."

"Ha, right. They'll bring me some thick-cut bacon and eggs swimming in grease with black pudding and beans on the side, will they?"

Felix wrinkled his nose at the mention of black pudding. "Your coronary arteries will thank you, Mike."

I snorted. "And what the fuck is acai? Oh my God, is this their version of a cooked breakfast? Almond dukkah? Are we the girls from *Sex and the City* all of a sudden? Fucking brunch. God. Oh, here's the Duke of Fuckingham. You two can get excited about your acai together now."

Ollie was on the phone as he walked over to our table with an intent expression on his face. He jerked his chin at both of us as he sat down but didn't hang up the call. Assuming he was doing his normal *Very Important Business* things, I looked back at the menu, but my head jerked back up when I heard her name.

"Isn't there anything on the menu that Vics would consider?" he asked and then sighed at whatever was said in response. "Have you tried the café around the corner?" He paused. "But could you get them to make it up without the packaging? Maybe bring the Tupperware she likes to put it in, so she wouldn't have to touch the paper?" He paused again for a moment, his head dropping forward as his frown deepened. His voice dropped so low that I had to strain to hear the next sentence. "She's lost way too much weight, Lottie. Maybe you could try to ask her again today. If we knew the trigger, we could work on sorting her out. Tread carefully, okay."

He paused, then his frown cleared as he smiled his *Lottie smile*. It was the sappiest, most pathetic expression I'd seen on my friend's face, ever.

Lottie had turned the Duke of Fuckingham into a giant teddy bear. He would do anything for her and her little sister.

"Okay, darling," he muttered and then rolled his eyes at me when I made a gagging gesture. "Gotta go. I've arrived at the restaurant, and Mike's being Mike." He paused and smiled that smile again. "Yeah, I'd like that, baby." His voice was lowered, and it was my turn to roll my eyes when he finally hung up the phone.

"Gross," I groaned. "Do we have to listen to you ear-fucking your girlfriend every time we go out now? Honestly, I think I just threw up in my mouth. Go home and bang her already if you can't get through one meal without hearing her voice."

"At least I've *got* someone to ear-fuck, you wanker," Ollie muttered.

Felix chuckled but managed to choke it down when I shot him a dark look—from the moment he started shagging my sister, he wasn't allowed to piss me off. He'd used up his pissing-me-off quota for the next decade, and the bastard knew it.

I gritted my teeth. Since my two best friends had gone all sappy, these meet-ups had become annoying. The bastards had started encouraging me to *find someone,* which just pissed me off even more. Of course, I wanted to find someone. Did they think I was happy holed up on my own in Little Buckingham? Did they think I appreciated the smug tone they used when they told me to stop shagging about and settle down? It wasn't as easy as that.

Yes, okay, the new barmaid at The Badger's Sett had made it clear she was up for it, and she was undeniably hot, but for the last few months I just didn't feel like flirting with women in general. I certainly didn't want to take them to bed. The only woman I saw when I closed my eyes was the last one I would ever consider.

I was stuck.

Just briefly, a vision of her hand shaking as she pushed her hair behind her ear that day swam into my brain. Her shaking hand and her slight stutter had been haunting me ever since. They were both so completely incongruous with the cool, emotionless woman I knew her to be that I just couldn't reconcile the two. Every time I thought about either, my chest would feel too tight, almost as if I couldn't breathe.

When I wasn't thinking about Dream Vicky, I was re-running the harsh words I'd said to real Vicky that day at her house, over and over again. Okay, so she'd pissed me off, but did I need to be that much of a prick about it?

When I thought I was dealing with the classic ice princess who just wanted to use me like a piece of meat, it hadn't seemed that bad. But that barest hint of vulnerability she'd displayed had me questioning everything.

"You making poor Lottie run around after that sister of yours again?" I asked, forcing my voice to casual indifference.

She's lost way too much weight.

That chest tightness was back again, and I frowned. Was Vicky on some sort of stupid rich-girl diet? I knew those types were prone to it—too wrapped up in their appearances to care about putting their health at risk by starving themselves. Christ, Vicky wouldn't actually starve herself, would she? I remembered a girl at school with anorexia who nearly died when I was a teenager. I looked up at Ollie because the fucker was taking too long to answer. He was staring at me with a frown on his face.

"Lottie doesn't 'run round after Vicky'," he said with an edge to his voice.

He'd always been protective of Vicky, even when we were kids. I hardly ever saw her back then, but the handful of times she did come to Mum's cottage, she didn't deign to speak to any of us. She'd barely even look at my little sister, who was a similar age, which just pissed me off, and she turned her nose up at my mum's cooking, which was the final straw in my young mind. For some reason Mum had to make her special sandwiches instead, adding to her already heavy workload by having to cater for yet another rich, entitled brat.

Ollie had always been cagey about her. When I'd asked him why she was such a snob, he just told me she was "a bit different" and wouldn't offer any further explanation. As I barely ever had contact with her anyway, I never brought it up again. I hadn't even seen her for over a decade until she and Felix threw my sister out of their office last year.

I snorted. "She's Vicky's assistant. Isn't that sort of the point?"

Ollie narrowed his eyes at me. "Lottie is Vicky's *executive* assistant, you dickhead. Not some sort of office gopher. Vicky needs Lottie for high-level stuff. Lottie's invaluable with her ability to read people. Vics, well she… let's just say reading people is not one of her strengths."

"If Lottie's so *high-level,* then why is she chasing around trying to get your sister the perfect lunch?"

Ollie broke eye contact and looked to the side as his jaw clenched. "She's not doing that because she works for Vics. She's doing it because she cares about her."

The waitress arrived before I could reply, and we all ordered from the fancy-schmancy menu. I went for the least spinach/acai involved option I could identify after establishing that, *no*, there was not any black pudding available.

Once the waitress left, Felix started to ask Ollie about his loser brother-in-law, but I wasn't finished.

"And your sister can't buy her own lunch?" I interrupted, and both Ollie and Felix turned to me.

"Yes, of course she's capable of buying her own lunch."

"So, why make Lottie do it?"

Ollie sighed. "Something's wrong with Vicky, okay?"

That tightness in my chest was back, so strong, I started to rub my sternum.

"What do you mean? You said she's losing weight. Is she sick or something?" I tried to keep my voice casual, but Ollie's sharp look, and the way Felix tilted his head to the side as he stared at me with a curious expression indicated that I was not quite achieving that aim.

"Why do you care so much about this, Mike?" Felix asked. "I thought you didn't like Vicky."

I cleared my throat and shifted in my seat. "I mean, she's not exactly my cup of tea, but I don't *hate* the woman or anything. What's wrong with her?"

Ollie reached back to rub the back of his neck. "Look, Vics would hate me to divulge anything, especially... well, especially to you."

"Why, especially to me?" I said in the most innocent tone I could muster.

Felix snorted, and Ollie's eyes narrowed on me again.

"You know exactly why, you tosser," he muttered.

I shrugged. "No clue."

"Mike, you know she's got a crush on you," Ollie said with real impatience now.

I frowned. We'd never actually openly acknowledged Vicky's obvious interest in me before, but there was something about Ollie's turn of phrase that didn't sit well with me.

A crush? That made Vicky sound like some innocent teenager harbouring romantic feelings.

Vicky was far from innocent, and I was quite sure the only feelings she harboured about me were related to the basic urge to bang me. None of that hearts and flowers bollocks. She was too much of a perfect princess to be considering that with me.

I snorted. "A crush? Let's be honest, mate. Vicky wouldn't mind shagging me as a bit of rough, but beyond that, I'm quite sure she's not interested."

Ollie had taken a sip of his coffee and started choking on it at my words.

Felix slapped him on the back.

When Ollie recovered, he looked at me with his eyebrows practically in his hairline. "Shag you?" he said in a tight voice. "You think that Vicky just wants to get her end away and have done with it?"

I shrugged. "Look, lots of your mates have wanted a piece of me at one time or another. Posh girls like to go slumming occasionally. Doesn't bother me—they're a good time."

That was a lie—when one of Ollie's posh friends had broken my heart at the tender age of fifteen, I'd been devastated. I'd overheard her taking the piss out of my accent and telling her mate, "You can't take townies home to Mummy and Daddy, but they're good for a few shags."

I never told Ollie or Felix, but after that, I made sure that when it came to any upper-class birds, I always kept things extremely casual. "Vicky's no different. And don't get me wrong, she's hot. But I like my women to have a bit more personality, even if it's just for a roll in the hay."

Ollie blinked. He stared at me for so long, I began to feel uncomfortable. "You really do not know my sister at all," he said slowly.

I rolled my eyes. "Believe me, I've known plenty of women like your sister."

"No," he said sharply. "No, you have *not.* If you think that Vics just wants to *shag you* in order to *rough it,* and if you think she's lacking in personality, then you don't know the first thing about her." His tone sharpened then, and his eyes flashed. "And you know what, you don't deserve to know her, either."

CHAPTER 5

It's creepy

Vicky

"Ah, you're here," Mum said, sounding disappointed, but I was used to that. I couldn't actually remember a time when my mother had been pleased to see me. This was just one of a long list of reasons why my therapist, Abdul, thought I should go no-contact with this side of my family.

"They make you sad, Vicky," he explained in our last session. *"I don't think you realise just how much their indifference affects you."*

That was part of my problem. It wasn't always easy for me to identify my emotions and label them for what they were. To an outside observer, it might have even seemed like I felt too little, and that I was unaffected by most things. But Abdul helped me see that, if anything, I felt *too much*.

It just all brewed around inside me, almost overwhelming at times. And the negativity directed at me from Mum and her family wasn't helpful at all. I understood that, but I knew I would not be able to shut these people out of my life. I owed my mother. She had taken care of me as a child in terms of food, shelter and education. My father was never very interested in me—but then again, I was a bit of an inconvenience, seeing as I was conceived as a mistake during an extramarital affair. That aspect of myself—the mistake part—had always been emphasised to me by both my mother and my father when he was alive.

Strangely, the one person who never told me I was a mistake was Margot, my father's wife. And Margot still got very, *very* cross whenever I mentioned the mistake part now, so I did my best not to do that. Margot absolutely hated my mother, which I could understand, given the whole affair scenario, so I did my best not to mention her either.

"You're early," Mum snapped.

"I was told 12:15," I said as Mum stood back to let me into the house. There were no hugs or kisses with Mum. She'd learned long ago that I didn't like to be touched, and she'd never bothered to work out what sort of touch worked for me, so there were none of the brief, tight hugs that I got from Ollie and Margot. "It is 12:17," I pointed out. "That makes me two minutes late."

"Victoria, most people do not arrive on the dot. It's actually rude to be pathologically on time. You need to give five minutes or so leeway."

I pressed my lips together to stop myself from pointing out again that I was, in fact, *two minutes late.* Luckily, I did manage to hold that bit of information in. It was a trick I'd only just mastered over the last year with Lottie's help, but it was extremely advantageous when dealing with my family. They found me difficult enough without my penchant for correcting people.

I wished Lottie was with me now, but that would be impossible. Not only would my family be unhappy with me dragging my executive assistant along with me, but the thought of Lottie seeing me with them filled me with horror.

The truth was that I was ashamed of how much my family hated me. It was why I rarely mentioned them to Margot and Ollie, and why I would *never* bring Lottie here. I knew I was a difficult person to like, but the open hostility and hatred from my own flesh and blood was too stark a reminder of just how unpleasant some people found me.

My mind flashed back to the morning with Mike two weeks ago, and I shook my head to clear it. The last thing I needed was to trigger myself with bad memories whilst creating new likely even more unpleasant ones.

"She's here," Mum announced as we made our way into the large kitchen diner.

I cringed at the mess on the work surfaces and the clutter piled up on the table.

My mother seemed to be almost allergic to putting her belongings away, and she loved acquiring new possessions—not a good combination. For a woman who hadn't worked a day in her life, she had a surprisingly large amount of stuff. Her house was a good-sized five-bedroom, detached in a leafy suburb just outside London, but she had sufficient belongings to fill three much bigger houses. As it was, my late father had only agreed to fund *one* house, so she was stuck filling just this one up with endless material goods. I'd paid for the extension on it two years ago, but it seemed she'd already filled that to capacity as well.

"Hi," my half-sister Rebecca said through a forced smile. I was so taken aback that I didn't quite manage one of my own. Smiles from Rebecca, forced or otherwise, were a rarity when it came to me.

"Hey, Vicky," my stepfather, Gareth, said from his place next to Rebecca at the kitchen table. Now, Gareth did smile at me, but then, that was just his way. Gareth was a very kind man. I'm sure he disliked me just as much as his daughter and wife, but he'd always managed not to show it quite as openly. He was also the only one who called me by my preferred name. I'd always hated the more formal Victoria. I knew that I myself could come across as stiff and formal in my interactions with people, so the last thing I needed was a stuffy name to match. "Everything okay with you, cariad? Business going alright?"

I smiled at Gareth. I'd always really liked it when he used Welsh endearments like cariad with me as if he considered me a real member of the family. Mum hadn't indicated I should sit yet, so I was left standing in the middle of the kitchen, trying not to look at all the mess. Clutter and mess were really difficult for me to deal with. I found it too overwhelming and distracting, and it made my thoughts murky, like I was underwater and couldn't quite get to the surface.

"Profits in this quarter are higher by seven-point-five percent," I told Gareth, and then went into some detail about the way the investment structure had improved.

When Rebecca rolled her eyes and faked a yawn, I blinked and snapped my mouth shut. Talking to Gareth about my business with what I considered to be a thorough answer was a mistake. I was always falling into this trap.

I found it difficult to spot a polite question that only required a cursory, brief response. Without Lottie here to squeeze my wrist, I didn't have a failsafe to stop myself from "banging on", as Mum and my half-sister would call it.

I felt heat hit my cheeks and looked down at my feet as Rebecca snorted.

"There you go, Dad," she said in a snide voice. "Aren't you glad you've got the exact percentage improvement? Super important info. *Fascinating.* Still a fun sponge then, Victoria?"

Fun sponge was relatively mild when it came to the insults Rebecca could throw at me, but it still cut as deep as the rest. I knew what it meant—that I, as a person, extracted the fun out of any situation. That was Rebecca's opinion of me. All the confidence I'd built over the last few months with Lottie and Lucy just seemed to crumble with her words.

Did Lottie and Lucy think I was a fun sponge? They gave no indication that this was the case, but then, I knew people didn't always say what they truly felt. Not everyone went around blurting out uncomfortable truths every five minutes. They were both kind women. They could be putting up with me out of guilt.

Then, an even more horrifying idea occurred to me as I stood there in the middle of the kitchen. What if Lottie only put up with me outside of the office because she was worried about her job and she was trying to please my half-brother?

For some reason, Ollie was ridiculously protective of me. Lottie could easily be under the impression that she *had* to see me outside work out of some sort of obligation.

"Earth to Victoria," Mum snapped, waving her hand in front of my face to get my attention. "Are you going to bloody well sit down or what?"

"Yeah, can you not just stand there like a weirdo?" Rebecca said. "It's creepy."

"Yes, come on, Victoria."

I froze at the sound of his voice and heavy footsteps as he walked into the kitchen.

Had I known Darrell would be here today, I definitely would *not* have come.

My sister's boyfriend was my least favourite human in the world. I hated him with every fibre of my being. So, when his large hand enclosed my elbow to propel me to the kitchen table, I reacted on instinct, jerking away from him so wildly that I stumbled to the side, catching my hip hard on the granite work surface. After wincing in pain, I decided to put even more distance between us by darting around the kitchen island, feeling much happier with the vast expanse of clutter-covered granite between us.

"Woah!" he said, both hands held up in mock surrender and a smirk on his smug face.

Darrell would probably be considered conventionally attractive with his perfectly styled blond hair, tall, lean physique, and chiselled features, but he made me feel physically sick.

"For God's sake, Victoria," Mum snapped. "Can you stop being so bloody strange? Darrell was just trying to be polite. I'd have thought you would have gotten over this whole phobia about any form of even polite physical contact now. Aren't you in therapy, for goodness sake? Isn't that supposed to *fix* you? Can't you try to be a bit more normal?"

"As if Darrell wants to touch you anyway," Rebecca said as she scowled at me.

I didn't bother correcting her. I may have been bad at reading people, but I knew that Darrell definitely *did* want to touch me.

The second time I met him, a year ago, he'd pinned me to the wall outside the ladies' toilets and groped my breast. The breast groping wasn't even the worst part. The worst part was his hot, awful breath on my neck as he whispered in my ear, *"I hear you don't like to be touched. This is going to be fun, isn't it, little sister?"*

When he finally let me go, I ran into the toilets and only just made it into a stall before I threw up everything I'd eaten that evening, then had a silent meltdown for over an hour on the cubicle floor. I was too scared to face him again, so I just left the restaurant and then walked all the way home, all three miles from central London to my house in Chelsea, in four-inch heels.

I didn't speak for three days.

Eventually I'd snapped back to reality, and I went to Mum's house to tell her—as usual, blurting out the full, unvarnished truth. I knew my mother didn't like me, but when she rolled her eyes and told me I was too sensitive and highly strung, that I must have misinterpreted Darrell, and that he was just being friendly and teasing me, I was stunned.

Rebecca screamed at me when I tried to tell her, calling me a "lying bitch," and telling me I was just jealous because nobody would shag me, seeing as I was "so bloody weird."

Gareth hadn't been there during my admission, and Mum had made sure to ring me afterwards, threatening all manner of retribution should I ever mention any of those accusations in front of him.

The only other person I told was Abdul. And Abdul's reaction was very different and somewhat strange. After I told him what had happened, he stood up suddenly from his chair, paced from where we were sitting to the middle of the room and then back again, but did not sit down. He stood behind his chair, gripping the leather until his knuckles turned white whilst he stared at me.

"For fuck's sake," he'd snapped, and I flinched.

Abdul was normally the epitome of a calm therapist, as he should be. I didn't think that stalking about his room and throwing expletives around was really his normal operating procedure.

But what did I know? I wasn't a qualified therapist.

"You seem angry," I'd said, actually quite proud of myself for identifying his emotions. It was something I'd been working on.

Abdul closed his eyes slowly as his head fell forward.

"Yes, Vicky," he'd said in a carefully controlled voice. "I am really fucking angry. Please tell me you intend to contact the police."

My eyebrows went up. "The police?"

"Yes, the police. That man assaulted you."

I'd shaken my head. "There were no witnesses, and my own family doesn't believe me. Also, I am aware of the rate of conviction when women report sexual assault to the police. Statistically speaking, that would be a waste of time."

"Fine. If you won't report him, then at least tell your brother."

"Half-brother."

Abdul's jaw had clenched in frustration.

"Tell Ollie."

I'd looked out of the window and pressed my lips together.

I wouldn't have told Ollie anything. I was aware that I was already a burden to my half-brother. I would not be adding to that by running to him every time I was scared or sad. I'd spent a lot of time scared and sad—it would be a full-time job sorting me out, and I was old enough to do it myself.

So, much to Abdul's frustration, I didn't report Darrell. My solution was simply to avoid him. The avoidance tactic did not involve or inconvenience anyone else, which is why I would never have gone to Mum's house that day if I'd known he would be there.

I was on the other side of the kitchen from Darrell and the rest of my family. My heart was hammering in my chest as I forced my hands into fists to stop them from shaking. My eyes were still focused on Darrell. Fear had crawled its way up to my throat, and I couldn't actually speak.

"Vicky, love," Gareth's gentle voice sounded from close by, and I startled when I realised he'd gotten up from the table and was now at my side.

I spared Gareth a glance, but then refocused on Darrell, who was trying to hide a small smirk. "You okay?"

If I could have spoken, I would have said *no*, I was not okay. Because lying was not something I'd ever been able to master. But I *couldn't* speak, so I just shook my head.

"Honestly, Gareth," Mum snapped. "Don't pander to her. It only makes it worse."

I'd heard a lot of that growing up. *Don't pander to her* was one of Mum's favourite sayings when it came to my meltdowns, my mutism, my fear of school when I was being relentlessly bullied, and to my teachers when they suggested assessments for autism spectrum disorder. I'd only been diagnosed in the last few years after Margot and Ollie talked me into having some therapy.

"Darrell," Gareth said with an edge to his voice. "I think it'd be better if you leave now."

"Daddy," Rebecca whined. "That's ridiculous. It's just Vicky being crazy. She needs to get over herself."

Gareth was staring at Darrell and ignoring his daughter. After a few moments, Darrell held his hands up again. "Of course. No problem, folks. I'll go. Vicky, I'll be seeing you."

Once I heard the front door close behind him, I swallowed and fully straightened from the slight crouch I hadn't even realised I'd dropped into.

"Come and sit down, cariad," Gareth said in that gentle voice.

For a moment, I stared at the door Darrell had left through. Only when I was convinced that he wasn't coming back did I move to the kitchen table.

“Cup of tea?” Gareth offered and I nodded, eyeing my sister and mother carefully as I slid into the vacant seat across from them.

“You need to stop being a crazy person about Darrell, Victoria,” Rebecca said. “It will look really fucking odd at the wedding if you go mental like that in front of everyone.”

CHAPTER 6

What's there to be stressed about?

Vicky

"Wedding?" I managed to force out as my eyes went wide with horror.

Please don't tell me Rebecca was going to marry Darrell.

"Yes, wedding," Rebecca said with a fake smile. "You know, that ceremony people have in the course of a *normal committed relationship*?"

I wasn't great at reading subtext in conversations, but even *I* knew what Rebecca was getting at with that comment—that I'd never had anything even approaching a normal relationship, and likely never would.

Gareth put a steaming mug of tea in front of me. It was the incorrect strength for this time of day, but then, Gareth was not in possession of my tea colour chart, so I couldn't realistically expect him to get it right.

I unclenched my fists enough to put my cold hands around it.

"I see," was all I could manage to get out past my tight throat.

"And you're my sister, so you'll have to be a part of it all," Rebecca told me begrudgingly.

"Yes, we'll need you to be normal for a day if you can manage that small favour," Mum said, and then we all jumped when Gareth's chair scraped back in a sudden movement.

I looked up to see him looking at his wife with a furious expression on his face.

"I've heard enough of this shit," he growled, then softened his tone when he turned his attention to me. "Don't let them bully you, love. If you want to be there, you're welcome. If not, I'm sure they'll survive."

"Daddy!"

"Don't 'Daddy' me, young lady," Gareth snapped at his daughter, and my eyes went wide at this unusual turn of events.

In general, Gareth did not snap at anyone. He was mild-mannered and avoided confrontation like the plague. Whenever Mum and Rebecca had a go at me when I was younger, he never said a thing. Truth be told, he usually couldn't leave the room quickly enough.

Granted, he was leaving now, but not before he'd spoken his mind.

"I'm paying for this shindig, so if you want all those bells and whistles, you'll do what I'm asking of you and respect your sister for once, for God's sake."

Then he stormed out, and I was left with the uncomfortable silence that followed.

"Great," Rebecca said when she was sure Gareth had really left. "You know you really—"

Mum's hand shot out to squeeze Rebecca's wrist, reminding me of the way Lottie communicated with me when I needed to cease and desist one of my verbal tirades, which was strange, since Rebecca did not have the same difficulties as me with reading social cues.

"So. Of course, you'll come to the wedding," Mum said to me through a forced smile. "It's not for two months, so you've got plenty of warning. We're family. We're *your* family. You wouldn't forget that, would you, Victoria? Not after everything I've done for you."

This was another favourite of my mother's sayings: *after everything I've done for you*. It was relatively effective. My mother had sacrificed a lot to have me and to raise me. On top of that sacrifice, I hadn't been an easy child, not by a long way. Then again, after the age of six when I stopped talking altogether, I didn't really bother Mum with meltdowns and such, as they were all conducted silently, for the most part.

But by then, I was labelled as *a problem*. This was compounded by the constant pressure from teachers to have me assessed—these calls were studiously ignored by Mum as she didn't want to "pander to my difficult ways," believing it would only exacerbate them.

Everything I'd learned since being diagnosed as an adult would suggest otherwise, but there was no point confronting Mum with that information.

"If you require me to be there, then I will be there."

Rebecca rolled her eyes. "God, anyone would think we were asking you to drink acid. It's a party. It's going to be a laugh. Not that you've ever had a laugh in your life."

I cleared my throat and decided not to address the "it's going to be a laugh" comment. I wasn't sure how an event featuring a man who had sexually assaulted me marrying my sister who hated me was going to be *a laugh*, but then again, I had long since given up trying to understand the way Rebecca's mind operated.

I looked down at my tea and realised I hadn't even taken a sip. I would have tried, but the stress of the last few minutes would have prevented me from swallowing it anyway. I looked up at the clock on the kitchen wall and then back at Mum. It was difficult for me sometimes to gauge how long interactions should go on for. At work, I had Lottie there to guide me on this, but of course, Lottie wasn't here now. I was not enjoying this interaction at all, and I doubted Mum or Rebecca were either. I'd been here for sixteen minutes now, which I knew was short, but we seemed to have discussed all the salient points, and I wanted to go home.

I cleared my throat. "If that's everything to be discussed, then I'll leave."

"You haven't even drunk your tea!" Mum's voice was pitched high with indignation.

Maybe I had misjudged the required time frame. Lottie and Abdul had told me to be more open about my difficulties so that people understood when I did something that could be interpreted as aberrant or rude, so I took a deep breath and explained.

"I can't actually swallow fluids or solids during a period of stress," I told Mum, to explain my lack of tea drinking and eliminate the appearance of rudeness.

"Why the hell are you so stressed?" Mum's voice pitched even higher, and I bit my lip to stop myself from replying honestly, which was the only way I would have been able to reply. "This is your family home, and you've popped in for a cup of tea. What's there to be stressed about?"

I pulled my lips in between my teeth and bit down to stop my reply since I had the feeling it would only make Mum angrier. In fact, anything I said seemed to inflame the situation. Even trying to explain that I wasn't being rude by not drinking tea had only made things worse. A lot worse.

"Let's cut to the chase, now that Dad's out of the room, shall we?" Rebecca cut in, and I turned to her. She had a calculating look in her eyes. "Victoria, you need to pay for my dress, the flowers I want, and the booze. Dad's talking about shelling out for a few glasses of champagne and then making everyone go to a *paying bar*." Rebecca grimaced. "I can't ask my mates to pay for their drinks at my wedding. It would be mortifying."

I blinked at her. "I thought your friends were all wealthy?"

My father may not have been the best in terms of emotional support or even acknowledgement when it came to me, but he did pay child support. A lot of child support. In addition to owning the house Mum currently lived in, he'd also paid the exorbitant fees for my boarding school. As for the additional child support money, Mum had spent most of it on herself and her other daughter. This meant that Rebecca had also gone to posh boarding schools, and, not being as unlikeable as I was (Rebecca may have been a raving bitch to me, but she could certainly turn on the charm when she needed to), she made a lot of friends there. Then made even more friends when she attended Durham University.

So, all Rebecca's friends were affluent in the extreme. They could easily afford their own drinks, whereas my stepfather, who worked hard as an accountant but only had a moderate income, could likely not afford all-night champagne.

"It's not that they can't afford their drinks," Rebecca said through her teeth. "It's how embarrassing it would be to ask them to pay. I'd be completely humiliated."

"Gareth does not understand the situation," Mum put in. "He expects Becky to wear a dress costing a *maximum* of one thousand pounds."

"That's not even going to buy the bloody veil," Rebecca muttered.

"A wedding dress is a very poor investment," I put in, thinking this information would be considered helpful.

Judging by how red Rebecca's face turned, it was not.

"The ROI is abysmal," I explained, hoping to get my point across without her head exploding. And I was actually telling the truth. I'd never understood how anyone could spend tens of thousands of pounds on a dress they only wore for one day. "The re-sale in general only yields approximately a third of the market value for the dress once it's been worn."

"Why the fuck are you talking ROI and market value, you freak?" Rebecca's face was a really ugly shade of puce now.

Clearly, further explanations on the economics of the wedding industry were not welcome at this point.

Mum sighed. "Victoria, just give us the money and stop being difficult. We can't afford it, and Gareth's not changing his mind."

I frowned. "But what about the allowance I pay you?"

Mum's eyes went wide, and she shushed me, looking over my shoulder, presumably, to check that Gareth hadn't snuck back into the kitchen.

"I thought I told you not to ever mention that."

"But it should be more than enough to—"

"I've spent it, okay?" she snapped, and Rebecca sat back in her chair with a mutinous expression on her face and her arms crossed over her chest.

After Dad died, his child support payments stopped. I was, at that point, twenty-three, so technically they should have stopped five years prior. But I think my father knew that continued financial support kept Mum from harassing me, and if he didn't carry on paying, she would simply use me to extract the money anyway.

He might not have been the most interested father, but he did tell me that he didn't want Mum "fucking me up any more royally than she already had," so it was easier to keep her paid off.

Dad's funeral was the first time Mum approached me about money. When she could corner me, away from Margot and Ollie, who had very kindly included me in the event as if I were family, when really, I was nothing of the sort, she told me that I needed to continue the payments now that Dad was dead.

My inheritance from my father was very modest compared to that of his *real* children. It only really lasted until I was earning for myself after university. So I had to pay my mother's allowance out of my own earnings. To be honest, it seemed to be the most expedient option. I never really bought anything for myself, nor did anything, so I didn't actually require unlimited wealth.

Then, of course, I started working at Felix's company, and my income sky-rocketed, so I simply forgot about the payments to Mum. But they were substantial. So substantial that drinks and a wedding dress shouldn't be an issue if she'd saved any at all. But then, looking around at all the clutter, I could guess where the money went.

"You owe me." Mum hissed as she grabbed my arm.

I tried to flinch away, but her grip was way too tight.

"You know you owe me. This is pennies for you, and your sister has had a hard time recently."

The *hard time* Mum was referring to Rebecca's firing from her employment at a high-end fashion boutique for "borrowing" the clothes. Borrowing was the term Rebecca used for it. Stealing was how the boutique termed it. She was furious about it at the time, saying that she was a "walking advertisement" and her Insta following alone would be worth the price of the few pieces that she "borrowed".

I suspected that it was more than a few pieces, seeing as Rebecca rarely wore anything twice, and it was nearly always designer.

I really needed Mum to let go of my arm, and I knew the only way that was going to happen was if I agreed to her terms.

"Okay," I said and then breathed a sigh of relief when Mum released her grip.

CHAPTER 7

A lot of people are mean to me

Mike

"Hello, ladies," I said as I passed my sister Lucy, then Lottie and Vicky on the sun loungers on my way to the pool.

Christ, she was wearing that goddamn bikini again. I'd only risked the briefest of glances, but the image of her slim, golden body laid out on a sun lounger with her golden hair splayed all around her was burned into my brain.

This was not going to be good at all for the ejection of Vicky from my late-night appointments with my hand, which seemed to be the only way I wanted to get off nowadays.

Or the fevered dreams I still had about her every night, which had ramped up significantly since that day at her house.

All the women turned their heads towards me as I passed, and to my absolute shock, Vicky squeaked. The woman actually made a squeaking sound.

When I risked a glance back at the trio, the other two were staring at Vicky in open-mouthed shock. But Vicky? She was staring at *me*.

Lottie whispered something to her, but she didn't respond

to whatever the other woman was saying. So, as usual, fucking weird.

"Hey girls," I said when I came up from my dive into the pool to smile at Hayley, Lottie's little sister and Florrie, Ollie's niece.

"Hey, Mike," Florrie said, and Hayley gave me a shy smile.

"Uncle Ollie, do the thing! Do the thing!" Florrie shouted, then squealed as he plucked her off the side of the pool, lifted her high above his head and then launched her into the deep end, where she swam to me then stood on my shoulders until I launched her into the air again.

Hayley even managed a much gentler launch and came up with a proud, smiling face.

"That's brilliant, Hayley!" I said. "I'm amazed you've learned anything from these losers, to be honest. You must be natural. How about you learn from the master?"

"Get over yourself, mate," Felix said as he balanced Florrie on his shoulders. "We're *way* better swimmers than you."

I snorted. "Only because you overprivileged losers had your own pool."

Florrie was on my shoulders now, and I launched her high in the air, back towards Ollie.

Felix rolled his eyes. "You had use of the pool."

"Okay, well *I* taught Lucy to swim."

"I taught Vicky to swim," Ollie said.

"Lucy was younger."

"Well, that's nothing, Vicky was..." Ollie was interrupted by the sound of a sun lounger scrapping back.

We all looked over to see Vicky stand, shove a man's large T-shirt over her head and run from the pool.

"Shit," Ollie muttered.

"You swore again," Florrie shouted. "I'm telling Granny!"

Ignoring Florrie's threats to her uncle, I swam over to him. He was still staring after Vicky.

"Vicky was what?" I asked, and his gaze snapped to me before he frowned.

"My sister was and is none of your fucking business," he said.

"Granny's gonna be super mad, Uncle Ollie," Florrie put in helpfully.

I stared at Ollie for a moment but then he broke eye contact when his sister Claire, and her dickhead husband, Blake arrived.

"Come on, Hails," Florrie said, her expression now grim as both girls glanced up at Claire and Blake before exchanging a look. "We'd better go and muck out Legolas and Bertie. We said we would."

Christ, that kid really did not like her stepdad.

Was that why Vicky ran? But they only just arrived. No, it was when Ollie was about to say something about her to me. Why would she run? I knew I'd spent way too much time thinking about Vicky lately, but I couldn't shake the gnawing thought that I was missing something. And the way her hands shook after I'd been a shit to her that day was still playing on repeat in my mind, making my chest tight.

I made a decision and hauled myself out of the pool.

"I'll see you later," I muttered to Lucy as I stalked by her and Lottie on the sun loungers, grabbing a towel from my sister to dry off as I went.

Lottie gave me a narrow look, but thankfully, didn't say anything about me going in the same direction as Vicky. Lottie was like Vicky's personal security or something, which I didn't really get. The woman was perfectly capable of looking after herself from what I'd seen.

When I was sure I was out of sight, I jogged up the lawn towards the main house. The motherfucker was huge, and I'd always been really intimidated by it as a child. Felix's modern monstrosity of a family home was bad enough, but the Buckingham Estate was on another level.

Luckily, I knew my way around this place like the back of my hand, and I knew which of the many entrances Vicky would have used. By the time I made it up to the house, I wasn't soaking wet, but I still left watery footprints on the wood floors, which I decided I'd take the flak for from Margot later.

I caught up with Vicky as she was traversing the vast expanse known as the orangery. Weird as no oranges featured, but it was about fifty feet long and almost entirely glass, like a mega posh conservatory built over two hundred years ago.

"Hey!" I called, and Vicky came to an abrupt stop before she spun round to face me. The light shimmered off her long, blonde hair as it swung out and over her shoulder with the movement. Fuck me, she was beautiful. Possibly even more beautiful with no make-up, her hair down and left to dry in natural waves after swimming. The only thing spoiling the picture was the fact she was standing there in another man's T-shirt. This made my temper spike for some unknown reason, so I forgot what I meant to ask her and said the first thing that came into my head instead.

"Whose T-shirt is that?" My voice was a low, territorial growl that I barely recognised.

Bloody hell, I was losing my goddamn mind.

"W-w-what?" Vicky whispered, and I gritted my teeth. One of the things that kept replaying in my mind after my confrontation with Vicky when I delivered her table was when she stuttered. It was so un-Vicky like, so vulnerable, that the thought of it made my stomach hollow out.

"Shit," I muttered, my hand going to the back of my neck to grip it in frustration as I forced myself to break eye contact with her and stare out of the glass wall.

I was scaring her again. Why was I driven to be such a prick around this woman? The bottom line was that she was into me. Way, *way* into me, and I'd been fucking rude. I needed to apologise, and then get us to a place where I could find out why she wasn't bloody well eating. I did *not* need to bark at her and interrogate her in her home. But then, I looked back at her, and I saw her eyes were no longer on my face; no, they were focused on my chest, on the muscles I knew were now flexed there and on display, seeing as I had yet to get dressed and was still wearing a pair of low-slung board shorts with a towel in my hand.

Okay, not *totally* scared of me then. Despite the tense atmosphere, I had the sudden desire to smile. And I decided that if Vicky was going to eye-fuck me like this, then I did, in fact, deserve an answer to my question. I took a step towards her. She startled and took a step back, tearing her eyes from my chest to look at my face. But she didn't make direct eye contact, instead, she stared at my left ear.

"I asked whose T-shirt that is that you're wearing, love?" I said, my voice no longer a growl, but still low and firm. She blinked at the endearment, and her mouth parted for a moment before she snapped it shut.

"It's my half-brother's," she said, her voice still just above whisper. Half-brother. Never brother, or just Ollie. It was almost as if she had to clarify the distinction, and, not for the first time, it struck me as odd. But the knowledge that Ollie had given her the T-shirt, and she was most definitely not fucking her half-brother made my tense body relax.

"I was an arsehole," I told her.

Her body jerked slightly, but that was the only indication I had that she'd even heard me.

I cleared my throat.

"You were?" she asked as she tilted her head to the side.

My eyebrows went up. "Er… yes, love." Again, that blink at the endearment, then the briefest bit of eye contact, her crystal blue ones locking with mine for a split second. "I was a *total* arsehole. I'm here to say I'm sorry."

"I don't understand," Vicky said.

"Vicky, I was mean the other day. It was completely unwarranted." My voice was soft then. I still wasn't sure what was going on here.

Surely a girl like Vicky should be taking my apology as her due and being a total bitch about it? She had me over a barrel. If she told Ollie what I'd said to her, he would be furious, but she clearly hadn't said a word. Which was unusual in itself.

Lucy would've definitely come to me if Felix had been a shit to her. In fact, she had come straight to me after he threw her out of his office, and I'd punched Felix in the face in short order.

Where was my face punch?

"I should have been kinder when I turned you down."

Vicky just shrugged, which pissed me off even more. "It's not your fault," she told me in a neutral tone. "A *lot* of people are mean to me. I'm told I can be extremely irritating."

White hot anger shot through me at her words. "Who the fuck is mean to you?" I said with that growl back in my voice now. She frowned up at my left ear as if confused by my words.

"Mr. Mayweather—"

"Mike," I corrected her.

"Er... Mike."

Hearing my name on her lips was something I didn't realise I needed until that very moment, but it shot through me like a knife.

"I can be an exceptionally annoying person. I don't read people well, and I very often insult people. Thus, people are inevitably... well, *mean*. It's not a—"

She broke off as I took another step towards her, saying in a low voice, "Baby, I asked *who* was mean to you."

"Baby?" she whispered, her eyes flying even wider as she took another faltering step back, but she stopped when she came up against the large oak table behind her.

My eyes flashed down to her legs, and I frowned at the large bruise I hadn't noticed there. Before I could think better of it, or in fact, think anything at all, my hand came up and I traced my fingers along the edge of the discolouration without actually making contact with her skin.

"How did this happen?" I asked.

"W-what?" She shook her head, her voice breathy now, and she looked dazed rather than scared.

"The bruise on your leg, love," I said softly.

She shook her head again. "It's nothing."

"It's not nothing."

Her chest rose and fell on a deep breath, and she pressed her lips together in a thin line. Clearly, it wasn't nothing, but she didn't trust me enough to tell me about it. Suddenly not having Vicky's trust felt very, very wrong.

I swore under my breath as I pulled my hand back. "I really am sorry for what I said, Vicky."

"It's not—"

"Do you forgive me?"

"I… there's nothing to forgive."

I decided to let that lie for the moment and move on to my next line of questioning.

"Why aren't you eating?"

Her eyebrows went up. "It's not currently a mealtime. In fact, there are…" her eyes flicked to a clock on the wall, then back to my ear. "Three hours and thirty-eight minutes until the next mealtime. Approximately."

I smiled again. "Approximately?" I teased.

"Well, yes," she said with a small frown. "I only have the wall-mounted clock to estimate with. I've tried to convince the Hardings to install digital clocks in their house, but my half-brother is resistant to the idea. So, I have to rely on inaccurate, often very old analogue devices. The one over there is two hundred years old and loses three minutes and thirty-eight seconds every year. I adjust it every six months, or however often I'm here if the frequency is less, but in general, the Buckingham Estate is running on inaccurate timings. So that was an approximation of the—"

She broke off as my hand came up to her delicate jaw, tilted her head back slightly, and my mouth closed over hers. In my defence, she looked so gorgeous with the sunlight still shimmering off her hair, and tiny freckles that must normally be hidden under make-up across the bridge of her nose, that her adorable little clock accuracy rant simply tipped me over the edge.

Given how dilated her pupils were, how rapid the rise and fall of her chest was, and how I *knew* that she found me "extremely attractive", her instant reaction was unexpected.

My lips were only on hers for a fraction of a second, enough to feel how unbelievably soft they were, and enough to notice the sharp, indrawn breath she took before suddenly wrenching away from me.

Blocked by the table at her back, she scrambled to the side until she was clear of it, backing away, her hand up in front of her as if to ward me off. Her eyes were wide, her breathing was way too fast, and her hands were shaking.

What the fuck was going on?

"Christ, Vicky, I'm sorry," I said, taking a step towards her, but halting in my tracks when she took another one back. I held up my hands in surrender. "It's okay. I'm not going to touch you again. I promise. I would *never* have kissed you if I didn't think you'd be right there with me."

Her lips were pressed together, and her hands had slowly crept up to her ears—not to cover them, but to sort of rest near them under her hair. And I noticed that she was rocking. It was a *tiny* movement, and I only caught it because I was watching her so closely, but she was *very* slightly rocking backwards and forwards.

My chest tightened as real concern shot through me.

What had I done?

"Vicky?" I said, taking another tentative step towards her.

She was so wrapped up in her own world that she didn't seem to notice.

"Baby, are you okay?" The endearment seemed to break through.

She blinked a couple of times and made very brief eye contact before focusing back on my left ear.

I was within touching distance now, but I kept my hands by my sides.

She swallowed, and her hands came down from her ears almost as though she was forcing them to. After a few moments, she held onto the table that was now by her side, and she stopped rocking as if using the solid wood to anchor herself.

"I have to—" she started to say, but her voice broke off. Her eyes closed briefly, and she swallowed before she spoke again. "I have to have warning." She was whispering now, as if she was telling me something deeply shameful.

I frowned. "Warning? Before I kiss you?"

She cleared her throat. "Before *any* physical contact."

I nodded. "Right, okay. Warning."

She was shaking very slightly now. I wasn't sure if it was because of the slight breeze going through the orangery, or whether she was still scared, but something deep in my psyche seemed to sense what she needed.

"Would it help if I… held you?" I asked, then held my breath for her answer.

"I… yes, but…" she paused for a moment. "It has to be a tight hug."

I smiled as I closed the distance between us. "Got it. Tight hug."

Then she was in my arms, her softness pressed tightly to me, my chin resting on top of her head, and my arms enclosing her small body completely.

At first, her body was stiff with tension, and there were small tremors running through her, but after a few moments, she relaxed against me, her hands flattening against my chest, and her face burrowing into my skin.

As I gathered her even closer, I felt like I'd scored a massive victory.

This was significant—that my embrace could comfort her meant something.

I have to have warning.

I can be extremely irritating.

A lot *of people are mean to me.*

There's nothing to forgive.

I wasn't sure what the fuck was going on with this beautiful woman who seemed to think it was okay for people to treat her like shit, who freaked out at a closed-mouth kiss, who'd told me she found me *extremely attractive,* but at the same time, seemed to be totally terrified of me, but I was sure as fuck going to find out.

CHAPTER 8

Am I interrupting something?

Vicky

The thoughts whirling through my mind were slowly quieting.

Mike's huge body enclosing mine was bringing me back to myself. I'd dreamt about being in his arms so many times—how strong he would be, how warm—but the reality was so much better.

Tight hugs were always calming for me. Sometimes, they were the only way to bring me out of a meltdown, the only way to calm the storm that my mind became when I was overwhelmed, but I'd never felt this level of peace before in someone's arms.

But then, very gradually, reality started to creep in.

The realisation of how I'd lost it when he kissed me. That I was so defective, so totally weird, that I couldn't even let a man I wanted more than my next breath kiss me spontaneously.

This was not the way to convince Mike Mayweather I was a normal human being.

I felt completely mortified.

"Vicky?" His tone was concerned. He'd clearly felt me stiffen in his arms. He was probably worried I was going to freak out again. And who could blame him? I'd made it clear I wanted him two weeks ago, and now, I'd reacted like he'd assaulted me, when all he did was touch his mouth to mine.

The memory of that kiss tore through me like fire. It was, hands down, the best moment of my life, and I'd proceeded to ruin it. "Hey, princess. You okay?"

Princess.

As soon as I pushed against his chest, he loosened his arms, and I stepped back. Then, as if a switch had been flicked, other memories invaded:

Well, I've got news for you, princess. I wouldn't touch you with a barge pole.

You can stop with this bullshit, staring at me all the time.

You want some fun with a bit of rough, and I'm not interested.

You, you're like a beautiful vase—great to look at but empty inside.

The trouble with my memory was that I could recall everything with absolute accuracy. Every word Mike had said to me was still burned on my soul. I wasn't lying when I told Mike I didn't blame him for his unkind words. I knew how I "wound people up" as Rebecca would say—it was one of the reasons I didn't push myself on Margot, Ollie or Claire, and why I only came to Buckingham House when I was specifically invited. I didn't want to use them up. I didn't want them to tire of me. I could be very tiring.

Now, for some reason, Mike had kissed me. I analysed the facts for a moment. I was very physically attractive, I knew this—it was simply a fact. I could never understand beautiful women who denied what they were. If you were physically attractive, the attention you garnered was obvious and constant. I may not have been able to read people very well, but I knew when men were attempting to *get in my knickers,* as Lottie would say. I wasn't *that* oblivious.

So if you combined the fact that I was physically attractive with the other facts about the situation, it made perfect sense for him to kiss me.

Number one, I'd been in just a bikini. It was something I already knew Mike found arousing—there was no hiding that physical reaction either. Number two, I was still only half-dressed, and number three, the last time I saw Mike, I'd made it clear that I found him extremely attractive, and his interpretation of this declaration was that I wanted an immediate sexual relationship with him. Due to my poor communication skills, I hadn't been able to correct this assumption.

I had my answer.

I'd had a particularly uncomfortable session with Abdul in the aftermath of my previous confrontation with Mike. When I told him what had happened, he was open-mouthed with shock for a full minute.

"Let me get the straight, Vicky," he said slowly. "You order furniture from this man, and when he delivers it, you launch straight into how you find him attractive and want to propose *something to him? But he cuts you off before you can get any further?"*

"Well, yes. I thought the direct approach would be the most expedient."

Abdul sighed. "Vicky, have you ever watched any pornography?"

I wrinkled my nose in disgust. "Pornography? No, I have not."

"What you've just described is a pretty standard scenario of a rich woman wanting to have casual sexual relations with an attractive, blue-collar delivery man-slash-plumber-slash-builder, take your pick. He probably felt like you were just wanting a quickie, and he got offended."

"Oh."

Abdul sighed again. "Look, Vicky. I know you like this guy, but from what you've told me, he's not interested. And I'm sorry, but he sounds like a bit of a di–." Abdul broke off and cleared his throat. "He sounds like an unpleasant individual. What he said to you was not okay. I don't think you'd be safe with him."

I shook my head. "No, he's not dangerous. He—"

"I don't mean physically unsafe, Vicky. I mean emotionally unsafe."

I took another step back. My mind flashed to the hours I'd spent under that coffee table. I didn't think I could go through that again. I still wasn't managing proper meals, but then the added stress of Darrell and the upcoming wedding was contributing to that as well.

And now, Mike had witnessed how, behind the mask, I was vulnerable. *Masking*—that was how Abdul described it. With Lottie's help, and if I avoided becoming overwhelmed, I was able to do it pretty successfully.

But I knew that long diatribes on the inaccuracies on analogue timekeeping and wrenching away from someone when they kissed you, even though they knew you were outrageously attracted to them, was not successfully masking. Not even close.

And that didn't even include me running away from the pool like a mad woman earlier.

But I simply couldn't stay to hear Ollie tell the others how painstaking it had been to teach me to swim. He'd had the patience of a saint back then, slowly getting me over my aversion to water, one meltdown at a time.

I couldn't bear the thought of Mike thinking I was a freak, of him seeing behind the mask any more than he already had. Maybe if I'd known I could be safe with him it would've been different, but after what happened two weeks ago, and with Abdul's advice ringing in my ears, I knew that wasn't the case.

I couldn't trust Mike.

"This isn't a good idea," I whispered at my feet.

"What?"

I shook my head from side to side, trying to find the right words. "You said it yourself. I'm not the right person. And that was before you knew that I'm..." my voice dropped lower. "Not normal." I chanced looking up at him.

His arms were crossed over his chest, and he was frowning down at me. "Who says you're not normal?"

I tilted my head to the side in confusion. "Um... everyone."

He shrugged. "Well, I don't give a fuck about normal."

"I'll stop staring at you," I blurted out. "I can get really focused on... some things. But I'll try to stop focusing on you."

"What if I don't want you to stop focusing on me?" he asked, his frown melting into a small smile.

I shook my head again in jerky movements. "I am incorrect for you. You like your women 'warm, cute, kind, able to express actual emotion, and equipped with a personality'."

He blinked at me, his smile fading as I repeated his words back to him. "Christ, I'm a fucking dickhead."

"No, you were honest. I actually appreciate honesty. It helps me judge situations better."

Mike's jaw was clenched tight. "Can we just forget what I said two weeks ago? I made some stupid assumptions, and I've already said I'm sorry."

"And I've said you don't have anything to apologise for."

"If I've nothing to apologise for," he said, frustration leaking into his tone. "Then why the fuck are you telling me this isn't a good idea?"

"You have nothing to apologise for because you were simply being honest. And we won't work because I'm not your type."

"How about I decide what my type is, baby?" he said in a low voice as he stalked a couple of steps closer to me and frowned when I took another one back.

"You already did. You said—"

"Fucking hell, can we just forget what I bloody said?"

I flinched at his sharp tone, and he let out a shaky breath.

"I'm sorry, love," he said, his voice soft now. "I'm not angry with you. I'm angry at my stupid self."

"Mike?" Lucy's voice sounded from inside the house, and both our heads whipped in that direction. "Legolas has gotten out again, and we need to… oh, Vics. What are you guys…?"

Mike turned back to me and closed his eyes for a moment as frustration crossed his features, and he swore under his breath.

Lucy was standing next to us by then and looking between us with a curious expression. "Am I interrupting something?" she asked cautiously.

"Yes." Mike snapped at the same time that I said a firm, "No."

"Okay," Lucy said slowly, one of her eyebrows winging up, and a small smile on her lips. She seemed happy. Happy that I was here with her brother. That arrow of guilt shot through me again. Lucy shouldn't be happy for me in any capacity. It may have been months ago, but I remembered with perfect clarity everything that had happened to her in our office, and how I had let her down.

Lucy had forgiven me. She was in love with Felix, who was head over heels for her, and who had managed to claw his way back to her after much grovelling.

But I would *never* forgive myself. And now, here she was, looking between me and her brother, her expression bright and hopeful, as if the chance Mike might be finally caving to my obsession was fantastic news.

I didn't deserve her, and I definitely didn't deserve her brother.

The Mayweathers were a close family. They didn't need someone *empty inside*, someone who would never fit in. I took another few rapid steps back.

"I've got to go," I muttered, nearly tripping over the chair behind me but righting myself at the last minute.

Mike made a move to come after me, but Lucy must have seen something in my expression, and she put a hand on his arm to stop him. I knew it would look weird if I ran, but the Orangery was really, really long, and I was starting to spiral. So, like the freak I was, by the time I was at end of the long space, I was full-on sprinting.

CHAPTER 9

You've got a deal

Mike

"Hello, young man."

"Sh–sugar—hey, Margot."

Bloody hell, the woman came out of nowhere. Totally freaky. But that was Margot for you, always popping up where you least expected her. It was the same when we were kids. Margot would suddenly appear out of nowhere, and she always seemed to know what was going on. She was the type of woman who'd know everything about everyone and would manipulate things as she saw fit, which made her a scary motherfucker in my opinion.

Despite that, I still liked Margot. She was so posh, it was almost as though she broke through class divides with the sheer force of her aristocratic bearing. Nobody said no to Margot. But she was fucking hilarious as well. Always up for a laugh and always had a twinkle in her eye.

"Gosh, aren't you jumpy," she said with a small smirk.

I was sitting on one of the many garden benches at Buckingham Manor, kicking a stone with the toe of my boot and thinking that I should probably be getting back to my workshop, but not wanting to leave just yet without seeing Vicky again. There was open lawn all around me. Margot really had appeared out of nowhere. Like I said—scary, but kind of cool.

"But then, in my experience," Margot said with that eye twinkle again. "It's always the big, burly chaps who have the most nervous dispositions."

I narrowed my eyes at her. "I do not have a nervous disposition," I said through my teeth, and one of her eyebrows went up.

"Tell that to the little boy who ran away screaming when The Hulk arrived for my son's birthday party."

Heat flooded my face. When was I going to live that down? "I was four, Margot. And that bastard was massive. How was I to know it was just Jimbo from The Badger's Sett?"

"None of the other children were scared, darling. It's okay to be sensitive, you know."

I rolled my eyes. "I'm not sensitive."

She hummed but didn't reply as she sat next to me on the bench.

"I love Vicky," she said out of the blue after a full minute of silence.

I shifted uncomfortably on my seat and aimed a good bit of side-eye at the old bird. "Yes, okay."

She turned further to me before she spoke again. "She thinks she's difficult to love. But she's not."

My throat felt tight. How much did Margot know?

"She thinks she doesn't fit here, that we're not her *real* family, so we're just putting up with her. Have you noticed how she emphasises *half*-brother and *half*-sister when she talks about my biological children? How she won't claim Buckingham Manor in any way as one of her homes, just somewhere she's allowed to visit?"

I cleared my throat. "Is that... is it because she—?"

"Because she's my husband's bastard?"

My back shot straight at Margot's words. "Hey." I growled, fully ready to throw down.

How dare Margot call Vicky that?

"It's okay, Mike," Margot said with amusement in her tone. "You can relax. I didn't mean that as an insult to Vicky. She can't help the circumstances of her birth. But that *is* how she thinks of herself. How she's been made to feel by everyone, and even, I'm ashamed to say this, but even by me at first. It took me longer than it should have done to warm up to that little girl, and I'll carry that guilt around for the rest of my life. She was six when I first met her, and it was all quite a shock. My feelings were hurt, and I was humiliated. I put up with her like the martyr I felt I was, and interacted with her the minimum amount I could get away with that summer. This wasn't hard. As you know, the child didn't speak.

"Now, Ollie, my beautiful, wonderful Oliver, was different. He accepted her immediately. All his anger was directed rightfully towards his father. Claire still struggles with it, and that's made her… distant from Vicky.

"But for me… one day, I came into the kitchen, and there she was. This silent child just staring out of the patio doors. So still and small. My kids were good eaters. They were loud, and they seemed to be always moving, but Vicky, even though she was a lot younger than both of them, was so *so* still. The only way I even knew she was alive was the rise and fall of her chest. Then she looked at me. I think it was the first time I really made eye contact with her. Vicky's never been the best with eye contact, and it wasn't like I was seeking it out either. When I looked into those blue eyes, carbon copies of my own children's, I could suddenly see so much working behind them that I had to look away. That's the thing with Vicky—a lot of the time, the calmer she is on the surface, the more is going on inside. I vowed that day to treat Vicky like one of my own children. And I did. Her mother is… well, of course, I don't have a high opinion of the woman, seeing as she slept with my husband for years behind my back, but she is also one of the most vile people on the planet.

"So Vicky's had a raw deal overall, and I'm simply not prepared to let it continue. I want that girl to have what she wants. I want her to have *everything* she wants. And as I'm sure you're aware, Michael Mayweather, she wants *you*."

I started coughing then, the shock of her words prompting me to choke on my own spit. What the hell? Was Margot trying to act like Vicky's pimp or something? Or maybe, as *my* pimp? What was going on?

"Margot, I'm not sure what you—?"

"Oh, don't be tedious, Michael," Margot said as she waved her hand in the air dismissively as if to dispel my so-called tediousness. "You know exactly what I'm talking about. Now, down to the negotiations."

"Negotiations?" My voice was pitched higher than it had been for many years now. "What the hell are you talking about?"

"I want you to make a concerted effort to woo Vicky."

My eyebrows went up. "*Woo* her? You do realise this is not the eighteen-hundreds anymore, Margot?"

She rolled her eyes. "Men have been wooing women since the beginning of time, young man."

"What if she doesn't want to be wooed?" I said, some grumpiness leaking into my voice. I was still a little salty at how Vicky reacted to that kiss, and the fact she now thought we wouldn't work.

"Believe me, she does. I have a schedule for you. There are some upcoming events that the whole family will be attending, and now, so will you."

"Events?" I said warily. "What kind of events?"

"Black-tie kind of events. I presume you have a dinner jacket?"

"I'm not being trussed up in some monkey suit just to act as your gigolo, Margot," I said, my tone even grumpier now.

"Yes, you will," she said simply.

"What makes you so sure?"

"Michael, have you heard of Highcliffe Investments?"

I blinked, and my mouth went dry. "Of course, I'd heard of them. They were my main backer to expand the business." Lucy had offered, as had my two billionaire best friends, but I wanted to do it myself. The chip I had on my shoulder wouldn't allow any other way. And my sister had already helped Mum out, buying her a house of all things. I didn't want her giving me money as well.

"Hmm." Margot hummed, looking out at the garden now instead of making eye contact. "That was fortunate, wasn't it? An outside investor coming in at *just* the right time. Just when you needed the capital to expand but didn't want to go to your successful author little sister and her billionaire boyfriend."

My heart was hammering now. Everything I had rested on that investment. I'd just taken on an apprentice. We were making more profit than ever, and it was all possible because of the amazing deal I managed to get with Highcliffe Investments, who valued the company much higher than anyone else I'd approached.

"It would be a shame if that investment was pulled, wouldn't it?" she said as she continued to study the horizon.

I felt a surge of anger as my pulse beat in my ears.

"I do not enjoy being manipulated, Margot," I said in a low, angry tone that would make grown men shudder in fear.

This little middle-aged lady just shrugged and gave me a small smile.

"And I don't enjoy seeing my beautiful, sensitive stepdaughter being turned down repeatedly by the blind idiot who I *know* could make her happy if he stopped being so bloody stubborn. Hence my founding of Highcliffe Investments for the sole purpose of providing you with the incentive you needed to *make Vicky happy.*"

I blinked at the ground and took a deep breath. If it were a couple of weeks ago, before I'd delivered that damn coffee table to Vicky's scarily tidy but soulless house, before I'd seen her in that oversized T-shirt with no make-up on and her hair shimmering in the sun, before I'd tasted her, then I know I would have told Margot to fuck off and take her investment with her. I'd built up my company before, and I could do it again, with or without Highcliffe Investments.

But seeing as I'd been tortured by dreams of Vicky for weeks, and no other woman even vaguely appealed to me now—plus, in my mind, the moment she swayed towards me in the Orangery Vicky became mine—there was no harm in letting Margot think her blackmail worked. Okay, so I had to wear a monkey suit—it meant I got to see Vicky again, which is something I'd fully intended to engineer anyway. Why not let Margot think she'd won this one?

"You've got a deal," I said.

I didn't realise at the time, but I would come to regret those words more than anything else I'd ever said in my whole life.

CHAPTER 10

Nobody touches her

Vicky

Lottie squeezed my wrist lightly, which was my signal to stop, take a breath, and give someone else a chance to speak.

When I turned to her, she gave her head a very subtle shake. I tilted mine to the side with a small frown, but did manage to snap my mouth shut, which was annoying because I had way more to say on the economic principle of comparative advantage in trade.

My mind stalled for a moment. What was it Lottie said I should do next in this situation?

Lottie had such a high level of emotional intelligence and was so in tune with others that it was like she could almost read their minds. That's why she was invaluable to me. My emotional intelligence was in my boots, and I struggled with reading people. Before Lottie came on the scene, I was unwittingly insulting various investors and business associates on a daily basis. Now, if she was with me, she could help direct my aberrant behaviour with the non-verbal signals we'd developed together.

She squeezed my wrist again.

If in doubt, just smile at them, I heard Lottie say in my head, and I turned back to the men in the circle around me to do just that.

A couple of them blinked in shock at the abrupt transition, but most smiled right back.

Lottie's voice filtered into my thoughts again…

"Use that thing carefully," she'd warned me.

"What thing?"

"That smile."

I frowned at her. "What about my smile?"

"Vics, do you have any idea how stunning you are when you smile?"

I shrugged. Of course I was well aware that I was conventionally attractive, but what did that have to do with my smile?

She gave me a patient look. "What happens when you smile at people?"

"I don't really smile at anyone."

Lottie sighed. "Okay, then just try it for me. I guarantee that with men, they'll either smile back or be too stunned to do anything at all."

Lottie was right. Even in the most difficult negotiation, if I smiled, I could gain a huge advantage.

"I'm sorry, gentleman," I said in the self-effacing tone I'd practised with Lottie. It annoyed me, really. Why should I say sorry when I wasn't? Why should I apologise for knowing more about economics than them? I didn't understand the point. But Lottie explained that if I wanted people on my side, it was what they wanted to hear. "I tend to get carried away with economics."

"Money is Vicky's jam," Lottie said with her own smile.

There was a snort from the side.

My gaze flicked across, and I froze.

Mike was standing there in a dinner jacket perfectly fitted to his huge frame. He was pulling at his collar and shifting in his shiny Italian leather shoes. The contrast between this Mike and the normal Mike was so stark that my brain somewhat short-circuited.

"Well, I can attest to that," one of the investors said as he smiled at me. "The investments you've managed for us have doubled in the last quarter."

Someone else started speaking, but I lost the thread of the conversation. The importance of making a good impression on the men around us, which was one of the main objectives of this evening, faded.

All I could see was Mike.

"You're wearing a suit," I blurted out as I stared at him, ignoring everything else around us.

Once I slipped into hyperfocus mode, there was no stopping me.

Mike's eyebrows went up. "Er... well, yeah. It's kind of required," he said in his gruff voice.

"You never wear suits."

I vaguely registered everyone around us muttering in confusion, but I simply could not tear my focus away from Mike. I barely even felt Lottie's wrist squeeze to attempt to bring me back to the real world this time.

"I prefer you in your normal clothes," I said. My smile had dropped now, and I was frowning across at him.

The suit was *wrong.* I'd never been a fan of change. It felt imperative that I get this across to Mike right in that moment, so I didn't filter my words or think about what they might be implying.

"In particular, I like the thermal shirt you wear that has a small rip in the left sleeve."

"Jesus Christ," Mike muttered, and two flags of colour appeared on his cheekbones above his beard.

"Who *is* this guy?" I heard the Hyde Park investor whisper to his colleague. Both of them had made their sexual interest in me known previously.

I had improved on how I turned men down now. Instead of my standard "no" accompanied by a blank stare, I pretended to be flattered and faked remorse for the fact I wasn't free to pursue any further relations with them.

To be honest, I'd not quite managed this form of lying yet. Both of those men had received a blank *no* from me, and I'd overheard both of them call me *ice princess* more than once.

"Vics," Lottie said in a low voice, trying to draw my attention. "We need to keep an eye on the time, yeah? Gentleman, ladies, excuse us for a second."

I registered her pulling on my arm, but I couldn't tear my eyes away from Mike.

"Victoria," she snapped, her voice raised just enough to penetrate my hyperfocus.

I blinked before turning to her.

"We need to *go*." She breathed a huge sigh of relief as I nodded. Lottie muttered our excuses, and we left the circle to start across the ballroom.

"I was doing it again, wasn't I?" I asked in a dejected tone as Lottie headed for the exit with me in tow. There was a certain amount of panic in her movements now, and I knew it was because she was worried about the fireworks. Well, not about the fireworks, but about my reaction to the fireworks. I wasn't good with fireworks. Ollie hadn't even wanted me to come tonight because of them.

Ugh. What kind of person couldn't even tolerate a few loud bangs?

Once Lottie and I were around the corner in the corridor leading to the toilets, she turned to me and gave my hand a quick squeeze, which was all I could tolerate in terms of handholding.

"It's okay, hun," she said in a soft voice.

"It's not okay," I snapped, as my hands bunched into fists at my sides. "I'm never going to convince him to sleep with me if he thinks I'm defective."

After what happened between Mike and me at Buckingham Manor, I'd been thinking. Okay, so maybe Mike didn't like me, which made him a poor choice as a romantic prospect. But the kiss would suggest that he had changed his mind about pursuing something physical.

If I could convince him to take me on as a project in the sexual sense, then I might finally be able to lose my virginity. And given the fact that he was the first man I had ever been attracted to, this was probably my only opportunity to do it. It was ridiculous to be a twenty-nine-year-old virgin. If I didn't sleep with Mike, that was never going to change. I'd decided it was worth the risk, despite the fact I wasn't "emotionally safe" with him.

Plus, I simply could not stop thinking about him. The kiss and being held in his arms had made my obsessive thoughts ten times worse. I was actually thankful that I'd had a blissful twenty-nine years without being tortured by the kind of unrelenting yearning I was experiencing now. I woke up most nights aching and sweating after dreams of Mike kissing me, on top of me—all kinds of things I'd never imagined before. It was completely taking over my life.

Lottie frowned. "Vicky, you're not defective."

"Yes, I am. I'm defective and weird."

"Who wants to be normal? What even is normal?" she said with a smile, clearly trying to coax me out of my black mood. "It's probably blooming boring. I'd rather hang out with you than someone boring. And you are *not* defective, Vicky. Not at all."

As she linked arms with me and propelled us to the ladies' toilets, I had a warm feeling spread from my chest. Yes, I employed Lottie, so I knew deep down that she wasn't a *real* friend. It was a transactional relationship, which in reality, was the only type of friendship I was able to cultivate—but when she made comments like that, the warmth in her voice made it easy to pretend.

"Why are we going to the toilets?" I asked.

"It's what women do to catch their breath," she explained.

I wrinkled my nose. "Sometimes I think that the whole world is weird, and I'm the only normal one."

Lottie snorted a laugh as we pushed through into the cavernous bathroom. She moved to the mirrors whilst I headed to the nearest cubicle.

"You're not even going to try and use the opportunity to empty your bladder?" I asked, completely incredulous.

Honestly, people made no sense to me. After I shut the door behind me, I could hear someone else come into the bathroom and talk to Lottie, but the space was too vast to make out what they were saying. When I came back out, to my surprise, my half-sister was standing next to Lottie by the mirrors, glaring at her in the reflection.

Claire and Lottie had always seemed to get on okay.

"Stop it," Claire hissed at Lottie as I approached. "Leave me alone."

"Claire?" I asked as I drew up next to them and looked between them. Something was wrong with Claire's face. In the harsh light of the bathroom, I could see an area of darkening high on her cheekbone, and I noticed some swelling there. "Why have you got a bruise on your cheek?"

Claire glared at me for a moment, then tore out of the bathroom.

I frowned after her. Claire and I weren't very close. She only really tolerated me, but she was never unkind. And the last thing I wanted was for her to be hurt.

Lottie put her hand on my arm to get my attention.

"Vics, we need to go really soon. Why don't you find Ollie and let him know, and I'll go after Claire."

I nodded at Lottie, well aware that managing the Claire situation was far beyond my capabilities. She wouldn't welcome me coming after her. I knew that at least. But I also knew that if my half-sister was hurt, then my half-brother needed to know. Informing him was a task I *was* capable of. So I took a deep breath and forced myself into the crowd to get across the ballroom.

Crowds like this were not good for me. I could feel my anxiety levels slowly climb as I weaved through all the people, but all I could see in my mind was that bruise on my half-sister's cheek.

If anyone could sort it out, it was Ollie. He wouldn't let anything happen to Claire. He'd protect her.

But the more time I spent closed in with other people, the worse I started to feel. Where was he? Seeing a gap open up a pathway towards the bar, I made a break for it, but just as I was squeezing past the group of investors I'd been talking to earlier, one of them caught my arm, bringing me to an abrupt halt.

"Ice princess," he said in a booming voice, and the people around him started laughing.

I yanked on my arm, trying to pull free, but he held fast.

The feel of his large sweaty hand around my biceps made me feel physically sick. For an awful moment, I thought I might meltdown.

I knew what Lottie would tell me to do. She'd say to use my smile and make a polite excuse. Maybe if I'd been able to do that, he might have let me go. But when hit with the reality of this situation I just froze, blinking up at him with a blank expression.

"So, we're curious," the horrible man went on in a slurred voice. "Do you let anyone have a go with your royal snatch, or has everything iced over completely now?"

I pulled on my arm again to try and step away, but he only tightened his grip. Bile rose in the back of my throat, but just as I thought I would vomit on his shoes, suddenly, his hand was gone.

"What the fuck do you think you're doing, you tosser?" Mike shook the man by the arm he had snatched off me. He towered over him, and I watched as the man's face paled. "Answer me, you piece of shit."

"Fucking hell, let go of me!" the man shouted.

Mike dropped his arm, and the man took a step back, rubbing it with his hand.

"Doesn't feel good when someone bigger than you grabs you and won't let go, does it?" Mike's voice was low and furious.

"She didn't say anything," the man whined. "I would have let her go if she'd *said* something."

I shuffled back and hugged myself, suddenly feeling very cold. Of course, I should have said something. A normal woman would have been able to tell this odious man to cease and desist the minute he put his hands on her. But I wasn't normal.

Noticing my movement, Mike's gaze flicked from the man to me, then, to my complete shock, he walked in my direction, and as if we belonged to each other, he took my hand in his.

For the first time in my life, I tolerated someone holding my hand. There was something different about Mike's large, dry, calloused hand, something calming.

"Stay away from her," he growled at the man, then turned to the rest of the group, who were all cowering away from him. "The same goes for all you pillocks. Nobody touches her. Got me?"

They all nodded. The one who grabbed me looked mutinous and was still rubbing his arm, but he nodded along all the same.

Then Mike turned and pulled me through the crowd, successfully negotiating all the people far more effectively than I had managed. When we were in a relatively clear area next to the floor-to-ceiling windows and the huge open double doors leading outside, he pulled us to a stop, his hand still in mine, and glared down at me.

"Why the fuck are you alone?"

CHAPTER 11

What's wrong with her?

Mike

"W-what?" Vicky blinked up at me.

I felt like an utter bastard to have brought out the stammer again, especially after what just happened, but I tended to get angry when I was worried and seeing that man grab Vicky had taken five years off my life.

I took a deep breath and made a concerted effort to soften my gruff tone.

"Sorry, Vicky," I said, my voice softer now, with only a hint of growl. "I didn't mean to snap at you. Where's your brother and Lottie?"

"Lottie went after my half-sister. Claire has a bruise on her cheek."

Fucking Blake. That drunk prick always did give me weird vibes.

"Stay away from Blake."

Yep, I was just spouting off commands to this woman now like I owned her. But she still hadn't let go of my hand. She looked absolutely stunning in the long, fitted white dress she was wearing, and I was still seething after seeing some bastard grab her.

The thought that she could ever be alone with her brother-in-law made me vibrate with rage.

"I don't understand what you—?"

"And what the fuck were you doing with those idiots earlier?"

She frowned at me and snatched her hand back from mine. I could feel her retreat, and I knew I needed to reign in my temper and soften my tone again, but I simply couldn't manage it.

I'd been furious throughout this whole shitshow of an event.

Vicky and Lottie had been going from one group of complete twats to another, charming the pants off all of them. And I could tell from the various expressions on Vicky's face that she hated every minute.

I tried to stay in the background, but when I saw that forced smile she directed at one particular group of leering dickheads, I had to approach. And I'd felt a deep sense of satisfaction when Vicky's focus went from the other men to me in a matter of seconds.

But I was still recovering from the shock of her describing her favourite of my work outfits in great detail to everyone around us. Despite the fact I'd hated the attention on me at the time, I still felt huge satisfaction at the further demonstration of Vicky being mine. Especially after I'd had to endure overhearing all of these pricks talking about the *ice princess* and making bets on who was going to be the first to fuck her when she was out of earshot.

But before I could say anything to Vicky, Lottie had dragged her away, and I'd been searching for her ever since until I saw that grabby piece of shit holding onto her arm with her looking terrified.

Her eyebrows went up, and pink stained her cheekbones. "He grabbed me. I didn't—"

"I'm not talking about what just happened. I'm talking about earlier when you smiled at all those groups of motherfuckers and made them think they might stand a chance with you."

She blinked up at me, and the red on her cheeks deepened. "Lottie's coached me on smiling. It makes me more socially acceptable."

"Who the fuck cares if you're socially acceptable to those twats?"

"I have to do business with them."

I glared at her. "You are *not* doing business with *them*."

"I-I..." She looked so completely and adorably confused then that I just wanted to kiss her again, but the fire building behind her eyes told me that may not be the best plan. "You can't tell me what to do."

"I can if it keeps you away from bastards like that."

Okay, I was aware at this juncture that the wooing portion of the evening seemed to have gone seriously awry. I wasn't sure how wooing translated into modern times, but I knew it probably didn't involve barking orders and getting cross at the object of your affection.

Vicky had dropped my hand to put both of hers on her hips, and her eyes were narrowed. I'd grown up with a sister—I knew the warning signs. But just as I was about to try and claw things back, the event organiser's voice filled the space.

"So, if we're all ready, it's that part of the evening where you can start oohing and aahing as we light up this entire county!"

Vicky blinked before her eyes went wide, a look of sheer panic flashing across her features.

What was going on?

Then the first bang shook the room, and her hands flew to her ears.

The sky outside transformed with multi-coloured sparkles, and the floor trembled with the force of the explosions. Then one of the rockets that must have been set off too close to the open double doors suddenly misfired.

Sparks flew across the ballroom floor, and the crowd surged back amidst squeals of slightly panicky excitement.

Meanwhile, as the bangs from outside escalated, I realised that something was wrong with Vicky. She'd started shaking like a cornered animal.

I uncrossed my arms and started toward her, but she flinched back. I felt completely helpless as her hands at her ears started flapping. Then my heart stopped with her first awful scream.

She dropped into a half-crouch, hands still flapping at her ears, completely lost in her world of fear.

"Hold her!" I heard Ollie shout and glanced over to see him and Lottie trying to get to us through the crowd. "Mike, hold her! Do it, *now*."

It has to be a tight hug.

That's what Vicky had said in the Orangery. That's what calmed her down. Before I could doubt myself, I strode forward and pulled her small body into my arms.

The screaming stopped just as Lottie and Ollie made it to us, but Vicky was still shaking.

Lottie bent down to scoop up Vicky's bag, which had fallen to the floor, and pulled out noise-cancelling headphones.

"Keep firm pressure," Lottie told me as she put the headphones over Vicky's ears. "Don't stroke to soothe her. Just use the pressure. You can sway her very slightly from side to side. But *no* light touch. She can't *stand* light touch."

I gave a sharp nod as Vicky burrowed further into my chest.

Ollie's heavy hand fell on my shoulder when he arrived next to us. "Give her to me," he snapped, all ducal authority, which just pissed me off.

Where was he when his sister was being grabbed by some random bloke?

"I've got her," I said firmly, glaring at Ollie. Then in a much lower voice, I asked, "Why's she reacting like this?"

"She's Autistic," Ollie said, and suddenly, the puzzle pieces all seemed to fall into place.

"Why has nobody bothered to tell me that?"

Lottie shook her head. "She doesn't want people treating her differently." Then she bit her lip as if deciding whether or not to continue. When she spoke again, I could only just hear her above the fireworks. "Especially *you*."

I shook my head at the level of fuckwittery happening here.

So Vicky's mind worked differently. There was no shame in that. What's with all the secrecy? Christ, when I thought about all the jacked-up crap I'd said to her when I thought she was just a cold, stuck-up lady of the manor wanting to get her end away with a bit of rough, I felt ill.

But I didn't have all the information, did I?

"Well, how the fuck did you let this happen?" I said, furious with myself, but even more angry with her useless fucking brother. "You must have known how this was going to go down. Why is she even here?"

Vicky whimpered, and I felt my heart break right then and there, in the middle of this poncy bloody party.

I shifted her to encase her further into my arms, and she burrowed into me again.

"Lottie was *supposed* to make sure she left," Ollie said through gritted teeth.

"*You're* her brother, mate." I snapped.

"Where were you when *your* sister was hurt?" Ollie cracked back, and I stiffened.

I was about to blast him for this latest blatant bullshit—I was a *great* brother, thank you very much—but another small whimper from Vicky stopped me from unleashing on the Duke of Fuckingham. I needed to make the small woman in my arms a priority. I could haul this prick over the coals for neglecting her later.

"Look, can we just concentrate on sorting Vicky?" Lottie asked.

"Right, well, *I'm* going to be the one sorting Vicky out," I told them both.

We were now attracting a fair bit of attention, and I had a feeling Vicky would hate to be seen like this. Making a snap decision, and before either of them could say anything, I scooped Vicky up into my arms, held her tightly so that her face was still planted in my chest and hidden from the overly interested crowd, and strode off towards the exit with Ollie and Lottie trailing after me.

Once we were outside in the driveway, I went straight to my massive, ancient, mud-covered Land Rover and put Vicky on her feet to wrap her in my dinner jacket, which was so huge on her that it came down to her knees. I then lifted her up and deposited her on the front passenger seat.

Ollie blocked me as I tried to round the vehicle to get in myself.

"*I'll* take her home," Ollie growled. "You don't know what you're—"

That was when my temper snapped.

"No, I don't know what I'm dealing with because *none* of you fuckers bothered to tell me," I semi-shouted. "You've dropped this ball, Harding. It was me she wanted to go to in there. Me who held her through it, and it'll be me that makes sure she's okay."

Ollie glared at me, clearly not going to move, but then Vicky's shaky voice piped up through the now-open window of the Land Rover.

"I'll stay with Mike," she said, and that was all I needed to hear.

Despite my complete dickbag tendencies, she was still choosing me.

So I tuned both of them out to concentrate on her. Once in the truck, I put my arm over the back of Vicky's seat to look over my shoulder and reverse, then tore out of the driveway.

CHAPTER 12

No frame of reference

Vicky

Mike's hug had started my recovery from the meltdown, but what fully snapped me back to reality was his supremely masculine reversing manoeuvre.

I'd never found the way a man drives a car attractive before, but as Mike put his arm over my headrest to look back over his shoulder, with all his muscles flexing under his tailored shirt, I forgot about the fireworks, and my mouth went completely dry.

But now that he was tearing along the country road, changing gears with one hand whilst the other rested on the steering wheel (all unreasonably attractive manoeuvres for driving an ancient manual vehicle) the reality of the evening was starting to filter back in.

What's wrong with her?

She's Autistic.

I knew Ollie, Margot, Abdul and Lottie were right. There was nothing to be ashamed of. My brain just worked a bit differently. I saw the world and everyone in it in an unusual way. Not everyone can work the same or behave the same. In fact, as I've said before, if the world were full of Vickys, everything would run a lot more smoothly.

Certainly, everything would be on time, and everybody would say what they really meant—it would actually be a lot more efficient and less confusing. But seeing as I was the aberrant one, and everyone else ran on white lies and subtleties, it was difficult not to carry any shame.

Abdul put the blame for that firmly on my mother and half-sister. Mum's refusal to let anyone "put a label" on why I had difficulties meant that I internalised the idea of having a label as a bad thing.

Not to mention, Rebecca repeatedly called me a freak and a weirdo. I'd only been diagnosed a few years ago, and in general, I didn't want people to know.

With Mike, back when I was entertaining romantic fantasies about him, I had hoped he could overlook my quirks and just focus on my above-average attractiveness level, but I guess there is a limit to how far looks can override personality, or a lack thereof.

I had thought it would be better to ease him into the Autistic label, but I had also conceded he would need to know eventually. Now that I wasn't harbouring any romantic fantasies, but rather an intention to pursue a purely physical arrangement—if he would agree to it—I had hoped he might never *need* to know. But my meltdown tonight had well and truly outed me.

There was no hiding anything from him now.

I stiffened as we turned in the opposite direction to Buckingham Manor.

"Where are we going?" I managed to ask. I was not particularly good with unknowns, and driving off in the opposite direction of my family's house where I was staying was definitely an unknown.

Mike had both hands on the steering wheel now, and he tightened them until his knuckles turned white.

"I'm taking you back to my home," he told me.

"But… why?"

"Why?"

"Yes… why are we going to your home?"

"I live there."

I snapped my mouth shut and blinked at the windscreen. "But I don't live there."

"There's nobody at Buckingham Manor now. They're all at the party. You're not going home to that great big empty house after what just happened. You'll be coming home with me."

"That makes no logical sense."

His eyebrows went up. "Why not?"

"You don't like me."

Ah, my special talent—blurting out uncomfortable truths.

Mike let out a long breath, muttering, "shit" under his breath before he glanced at me then back at the road. "I like you, Vicky. Okay? And someone needs to look after you."

I blinked at the windshield, still feeling numb and shaky after my meltdown.

"You don't need to look after me," I whispered, horrified he thought me that incapable, but I was guessing after witnessing that meltdown, I should have expected it. "And anyway, if I do need to be looked after, then Ollie and Lottie can—"

"Fine bloody job they were making of it," he said in disgust. "First, you're carted around, smiling at a bunch of absolute gobshites that you shouldn't have been within a country mile of, *then* one of those gobshites grabbed you, leaving red marks which will probably bloody well bruise by tomorrow."

The absolute fury in Mike's voice when he mentioned even a possibility of a bruise on my arm made anything I was going to say die on my lips.

"And *then* when those fireworks go off, neither of those two were anywhere near you. So, no. I'm not keen to leave you with them after you've just had a massive shock. You're coming home with me."

I actually made a harrumph sound of frustration at Mike's little speech, which was entirely out of character for me. But I decided that I would just have to put up with this detour for now. I'd call a taxi from his house to Buckingham Manor. It would involve waking up Janice, who was the only taxi driver in Little Buckingham and would be less than pleased, but this was an emergency.

It was then I realised that I had no idea where Mike lived. He had a workshop at Moonreach, his mum's house, but I knew that he didn't actually live there.

We went through Little Buckingham, past The Badger's Sett and down one of the tiny lanes into the woodland by the side of the village.

When the trees thinned, I sucked in a shocked breath at the small house in the middle of the clearing. I'd never seen anything like it in my life. It was entirely made of wood, but not wood like I had ever seen it before. All the wood was cut in a sort of fluid way, following the grain and patterns of the trees it came from. There were no straight lines.

Even the fence around the wooden terrace at the front of the house wasn't straight; instead, it was made of sanded-down and varnished natural branches.

The windows were all different shapes, as if the wood itself had dictated how they should fit in.

I usually really liked straight lines and order, but as I stared up at this breathtaking house, I didn't think I'd ever seen a more beautiful building. I was still sitting in the passenger seat staring up at the house when Mike startled me by opening the car door.

He looked between me and the house for a moment and scratched his beard. "Right, so it's not much, but this is my gaffe."

"You *live* here?" I breathed, still unable to move.

Mike shrugged, and two flags of colour appeared high on his cheekbones.

"Uh, yeah. Of course." He sighed. "Look, I know it's not exactly what you're used to, but—"

"No, it's very, *very* different to what I'm used to," I said the absolute truth.

I'd never even seen a house like this before.

"We can't all live in fancy mansions, you know," Mike said through gritted teeth. He sounded annoyed, and I didn't understand why. "Are you getting out or what?"

Maybe he was annoyed that I was sitting there staring at his beautiful house and not getting out of the car, and therefore, wasting his time.

I cleared my throat, undid the seatbelt and then turned to jump down.

"I'm going to put my hand on your elbow," Mike said in a gruff voice.

"What?"

"To help you down. My Land Rover's high up, and you're wearing those crazy heels. You'll need a hand down, and you said you need a warning before physical contact, so..."

"Oh, right, thank you."

He nodded, and his large hand encircled my elbow, supporting me as I climbed out of the car.

I still couldn't take my eyes off the house. Small details were jumping out at me all the time: the flowers planted around the outside of the deck, the wooden door which formed an archway shape and had a small window in the upper part, the climbing rose up the side of the far wall.

"Do you own this?" I asked in a bewildered voice.

There was a small silence. I glanced at Mike, who was frowning down at me; he still hadn't taken his hand off my elbow, and I was finding I quite liked it there.

"Yes," he told me, then after another long pause, "I built it."

"You built it?" My eyebrows went up.

"Come on, it's cold." His voice was gruff now. "Come inside."

I nodded and felt oddly sad when he let go of my elbow to lead the way up the wooden steps onto the deck and into his house.

"You leave it unlocked?" I asked as he pushed open the door.

"Got nothing worth stealing, and we're not exactly in a crime hot spot."

He flicked a switch, and a soft glow filled the house.

I didn't agree that he had nothing worth stealing. Every piece of furniture was hand-crafted from beautiful wood. His kitchen had a massive, thick piece of wood as the countertop, which again, had that wavy edge where the grain had dictated the shape. There was a table and chairs matching the countertop, and across the room, an armchair and a small sofa with wooden frames, containing what looked like comfy, squishy sofa cushions with colourful throws over the top.

The entire room was double height. I looked up to see a central skylight right at the top of the house. There was a wooden spiral staircase leading to a mezzanine level, which was clearly the bedroom area, with one double bed up there.

When Mike broke the silence, his voice sounded strained. "Look, I know it's not up to your standards but—"

"Why are you cross with me?" I asked.

Abdul said it was better if I asked people directly what was going on if I didn't understand an interaction. He said that was preferable to allowing miscommunication to continue. That if I sensed something was wrong then I should just directly call it out.

Relying on social cues simply wasn't an option for me, especially without Lottie here.

"I'm not cross with you, Vicky."

"Your tone of voice is angry. I can pick up on anger quite well."

Anger and frustration directed at me had featured heavily in my childhood, and I had trained myself to spot the signs early on. Mike took a deep breath in and let it out slowly.

"Shit, sorry, I don't mean to sound angry with you." His tone was softer now. "I'm just a bit touchy about my house."

"Why would that make you angry with me?"

His hand went to the back of his neck, and those flags of colour appeared on his cheekbones again.

"Well, you seem a bit thrown by it, and not in a good way."

"Not in a good way?" I repeated.

"Yes. Look, sorry, it's okay if you don't like my house. I know it's not everyone's cup of tea."

I frowned. "You think I don't like your house?"

"Vicky, I know the type of posh places you're used to, and this—"

"This is the most beautiful building I have ever seen in my entire life," I told him the absolute truth.

His hand came down from his neck, and he stared at me with a new intensity. Both his fists bunched by his sides then unclenched as he took a step towards me.

I was proud of myself that after everything I'd been through that night, I held my ground.

When he was only inches away from me, his hand came up towards my face but stopped a hair's breadth away.

"Baby," he said in a low, growly voice. "I really *really* want to kiss you. Can I do that?"

"Yes, um... please," I managed to choke out.

"I'll be touching your face as well, if that's okay?"

"Y-yes, face touching is acceptable."

The corners of his lips turned up in a small smile before his hand made contact with my jaw and cheek.

I could feel the rough callouses on his fingers as he slid his hands from my cheeks, up and into my hair. I had to tip my head right back to look at his brown eyes, which were searching my face.

"You are so fucking gorgeous," he whispered, his lips almost touching mine, and my mind blanked.

The magnetic pull of this man was simply too much to take. So instead of waiting for him to close the distance between us, I pushed up onto my tiptoes as both of my hands went to the sides of his face, and my lips sealed over his.

He gave a startled grunt of surprise, and for a horrified moment, I thought I may have made a huge mistake. What was I doing, initiating a kiss like that? I had no experience of kissing protocol. What on earth did I do now?

But just as I was about to stiffen and pull away, Mike's other arm came up and around me, pulling my body into his, and he kissed me back.

At first, I felt awkward—worried he'd be able to tell that I'd never kissed anyone before. But as my body melted into his, surrounded by his strength and immense warmth, his woodsy, clean, manly smell invading my senses, I forgot to be awkward.

I forgot my own name.

So when his mouth opened over mine, my body took over, and I did the same.

I moved one of my hands into his thick hair, the other to the muscles of his chest, as I pushed up against him.

I couldn't get close enough. It was like a fire had been lit inside me. I almost felt like I was going to pass out with need. I could hear small, desperate moans, and after a moment, I realised they were coming from me.

Then Mike lifted me up effortlessly as he walked backwards, still kissing me before placing me on the wooden kitchen countertop and moving so he was standing between my legs.

Without the height difference, he didn't have to bend down so far, and our bodies could be even closer.

One of my hands went down to the hem of his shirt then up to the warm skin over the firm muscles of his back.

He groaned into my mouth, and I'd never felt so powerful in my life.

All I wanted in that moment was him. All the other turmoil in my mind was silenced, which was extremely rare for me. But all I could *feel* was him; all I could focus on was him.

It was the most peace I'd experienced in years, and I needed more.

I needed him closer.

I pulled on his hair and slid my hand further up the back of his shirt, trying to get to as much of his heated skin as possible. I felt like I was burning up from the inside. I wanted him more than I'd ever wanted anything before.

I started moving against him, more small moans still coming from the back of my throat.

He growled against my mouth, and then suddenly, his heat was gone.

When I opened my eyes, he was standing just out of reach, breathing heavily and pushing his hands through his hair, making the dark strands stand up at all angles.

I frowned.

"Why did you stop?" I asked when I could catch my breath.

"You've had a shock tonight," he bit out. His hands were clenched into fists at his sides again. "I'm taking advantage of you."

"You're not taking advantage of me at all," I said in confusion. "Is this because I'm not very competent?"

"What?" he asked in confusion.

I sighed. "The logistics of kissing," I said, then shrugged. "I'm not at all familiar with the standards logistics. I'm afraid I've no frame of reference."

"The logistics of kissing?" His lips tipped up in small smile for a moment before his eyes went wide. "Wait a minute. What do you mean by 'no frame of reference'?"

"I don't have any data to refer to as far as kissing goes."

Surely this had all been obvious to him?

"You've never..." Mike shook his head slowly. "I'm sorry, but are you saying you've never been kissed? Vicky, I... how is that even possible? You're beautiful."

"I've never wanted to kiss anyone before. In fact, the very idea of kissing any other human makes me feel physically ill."

My cheeks started heating as my embarrassment increased.

"Until I met you that is. Kissing you does not make me feel physically ill."

I thought I should clarify this point as I didn't want Mike to be deterred from further kissing activities should further opportunities arise.

"Kissing you makes me feel like I'm…" I needed to find the words to describe the feeling. I wanted to be accurate. "Like I'm burning from the inside out. Like I'm finally breathing after years of feeling suffocated. Like I'm in pain but a good pain. Kissing you silences the noise in my head and that's never happened before, not to me."

Mike was staring at me, the intense brown of his eyes lighting with golden flecks and burning into mine. His jaw was clenched. His body vibrating with energy, like every muscle was pulled tight.

"Um…" I started, not quite understanding what was happening, "Mike? Are you okay?"

"No, Vicky." His voice was hoarse as his fists bunched by his sides. "I'm not okay."

"Oh, why?"

"Because I've just found out that I'm your first kiss and—"

"If it's a problem, that's quite alright." His eyebrows went up. "I would understand it being a bit off-putting, so—"

"Off-putting?" Mike said in a strangled voice.

"Yes, well. I supposed the other girls you kiss are all much more proficient and—"

"Vicky." His voice was still hoarse. "That was the best kiss I've ever had, bar none, experienced or otherwise. And I realise this makes me a goddamn caveman, but I'm fucking thrilled you've not kissed any other bastard before. And after that description you gave me, I'm using all of my self-control not to pick you up off that counter, carry you up to my bed, and make you mine in every other way there is."

I smiled at him. "Oh, that sounds great. Let's do that."

He groaned. "Baby, please. I'm hanging on by a thread here." He tore his hand through his hair again. "I am not going to take advantage of you after what happened tonight. I'm enough of a bastard already to have kissed you like that. If I take it further, I won't have to wait for your brother to punch me in the face—I'll do it myself."

CHAPTER 13

Stop talking

Mike

"Hey."

I looked up from the frying pan to see Vicky standing at the bottom of my spiral staircase in my flannel shirt, looking at me with wide eyes. In a superhuman feat of self-control, I'd slept on the sofa last night after showing her up to my bed and leaving her there to sleep alone.

She cleared her throat.

"I'm sorry I slept so long. I should have warned you. After a period of stress, I… well, I tend to sleep a lot. I think it's a way of my brain protecting itself, of recharging. At least, that's what Abdul says."

I abandoned flipping the bacon as my eyes shot back to her and narrowed. "Who's Abdul?"

My attempt at a casual tone came out distinctly growly, but I suspected it was the best I could do after last night.

I knew it wasn't reasonable, but the Neanderthal in me had claimed Vicky already.

She was mine.

I've never wanted to kiss anyone before.

The overpowering sense of possessiveness that swept through me at that statement was definitely in caveman territory. But now hearing another's man name on her lips had sent me and my monkey brain into a flat spin.

She shrugged, completely oblivious to my internal struggle not to march over there, sling her over my shoulder, and make sure my name was the only thing she was calling out.

My grip tightened on the spatula until my knuckles turned white.

"He's my therapist," she said in a small voice, and I felt that animal part of me relax.

But then I noticed the pink in her cheeks and her hands coming up to her ears. She covered the movement by tucking her hair behind them, but I could tell there had been some sort of minor trigger in admitting to me that she had a therapist.

I wasn't sure why she would be embarrassed about that, but I knew I should tread carefully here.

"Oh right. That's good that you have..." Christ, I wasn't great at this sensitive stuff. "I mean, he sounds like he knows what he's on about. So that's good."

"I..." she shifted on her feet, still at the bottom of the stairs, and still too bloody far away from me. "I never used to see therapists. My mother..." Vicky broke off and looked to the side for a moment until focusing back on me. "Well, I do now, and he does help me."

"That's really good, love," I said in a soft tone.

She bit her lip and wrapped her arms around herself as she glanced around the cabin.

"Vicky?" I said, my voice still soft. Her gaze snapped to me. "Is there a reason you're all the way over there?"

"What?" she asked in confusion.

"Baby, do you regret what happened last night? Because—"

"Absolutely not," she said in a firm voice.

I turned the hob off and pulled the pan away from the heat to rest on the heat-proof pad on my worktop. Then I rounded the kitchen counter.

Her eyes widened as I stalked towards her, but she didn't back away, which I took as an encouraging sign.

When I reached her, I dropped my voice lower. "I'm going to kiss you now. Is that okay?"

Her eyes widened, and she nodded.

Then I cupped her delicate jaw with my big mitt of a hand, using the other hand to spread across her back and pull her to me as my lips fell on hers. Softly at first, but just like last night, Vicky was the one to deepen the kiss, also just like last night, in a mammoth feat of self-control, it was me that had to finish it.

But instead of stepping back from her, I rested my forehead on hers and closed my eyes.

"So," I said, my lips nearly touching hers, but not quite. "If you wake up in my cabin with me, that is how I want you to start the morning. In fact, you can make this your standard greeting for me in future."

"Kissing?"

"Yes, kissing. And I want you to come to me, not stand at the bottom of my stairs looking lost."

"You are a very bossy human."

"I know," I said on a grin. "Get used to that." Then I grabbed her hand and pulled her towards the kitchen island. "Right, I need to feed you."

Vicky climbed up on the stool facing the stove, and I switched the heat back on so I could finish making her breakfast.

"I'm not good with new places," she blurted out as I was putting some bread in the toaster.

"Okay," I said slowly, not sure where she was going with this.

She bit her lip and glanced around the cabin. "I wouldn't normally be able to sleep somewhere I'm not used to, or without all my things, but this house is... different."

"Different good?"

She nodded vigorously. "Different *very* good. Being in this house feels like being hugged all the time. It feels calming."

Jesus. I turned away from the kettle to smile at her. "That's great, love," I said in a now hoarse voice.

Her description of the house that I built with my own two hands was one of the most beautiful things I'd ever heard.

"But I'm still not good with interactions that don't have defined boundaries and social norms that I can understand."

I tilted my head to the side as I slid a plate in front of Vicky. "I'm not sure what you mean."

She sighed. "I struggle if I'm not sure what I should be doing. I've never woken up in a man's house before."

That possessive part of me surged to life again at that statement.

Christ, I was basic.

"And I didn't know if you would want me to leave or stay, or whether I should be getting dressed into what I wore last night because I still have on your shirt, but I like your shirt, because it's really soft, and it smells of you. And I like the smell of you because it's like freshly cut wood and man mixed together—I'm very sensitive to scent. Anyway, when I'm not sure, I just sort of freeze."

After all that, I decided I didn't like the distance of the kitchen island between us, so I picked up the tea that I'd made for Vicky and brought it around to her side, stopping just in front of her as she twisted on the stool to look at me.

"Can I touch your face?" I asked her.

She nodded, and my hand came up to her temple to stroke into her hair.

"There's so much going on in here all the time, isn't there?" I said softly. "All those thoughts churning around and around. It must be exhausting."

She nodded against my hand, her soft silky hair gliding through my fingers.

"Is it ever quiet up there?" I asked.

"It was quiet when you were kissing me," she whispered.

A low, almost-growl came from the back of my throat, the urge to silence her thoughts again surging through me, but she hadn't eaten in hours, and yesterday had been tough, so I took a step back and put her tea in front of her.

As I moved back to the stove, she took a cautious sip of her tea and then shot me a surprised look.

"How did you know how I take my tea?" she asked, then belatedly looked down at the plate in front of her. "And how did you know what I liked for breakfast?"

Her toast was sliced into triangles, and there were two rashers of bacon on top of them.

Lottie had said that eggs would be "too high risk". Apparently, Vicky was pretty extreme about her eggs. The actual colour chart Lottie texted over for Vicky's tea was quite something, so I decided not to attempt eggs.

"Lottie," I told her.

"Lottie? But Lottie's not here."

"I spoke to Lottie."

"What? Why would you—?"

"I had about a hundred missed calls from Ollie and Lottie, and I wanted to know what you would eat. You were asleep, so I rang Lottie back."

She blinked down at her plate and then back up at me with a stunned expression.

"It's not a big deal, love," I told her. "I knew you'd lost a bit of weight, and I wanted to give you something you could eat. Okay?"

"Not a big deal," she muttered, shaking her head. "That is an inaccurate statement. It is a *very* big deal to me."

I smiled at her, but my chest felt tight at the realisation that someone making her some food that she would like and eat would feel like a big deal to her. But instead of demanding a list of all those other thoughtless fuckers, I picked up my plate and sat down on the handmade wooden stool next to her.

"So, I was thinking," Vicky said, and I braced.

Over the course of the few conversations we'd had, I realised that literally anything could fly out of her mouth.

"I did want a romantic relationship with you in the conventional sense."

I almost choked on my tea but managed to swallow the rest down without incident.

"You *did* want that?" I asked after I'd recovered. "You mean, past tense?"

"Yes. Well, now, I realise that it's unlikely you would be amenable to a romantic type of situation with me."

My eyes went wide. "What the fuck about the last twelve hours makes you think that?"

She shrugged and broke eye contact to concentrate on her food. "Because you think I'm *empty inside*, devoid of *personality,* and you wouldn't touch me with a *barge pole*."

I closed my eyes as I dropped my fork to rub my temples.

Bloody hell, I was such a prick.

"Vicky, I—"

"You don't have to explain," she said, cutting me off in that matter-of-fact tone that she seemed to adopt when she wanted to mask her emotions, but I could just about detect the small thread of hurt through her words. "But last night and this morning would suggest that you have now got over your aversion to touching me. So maybe you're not open to a romantic relationship, but you might be interested in continuing the touching element?"

"Touching element?" I asked, taking a very ill-advised sip of my tea.

"Touching, as in sexual intercourse."

This time I really did choke, so much so, that Vicky had to pat me on the back.

"Are you okay?" she asked.

"Yes, I'm fine," I said in a strangled voice. "You just might want to warn a man before you say sexual intercourse."

"Is that a no?" Vicky sounded very disappointed.

"Jesus, Vicky, it's not a no, but—"

"Because you see, I have never found another man attractive in my life. And that's twenty-nine years. Or, I guess it would be fifteen years since puberty. Of all the men I've ever met, imagining intimacy with them made me feel unwell. I thought there might be something wrong with me. Well, apart from all the other obvious things that are wrong with me that is. But the thought of sexual intercourse with you is…"

She broke off as her cheeks went pink.

"Well, it doesn't make me feel unwell. It makes me feel achy, but in a good way. And to be honest, I can't stop thinking about it. It's actually really distracting at work, and I'm normally very focused about my work. But now, Lottie will ask me something, and I'll realise that I've been thinking about the way your chest looks under your thermal top, how your weight would feel on top of me, what your body looks like in swimming shorts, and what might be underneath said swimming shorts, so much that I've totally lost my train of thought. The dreams at night are even worse. I've actually orgasmed in my sleep from just a sexual dream about you. They're so strong, they wake me up, and I haven't even touched myself—it's just the *thought* of being with you."

"Vicky," I growled.

"Yes?"

"Stop talking."

"Um… are you okay?"

No was the answer to that.

No, I was not okay.

I had the most beautiful woman I had ever seen, the one I'd been secretly fantasising about for months, sitting in my shirt, at my kitchen island, having slept in my bed, and now describing her sex dreams about me and how they made her feel, in an effort to coax me into touching her more.

Jesus, Mary and Joseph, didn't the woman realise that all I wanted to do was touch her?

I swallowed as I slid off the stool and took two rapid steps back from her.

She frowned, her expression hurt, and I felt awful, but if I didn't put some distance between us, I'd be dragging her off her stool and up to my bed in under a minute.

If Vicky had never been kissed, and the thought of touching any other man had made her feel sick, then she was obviously a virgin. I wasn't going to lose control and shag a virgin without... oh, bloody hell, I was going to have to use that word... without *wooing* her first, even if she didn't seem to think that was necessary.

My stomach hollowed out when I replayed her words in my head.

That day at her house had been her clumsy attempt at a serious first move, and I crushed her.

"Vicky, all those things I said when I delivered your coffee table. I was wrong. I'd got you all wrong. So I'll say it again—I'm so, *so* sorry, love. Do you think you can forget what I said? Can we start over?"

She frowned and tilted her head to the side. "I can remember conversations with absolute clarity, down to the smallest word and gesture. It would be impossible for me to forget. I don't forget anything."

I sighed. "Well, could you try to remember this? Could you try to remember what I'm going to say now? That even when I had the wrong impression of you, I *still* dreamt about you for months. That the Vicky I've been with since last night is anything but empty or cold, and I'm fascinated by her. That I really, *really* like you. And that I want to give things a go properly with you, which should not include me throwing you over my shoulder and onto my bed before we've even had an actual date."

She blinked at me for a long moment. When she spoke again, her voice was just above a whisper, as if she didn't want to risk saying the words too loud.

"You like me?"

The way she said it was so heartbreakingly vulnerable, I had to rub my chest to ease the ache that was building there.

"Yes, love," I said in a hoarse voice. "I like you very much."

"Even though I'm… weird?"

I scowled and crossed my arms over my chest. "You're not weird."

Vicky shook her head. "Mike, I am well aware that I don't meet standards of normal behaviour. I'm an outlier in society."

"Well, maybe that's why I like you so much. Who cares about standards of normal behaviour? I like that you're unpredictable."

She bit her lip. "You do?" Her voice was so small now, that even in the complete silence of the cabin, I had to strain to hear her.

That was it. There was no way I couldn't go to her after that.

I strode forward and when I was a foot away I asked, "Can I hug you?"

She nodded, and my arms closed around her. As she burrowed into my chest and her small hands clutched at my shirt, I released a long breath, only then aware of the tension I'd been carrying with not having her in my arms.

CHAPTER 14

Green salad with no dressing

Vicky

I felt a trickle of sweat roll down my back as I stared at the menu. There was nothing here that I could realistically tolerate.

When I glanced up at Mike, I could see he was watching me for a reaction, and I managed a smile, at least I hoped I did—Mike's frown in response would suggest it was more of a grimace.

Right, I told myself, *get it together and woman up*, as Lottie would say. I needed to get these ridiculous food aversions under control.

I had come a long way since childhood, when for years, I'd only been able to tolerate plain pasta, cheese sandwiches, and fish fingers. It had driven my mother crazy. She once didn't give me anything I could eat for three days, trying to break me of the habit under the assumption that if I got hungry enough, I would eat.

I didn't eat.

It was only when she was called in to the school after I nearly fainted in assembly that she gave in.

"You can't even eat like a normal human," Rebecca had taunted me.

I could still hear her voice in my head now. She was right.

But I'd come a long way. Nowadays, I could eat a varied diet, and I approached that with military precision, consulting nutritionists and focusing on health. I only lapsed back into old habits of not eating when I was stressed or unhappy.

But I couldn't stand rich food. Sauces were a complete no-no, as was shellfish and rare meat. To be honest, when I was feeling as anxious as I was in that moment, I could only really manage absolutely plain chicken, undercooked broccoli—I couldn't stand it squishy—and plain potatoes or pasta.

I certainly wasn't going to be able to eat chateaubriand, Dover sole in lemon sauce or lobster thermidor.

"Vicky?" Mike asked, and my eyes snapped up to his from my frantic perusal of the menu. "Is this okay?"

He cleared his throat and shifted his big body on the delicate chair.

This restaurant didn't suit Mike at all, and I was surprised he'd brought me here. It was pretentious in the extreme, with a Michelin star and rave reviews in the *Guardian*.

And Mike looked different as well. He was wearing a shirt, smart jeans, and a pair of dress shoes. Apart from the black-tie outfit the other night, I'd never seen him in anything other than his work boots or trainers with well-worn combat trousers that had multiple pockets all over them, or paint-stained jeans.

His beard was trimmed tonight, and I missed the unruly wildness of before.

"This was the fanciest one I could get a booking on short notice." He shrugged. "You're probably used to better, but I didn't want to wait and—"

"No," I said with a frown. "No more waiting."

He smiled at me, and I felt my cheeks heat.

After that morning at his cabin, Mike had told me that he didn't want to rush things. He wanted to take me out on an official date before we did any more of the touching stuff.

I'm afraid I was a little grumpy about this. But when I'd been wrapped in his arms in his beautiful house, having eaten the breakfast that he'd prepared after taking great pains to find out what I liked—something nobody had ever done before in my life other than Margot, who didn't really count because she felt obligated to look after me, and she was a good person—I was fully ready for the sex.

I was ready for all the sex with Mike, and I knew he was ready for that too—at least I could feel the evidence that he was ready for sex.

When I explained this to him, in the interest of full disclosure, he'd made a pained groan and set me away from him, telling me in a strangled voice not to *say stuff like that,* and that he was *trying to be good here* and to *give him a break.*

Those two flags of colour had appeared on his cheekbones again, and his pupils were so dilated, only a thin rim of golden brown was visible.

I found this all immensely frustrating.

Mike Mayweather was clearly a gentleman. He had found out about my inexperience and was under the false assumption that he needed to orchestrate a series of non-sex-related interactions prior to intercourse.

I like you very much.

Okay, so there was that confession of his as well. I'd replayed it over and over in my head since the weekend. But I knew better than to put my trust in what he'd said then. I knew that, unlike me, people didn't always say what they meant.

I knew that there were often multiple agendas at play, and I could also still recall with perfect clarity the other words Mike had said to me just a few weeks ago.

Mike smiled at me, and I was momentarily frozen to the spot. His white teeth against his tan skin and dark beard was such a glorious sight that I almost dropped my menu.

"You're an impatient little thing, aren't you?" he said through his smile, and I rolled my eyes.

"I just don't see the need for this rigmarole," I said, still fascinated by his smiling face.

"Humour me," he said softly, and I shrugged.

I was staying at Buckingham Manor again this weekend. Margot had asked me to come down to look at some of the Buckingham charitable foundation accounts.

I did explain to her that this could be achieved remotely, but she was insistent that I come in person. When I told Mike I was coming down, he immediately arranged this date, something Margot seemed to be unreasonably excited about.

But then Margot was acting very strangely overall. It took me all of ten minutes to ascertain that the accounts were, in fact, in perfect order, which was not surprising, seeing as Margot already had a team of financial advisors keeping them that way.

Clearly, she did not need any help with them. She *did*, however, want to talk about Lottie and Ollie's break up. Margot was devastated that my half-brother had "fucked up so stupendously," as she put it.

Truth be known, I was devastated too. Ollie had said some terrible things to Lottie after my breakdown at the gala, blaming her for what happened, and Lottie and Hayley had moved out of Buckingham House the following day.

So far, Ollie's sustained attempts to win her back had been firmly rebuffed.

Now, I carried the guilt of that too. If I'd been able to tolerate some fireworks like a normal human, Ollie would never have said what he did to Lottie.

And Lottie was sad. Even I, with my terrible empathy, could intuit this. Lottie was one of my favourite people, and I didn't want her sad. She helped me so much, in so many ways, and I found it incredibly frustrating that I couldn't in turn help her with this, especially as I viewed the whole thing as my fault.

I'd decided to keep the Big Mike Date a secret from Lottie and Ollie. They had enough on their plate at the moment, and I knew that Ollie would be worried for me. Seeing as his overprotective tendencies towards me were what led to the breakdown of his relationship with Lottie in the first place, I didn't want to involve him yet.

Margot had agreed to keep the date a secret as well.

When Mike picked me up tonight from Buckingham Manor, I'd explained to him, *again*, that he didn't need to go through any of this in order to have sexual relations with me. That he didn't need to lie about liking me.

He looked furious for a moment but then cleared his expression before checking if he could take my hand and leading me to his Land Rover.

Before I could say anything more, he'd wrenched open the passenger door, lifted me into the seat (after asking if he could put his hands on my hips), and then stood in the door, caging me in and frowning down at me.

"I can see that our discussion on Sunday didn't quite penetrate," he said through gritted teeth. "But that's okay. Actions speak louder than words anyway, and so we're going on this goddamn date and getting to know each other whether you like it or not. Because, baby, I like you. Remember?"

All I could do was nod wordlessly, and he'd slammed the door and stalked around to his side of the car. As we drove in silence to the restaurant he still seemed cross, so I didn't want to question where we were going.

I should have questioned it though, because now I was going to look like a freak again.

"So, what can I get for you this evening?"

My anxiety ramped up another notch as I glanced up at the waiter who was now hovering next to our table. There was a long silence.

"Vicky?" Mike prompted. "What would you like, love?"

I swallowed against my dry throat, and to my horror, I felt my eyes start to sting. Ugh, please don't let me be this pathetic and cry over a simple food order.

The writing was swimming in front of me now as I tried to focus on it.

"Um… I…" I cleared my throat. "C-could I have the green salad with no dressing please?"

Mike slammed his menu down on the table, making me jump. When I looked up at him, his expression was furious.

"Listen, mate," he said to the waiter. "Could you give us a sec?"

"Yes, of course." The thoroughly confused waiter backed away.

"Vicky, look at me," Mike said in a gentle voice, which was in sharp contrast to how angry he seemed a second ago.

When I looked up at him, I saw the fury in his expression had morphed into concern and a little frustration. "You know I think you're beautiful, right?"

"Er… yes, you have consistently expressed your satisfaction with my outward appearance."

"You know I wouldn't want you to change anything about yourself, about your appearance?"

I frowned at him. "What has that got to do with anything?"

He sighed. "Vicky, you've been losing weight."

I looked to the side to avoid his searching gaze as he continued.

"Look, I don't want to push you on this, but when I take a woman I care about out to a restaurant with the intent of spending time with her and feeding her up a bit, I become a bit concerned when she only orders a side salad with no dressing. Baby, please, you don't need to lose weight. You can't afford to lose weight. There's nothing of you already."

I shook my head. "I'm not trying to lose weight, Mike. That's not why I ordered a salad."

"You're not?" His eyebrows were raised, his expression disbelieving. "You haven't been on some mad diet?"

I sighed. "No. It's just that if I get… stressed, my appetite is the first thing to go. I used to be quite restrictive when it came to the types of food I could tolerate, but I've worked on that and improved over the years. However, if something triggers me, then it becomes too hard to make myself eat."

"What's triggered you recently then?" he asked, his eyebrows were pulled down in concern now.

I stared at him and bit my lip, not wanting to admit the truth, and also not trusting my ability to lie.

He blinked once then his face paled.

"Vicky, I..." He swallowed, his hand going up to run through his hair before it came back down onto the table. "*I* didn't trigger you, did I?"

I had to look away from him then, glancing out of the window to avoid his concerned gaze.

"Oh God," he said on a pained groan. "I did, didn't I? My dickhead comments when you made that move on me stressed you out so much that you stopped eating."

I looked down at my hands, shame blooming in my chest.

When I spoke, my voice was small. "It-it wasn't just you, Mike. There's been other... uh, stressful interactions as well. Other triggers."

"Vicky, can I touch your hand?" he asked quietly.

I gave him a small nod.

He reached over the table and enclosed my small fist with his large, dry, warm hand.

I blinked a couple of times, forcing myself to look up at him.

The expression on his face was pained as he stared across at me, and when he spoke, his voice was rough.

"I can never take it back, love. What I did that day can't be undone. It kills me to know that I was one of those *stressful interactions* that made you sad enough to lose your appetite. But just know that I'm going to do everything in my power to make it up to you. Understand?"

"Mike, if I was normal, I could have handled what you–"

"No," he snapped, then gentled his tone. "No. I was mean, and I said what I said without knowing you well enough to make the judgements I made."

I looked out of the window again and pressed my lips together to stop myself from arguing the point with him.

He sighed and gave my hand a squeeze. "But, Vicky, you managed breakfast at my house. I thought that you might be eating a bit better now, so I just don't understand the salad ordering here. Do you think you could order an actual meal?"

I closed my eyes in defeat, realizing that I may as well admit the truth, at least then he wouldn't believe I was deliberately starving myself to death.

"I can't eat anything on this menu," I said in a small voice.

"What?" Mike asked, confused.

I gestured towards the leather-bound paper in front of me. "I just can't manage any of this stuff."

"Oh shit, I knew I should have booked somewhere fancier. Maybe I should have thrown Ollie's name around. That bastard gets a table anywhere he—"

"No, no, you don't understand," I said, panicked by the thought of suffering through a meal at an even *fancier* restaurant than this, maybe even one with the tiny courses, all of which consisted of awful, rich food I couldn't eat. "I can't really eat at restaurants like this."

"Like this?"

"Expensive restaurants."

"What?"

"The food here is too rich. There's nothing plain and familiar on the menu. And it's too formal. I know it sounds really odd, but I can't eat in formal settings. If I have a business dinner, I eat before. I think most people suspect I may have an eating disorder, but really, it's just I'm a bit… difficult when it comes to food."

I was on a roll now, so I decided to simply lay it all out.

"Also, I bought this dress for tonight, and I thought the fabric was soft, but now, it feels *really* itchy, and I don't think I managed to cut out the *entire* label, so that's driving me crazy."

I let out a long breath and collapsed back into my chair. It actually felt good to get all of that out.

Mike blinked at me, looking stunned, and then relief swept over his features.

"Well, thank fuck for that," he finally said. "Jesus, love, I was terrified that you were starving yourself. I had no idea you hated this fancy muck. I thought this kind of gaffe was right up your street, being a proper lady and all." He stood up from his chair and reached for my hand. "Well, if it's plain food you're after then I'm a bloody connoisseur of that shit."

I put my hand in his, and he pulled me up next to him, then tugged me along to the exit, muttering, "Sorry, chief," at the maître d', and slipping him a twenty as we passed.

"Pub food?" Mike asked, although I was too distracted by the reversing-arm-at-the-back-of-my-seat manoeuvre that he was doing as we exited the car park to hear him.

"What?"

He grinned at me before concentrating back on the road. "Can you eat pub food?"

"It depends on which pub. If it's like a gastro pub, then it's a firm no."

Mike snorted. "Never heard anyone describe The Badger's Sett as a gastro pub. So you're in luck."

CHAPTER 15

Hedgehogs

Mike

"Order at the bar, you lazy sod," Jimbo barked. "Bloody Ruby's off sick again, so we've no waitress, and I'm certainly not shifting *my* arse to serve you."

I rolled my eyes.

"No offence, love," Jimbo added to Vicky.

"None taken," Vicky told him. "I appreciate your candour."

He nodded and lumbered off to get behind the bar again.

I sighed. "Well, I promised you *not fancy*. I think this place fits the bill."

Vicky grinned at me, and I relaxed.

Bringing her here was a bit of a risk, but plain, non-nonsense food was definitely on the menu at The Badger's. And looking at her now, it was worth it.

She was no longer sitting stiffly across from me and looking green around the gills.

I'd taken her to Buckingham Manor first and told her to change out of her itchy dress into whatever she found the most comfortable. She came back downstairs looking unsure and wearing leggings and a hoody with her hair up in a ponytail.

When I said "bloody gorgeous" to her and kissed the side of her head, she gave me the first smile of the evening.

I was now completely addicted to making this woman smile.

Margot, who had been almost beside herself when I picked Vicky up the first time, was clearly worried that we'd returned so soon. But when Vicky changed, and I'd coaxed that smile out of her, Margot's excitement was off the charts.

"Have fun, kids!" she'd shouted after us as we left, like we were both still teenagers.

Margot was a pain in the arse, but she clearly cared a lot about Vicky. And from her almost unnerving levels of excitement about me taking Vicky out, it was obvious that she'd been worried about Vicky. Very worried.

"Is the food okay, love?" I asked, leaning forward so nobody else would hear me. "We can go back to my mum's for something if you don't fancy the stuff here."

Vicky's eyes went wide. "Your mum's?" she breathed. "You'd take me to your mum's?"

I shrugged. "Of course. Mum can cook anything you like, and her fridge is always fully stocked."

"Your mum would be okay if you just barged into her home late on a Saturday night and demanded supper for you and a random woman?"

I glowered at her. "You're not a random woman. Mum knows you. And she'd be beside herself if I took a lass home to her, believe me."

Vicky cleared her throat. "I'm not good with... families. I don't tend to make a very good impression."

She tucked her hands under her legs and rocked very slightly back and forth before she seemed to catch herself doing it and stopped.

I got the feeling that she'd tucked her hands there to stop them from creeping up to her ears and giving her away.

Something about what she'd just said stressed her out. I thought about my first impression of her, and I internally winced.

"You already know my family," I said gently, and she shook her head.

"I know Lucy, but I only met your mum a couple of times when I was a child. Seeing as I wasn't speaking then, I don't think you can say she really *knows* me."

I thought back to those few times Vicky had been in the cottage and winced again.

"Vicky, listen. I'm sorry I was a bit of a prick back then. I couldn't understand why you weren't speaking. Mum told me that she didn't think it was something you could help, but I just wrongly assumed you thought you were too good for us, seeing as we weren't blue bloods like you lot. I have a bit of a chip on my shoulder about all that class stuff."

Vicky snorted. "You know I blanked Ollie's cousins when I met them?" she said.

"Ollie's cousins?"

"Yes, his *cousins*."

"Oh! Right *those* cousins." Ollie's cousins had some of the bluest blood in the UK. "You blanked *them*?"

"Didn't say a word, apparently. My mother was really, really angry when she found out. My point is that I didn't used to speak to anyone, blue blood or no."

I smiled at her. "I'd like to have seen that." Then I let my smile drop. "I really am sorry, Vicky. All I understood was that the prettiest girl I'd ever seen didn't want to speak to me or my sister. I was already salty about not being one of the posh boys like my two best mates. I'd overheard their school friends asking why they hung out with a townie when they came to stay in the holidays."

Her mouth dropped open as she stared at me. "You thought I was pretty?"

I grinned. "Baby, you were pretty then; you're beautiful now. I was an idiot then and an even bigger one now, but hopefully, you'll keep speaking to me this time—I like the sound of your voice too much."

"I like the sound of your voice too," Vicky said quietly as she let her hands loose from under her legs and rested them on the table in front of her.

"Mikey boy!" A large hand clapped me on my back, and I resisted the urge to roll my eyes.

I loved my mates, but this was bad timing.

Vicky didn't need any more stress tonight, and new people seemed to trigger stress for her, especially if Lottie wasn't there as a buffer.

Our table was suddenly surrounded by four big blokes.

Vicky shrank back in her chair, her hands shot under her legs again, and I held back a sigh.

"Alright, boys," I said, receiving a few more back slaps and various greetings. "Lads, this is Vicky."

Jonny's eyebrows shot up. "Ollie's sister, Vicky?"

"Half-sister," Vicky muttered automatically at her menu. It seemed to be an ingrained reaction whenever Ollie was labelled as her brother.

The boys looked at her curiously, no doubt a bit confused by the lack of eye contact.

"Oh, er... alright then, half-sister." There was an awkward silence followed by the boys mumbling various greetings at Vicky.

She managed to glance up at them and give them a forced half-smile, but by the end of the introductions, the boys were frowning in confusion.

See, these were friendly salt-of-the-earth lads. They called women *love* and *sweetheart* and were used to warm interactions and banter.

I knew exactly what they were thinking of Vicky—cold, stuck-up, posh bird who thought she was too good to talk to a bunch of blue-collar blokes.

I didn't think it could get more awkward, but then...

"So, you're out with this one? Slim pickings in the big smoke, is it?" Mark said in a teasing tone, putting his hand on her shoulder as he pointed to me.

Vicky, already clearly wound up by the situation, wasn't ready for any physical contact. She flinched so hard away from Mark that she almost fell off her chair.

I stood up suddenly to pull Mark away from her before he could make anything worse.

He put both of his hands up in the air in a gesture of surrender.

"Woah!" he said, looking shocked. "Jesus, okay. I was just being friendly. I didn't mean anything by it." His face was flushed red, and he looked genuinely upset.

The rest of my friends were all scowling at us now. Most of them had taken a step back as if Vicky was an unexploded bomb, their body language closed—arms crossed over their chests, hands shoved in their pockets.

Vicky was still staring down at her menu.

I weighed up my options and thought, fuck it.

"Guys, listen," I said. "Vicky's a little different, okay?"

Vicky's eyes shot from her menu to me, and I really hoped I wasn't fucking this up.

This was hers to share, and I was being the typical bulldozer I always was. But I couldn't sit there and let the guys treat Vicky like I had treated her when it wasn't bloody necessary if they just had an honest explanation.

"She takes a little while to warm up to people, and she needs some warning before you touch her. And if any of you have a problem with that or upset her, then I'll be dealing with you outside."

"Mike!" Vicky snapped, and my heart sank.

Was she angry that I revealed all of that? I really should have checked with her first, but I couldn't let all the awkwardness and misunderstandings carry on when I could see how upset she was.

"Are you threatening to physically harm your friends?"

My eyebrows went up. "Well… yeah, if they piss me off."

Her eyes went wide. "You can't do that. They all seem like very nice gentlemen, and they're your *friends*."

There were a couple of chuckles from the lads, which quieted when I glared at them.

Pete joined us from the bar then, carrying a couple of beers, his head tilted to the side as he surveyed the scene.

"They're dickheads is what they are," I told her. "And Mark shouldn't have put his hand on you."

Vicky sucked in a shocked breath. "He didn't know I'd react like a freak, Mike."

"You're not a freak. And he can keep his hands to himself. I don't care if—"

"Hey, Vics," Pete said in a soft voice as he crouched down next to the table so that he was eye-level with her, but still at a safe distance so she wouldn't flinch.

Vicky stopped glaring at me to turn to Pete and then blinked in surprise. "Oh, hey, Pete," she said in a quiet voice.

It was clear they knew each other.

"Mike's a pain in the arse sometimes," Pete said, and it would have pissed me off had it not coaxed a small smile from Vicky.

"He can be, but I still like him a lot. Even though he's high-handed," she told him.

"No accounting for taste. Listen, the hogs are doing okay now. We get regular visits, though, and Emily's still putting down the food you recommended."

Vicky's face transformed from wary caution to unbridled enthusiasm. "How many babies did she have in the end?"

"We've counted four, but Jimbo thought he saw a fifth the other night. We spoke to Mrs. Gibbs about the slug pellets she was using, by the way, and she's agreed not to put them out anymore."

"Oh, thank goodness," Vicky said with real feeling.

I'd had enough of this. "What the fuck are you two talking about?"

Vicky turned to me, and I was relieved to see all her previous tension was gone. "Hedgehogs."

CHAPTER 16

"I really really like you, Victoria Harding."

Mike

"Hedgehogs?"

"Vics here is Little Buckingham's resident hedgehog expert," Pete said. "We found a hog out during the day, and Emily heard from Lucy about Vicky's website and Facebook group. To be honest, we were expecting just a bit of advice over the phone. Not for Vicky to book it straight out of London and arrive in that fancy car with driver in under two hours."

"I needed to assess the situation directly," Vicky explained. "Pregnant or nursing mothers need to be out in the day, but otherwise, the hedgehog might be injured or sick. This one—"

"Barry," said Pete, and Vicky nodded.

Was I going mad? Were they *naming* hedgehogs?

"Yes," Vicky said. "Barry was loaded with parasites. You see, if it's a broken leg, then the hog needs a vet, but parasites can be dealt with at the local rescue centre. I work with the British Hedgehog Preservation Society."

"Well, Barry was sorted out thanks to Vicky, and now he's a proud dad. Hey Vics, do you want to come over and see them? They come into the garden most nights."

"Oh, could I?" Vicky was nearly bouncing in her seat with excitement now. Then she glanced at me, and her expression faltered. "I mean. If it's okay with Mike, that is." She looked nervous again, and I hated that expression on her face.

"I'd love to see your hedgehog, love."

Mark snorted, and I punched him in the arm.

"But, for now, all you bastards can bugger off so I can feed my woman."

"I'm sorry about earlier," Vicky said in a small voice to Mark. "I sometimes get a bit jumpy, and I'm not great in new environments."

"Don't even mention it, love," Mark said in a soft voice. "I shouldn't go about landing my big mitts on unsuspecting women's shoulders."

"Oh no, I—"

"Seriously, it's fine. My cousin has... some similar stuff going on as you. I totally understand."

"Right, you lot, bugger off," Jimbo, the bartender, snapped. "This one needs to order, don't you, love?"

"Oh... okay," Vicky said to Jimbo, her voice unsure. "I thought the procedure was to order at the bar?"

"The procedure is whatever I bloody well want it to be, and Vernon's likely to sod off back home in the next half hour. I'm not having Lady Harding sitting in my pub unfed. You're too skinny anyway, love."

"Jimbo, you know I'm not a lady," Vicky said quietly.

He shrugged. "You are to me. Now what'll it be?"

*

Vicky

I'd eaten at The Badger's Sett before, seeing as the Hardings were regulars there. I mean, the Hardings owned the whole village, and therefore had to support the village pub. So I knew the menu, and Jimbo knew how plain I liked my burger to be; how I liked the salad on a separate plate with no dressing. And for once, when I was out, I actually ate. Which was good, because Mike was right: I did need feeding up. Margot, Lottie and Ollie had been on my case about it for a few weeks.

"Are you sure you don't mind this?" I asked Mike as we walked the short distance to Pete's house. Mike smiled at me and tucked me under his arm. I'd never walked arm-in-arm with anyone before. It wasn't the most efficient method of ambulation, but it was warm, and it felt unbelievably safe, so in this particular case I was willing to sacrifice some efficiency.

"Of course I don't mind, love," he said into the hair on the top of my head. "I want to meet Barry and his family as well."

"Oh, well we're not actually *guaranteed* to see the hedgehogs. Their nocturnal behaviour is not always predictable and—"

"Vicky, love. I'm just happy to be with you, okay?"

"Oh, okay," I whispered as I buried more into his side.

We did get to see the hedgehogs.

Pete, Emily, and their two kids were already excited when we arrived, as Barry was out with the full contingent of his family.

I sat down on the kitchen floor with the kids facing the garden next to the glass double doors. I liked kids in general: they were less complicated than adults, and they said what they meant. Pete and Emily's little girl, Maisie crawled into my lap and played with my hair, which was the extent of communication with Maisie, who was only two. Their eldest, Marcus, asked me many *many* hedgehog questions. At eight years old, Marcus was nearly as informed about hedgerow animals as me. I'd inducted him into my hedgehog squad last year.

After we left and got back into Mike's Land Rover, he sat there for a moment before he turned to me.

"Er... look," I said quickly. "I know it's been a bit odd. You probably don't have dates where the woman is too fussy for the really nice restaurant you chose. Or who drags you off to watch hedgehogs for an hour."

I bit my lip, thinking now that I shouldn't have accepted Pete's invite. And I *definitely* shouldn't have gone into hedgehog hyperfocus mode when I got there.

Men like Mike probably don't enjoy being ignored.

"I'm really so—"

"I'm going to kiss you now, okay?" Mike said in that growly, bossy tone I was starting to really appreciate.

I nodded, and he reached forward with both hands, cupping my face over the central console and sealing his mouth over mine. One of my hands went into his thick, glorious hair whilst the other gripped the front of his shirt. When he broke the kiss, we were both breathing heavily as he rested his forehead against mine.

"So," I whispered. "You don't mind about the hedgehogs?"

"No, baby," he said in a soft voice that was just a little fierce at the same time. "I don't mind about the hedgehogs. I love that I got to share that with you."

He set me back into my seat and pulled my seatbelt over me like I was a child, which was unusual, since I wasn't actually a child, but seeing as I got to smell him again and have him in my space for longer, I wasn't going to object.

Before we pulled away, Mike smiled at the windshield and said, again in that soft but fierce tone, "I really *really* like you, Victoria Harding."

"Um… okay," I said. "I mean, I really like you too. But you already know that."

So, it seemed my general weirdness was not going to put Mike off, which was good. I didn't want to put Mike off. But then he drove me back to Buckingham Manor. When we stopped outside, I turned to him and frowned.

"Why aren't we going back to the cabin?" I asked.

Mike sighed. "Vicky, love, if I take you back to my cabin now, after this evening, I'm definitely going to fuck you."

"Well, that's kind of the point of all this."

He shook his head and chuckled. "Jesus Christ, I'm not going to survive you. Vicky, I'm not going to take you home and fuck you after just one date."

I made another completely unlike me harrumph noise to express my dissatisfaction with this plan.

Before spending time with Mike I don't think I'd ever made such a ridiculous noise before in my life.

"Okay, how many dates?"

Mike laughed again, but it was pained this time. "I'm not going to give you a countdown to us fucking."

I bit my lip. "But I'm really good with timelines, and having exact parameters and expectations."

He chuckled again and rubbed his hand down his face before he jumped out of the driver's seat, stalked around the car bonnet and opened my door. He did the seatbelt thing again and then physically lifted me out of the car until I was in his arms, all the while, asking those little checks to make sure I was happy with any touch.

I was happy to be in his arms, but I still stared up at him with a grumpy expression as I did not want to get out of the car. I wanted to go back to his cabin.

"I'm not giving you a number."

"Fine," I said as I burrowed my face into his chest and inhaled deeply. "But I have to go back to London tomorrow."

So we left it without a timeline until sex, which made me extremely unhappy.

CHAPTER 17

I'm supposed to go straight to him and kiss him

Vicky

Lottie squeezed my wrist under the table again, but I couldn't drag my gaze from beyond the conference room, because he was *right there*.

Felix cleared his throat.

"Vics? You had the figures on that? Did you want to...?" Felix trailed off as I stood up from my seat, turned on my heel, and practically ran out of there.

Mike's eyes widened as I burst through the double doors and headed straight to him.

I didn't stop until I'd grabbed onto the front of his flannel shirt with my body against his, tilting my head back to look up at him.

"Hi," he said with a bemused smile as he stared down at me, and his arms closed around me, pulling me closer.

"Hi," I breathed, then went up on tiptoes to try and press my lips against his, but he was too tall.

Seeing my intention, Mike closed the distance, dipping his head to kiss me.

It was brief and closed-mouthed, but just like everything with Mike, it was completely fantastic.

Being in Mike's arms, surrounded by his warmth and his clean, woodsy scent was better than anything I'd ever experienced. Better than making my first million, better even than hedgehogs. It was everything. He pulled back slightly to smile at me, and that was fantastic as well.

"What meeting did you just walk out of in there?" he asked.

I shrugged. "It's a new development Felix is planning. I'm securing the investment for it."

He glanced over at the wall of glass beyond us, where I knew everyone would still be sitting around the table. The negotiations were far from over.

Mike looked back at me, and gave me a squeeze.

"Baby, were you supposed to just walk out? Felix looks like he might have a heart attack."

I frowned. "Of course I was supposed to. You said, remember?"

His eyebrows went up. "I said what?"

"You told me that when I greet you, I should come *straight* to you and kiss you."

His arms gave me another squeeze, his body shaking with silent laughter as he leaned down to give me another brief kiss.

"Why are you laughing?" I asked in confusion. "Did I do the wrong thing?"

Mike glanced at the conference room again, then back at me.

"Nope," he said in a smug voice. "This is perfect. Exactly right, love."

I smiled up at him. I very much liked hearing that I had done the right thing, and I was finding that I responded very well to praise, especially when it came from Mike.

It had been three weeks since our first official date, and a whole week since I'd seen him again.

I'd missed him so much, I was worried that it might be an abnormal amount.

When I focused on something I never really managed to do it in half measures, and I was *very* focused on Mike.

All this waiting for sexual intercourse he seemed to insist on didn't help matters. Nor did the fact that being with Mike was just so… easy.

He hadn't *once* told me I was weird.

That first date, as soon as he knew I was uncomfortable in the restaurant he'd taken me to, he didn't roll his eyes or call me a "fussy bitch," both of which I'd experienced with other men in the past. No, we just up and left.

Since then, I'd come back to Little Buckingham again once to see him. He'd offered to come up to London, but I wanted to see his cabin again. This time, he made sure that I'd like the food. When I told him that the fish and chip shop in the next-door village was one of the only options, he'd frowned at my apologetic tone.

"I bloody love fish and chips, sweetheart," he told me firmly. "Got to say, I'm relieved as fuck that you're not dragging me to those fancy shitholes your brother likes."

We'd taken the fish and chips back to Mike's comfy sitting room and eaten them from his beautiful coffee table, watching *Britain's Secret Hedgerows* on the television.

Apart from the fact Mike still wouldn't have sex with me, it was just about the most perfect evening I'd ever experienced in my life.

Lottie and Ollie's ongoing dramas had taken up much of the following week.

Thankfully, they were back together now, which meant Lottie was back to smiling, and Ollie wasn't ringing me twenty-four hours a day, asking her whereabouts, if she was okay, what she was eating, or how I thought he could earn her forgiveness. Given my limited social and emotional intelligence, I had no idea why Ollie asked my advice on that score. But even without my advice, Ollie had managed to win her back, and I was so, *so* relieved.

Lottie and Ollie were two of my favourite people. Just because I couldn't express emotion in the normal way, didn't mean I didn't feel it. If anything, I felt too much, and I'd been devastated by their unhappiness, and my inability to do anything helpful to heal the rift.

With all that going on in London, and Mike's huge projects he had to finish in Little Buckingham, there hadn't been time to see each other.

But now, Mike was here in my office, and I was in his arms again, which I took as a very good sign.

"What the fuck is going on here?" Felix's angry whisper-shout pulled me out of my Mike Haze.

"What do you mean?" I said, frowning at him.

He was standing next to Mike and me with his arms crossed over his chest, glowering at both of us.

Lottie was by his side, but she certainly wasn't glowering; if anything, I would have guessed Lottie was trying to suppress a laugh—her lips were pressed together, and her shoulders were shaking.

This was good, because ever since her fight with Ollie, Lottie's smiles had been few and far between.

"Vicky, we are in the middle of contract negotiations for a deal that's been in the pipeline for months, championed by *you*. I don't know the numbers. I don't even understand the numbers. Nobody in that room does. That's because no bastard can understand those numbers except *you*. But then, you simply stand up at one of the crucial points in a very sensitive meeting, leave the bloody room like someone's chasing you, then run out here to kiss this great big lug in front of the whole bloody conference room."

"Well, when I see Mike, I'm supposed to go straight to him and kiss him. He was very specific."

Felix's eyebrows shot up at this declaration as he turned to Mike. "That right, mate? You tell her to do that? Does Ollie know about this?"

Mike sighed. "Leave the Duke of Fuckingham out of this," he told Felix.

"Leave him out of it? Listen up, carpenter-boy. You've been deliberately ignoring Vicky for months. What's your game now? Neither Ollie nor I want her mucked about. So you better tread carefully. Understand me?"

"Look, I do understand what a dickhead I've been, believe me. But I didn't have all the bloody information, did I?"

"I don't think you're a dickhead," I told Mike, my voice annoyed.

He turned to me and smiled.

"I *was* a dickhead, love," he said softly. "And Felix is right. I don't deserve a chance with you, but I'm going to take it anyway."

"I just hope you're being careful with her, Mike," Felix clipped.

"I am being careful with her," Mike shot back. "Far as I can see, I'm about the only one who's been proper careful with her for a bloody long time, *mate*."

"Felix, why are you so cross?" I asked in total bewilderment. "Oh, of course. Sorry, I'm messing up the meeting, aren't I?"

Felix's expression softened as he turned from Mike to me. "Vicky, I'm not only angry about the meeting, although you do need to get your little genius arse back in there. I'm angry because I don't want Mike messing you about if he's not fully invested, and Ollie will feel the same."

"B-but why do you care?" I blurted out. "I mean, I'm your business partner. Oh, is it because I might not be at peak performance?"

Felix was frowning at me now. "Vicky, I care about you. Surely you…" he broke off and rubbed the back of his neck—a sure sign of Felix's discomfort. "Surely, you know I care about you?"

I bit my lip. This was one of those questions that Lottie would advise me not to answer.

"See what I mean, you tosser," Mike muttered, giving me a squeeze and then setting me away slightly as he turned from Felix to me. "Go do your *genius numbers stuff*, love. I can wait with Lucy."

I glanced over at the glass wall to Felix's office to see Lucy in her window seat where she tended to hang out and write whilst her fiancé conducted his business.

She was grinning across at me and Mike, waving frantically with an excited expression on her face.

I managed a small smile and waved back, relief surging through me that the sight of me in her brother's arms did not seem to be provoking anger.

Lucy was one of the few people who didn't have a pecuniary interest in me and still wanted to be my friend. I put that down to her slightly quirky, extremely forgiving and unbelievably kind nature.

"Okay," I said, a little sadness leaking into my tone.

I didn't want to go back to the meeting. I wanted to stay with Mike. It was the first time I'd ever truly not wanted to work. Normally, work was really all I had, to be honest.

"Great," Felix muttered. As we walked back to the conference room, he shoulder-checked Mike, which I thought was completely unnecessary.

"Well, that was interesting," Lottie said in an excited whisper as we walked to the double doors. "Don't worry. I'll deal with your brother."

"Half-brother," I corrected automatically.

CHAPTER 18

You'll do

Mike

Bloody hell. That was not what I'd had in mind when I decided to surprise Vicky at work.

To be honest, I hadn't really thought the whole thing through, but then, thinking clearly when it came to Vicky didn't seem to be my strong suit.

So when I completed my delivery early, I'd decided not to wait until later when we said I'd pick her up from her place.

No, like the normal bulldozer I was, I decided to go to her office. I'd been there often enough.

Felix was one of my best friends, and my sister's boyfriend. And I was tired of us keeping things on the down low whilst all the drama with Ollie and Lottie played out.

It was time for everyone to know that Vicky was mine.

I had not anticipated that Vicky would stand up in the middle of the meeting she was in, leave all those suits who had been hanging off her every word for dust, and run out of there, straight into my arms.

I mean, who *could* have predicted that?

But I should have remembered how very literal she was. If I'd told her I wanted to be greeted with a kiss when I saw her, then that's what she was going to do, appropriate circumstances or not.

And there was no way I was pushing her away.

Those suits could suck it up, and that included Felix.

B-but why do you care?

I tamped down the surge of anger as I remembered her small voice and the genuine confusion in it.

What the fuck was going on with these people? Why did Vicky think they wouldn't give a shit about her?

Now that their meeting was finished, I'd been told, in no uncertain terms, that the quiet meal for two I'd planned for Vicky and me had been hijacked.

Minutes later, Ollie strode into the office like he owned the place. To be fair to the bloke, he *did* actually own a large percentage of London, and some of his swagger was just innate aristocratic arrogance. His family had been bossing around a fair amount of the UK for over five hundred years after all. Well now his aristocratic, Lord of the manor gaze was fixed on me, and the man wasn't best pleased.

"Hi, Ollie," Vicky said, completely oblivious to the tension in the air.

When I put my arm around her and tucked her into my side, Ollie's eyes flared with surprise.

"Felix rang me," he said, looking between us and taking Lottie's hand automatically when she came up to his side. "Mike, this is a bit of a turnaround, don't you think?"

Bloody hell. I really wished I'd been a bit less of a prick about Vicky in the past. It was coming back to bite me in the arse now in a big way.

Why had I thought it was a good idea to ignore a beautiful woman with an obvious crush on me, and tell my friends how annoying I found her? What was wrong with me?

I could have been with Vicky for months at this stage if I hadn't been such a blind idiot.

"Ollie," Vicky put in. "Don't be mean to Mike. I like him,

and he doesn't think I'm *empty inside* or *devoid of personality* anymore."

Ollie's eyes flashed. "Wait a minute. How do you know he thought that in the first place?"

"He told me," Vicky said with a shrug. "He thought I was trying to–"

"Vics, why don't you go and have a chat with the girls a minute?" I said quickly, cutting her off before she could get me in any more trouble with her brother. "I'll sort things with Ollie, okay?"

"Come on, Vics," Lottie said, pulling Vicky away towards Tabitha and Lucy. "You've got some explaining to do, you little minx."

"What the fuck?" Ollie said once the girls were out of earshot in Felix's office. "I thought you couldn't stand my sister? What's changed?"

"I was wrong, okay?" I said for what felt like the hundredth time. "I'm a dickhead, and I was wrong." I shifted on my feet before clearing my throat. Talking about feelings with my mates was not something I relished. "I really like her, Ols," I told him in a quiet, sincere voice. "I wouldn't have started something with her if I didn't."

Ollie swiped a hand down his face, glancing over to where Vicky was being interrogated in Felix's office, then back at me.

"Vics has had a rough go of things. I worry about her, and I know I've taken my eye off the ball recently." He sighed. "Look, I know you saw her meltdown at the gala, but that's only really scratching the surface. A couple of weeks before that she..." he trailed off, and I felt a shiver of unease down my spine.

A couple of weeks before the gala was when I'd ripped into her at her house when I thought she was propositioning me.

Ollie shook his head as if to clear it. "Listen, I love you as a friend, and I trust you, but you've got to know what you're dealing with. Don't hurt her, okay? She's vulnerable, Mike."

"I'm not going to hurt her, Ollie," I told him, my voice firm. Clearly, I'd hurt her enough already. I needed to find out what happened after I stupidly gutted her at her house.

She must have had some sort of meltdown again. But I didn't want to push Ollie on it too much there and then, plus, the girls were now heading our way.

Half an hour later, Vicky, Felix, Lucy, Ollie and I were standing outside a Michelin-starred poncy nightmare, which I knew had precisely bugger all on the menu that Vicky could eat. Lottie had gone to collect Hayley from school so wasn't there to advocate for Vicky as she normally would.

"We're not going there," I said, gently pulling Vicky into my side, ignoring Ollie's death stare.

"It's okay, dickhead," Felix said. "They won't take away your working-class-salt-of-the-earth card just because you ate somewhere with a Michelin star, you know."

I glared at the inconsiderate bastard. "Choose somewhere else," I said through gritted teeth.

Holding Vicky against me just strengthened my resolve. There was literally nothing of her; I could feel her ribs, for God's sake.

"Mike," Felix snapped. "Stop being an awkward bastard and—"

"Mike's right," Ollie put in.

When I looked over at him, he was watching me and his sister with something close to approval in his expression.

"We're not eating here."

"How about that place we found the other day, Vics?" Lucy said in a gentle voice. "The Italian place. Remember?"

"The one that made me the sauce with no onion in it?" Vicky asked.

Lucy smiled. "Yeah, that's the one."

Vicky shook her head. "We should make a majority decision. That's the most logical way."

"Okay, well, I want the lobster, so let's go with the original one, that's—ow!" Felix glared at Ollie, who'd just kicked him in the shin. "Fucking hell, Bucks."

"We'll eat at the Italian place."

We made our way to the restaurant in uncomfortable silence. I refused to let Vicky go, despite the tense atmosphere.

"Right," Ollie said from across the table after we'd finally sat down. "Maybe now, we can sort this out."

"There's nothing to sort out. I'm seeing your sister," I told him, something that was completely obvious, seeing as I hadn't let her leave my side once, and I had my arm slung over the back of her chair now.

"Half-sister," Vicky added.

I gritted my teeth to stop myself saying anything.

"I want to know when all this started," Ollie snapped. "You've been ignoring her for months."

"I think you're forgetting the gala when you dropped the ball, and I saved the day. You're welcome, by the way."

"I *let* you take Vicky home from the gala," Ollie said through gritted teeth. "That does not mean I gave you permission to do whatever you liked with her. In fact, I specifically remember telling you to keep your bloody hands off her."

"Language, Ollie," Lottie snapped as she approached our table with Hayley in tow.

"Hey, stowaway," Ollie's voice was immediately softer, as was his way with this little girl.

Lottie's sister was just that cute.

Hayley smiled at him and gave him a hug, then a low wave to the rest of the table. She was a shy little thing. Up until recently, I'd never actually heard her speak.

Hayley had selective mutism triggered by trauma. Her mum had been an alcoholic and had neglected Hayley before Lottie took custody of her. For the longest time Hayley only spoke to Lottie, but now we were hearing her quiet voice more and more.

I frowned. Childhood trauma. Is that why Vicky didn't speak when she was little? What exactly *was* the trauma?

My chest felt tight at the thought, and I pulled Vicky's chair even closer to mine.

To my surprise, after hugging Ollie, Hayley went directly to Vicky.

They looked at each other for a moment, then even more surprisingly, Hayley spoke.

"Mikey has his arm around you," Hayley said.

"He tends to do that," Vicky replied, as Hayley pulled a chair over so she could sit next to Vicky.

"Good," Hayley said in a quiet voice, glancing around as she realised everyone was watching her.

Vicky shrugged. "*I* think it's good. He has very nice arms."

Lucy snorted so hard with a suppressed laugh that the little shit almost spat out her drink.

Then Hayley smiled at Vicky before peeking around her and smiling at me.

It was the first outright smile I'd ever got off the kid, and it was because I made her friend happy.

Hayley pressed her hand to her own chest before she pressed it to Vicky's.

Vicky repeated the move, and when I glanced at Lottie, her eyes were glistening with unshed tears. When her gaze met mine, she gave me a watery smile.

Vicky's layers just got deeper and deeper.

Ollie had been watching this exchange and saw Hayley bestowing her approval.

His jaw tightened for a moment, and I thought he was still going to go off, but instead, he looked at the ceiling for a moment before his eyes came to mine.

"Don't fuck this up, Mayweather," he growled.

"Ollie, you don't have to worry about when Mike decides he's had enough of me," Vicky said.

Everyone's shocked gazes flew to her.

"I promise, I'm anticipating that, and I will endeavour not to be an emotional burden to you, Lottie, or Margot when that happens."

"What do you—?" I began in disbelief, but Ollie interrupted.

"A burden?" Ollie was frowning at Vicky. "Vics, when have I ever told you you're a burden?"

"Isn't that why you're concerned about my relationship with Mike? I do understand that you are a very busy man. I wouldn't impose my distress on you." She turned to Felix. "And my work performance won't be affected. Actually, when I'm unhappy, I tend to be *more* productive. So you don't need to threaten Mike either."

"Vicky," Ollie said in a low, warning tone. "Are you telling us that you believe I only care how Mike treats you because I'm worried you might become a burden?"

"And that *I* only care in case your bloody productivity goes down?" Felix put in.

Vicky frowned then turned to Lottie. "I'm sorry, is this one of the times I shouldn't tell the truth?"

"No, honey," Lottie said softly. "If it's *your* truth, then I think we need to hear it."

"You're my sister," Ollie said, slamming his hand down on the table in frustration, causing Vicky to jump in her seat.

"Calm it down, Harding," I snarled as I felt Vicky tremble.

"Half-sister," she whispered.

"And stop with all this half-sister, half-brother bullshit. What difference does it make?" Ollie said in frustration.

"Hold on," Lottie said. "Vics, are we friends? You and me?"

"Is this one of the times when I—?"

"No, I want to hear what you think. It's not a time for a lie."

"Then, no. We're not friends, in the traditional sense of the word. I like you very much, and you are very kind to me. *Very* kind. I appreciate that. But you work for me, and you're my half-brother's girlfriend." She shrugged. "You don't really have a choice."

Lottie's face was turning red as she scowled at Vicky.

Ollie, clearly sensing she was about to blow, put his hand on her arm, but he was too late. Lottie shot out of her chair.

"You..." She pointed to Vicky. "Are one of the *best* friends I've ever had. I love you, you ridiculous woman. I love the way you make me laugh every day. I love the way your beautiful, complicated mind works, I love how generous you are, how kind, how much you care about people, even when they can't or won't try to understand you. So don't you *dare* tell me we're not friends!" Lottie was shouting by the end of her rant, and then she collapsed back into her chair.

Hayley signed something at her, and she snapped, "No, I will not calm down. It's okay for you. Vicky *believes* that you're her friend."

"And please stop with the half-brother stuff," Ollie said stiffly. "We love you. This big idiot is going to treat you well, or we'll break his fucking legs, and that's that."

Vicky was tense in my arms now, and I didn't like it. "Right, enough with all the shouting and carrying on, you lot," I warned. "Let Vicky eat her food, for God's sake."

"I love you too," Vicky whispered to Lottie, her voice a little shaky.

"I know you do, hun," Lottie said softly. "No more of this burden stuff, okay?"

Vicky looked down at the table but nodded in a short movement.

The rest of the evening was surprisingly drama-free. Felix and Lottie recounted the complete evisceration Vicky delivered to an unsuspecting group of lawyers representing a big fish investor earlier in the day. They started the meeting totally underestimating her and having no idea she'd done a deep dive into their financials for the last decade.

"It was beautiful," Lottie said. "I love it when I can just let you run. Honestly, those bastards deserved it."

Lottie could tell when people were lying; as a team, Lottie and Vicky rarely made a wrong move.

"I didn't want to *eviscerate* them," Vicky said through a frown. "You should have squeezed my wrist."

"What does the wrist squeeze do?" I asked. "I've seen you do that to Vicky before when..." I trailed off as I realised what I was saying.

"When I was hyperfocused on you," Vicky supplied.

Ollie choked on his wine.

"It means *stop*. Either stop what I'm doing, stop talking, or stop focusing on something I... shouldn't be."

"Stop talking?" I said in surprise. "Why would anyone want you to stop talking?"

Vicky turned to me. "Mike, you must have noticed. When I get going on a subject, I can be... intense. Remember how long I talked about the danger the UK's hedgerows are under the other night?"

"So what?" I said with a frown. "You always say interesting stuff. I don't think anyone should be cutting you off."

I caught Lottie's eye across the table. She was beaming at me.

"You'll do," she said decisively.

CHAPTER 19

Good girl

Vicky

Mike's van wouldn't start. Twice now, he'd turned the key in the ignition, and the engine had spluttered then died. His Land Rover, whilst ancient and mud-splattered, did seem to be somewhat reliable, but the van he used for his deliveries was another matter.

"You need a new vehicle," I told him.

"Aware of that, love," he said through gritted teeth.

"Your furniture," I started, my voice rising as I felt so strongly about this. "All of it, every single piece, is a work of art. You should have appropriate transportation for it."

Mike froze, then he turned to look at me, his expression intense. His hand left the steering wheel to reach up to my face, pausing so I had time to nod my agreement.

He swept the hair that had escaped my tight bun and fallen in my eyes behind my ear, cupped my jaw, and then gave me a brief, hard kiss before turning back to his task.

"Third time's the charm," he said through a grin as the old van roared to life.

"It shouldn't take three attempts for the van to start," I told him. "I am not a mechanic, but I do have a basic understanding of—"

"I'll replace the old girl when I have the money," he interrupted. "I've just expanded the workshop. Had to sink all the capital into that for the moment."

"I could—"

"No," he cut me off very decisively.

"Is this a male pride thing?"

"Partly, but also, didn't I just hear you tell one of your best friends that you thought the only reason she spent time with you was because of what you did for her? Do you think I want you believing that about *me*, even for a second?"

"Oh." I didn't know what to say to that. In my experience, if I offered money, it was accepted.

I'd funded my mother and my half-sister for years, and they didn't even pretend to like me. I'd never had someone decline my money in case it made me doubt their motives.

I was still going over what had happened tonight. As I ran Lottie's words over and over in my head I felt something start to unfurl in my chest that I hadn't really even realised was twisted before.

"I wish we could go to the cabin," I said as we pulled up outside my house. My voice sounded about as dejected as I felt about the prospect of going into my empty London home. "I don't suppose we have reached the magic number yet, have we?" I asked Mike hopefully.

He chuckled. "Come on, you. I'll walk you in."

He jumped out of the van and jogged around to my side to open my door for me.

I was noticing this about Mike. He might think he was rough, but as far as actions were concerned, he struck me as more of a gentleman than most of the men in the upper classes I knew.

It was little things like opening doors, keeping me on the inside of the pavement, pulling out my chair, putting his hand on the small of my back to guide me through crowded places.

The hand on the back thing was my favourite. I wasn't sure that Mike was always fully aware he was doing it, as usually he was very careful to ask consent before he touched me—but the hand on the back seemed to be instinctual. It made me feel safe.

I didn't always feel safe in strange environments, but with the heat of Mike's large hand on the small of my back, I simply knew that everything was going to be okay. I knew that he wouldn't let anything hurt me. I mean, it's totally illogical—a grown woman does not need guiding through any space, and I usually disliked illogical scenarios like this.

But, however illogical, that hand on my back made me feel safer and more valued than I had ever felt before.

Mike stopped dead in the hallway when confronted by the coffee table he'd made, which was still in the same position he'd left it.

"Why's it still here?" he asked.

I shrugged. "Ollie was here after…" I trailed off. I did not want Mike to know what happened after that delivery. "After you brought it round. And he offered to move it, but I wanted to keep it there.

"Slap, bang in the way?" he asked in confusion.

"It was a reminder."

"A reminder of what?"

I sighed. "A reminder to leave you alone. I'd come home, see the coffee table, and I'd remember what happened. It was to stop me slipping into hyperfocus mode again when it came to you."

His head tilted to the side as he looked at me. There was an intensity in his eyes now, like some sort of storm was brewing.

"Vicky, Ollie said something earlier about you. He mentioned that something happened with you two weeks before the gala. I… well, I know that was when I delivered the table; you told me it was a stressful interaction for you, and I just…"

"I had a meltdown," I said.

There was no point lying. Mike needed to know exactly what he was getting into, even if admitting to my level of dysfunction caused heat to rise up my face, and my stomach to twist.

"Ollie and Lottie found me under the table. It wasn't like the gala. No screaming and such. But they had to let themselves into the house, because I went missing, and I wouldn't speak or move when they found me. Ollie had to drag me out and hug me until I calmed down."

"Was it...?" he looked to the side, then swallowed before he met my eyes and spoke again. "Was it because of what I said? Because of how ugly I was to you?"

My chest felt tight as I shifted and looked away from his piercing gaze. I very much wished in that moment that I was able to lie successfully.

"You have to understand," I told him. "I was very focused on you, and I really *really* wanted to make a good impression. I even found a pair of jeans I could wear—but to be honest, that was a mistake. No jeans are soft enough for me to tolerate. So, yes, I reacted badly."

He groaned and moved to me. His hands came up to frame my face, but before they made contact, he whispered, "Is this okay?"

I nodded, and his fingers slid from my jawline into my hair as he looked down at me, his eyes burning with intensity.

"Vicky, I know I've said it before, but you'll never understand how sorry I am for what I said to you that day. Please tell me you know now that it was all bollocks, right?"

"You don't have to apologise to me again," I said in a small voice. "Honestly, anyone normal would have..."

"Stop saying that. Don't you dare put yourself down like that," he said in a firm voice with just a hint of growl to it.

I snapped my mouth shut.

"God," he muttered as he pulled me into him for a hug. "I'm a lucky shit that you're giving me a chance."

I snorted into his soft shirt, loving the feel of his firm body against mine. "I'm the *lucky shit* in this scenario."

His arms gave me a squeeze as he shook his head and muttered, "You have no idea how amazing you are, do you? How is that even possible?"

I didn't think any further argument was productive, so I just buried further into his chest.

After a few moments, he pulled back, and his stormy eyes moved from me to the coffee table.

"Right, well I'm getting rid of this now. No more reminders of how much of a wanker I was. I'll take it out to the van."

"No," I said, moving to stand between him and the table. "I *love* this table."

"I can make you a new one, love," he said softly.

"No." My tone was firm now. "I want this one."

He sighed. "Right, well I'll move it to a proper place. Where do you want it to go?"

He took his flannel shirt off and tied it around his waist so that he was only in a tight thermal, which showed off his muscles. Then he reached down and plucked the enormous coffee table off the floor as if it weighed nothing. "Vicky?"

I was frozen in place, lost in the sight of him. The only sign of strain was the way all the muscles of his chest and arms were flexed.

"Baby," Mike said through a chuckle. "If you've finished checking me out, you might want to tell me where to put this bloody great thing."

My cheeks burned as I pointed in the direction of my living room. Words seemed to be beyond me at that moment. I felt hot and cold at the same time. An aching sensation had overcome my whole body. Like I had flu. As if there was a fever, and my body knew the only way to help it was to be closer to Mike.

"Okay, I'll just put it here," Mike said when it became clear that I wasn't going to be able to speak once we were in the living room.

He put the table down and then straightened up, going into

a stretch as he put his hand on his neck, moving his head from side to side to work out the crick there.

I moved towards him, my body on complete autopilot. That fever in my blood taking over my actions. My hands landed flat on his glorious chest and started moving over the hard muscle there, but it wasn't enough. I needed to feel *him*, not his thermal. So I reached down under his top and onto the ridges of his abs, which flexed under my touch.

"Christ, Vicky," Mike said in a strangled voice. "Baby, I—"

"I just need to be close to you," I said, my voice edging towards the desperation I could feel building. "Please, Mike."

It was the *please* that flipped the switch.

Mike's arm shot around me, pulling me into his body, his other hand going into my hair as he kissed me.

I moaned into his mouth and pushed my hands up the back of his thermal to feel the hot skin over the hard muscles of his back. I felt lightheaded. Everything was blurry. The fever was worse now than before.

And Mike had too many clothes on.

One of my hands went between us to attack his belt, and it was his turn to groan.

He broke the kiss to rest his forehead on mine.

"Vicky, what are you doing? Let's… uh, bloody hell…" he broke off as I leaned into him and started kissing his neck, then, acting on an instinct I wouldn't have thought I had in me, I went up on my tiptoes to take the bottom of his ear lightly in my teeth.

I had no idea what I was doing. Was it weird to bite someone's ear?

Before Mike, the idea would have completely bemused me, but after hearing the noises he made when I did it, I didn't think he found it weird.

"Can you take your top off?" I asked.

My voice didn't sound like my own anymore; it was hoarse and rough with need. But I just *had* to be closer to him. I had to feel his skin against mine.

In the interests of moving towards that goal, I pulled my own shirt over my head, leaving me in just a bra. It was the first time I wished I could tolerate anything other than cotton, underwear-wise.

But Mike didn't seem to mind. In fact, the sight of my plain, light pink bra seemed to be the straw that broke the camel's back for his self-control.

"Holy shit, you're so goddamn beautiful," his voice sounded pained, and his breathing was fast. When he looked at me, his eyes were intense—dilated pupils with only a ring of golden fire around them.

"Please Mike," I panted, and he groaned again before lifting me up off my feet in a sudden movement, so that my legs automatically went round his hips, and my arms around his neck.

"Bedroom," he growled, and I smiled a very out of character, massive smile at him. He looked momentarily stunned. "You're gorgeous," he breathed then kissed me again.

I didn't want him to get distracted from the whole progressing to the bedroom thing, as this seemed to be the most expedient route to what I wanted, so as soon as I could speak after the kiss, I told him, "Up the stairs, first door on the right."

He took the stairs two at a time, not seeming to even notice my weight, and shouldered open my bedroom door without breaking stride until he'd laid me down on the bed. His large body hovered over mine, those golden-brown eyes searching my face as he smoothed my hair back from my forehead.

"You could have anyone you wanted," he said, his voice almost reverent. "You realise that, right?"

"All I want is you," I told him the honest truth, my hands coming up to either side of his face into his beard. "All I've *ever* wanted was you."

He growled as his body came down on mine, and I took his delicious weight whilst he kissed me again. But this time, I tugged at the bottom of his top until he took the hint and pulled it over his head in another incredibly attractive manoeuvre, using one hand to grab the back of the shirt and whip it off, all in a single motion.

"Oh my God," I breathed as I took in the perfection of his chest, and then he was back on top of me again, pressing me down into the bed and moving against me as he kissed down my neck.

Somehow, my bra was gone in another smooth move, and I arched when his lips closed over my nipple, moaning again, repeating, "Please, please, please," under my breath, not even having the experience to know what I was asking for, but knowing I needed *something.*

He moved back up my body until his mouth was by my ear.

"It's okay, baby," he whispered, low and husky, and I shivered. "I've got you."

He'd shifted slightly to the side so he could push up my skirt, then the heel of his hand was right there where I most needed the pressure.

My lower body moved of its own accord against him, trying to get more and more friction.

"Shh," he whispered in my ear. "I'm gonna take care of you, I promise. Now lift up for me."

I raised my hips, and he pulled my tights and knickers off in another smooth move, then the pressure was back where I needed it to be again.

"Good girl," he muttered in my ear, and it tipped me over the edge.

All the tension had been building and building. The reality of having this man in my bed, the knowledge that this wasn't a dream—that it was really his body on top of mine was too much.

My eyes rolled back in my head; I arched against him, and then the tension broke as I was overcome with wave after wave of incredible bliss.

I saw stars as everything in my body exploded. The release was immense.

Mike kept his hand there, cupping me as I came down from the high. His other hand was at my forehead, pushing some of the hair that had stuck to the sheen of sweat there back from my face.

"Christ, Vicky," he said, his voice hoarse. "We haven't even gotten started yet, baby."

"D-did I do something wrong?" I asked in a small voice, feeling exposed, and maybe a little weird now.

"No, love," he said firmly, moving so that he was fully on top of me and staring straight into my eyes. "That was perfect. You're perfect. You just..." He chuckled. "I guess you just arrived a little sooner than I anticipated."

My face felt hot, and I tried to break eye contact by turning my head, but his hands came up to cup my face and hold it still.

"Hey, that's not a bad thing, Vics. It just took me by surprise."

The ache was starting to build again now that his weight was back on me fully, pinning me to the bed. I liked feeling that I was held down like this, that he was enclosing me, claiming me.

"I think it was you calling me a 'good girl'," I admitted. "I think that might be my thing. I've always responded really well to praise and performance-based outcomes."

He groaned and started moving against me again.

"What am I going to do with you," he asked, his voice pained, and his jaw tight.

"Um... well, you could have sexual intercourse with me?" I suggested. I mean, it did seem like the most obvious course of action.

"Vicky, you're a virgin. I shouldn't even be doing what I'm doing with you right now."

"Please Mike," I whispered. "I need you. I can't bear waiting any longer."

Mike stared down at me with burning intensity muttering, "I'm going to hell," before he kissed me again.

CHAPTER 20

Standard procedure

Mike

Okay, I'm not a saint.

Yes, it was too soon for her. I knew that. I knew it was wrong. But having the most beautiful girl I'd ever seen in real life naked underneath me, knowing that I was the only one she wanted, having dreamed about her for *months*, there was simply no way I was strong enough to do the right thing.

After breaking the kiss, my mouth moved to her jaw then across to her ear, returning the bite she gave me earlier. As soon as her mouth was free, she started talking in that breathless needy voice again.

"I'm on the oral contraceptive pill," she told me. "The dosage of ethinylestradiol is 30 micrograms and Levonorgestrel is 50 micrograms. I've been taking it for the recommended time period to ensure efficacy. And I bought condoms. I bought all the condoms. There was a lot of choice. I didn't know what you'd like, so I got a wide range. So that side of things is covered. Also, if you're on some sort of tight timeframe, we could keep the after-sex part to a minimum. I did some research, and I know some men don't want to be crowded, so I can—"

She only broke off when I sealed my mouth over hers again. It was as if she was arguing her case in a court of law.

As if I needed convincing.

As if I'd be worried I was going to have to waste my time. Fuck.

"Vicky," I said against her mouth. "Shut up, gorgeous. Okay?"

"Okay."

"Good girl."

She shivered underneath me, and I grinned before moving down her neck with my mouth.

"W-what are you doing?" she asked in a shaky voice.

I'd made it to her smooth stomach now, paused briefly to tug her skirt fully off, and then kissed from her hip across to her centre.

"Oh my God!" She arched off the bed when I licked her. "Is this standard… uh, standard procedure?"

I grinned before licking her again, using one of my blunt fingers to test how tight she was as my mouth focused on her clit. The answer was she was very bloody tight, and I was not a small man. I felt a twinge of unease but then refocused my efforts, bringing her right back to the edge.

"Mike, Mike, Mike," she chanted my name like a prayer as her hands sank into my hair, her whole body trembling. "I can't… it's not… ah!" She flew apart with a scream, everything under my tongue contracting, and her whole body jerking with the force of it.

I moved up her body slowly, keeping my hand cupping her with some light pressure there.

The drugged look of pleasure on her face made me feel ten feet tall.

"I need you inside me," she breathed, trying to pull me down on top of her again. "Please Mike, I'm yours. Please."

I could feel how slick and wet she was under my hand. It might be too soon, but I knew she was ready for me.

"Okay, baby," I said, my voice now a low growl, my body aching with the tension of holding back. All I wanted to do was plough into her, but the memory of how tight she was and the concern I would cause her pain helped me keep control.

"Condoms," I muttered.

I was clean, but she'd mentioned the condoms, and knowing how Vicky researched everything, I expected that she would want to use them.

"Top drawer of the bedside cabinet," she said.

I kissed her and pulled back, getting to my feet by the side of the bed. I opened the drawer and despite the tension in the room, I let out a surprised laugh.

"You weren't joking when you said you bought them all." The drawer had every make, size and flavour of condom known to man.

"I didn't want to get it wrong," she said in a small voice, and I choked back the rest of my laughter. Her face was red again, and the last thing I wanted was for her to feel embarrassed.

"You did a great job, love," I said as I grabbed one at random then pushed down my trousers and boxers in one.

Vicky's eyes went wide as she stared at me. The colour drained from her face, and she swallowed.

I frowned at her as I kicked my trousers away.

"Hey," I said gently, and she tore her eyes away from my cock to my face as I moved back to the bed to lie beside her. "We don't have to do anything else today. Okay? If you've changed your mind, then that's totally cool."

She flicked a glance down then back up again before swallowing nervously.

"No, I haven't changed my mind," her voice was firm, but I could hear the slight shake to it. "I just wasn't sure of the exact logistics of everything, er… well, fitting."

I smiled at her. "It'll fit."

"Er, okay." She didn't sound convinced.

I pushed her light blonde hair back again and kissed the corner of her mouth.

"Let's pause everything for the moment." I wasn't sure that my dick would ever fully recover, but I *was* sure that I wanted Vicky fully on board if we were going to do this.

A look of determination came over her face, and she surprised me by pushing me back and then climbing on top of me, her heat now resting against my cock.

"No," she said in that stubborn voice. "I can't wait. I need you, and I…" My hands were at her hips now, and I was moving her against me in a slow rhythm. "Oh, I… yes, that's…" she broke off with a small moan that almost snapped my control.

"That's it, baby," I encouraged as she started to take over the rhythm, her body instinctively knowing what she needed. "That's a *good girl*." She moaned again, her clit rubbing the underside of my cock in an almost desperate pattern.

"Mike," she breathed. "I need you inside, but I'm not sure I know what I'm doing this way up. I think—"

Before she could finish her sentence, I flipped her over to her back, keeping the pressure and the rhythm going once she was settled underneath me.

"I-I'm ready," she said as her eyes rolled back. "Please, Mike. I think I'm ready." I paused to roll the condom on and then finally, I was right there.

"Okay, okay," I muttered, panting with the effort of holding myself back, every muscle in my body strung tight. "I can't… Vicky, are you sure you—?"

She reached up then and pulled my head down so she could speak in my ear.

"Please, Mike. I'm yours. I've always been yours. I want it to be you. I need you inside me."

That was it. Those words snapped my control completely.

I pushed slowly into her tight, slick heat, checking with her as I did. She gave me a short nod and a hoarse "yes" before I surged forward, muffling her cry with a kiss. When I was fully inside her, I held perfectly still, even as my body screamed at me to pound into her. When I pulled back from the kiss to see tears in her eyes, I froze.

"Oh God, Vicky, I'm so sorry," I said in horror. "Baby, are you okay?"

"I-I—" she hiccupped on a small sob, and my heart felt like it was being torn from my chest. "I'm not great with pain. And you seem to be quite… quite well endowed. I feel like I've been sort of torn open, and the pressure is huge, but… I don't know, now that you're there and it's done, I… well, the pressure feels *right*. Achy and full, but good… maybe?"

"Okay, so you're not in pain now?" I gritted my teeth with the effort of staying still with her tightness around me.

"No, I just feel full. But I also feel like I need more." She paused and looked up at me with a frown. "Mike, I don't mean to tell you your business when clearly, I'm the inexperienced party here, but is it standard procedure to pause in the middle of intercourse for a full-on conversation? I mean, I thought there was a lot more movement involved?"

I let out a pained but relieved chuckle. "No, it's not *standard procedure*, but I wanted to check you were okay." Of their own volition, my hips withdrew slightly and then thrust forward again.

Vicky moaned.

"Well, consider me fully checked," she said in a rush. "So, if you could resume then maybe… uh!"

I started with slow thrusts, watching her carefully to make sure she wasn't in any more pain. But as her eyes rolled back in her head, and she started to move with me, my control started to slip.

By the time she was moaning my name, her hands gripping my back, I was totally gone. All that was on my mind was claiming her.

The idea that she was mine and mine alone seemed to send me almost feral. I growled into her neck as she tightened underneath me.

"Mike, I'm going to… I—" I could feel her convulsing against me, and it sent me over the edge, my thrusts now erratic, until I came harder than I'd ever experienced in my life.

Fireworks exploded behind my eyes. It almost felt like I might black out from the strength of it.

For a moment, I just collapsed on top of Vicky, my cock still deep inside her, the need to pin her down and claim her still pumping through my veins. Then, as my head cleared, I realised she probably couldn't breathe and I put weight on my arms to push up and look down at her.

She had a sheen of sweat over her forehead; her eyes were unfocused, her mouth still parted from the small scream she made when she came.

I gave her a brief kiss, then she whimpered as I pulled out.

Without thinking, I moved quickly off the bed and to her bathroom to deal with the condom. My chest tightened at the sight of a not-insignificant amount of blood. I made a snap decision, grabbed a flannel—unfortunately white, but then everything in this house was white—wet it with warm water, then strode back into the bedroom.

When I made it back there, Vicky was sitting up in bed, holding the sheets up to her neck. Her usually perfect hair was a mass of tangled blonde down her back and over her shoulders, there was some mascara under both eyes.

She looked unsure, small, vulnerable and more beautiful than I'd ever seen her before.

"Um, so… that was very satisfactory," she said, her voice shaky. "I mean, from *my* point of view, it was. Obviously, with my lack of experience, you may not be of the same opinion. I'm not sure of the protocol from this point on." She swallowed nervously. "If you want to leave, then I—"

"I'm not fucking leaving, Vicky," I said, striding over to her.

She blew out a relieved breath, and my heart felt like it broke a little.

This woman had such low expectations that she expected me to take her virginity and then just swan out of the door.

I sat on the bed next to her and reached for the covers, pulling them out of her grip. "Lie back down, baby," I said softly.

"Er… w-why?"

"Just lie back for a moment."

She hesitated but then rested back on the pillow behind her. "W-what are you do—?"

She squeaked as I moved her legs apart and gently reached down with the flannel. Once I'd sorted that, I folded up the cloth to hide the blood and chucked it into the bin for me to deal with later.

Vicky was sitting bolt upright, looking at me with wide eyes. "I can't believe you just did that," she whispered.

"This is all standard procedure," I told her, bending the truth a little—I'd never done that before in my life, but then, I'd never slept with someone as wonderful as Vicky before, either.

"Oh, er… right."

I pulled her to me as I lay on the bed beside her, until her head was resting on my chest, and her small body was gathered close to me in my arms.

"Um…" She hummed. "Is this all standard procedure as well?"

"Oh yes," I said, smiling up at the ceiling as I felt her softness relax into me, and her tension gradually draining away. "Very much so, love."

CHAPTER 21

"Six, I think"

Vicky

I bit my lip as I stared at Mike across my kitchen island. He was in only his thermal because *I* was wearing his flannel shirt.

I had no idea if it was okay to continue to steal his clothing, but when he'd been brushing his teeth this morning, I'd picked it up and tried it on, wanting to be surrounded by the woodsy Mike smell and feel the soft material against my skin.

He didn't seem to mind. In fact, when I started to take it off, he'd yanked it back up onto my shoulders and buttoned the front, telling me he liked me in his clothes.

Then, before I could put my leggings on, he'd grabbed my hand and taken me downstairs. So here I was, in just my knickers and a huge flannel shirt, watching the most beautiful man I'd ever seen prowl around my kitchen.

"I want to cook for you, love, but you appear to be missing a toaster?"

I slipped off the stool he'd put me on and pulled open the cupboard doors that my toaster and kettle lived behind.

His eyebrows went up, and he smiled.

"You hide your appliances?" His tone was teasing.

Lottie had helped me to identify when someone was teasing and when they were being mean. I wasn't always that great at it, but I was much more proficient than I used to be at telling the difference.

"I really don't like clutter." This was an understatement, but I didn't want to elaborate more than I had to.

He turned away from the toaster and stepped into my space, giving the brief pause he always did in order to warn me, then gathering me in his arms and kissing my nose.

"I kind of realised that when I came back to bed last night, and my clothes were folded on your chair, socks too."

"I can be a bit obsessive," I whispered. The socks had definitely given me away. I just hoped that discovering all my quirks all at once wasn't enough to put him off.

He shrugged. "Me too. Maybe not about socks and toasters, but definitely when I'm working on a piece. Obsessed is putting it lightly. Right, let me make you food, woman. How do you like your eggs?"

I bit my lip again. "Mike, I'm really specific about eggs. It's… complicated."

His arms gave me a squeeze, and his voice softened. "How about you show me, and then I'm ready for next time."

At the mention of a next time, I stared up at him and smiled a huge smile.

An almost fierce expression crossed his features before he gave me a brief, hard kiss, another arm squeeze, and then let me go to start the eggs.

As I was getting everything out for them, I asked Mike how *he* wanted his eggs, and he just told me he'd have them the same as me.

That level of flexibility always intrigued me.

He didn't even know how I was going to cook my eggs: how runny the yolk would be, how brown I'd toast the bread. I *had* to have poached eggs. They *needed* to be cooked for exactly two minutes and thirty-five seconds. The bread *had* to be wholemeal, but not seeded, and toasted for one minute and ten seconds, exactly, in a pre-heated toaster.

"Hold on, let me write this down," Mike said as I rattled off what I was doing. "And what do you mean by a pre-heated toaster?"

My face felt hot, and I ducked my head to avoid his eyes. "I turn it on for thirty seconds so that it's hot when the toast goes in."

I continued avoiding eye contact as I bustled around the kitchen. When I eventually presented him with poached eggs on toast and sat next to him on the kitchen stool, I just stared down at my plate, my appetite gone now that I felt weird.

Was pre-heating your toaster weird?

"Hey." I glanced at Mike who was now turned fully towards me, but then ducked my head again, allowing my hair to block him from view. But in typical Mike fashion, he just put his hand on the back of my stool and turned me to face him by spinning the seat, then used his other hand to tuck my hair behind my ear. "What's up? Why aren't you eating?"

"I'm a little bit… specific about food," I said. "It's not an ice princess thing. It's not me being spoiled or deliberately awkward. I just—"

"Vicky, you're making *your* breakfast in *your* kitchen," he said. "You can be as specific as you like." His voice softened then. "And baby, I'm sorry I called you a princess. I didn't know you then, and I made assumptions. You know I don't think that now, right?"

He paused for a moment as an expression I couldn't read crossed his face.

"Vicky, you lost weight after I was a dick to you, and Ollie had to come and find you under that bloody coffee table. I will never forgive myself for that, but I'm going to do everything I can now to sort it. I don't want to stress you out again. I would never think you were being spoiled or awkward."

I managed a small smile. "Mike, you've got to admit, I can be a little bit awkward."

He raised his eyebrows. "I don't think so."

I sighed. "I have a colour chart for my tea preference according to time of day, Mike."

"Yes, well if anything, that makes you less awkward," he said casually. "If only everyone would do that, a lot less tea would go to waste."

I blinked at him. "I think that too," I whispered. "I told Lottie that, and she assured me that most people wouldn't agree. I'm not allowed to bring it out at meetings."

He frowned. "You take your chart wherever you like, love," he said in a grumpy voice. "You should have the tea you bloody well want."

I put down my fork and turned to him on my stool. "I really *really* like you, Mike Mayweather," I told him, and he smiled, his white teeth against his tanned skin and beard, so beautiful I felt stunned for a moment.

"I really, really like you too, baby," he said in a low voice that I seemed to feel everywhere.

Heat rose to my cheeks, and I bit my lip.

His gaze dropped to my mouth and then he cleared his throat and shook his head as if to clear it.

"Listen, eat your eggs, woman," he said, his voice now hoarse as he turned away from me. "I don't want to be the reason you lose any more weight."

"It wasn't just what happened that day," I blurted out, not wanting Mike to carry all this guilt anymore. "It wasn't just your rejection. There was other… stuff, and, well… it wasn't just because of you that I stopped eating."

Mike stared at me for a long moment. "You'll tell me the other stuff when you're ready?" he asked, and I was glad he wasn't going to push this now.

"Okay," I said in a small voice. Then he kissed my temple, gave me a brief side hug, and just like that, my appetite was back.

Or it was until my phone started ringing, and I looked at the display. It was as if I'd conjured her up just by mentioning the *other stuff* that had stressed me out.

Knowing that she would only keep ringing until I picked up, I decided to just get it over with.

"Hi, Mum," I said, pushing what was left of my poached eggs on toast away.

"You need to ring the florist to pay for the arrangements," she snapped.

This was the first time she'd spoken to me in over six weeks. No hello, no asking me how I was.

"Okay," I said slowly. "But Mum, I already paid for the flowers. The florist invoiced me last week. It was—"

"We've decided that we want both the table displays *and* the taller orchid cascades. It'll be an extra five thousand."

"Mum," I said quietly, aware Mike was watching me with a curious expression on his face. "Is Gareth aware that—?"

"Don't you stick your fucking nose in with Gareth," Mum semi-shouted.

Mike stiffened next to me, clearly having heard her shrill voice.

I sighed. Gareth would be deeply unhappy if he knew how much extra was being spent on the wedding behind his back, but there was nothing I could do about it.

"Okay, fine. I'll call them tomorrow."

"And don't wear anything to upstage your sister."

I blinked. "I'm not going to—"

"I won't have it, young lady."

"Mum, I paid for her wedding dress. It cost ten thousand pounds, and it's Oscar de la Renta. Nobody is upstaging Rebecca. It would be impossible."

"Just don't wear anything flashy."

"Listen, do you want me at the house before the ceremony? Gareth said that—"

"No. The house is only for the bridesmaids and close family."

"Right," I whispered. "I'll... um, see you at the church then?"

"Hmm," Mum hummed, non-committedly.

"Listen, Mum," I said, trying for a completely neutral tone. "Honestly, if you'd rather I wasn't there, I don't mind. I know I annoy you and Rebecca, and—"

"Oh, God. Stop with the martyr stuff again. Spare me, please. You have to be at the bloody wedding. It'll look strange if you're not. Just try not to speak to people too much. And for God's sake, don't mention hedgehogs, or any other of your little obsessions."

I nodded, even as my heart sank. I was really hoping that she'd let me out of going. But she needed me there. People knew she had two daughters. She was right; it would look strange if I wasn't at my sister's wedding. But the thought of a whole day with people who didn't like me made me feel like there was a heavy weight on my chest, and for a moment it was hard to catch my breath.

Rebecca's friends had never liked me, either. They teased me, but not the good kind of teasing. Even as a child, I knew it wasn't the good kind.

"Okay," I whispered, but she had already put the phone down. My hand was shaking when I transferred my phone onto the granite in front of me.

"That didn't seem like a very fun conversation," Mike said cautiously.

I shrugged. "It's about my half-sister's wedding."

"I didn't know you had another sister."

"Mum married Gareth three months after she had me. They had Rebecca a year after that."

"Was your dad ever with your mum? I know he left Margot after you were born. He never married your mum?"

"Oh no, dad *hated* her. He never lived with us. I was a mistake. He told me that I was her attempt to trap him, but he wasn't having any of it."

"He *told* you that?"

Mike sounded angry now. Maybe this wasn't such a good subject.

"How old were you when he told you that?"

"Six, I think."

"Your father told his six-year-old daughter that she was a mistake, and the result of an attempt to trap him?"

Oh dear. His voice was rising now. I didn't want Mike getting angry, so I told him the facts in an effort to calm him down.

"Well, it was the truth, and Dad knew I liked the truth, and that I wanted people to be honest in their dealings with me. It was only facts he was relaying to me."

Mike closed his eyes slowly and took a deep breath in and out through his nose. "You don't relay those kind of facts to a fucking six-year-old, Vicky."

"No, you don't understand. He—"

"How old were you when you stopped speaking?"

What on earth? Where had that question come from?

I blinked at him.

"How old, Vicky?"

"I was six," I said quietly, and he stared at me. I shook my head, putting what he was implying together. "No, that wasn't the trigger."

His eyebrows went up. "Worse shit than that went down when you were six? Is that what you're saying?"

I stiffened.

Yes, worse shit had gone down when I was six. But I wasn't going to go into that.

"I don't want to speak about my childhood anymore."

He watched me as I sat stiffly on the stool for a moment, and tracked the movement of my hand as I tucked some hair behind my ear. I brought it back to my lap when I realised it was still shaking.

"Okay, love," he said softly. "Eat your eggs."

I grimaced when I looked at the now-cold eggs. "I... um, well..."

"I'll make you some more," he told me, jumping off the stool.

"No, it's fine. I can—"

"Vicky, are you going to be able to eat a cold poached egg? Tell me the truth."

"No," I whispered, feeling like a fusspot, but that *was* the honest truth.

"Well then," he said simply.

"But—" I was about to tell him that I'd do it. He might have watched me, but he didn't know all the exact timings and—

"Don't worry," he said with a grin, holding up his phone. He'd typed a whole paragraph of notes and timings in his notes app with the title, Vicky's Eggs.

I smiled and felt my eyes sting, which was ridiculous. It was just eggs.

"Thanks," I said in a hoarse voice.

He gave a firm nod and set about making my second breakfast.

"When is that wedding?" he asked casually.

"W-what?"

"Your sister's wedding that you were talking about with your mum. When is it?"

"Oh... next Saturday."

"Right, what time am I picking you up?"

My mouth dropped open.

"Picking me up?" My voice was high-pitched with shock now.

"For the wedding."

"You're picking me up for the wedding?"

"Baby," he said firmly. "If you think that after overhearing that little chat with your mum, I'm letting you go to that wedding alone, you're crazy."

It hadn't even occurred to me that Mike might be willing to take me to Rebecca's wedding. That weight on my chest lifted at the thought of having him by my side.

"Vicky?" He'd paused what he was doing to look at me. "You okay?"

"Thank you," I said, putting as much feeling as I could into the words which came out a little choked as I had to force them past my tight throat.

He stared at me for a moment with a fierce expression before he put the pan down and strode around to my side of the kitchen island. He turned my chair towards him in that bossy way of his and kissed me. When he pulled away to rest his forehead on mine, his expression was soft.

"That's okay, love."

CHAPTER 22

C-could you stay with me today?

Mike

Vicky was sad, and I hated it.

Since I picked her up about an hour ago, all she'd done was stare out of the window of my ancient Land Rover. The contrast between this Vicky and the Vicky I'd taken out on a date two nights ago was stark.

After the first-date disaster of taking her to a fancy restaurant where she couldn't actually eat, a second date entailing fish and chips on my sofa—something she seemed thrilled about but which I considered well below wooing level—then a date crashed by all our nosy friends and family, I'd wanted *this* date to be perfect.

So I'd tried to come up with something Vicky would think was perfect. I'd told her to wear her most comfortable leggings and hoodie, picked her up from her house and taken her to a hide in Regent's Park used by the Zoological Society of London to watch the little prickly guys.

It was the first time I'd ever made a picnic, but I'd done my research. Lottie told me, in great detail, how to make a sandwich that Vicky would eat.

It was all worth it to see the look on Vicky's face when we arrived at the hide. The way she looked at me, like I'd hung the moon for her, when in reality, I'd made a sandwich and managed to sneak us into a park at night, was almost unreal.

"You like hedgehogs too?" she'd asked with wide eyes.

I'd pulled her into me and hugged her close, saying, "I like *you,*" into her hair.

When I pulled back, she was blinking rapidly, and I could see the unshed tears in her eyes.

Bloody hell, had I actually thought that this woman wanted designer clothes and fancy cars? Had I really believed she thought she was better than everyone else?

She talked about hedgehogs and wildlife preservation for an hour straight after that. When I had to gently tell her to eat her sandwich, she'd blinked as if coming out of a trance, and then a look of mortification had swept over her features.

"I did it again, didn't I?" she asked, her face flaming red.

"What, love?" I asked with a frown.

"Banging on about my obsessions. I did it again. Y-you should have stopped me."

"Hey, I want to hear about the hedgehogs too, you know. You can't be selfish with the hedgehog facts. That's not fair."

She tilted her head to the side. "You're teasing me, aren't you?" Her voice was steady, but I could just about make out a small thread of hurt running through it.

I turned fully to her on my camping chair. "Vicky, no. I'm not teasing. I *like* hearing about the hedgehogs. I like hearing about anything that makes you happy. You listened to me bang on about welding yesterday."

There was a long pause before she leapt on me and kissed me.

We'd had another standoff that evening when I told her we could sleep together but couldn't have sex because she'd be sore. That didn't go down well at all. Then I'd refused to teach her the "logistics of a blow job", which didn't go down well either.

We ended up in a ridiculous negotiation over it.

Vicky wanted an exact number of "dates" before I'd teach her. It was insane. Of course, I wanted a blow job. Fuck. But this girl was a virgin three days ago, and we were going to take it slowly, goddamn it.

But now sitting in my passenger seat, she was not babbling about hedgehogs or universal income—another of her pet obsessions, which I got her started on last night on the phone, setting off an hour-long explanation—it was actually fascinating stuff, and I just loved hearing that unbridled enthusiasm in her soft voice. No, she wasn't talking about anything. And she looked really, really far away. Like she'd retreated from me, like she was back behind protective walls.

I reached out and laid my hand on her leg.

She flinched as if she'd forgotten I was even there.

"Sorry, love," I said quickly. "Is this okay?"

Before I could pull my hand away, hers had clamped down on it and gripped hard, as if holding onto a lifeline. "Yes. Very okay."

"Are *you* okay?"

She bit her lip and took a deep breath in and out, but before she could answer we'd pulled into the church car park.

"We'd better go in," Vicky said, glancing at her watch. "It's seven minutes until the ceremony starts."

I nodded. "Right."

I wanted to ask her why she wasn't coming with the family. Wasn't that what normally happened at weddings with sisters? But then again, what did I know? My sister was getting married, and she'd asked me to walk her down the aisle, so I was definitely not sitting in the audience at the church.

But maybe rich people did things differently? Maybe they were meeting outside the church?

"Mike, do I look… do I look too showy?"

My eyebrows went up.

Vicky was wearing a soft blue shift dress. It was simple and elegant. She'd paired it with a small hat thing, the kind that I didn't really understand how it stayed on a girl's head.

"You look beautiful," I told her the truth.

She looked out of the window again with a frown as she chewed on her bottom lip. Somehow, it felt like I'd said the wrong thing.

As we walked into the church, Vicky kept her head down, muttering thanks to the ushers as they gave her a programme and moving quickly past them. Nobody greeted her. Nobody tried to hug her. It was completely bizarre.

Then, compounding the bizarreness, once we were in the church, she darted into the back row and sat down. This was her *sister.* Why the hell would she sit in the back row?

When I sat down next to her, she huddled close to me, as close as she could get, despite the fact we had the whole church pew to ourselves.

Not that I was complaining, but it was almost as though she was scared of something.

"Vicky," I whispered. "Shouldn't you be up at the front where the family sits? I can stay back here if you want?"

Maybe she didn't want to force a random into the mix on her sister's wedding day.

I mean, she'd seemed very keen, almost desperate for me to come, but I could see how awkward it might be to have me muscling in when I'd never even met this side of her family.

"C-could you stay with me today?" she said in a small voice. "Sorry. I know it's a bit clingy of me, but just for today, could you make sure you're with me? Um… all the time?"

I was starting to feel a bit uneasy. My instincts were screaming at me at this point to bundle Vicky up, carry her out of the church, and take her back to my cabin where she was safe.

Which was ridiculous, wasn't it?

This was her family. Surely, this should be a happy day?

The conversation with her mother had been a bit odd; why was Vicky buying her sister's ten-grand wedding dress? I definitely hadn't liked the sound of the woman, or the way she spoke to her daughter, but when I pressed Vicky about her family, she said they were *fine.* But why was she in this current panicked state if her family was fine?

Something else was going on here.

"Of course, I'll stay with you," I said in a firm tone.

"Oh, thanks," she said, her voice full of relief.

When I turned to her, she smiled up at me; it was the first one she'd managed all day. But when she turned back to the front of the church, the strangest thing happened. Her smile dropped, and her face drained of all colour as she sank lower into her seat.

I followed the direction of her gaze, and there was the groom. He was staring right at Vicky, and he was smiling.

Why wasn't she smiling back at him?

My sense of unease grew, especially when his eyes flicked over to me, and his smile wavered before he turned back to the altar. A hush fell over the church as a blonde woman in a huge hat came down the aisle and made her way up to the front, pausing on her way to greet people and wave at different groups.

I assumed this was Vicky's mother, but she didn't even glance at her daughter, and if anything, Vicky shrank further into me when her mother made her entrance.

I leaned down to whisper in her ear. "Vicky, is something—?" I was cut off by the organ playing, and the vicar telling us to be upstanding for the entrance of the bride.

My God, Vicky's sister was wearing the most complicated bloody dress I'd ever seen in my life. There was a lot of lace involved, and the train was almost the entire length of the aisle.

She had five adult bridesmaids, all in dresses the same salmon pink as the flowers the church was decked out in.

The service went on for a while. There were no fewer than five readings, and one of the bridesmaids sang a horrific song during the signing of the register.

And throughout the whole thing, not one member of her family acknowledged Vicky. Not *once.* It was beyond strange.

Outside the church, things got even stranger.

Vicky stood separately from everyone else as the ushers and bridesmaids organised people into rows to shower the happy couple with confetti and get photos of them emerging from the church.

Then the whole wedding party had photos together. Still, no acknowledgement of Vicky.

I was beginning to think that they hadn't actually realised Vicky was there, until suddenly, her mother was in front of her with a sour expression on her face as she glared down at her.

It was then that I remembered Margot's words from weeks ago:

I don't have a high opinion of the woman, seeing as she slept with my husband for years behind my back, but she is also one of the most vile people on the planet.

"You'll have to come for the family photo," Vicky's mother snapped, grabbing Vicky's arm above her elbow.

Vicky flinched at the sudden contact, and her hand tightened in mine.

"Honestly, Victoria," the woman spat. "Don't embarrass me, today of all days. And for God's sake, try and smile. It's not that hard."

I was already on the edge with the arm grabbing and the way she was speaking to Vicky, plus the fact that she hadn't hugged her or acknowledged her, other than barking out orders, but what happened next pushed me right over it.

"Well?" she asked, giving Vicky's arm a hard shake, which in turn, shook her entire body, forcing a small, distressed sound from the back of Vicky's throat—a very quiet version of the sounds she'd made when she was under really severe stress at the fireworks.

I stepped forward, pulling Vicky behind me with my hand that was still holding hers, and putting my other hand on her mother's arm to yank her off her daughter and set her away.

"What the fuck is going on here?" I said, my voice low and furious.

Vicky's mother blinked at me. "Who are you?"

"Vicky's boyfriend. Who are you?"

Her eyes went from me to Vicky and then narrowed.

I decided I didn't like that, so I snapped my fingers in front of the woman's face.

She jerked in shock, and her eyes went wide.

"Don't look at her," I snapped. "Eyes up here. Now you were going to explain who the fuck you are, and why the fuck you're assaulting my girlfriend in broad daylight."

"I'm her mother."

"Well, you'll forgive the confusion..." I deadpanned. "You see, the way you've just greeted your daughter did not seem very *motherly* to me."

"Mike, it's fine," Vicky said from behind me.

"It is not fine, Vicky," I said, keeping my eyes on this viper of a woman.

Vicky's mother looked between me and her daughter with cold calculation, then she plastered the fakest smile I've ever seen in my life on her face.

"Goodness, well this is all just a misunderstanding. Of course, I'm a little tense from all the organising." She turned to Vicky, her fake smile now looking like it was causing her actual pain. "Darling, do introduce me properly to your young man. You are naughty not telling me about him."

"Mum, this is Mike," Vicky said, still in that small voice. "And Mike, this is my mum. Mrs. Williams."

"Oh please, do call me Janet." She was all sugary sweetness now, and it was making me feel vaguely ill. But when she held out her hand to me, Vicky gave my other hand a squeeze, so I decided not to take any more of a stand..

"Janet," I said in a short voice, giving her hand a brief but maybe too firm shake.

"Would you forgive me if I steal away my daughter?"

Could you stay with me today?

Vicky's voice from earlier floated through my brain, along with that slight thread of fear that ran through it.

I tightened my grip on Vicky's hand. "Lead the way."

CHAPTER 23

Are you Vicky's carer?

Vicky

"How much did you pay him?" Mum hissed at me after the photographer had arranged us where he wanted us all to stand.

"W-what?" I whispered.

"That man. How much did you pay him to be here?"

"I-I didn't—"

"Now, ladies," the photographer interrupted. "Eyes to me, please, and big smiles."

I turned away from Mum and looked towards the camera, trying to force my mouth to cooperate so that the corners would turn up even whilst my stomach was churning with nausea.

"Lady in the pale blue?"

I blinked and looked from his camera to him.

He smiled at me. "Yes, you, beautiful. Can you try for a smile?"

"Fucking freak," I heard Rebecca mutter.

Darrell chuckled next to her, and my mother elbowed me sharply in my ribs.

I bared my teeth in what I hoped was a semblance of a smile. Thankfully, it was enough to satisfy the photographer, because after another couple of minutes, we were done.

"It's my wedding day," Rebecca snapped at me once the photo was over.

"Yes, I know," I said, looking over her shoulder to search for Mike, but he'd been intercepted by two bridesmaids.

Lucinda and Fiona were Rebecca's friends who took particular pleasure in being mean to me.

Fiona was leaning into Mike now, and she had her hand on the lapel of his jacket.

My throat felt too tight. Mike looked *so* handsome in his suit.

I should have expected this. I should have expected women to be all over him.

I tore my eyes away from the three of them.

Fiona was very beautiful and very charming. If she wanted to take Mike from me, she could. It was naïve of me not to think of this before.

Mike and I had only just started dating, and I was already proving to be hard work. I knew that. Everyone *always* said what hard work I was. So it stood to reason that eventually, he would be taken from me by someone like Fiona.

The hurt and jealousy I felt at that thought was almost enough to trigger another meltdown.

I had to get it together.

"If you know today's important," Rebecca continued, her voice still dripping with disdain. "Could you try and be a little less of a freak? I mean, how bloody difficult is it to smile?"

"Right, yes, I'll try," I told Rebecca automatically, taking a small step back.

I was really hoping this exchange would be over soon. Usually, once she'd called me a freak or a weirdo and made it clear how much I annoyed her, she would leave me alone.

When we were very young, things had been different. We would even play together as children, all of course directed by Rebecca, as playing wasn't really one of my areas of strength.

Even after I stopped speaking, it was years before Rebecca started being openly unpleasant. But then, as we grew into our teens, Rebecca began taking her lead from our mother more, and our interactions became far more adversarial. Things would escalate if Rebecca didn't get the reaction from me she wanted. I didn't cry easily, which often led to protracted name-calling and nastiness from Rebecca, who would go on to enlist her friends, Fiona being the main offender.

"Where are you going?" Rebecca was furious now as I took another step back.

I shrugged. "I assumed this interaction was complete."

"I'll say when I'm done with you, freak," Rebecca said. "Don't you dare—"

"Come on, Becs," Darrell put in as he slid his arm around her shoulders. "Chill out. She's here, isn't she?" He turned to me, and I felt my body tense with the perceived threat. "Hey there, sis. Let's hug it out. We're family now."

He took a step forward, and I panicked.

Running backwards in heels in a graveyard is not a good idea. One of my stilettos stuck into the soft grass, the back of my knee hit a gravestone, and before I knew it, I was sprawled on the grass in between two graves, with Darrell smirking down at me, and the sound of the bridesmaids' laughter all around me.

When he took another step towards me, I scrambled back further, uncaring about the stains I knew would now be all over my dress.

I held my hand up to ward him off, but then suddenly, my vision was filled with a frowning Mike.

Relief swept through me as I breathed in his now familiar, woodsy scent.

"Hey, love," he said softly. "You okay if I lift you up?"

And there it was.

The consideration my family never showed me.

Always checking before he put his hands on me. The irony was that Mike didn't even have to check now. His touch was so familiar, that I didn't need the warning anymore.

I nodded, and he put his strong hands under my arms, lifting me up and setting me on my feet as if I weighed nothing at all.

When I was upright again, he stood in front of me, blocking my view of Rebecca and Darrell. "You alright? Wanna get out of here?"

"I can't leave," I whispered at his feet.

"Hello?" Rebecca snapped from behind Mike, and his shoulders stiffened. "Who are you?"

"I'm Mike. Vicky's boyfriend," he said, turning towards Rebecca, keeping me slightly behind him, just like he'd done with my mother. He offered his hand to her. "Congratulations. You must be Rebecca."

Rebecca stared at Mike with her mouth hanging open for a long moment, not taking his hand, which was annoying as you were *supposed* to shake hands—even I knew that, not that I could often bring myself to do it.

Luckily, my stepdad came to the rescue.

Gareth joined the group and took Mike's hand himself.

"Great to meet you, Mike," Gareth said with a smile and a firm handshake. "You'll have to excuse my daughter; the whole day is all a bit overwhelming. I was so glad when Vicky told me she was bringing a plus one."

I heard giggles behind us—the bridesmaids again, no doubt.

"Vicky," he said to me after dropping Mike's hand. "It's good to see you, cariad." I stepped around Mike, and Gareth walked to me, hesitating until I gave him a nod, and then hugging me quickly, and with just the right amount of pressure.

"Daddy," Rebecca whined from behind us. "Do you mind sorting the cars instead of fussing over her? It is actually *my* wedding day."

Gareth sighed as he released me.

"Good luck, man," Mike said to him, clapping him on the shoulder in that manly-I-respect-you kind of way.

Gareth smiled at him. "Cheers, I'm gonna need it."

"Daddy!"

Gareth rolled his eyes and then gave me a warm look and a wink. "I'll see you later, Vicky," he said before ushering his daughter, new son-in-law and wife to the waiting cars.

Darrell was eyeing Mike with annoyance as he walked away.

When he caught me looking at him, he raised one eyebrow and smirked, and I felt a cold shiver run down my spine

Mike's hand went to my lower back, and he guided me across the graveyard to his truck. On the way there, we had to negotiate my aunt Teresa, who spoke to me like she always did—as if I was mentally challenged.

Her shock when Mike introduced himself was palpable.

"A boyfriend, dear?" she said, looking Mike up and down, her eyebrows in her hairline. "That's a bit of a turn-up with your, er... difficulties."

"What difficulties are those?" Mike asked with an edge to his voice. "Her wildly successful career? Her intelligence? The fact she's the most beautiful woman in any room? How kind, funny and generous she is?"

Aunt Teresa gaped at him for a moment and then, with a vague noise intended to excuse herself, made her escape.

"What's her deal?" Mike asked me when she was out of earshot.

"What do you mean?"

"Why does she speak to you like that?"

"All my family think I'm a bit... well, my Uncle John would call it 'touched' or 'a few pennies short of a pound'. I wasn't an easy child, and, as you know, I didn't speak for many years." I shrugged. "It's what Mum told everyone to explain it."

"Bloody hell, your family's a bunch of dicks, and your mum is queen of the dicks."

"Queen of the dicks?" I repeated, feeling my lips twitch, and then something happened that I wouldn't have thought possible on my sister's wedding day, a day I'd been dreading for weeks...

I laughed.

It started as a nervous giggle, but by the time we made it to Mike's Land Rover, I was laughing so hard, a tear had made its way down my cheek.

Mike opened the car door for me with a huge smile on his face.

Once I was sitting in the seat, and my laughter had subsided, he swiped my tear away with his thumb and kissed my still-smiling lips.

"Think that might be my new favourite thing to do," he told me softly.

"What?" I asked.

"Watch you laugh."

His gaze scanned my face as my smile faded.

"Just got to figure out how to make it happen more often, is all."

Then he gave me a firm, closed-mouthed kiss before he moved back to close the car door.

I tried, but I couldn't hold onto the light feeling that Mike calling my mother the queen of dicks gave me as we drove to the reception.

I was back to staring out of the window in silence. I didn't want to be silent with Mike, and I knew it was a bad habit to slip back into, but the prospect of this much time with my family was simply too overwhelming.

"Your stepdad seems like a decent guy," Mike said. "Even if the rest of your family are really fucking questionable."

I shrugged. "Gareth is kind."

Mike huffed. "It's not *kind* to greet your stepdaughter with some semblance of affection. It's bloody normal."

I hummed in a non-committal agreement. I just wanted to get this whole day over with.

Luckily, when we arrived at the reception, and I checked the table plan, Mike and I were the furthest we could possibly be from my immediate family.

Mike didn't seem to think it was lucky.

"What the fuck?" he growled as he plucked a champagne glass off a passing waiter to give to me, then asked for a pint of beer for himself. "First the church, and now this. Vicky, what is going on with your family?"

I felt my face heat and ducked my head so that I was speaking at the grass at my feet. "It's fine, Mike. My family, they… you've got to understand, they've had to put up with me since I was a child. And I was a very difficult child. I still really annoy them, so it's hard for them to be—"

"What in the fuck are you talking about?" Mike ground out.

Oh dear, my explanation did not seem to be calming him down at all.

"Difficult child? Is that their excuse for treating you like shit?"

"Mike, honestly, I *was* hard. I used to have a lot of meltdowns. Until I was about six, I could be really loud if something set me off. It was extremely embarrassing for Mum. That issue resolved of course with the mutism, because then, my meltdowns were mostly silent. But the not speaking was considered aberrant also. It annoyed Mum a lot. And she didn't believe in having me assessed, so—"

"Hold on," Mike cut me off. "You had regular meltdowns *for years*, then you were mute, again *for years*, and your mother never had you assessed?"

I shrugged. "The school tried, but Mum blocked it. She doesn't really believe in labels. And she thought if they pandered to it, that would make me worse."

"What about your dad?"

"Oh well, I didn't really see much of him. Margot was the one at Buckingham Manor. As you must know, my father rarely visited."

"So, he told his estranged wife to look after his mistress's child and just buggered off?"

"Well, there wasn't another option, really. Mum couldn't cope with me for the whole summer, and Dad just sort of dumped me at the Manor. Margot wasn't very happy at first, but after a while, she just got on with it—you know what she's like. Ollie was brilliant, though; he accepted me immediately."

"And Claire?"

"Claire's seven years older than me. I was only there for a couple of weeks for few summers at the same time as her, and she mostly ignored me. Then she had Florrie quite young with no support from Florrie's father. Things were a little better between us then. Florrie has always been quite attached to me and I like her direct nature very much. But after Claire married Blake things deteriorated again. I hate Blake."

"Well, we all hate Blake."

I shook my head. "No, I *always* hated Blake. And I'm not good at lying. So, Claire had a few reasons why she didn't like me. Firstly, she loved her father and saw me as the one who pushed him away from her mother, and secondly, she could tell I hated her husband. It's fine."

What I didn't say is how very heartbroken I'd been when Claire had rejected me. How much I'd longed for a sister who didn't hate me. How Claire's disdain for me only solidified the knowledge that I was unlovable.

Mike's jaw clenched. A waiter handed him a pint of beer, and he took a long sip before focusing back on me.

"But *Ollie* was never a dick to you, right?"

I shook my head. "Ollie is naturally very protective. He feels obligated to me, and he's not the type of man to shirk his obligations."

"You think you're just an obligation to Ollie?"

I nodded. "Of course. And Margot felt sorry for me, so eventually, I became an obligation to her, too."

"They love you, Vicky," he said softly, and my chest tightened as I gave him another non-committal hum. "Your fucking family have a lot to answer for."

I sighed. "I don't think I've explained it right. You've got to understand how—"

"If you say anything else about being a difficult child or annoying, I'm gonna lose it."

I did not think this was an ideal environment for Mike to *lose it*, so I pressed my lips together to stop myself from saying anything more.

It wasn't long until the drinks reception was over, and we were seated at our table, a safe distance from my family. I was next to my uncle, who also spoke to me like I was mentally deficient, but it was better than open hostility.

Unfortunately, Mike had Fiona on his other side, who kept pawing at him. Fiona was very obviously drunk by the time the main course was served and seemed oblivious to Mike's growing annoyance.

"How much did she pay you?" I heard her slur in his ear. She probably thought she was whispering, but she may as well have shouted her question across the whole table.

Mike, who'd been valiantly trying to eat his meal up until that point, lowered his fork slowly down to his plate.

"What the fuck are you talking about?" he asked.

Fiona giggled. "Vicky. How much is she paying you to be here? Come on, you're like something out of a catalogue. Did she mail order you?"

"I'm Vicky's boyfriend, and no, she did not *mail order* me."

Fiona snorted. "That freak has a boyfriend like you? You must be joking. Is this some sort of community outreach programme or something?"

"Oh, is that it?" asked my aunt in a curious voice from across the table, clearly having caught the tail end of the conversation. "Are you Vicky's carer?"

I felt my face flame, and I simply couldn't take anymore. "I'll be back in a minute," I whispered into Mike's ear before darting off in the direction of the toilets. At least, I'd hoped it was the direction of the toilets.

The reception was in a stately home, and I seemed to have taken a wrong turn down a portrait-lined corridor. But when I spun around to retrace my steps, my heart sank.

Darrell was blocking the corridor and my exit, and he was smiling that shark's smile, which showed all his teeth.

"Where are you off to, little sis?" he asked, taking a step towards me.

I took a corresponding one back as my heart began to pound.

CHAPTER 24

Last time?

Vicky

"S-s-stay away from me." I'd meant my voice to come out strong, but it was so small, it was only above a whisper.

His eyes flashed as if relishing the challenge.

"Tell me," he said in a conversational tone as if we were having a normal chat, and he wasn't stalking me with intent. "Are you still a little virgin like your sister told me you were? Or has the Incredible Hulk in there managed to fuck the ice princess out of you?"

"You shouldn't s-s-speak to me like that," I said. "I'll tell my—"

Darrell let out a bark of laughter. "Who will you tell? How did that work out for you last time?"

He lunged forward, and I wasn't quick enough to get away.

Freezing was the most useless human defence mechanism.

I wished I was a runner, although I wasn't sure how far I would have made it in those heels, and I had a suspicion Darrell would enjoy the chase.

He had hold of both my arms now and dragged my body flush with his.

I struggled for a moment, but then he gave me a hard shake, which was enough to make me freeze again.

He took advantage of my lack of movement, dragging me across to a free patch of wall in between two of the portraits, and pinning me there.

Claustrophobia enveloped me, and I started to struggle for breath; my head was swimming, and then it was like I had left my body altogether. Like I was floating above Darrell and me, watching as he yanked up the hem of my dress to my hip.

Deep in terror now, knowing I couldn't fight him off, I hung in his arms and closed my eyes.

But then a vision of Mike's face swum into my consciousness: Mike hesitating before he touched me, Mike holding my hand, Mike telling me he liked me, Mike finding out exactly the type of sandwich I can eat.

How fucking *dare* Darrell touch me?

I wasn't his, I was *Mike's*.

And so I took a deep breath in, and I screamed at the top of my lungs.

"You crazy bitch," Darrell snapped in horror as he tried to cover my mouth with his large hand whilst grappling to keep me pinned to the wall with the other.

But I was no longer frozen. I was fighting, and I remembered Ollie's go-to advice: *Always go for the balls, Vicky.*

I brought my knee up and smashed it into Darrell's crotch.

He howled in pain, the hand over my mouth dropping to his groin as he used the other hand to grab my hair by the roots and smash the side of my face into the wall. But then, suddenly, he was gone.

To be more precise, he was actually flying backwards through the air.

Mike had grabbed him by the back of his jacket and shirt, and literally lifted him up and off me, as if he weighed no more than a bag of flour.

Darrell tried to get away. His arms were whirling all over the place in his attempt to escape, but Mike just held him at arm's length, suspended slightly off the floor by the scruff of his neck, like he was a naughty kitten.

"What the fuck is going on?" Mike shouted, giving Darrell a rough shake. I was a non-violent person, but it did feel good to watch Darrell get a taste of his own medicine.

"She was asking for it," Darrell, very unwisely said. "She's a little fucking tease. All that ice princess stuff is just—" Darrell broke off because Mike punched him in the face, and he crumpled to the floor at Mike's feet.

"Er... sorry to interrupt," the wedding planner—I knew who she was because I'd had to go onto her website to pay her for her services—said from a few feet away down the corridor. Her wide eyes were fixed on the three of us.

I realised that my dress was still up around my hips, and I jerked it down.

Mike's eyes flashed with fury when he saw me do that.

"B-but the speeches are about to start and—"

"Go and get the bride *and* the mother and father-of-the-bride and bring them here," Mike snapped at her. "Right fucking now."

"Oh, er... okay." Wedding planner lady seemed relieved to be making a hasty exit.

Meanwhile, Darrell started scuttling back from Mike. He was bleeding from his nose, all down his pristine white shirt and that horrible salmon pink tie.

"Oh, no you don't," muttered Mike, striding over to him and grabbing him by the scruff of his neck again to lift him up onto his feet. "You're not going anywhere, mate."

"What the hell is going on?" Mum stormed down the corridor, her face puce with rage, followed by Gareth and Rebecca.

"Oh, Darrell!" cried Rebecca when she saw her new husband. "What's happened? Baby, are you okay?" She walked to him, and her hands fluttered around his bloody face—there was no way Rebecca would risk blood stains on her dress, no matter how badly her new husband was hurt. "What have you done to him?" she accused Mike and then turned to glare at me. "What have you both done?"

"I knew this would happen," Mum said in a hysterical voice. "I knew you'd come here and ruin everything. You can't just be bloody normal and let everyone else live their lives? You have to sabotage everything. Just like you did my *entire life*. Just like you've always done."

"Janet, shut up!" Gareth snapped, then turned to Mike. "Er… Mike, maybe you could put Darrell down for a moment, son?"

"Gladly," Mike said gruffly, dropping Darrell abruptly so that he collapsed onto the floor, before staggering to his feet, looking wildly between Mike and me.

"That bitch kneed me in the balls and then Arnold bloody Schwarzenegger here punched me," he said in a high whiny voice, which came out very nasal due to the blood still pouring from his nose.

"Oh my God," said Rebecca, glaring at me. "You'd do anything to ruin my day, wouldn't you? I just knew you'd be lying in wait to pay me back. I just knew that—"

"Pay you back for what?" Gareth asked. There was some steel in his voice now that I'd rarely heard before as he crossed his arms over his chest.

"Nothing, Daddy," Rebecca waved him away dismissively, but I saw a flash of panic in her expression.

Darrell was slowly edging backwards again.

"Stay where you are, you piece of shit," Mike snapped at him, halting his progress towards the exit. Then, ignoring everyone else, Mike strode over to stand right in front of me.

"Okay, love?" he asked softly.

I gave a shaky nod as he reached up to my hips slowly then gently pulled my skirt fully down. There was silence in the corridor now, and when I glanced around, I realised that they were all watching us.

"Let me see, okay?"

I nodded and his jaw flexed as he gently tilted my head to the side to look at my cheek, which was feeling tight and achy now.

"What else did he do, love?"

"He pinned me to the wall," I whispered. "But he didn't… er, he didn't have the chance to… do what he did last time."

Mike's whole body tensed, pure and absolute fury flitting through his expression now.

"Last time?" he growled.

"Listen, Vicky's always making up stories," Mum started to tell Mike. "She's not normal. She has mental health problems. Whatever she's told you, she—"

"Shut the fuck up," Mike snapped.

I flinched with the force of his words and the anger behind them.

"I just saw this evil fucker assault your daughter. Her skirt was pushed up round her hips. She was fucking *terrified*." Mike was turned towards all of them now, yet again, shielding me.

I reached up and laid my hand on his arm, feeling the bunched muscles there trembling with suppressed rage.

"Mike, honestly, just leave it. I tried to tell Mum and Rebecca the last time it happened. It's not really worth—"

"You told them?" He turned to look at me.

"Well, yes, but—"

"She told you?" he shouted at Mum.

Mum, very, *very* unwisely, rolled her eyes. "Vicky was just trying to get attention and I—"

"What the fuck did you do, boy?" I blinked in shock as I saw Gareth grab Darrell and shove him up against the wall, his face a mask of rage.

"Daddy! What are you doing?" Rebecca shrieked.

"Stay out of this, Becky," said Gareth. "I'll deal with you in a minute. My fucking son-in-law is going to tell me what the fuck he's been doing."

"Gareth, language!" Mum breathed in a scandalised whisper.

"Janet," Gareth said in a low, dangerous voice. "Why am I paying for a wedding so that a rapist can marry my daughter?"

"I didn't rape her," spluttered Darrell. "For fuck's sake. I barely touched her this time, and last time, I..." his bloody face drained of all colour as he realised what he'd revealed. "Well, I didn't actually rape her," he said in a weak voice.

"You're not even paying for most of the wedding, Gareth," Mike put in. "I know for a fact that Vicky is paying for the wedding dress, the alcohol, the band, and most of the venue. I've *seen* her pay the balance for that stuff."

"Jesus Christ," Gareth clipped, still pinning his son-in-law to the wall, but now wearing a broken expression. "I'll pay you back, cariad," he said to me, then turned to his daughter, his voice dropping to ice cold. "I told you we couldn't afford a big wedding. I knew you were lying to me about the costs."

A mutinous expression crossed Rebecca's face. "Why should I have to have a shitty reception in a village hall? It's not fair that she's got all this money, and we have to scrape around for the bare necessities. We had to put up with her all those years when she was being a bloody weirdo. Why shouldn't she pay us back now? Her dad will have left her a ton of cash and—"

"I did not receive a large inheritance from my father," I said. "And after my father died, I continued the payments he used to make to Mum out of my *own* money."

Rebecca snorted. "As if the bloody duke wouldn't have set up a trust fund for you."

"I only had a small trust fund, which I used for university."

"How have you got all this money then?"

"She earned it, you spoiled brat," Mike snapped, then turned back to me. "That's why earning money is so important to you, isn't it? You needed it to get away from this lot?"

I shrugged. "Money gives security. I needed to feel..." I trailed off, looking down at my feet.

"You needed to feel safe," Mike filled in for me. "Did you hear that?" he said to my family. "She needed money to feel safe, from *you*."

Mum snorted. "You've no idea how difficult she was when she—"

"Janet," Gareth snapped, cutting her off. "She didn't bloody well speak. Even when you and our daughter put her down again and again, she didn't say a word."

"Because she's a freak," spat out Rebecca, her face bright red and furious.

"What did you do to her, young lady?" Gareth said, turning on his daughter. "What did you think she was going to pay you back for?"

Rebecca's hands bunched into fists at her sides as her face screwed up into an ugly scowl. "This is *my* fucking day!" She stamped her foot. "She's ruining my day, and you're letting her!"

"Right," Mike said, pulling me close to him and tucking me under his arm. "I've had enough of this shit. Good luck, Gareth—you're going to need it. Vicky and I are going to make the long overdue, it seems, trip to the police station to report this assault and the previous one."

"The police aren't going to be interested in—" started Darrell in a panicked voice, but Mike cut him off.

"Oh, they'll be interested. Aside from the physical evidence—"

"What physical evidence?" Mum asked in a high voice.

"The swelling on her face and bruises that are already coming up on her arms."

"That doesn't mean anything," Mum snapped. "She's always bruised very easily."

Mike froze, and it was like all the air was sucked out of the corridor.

"Please, tell me that what you just said doesn't mean what I think it does?" His tone was so threatening that Mum took a step back towards Gareth. "My God," Mike breathed in disbelief. "You evil bitch. You put your hands on a child?"

"I-I-I you can't speak to me this way. Gareth, tell him he can't—"

"Shut up, Janet," Gareth said in what now sounded like a completely defeated tone. "Just please *shut up*." He turned to Mike. "Can you take her out of here, please son?"

Mike nodded and started to move past them, with me still held close to his side.

As we passed Gareth, he reached out to catch Mike's arm. "You'll look after her?"

Mike nodded again, and then Gareth turned to me. "I'm sorry, cariad," his voice was hoarse now. "I should have said that a long time ago, but I *am* sorry."

CHAPTER 25

Why is your mum here?

Mike

There was a low buzzing in my ears from residual fury as I gripped the steering wheel so hard my knuckles turned white.

Vicky kept darting me small glances as we drove, no doubt worrying about me.

Yes, worrying about *me.*

As we'd driven away from the shitshow of a wedding where my girlfriend was goddamn assaulted, she'd asked me if *I* was okay.

She'd been assaulted, and yet she was asking me how *I* was.

I'd given her the honest truth, that no, I was not okay, and it was taking all of my restraint not to turn the car around and go back to finish off that piece of shit before fucking up the rest of her family.

I'd never had such a strong urge to hurt a woman as I had with Vicky's mother and sister.

She's always bruised very easily.

What the fuck was *wrong* with that woman?

"Oh," Vicky had replied in a small voice. "I'm sorry."

"You're sorry?" I said through gritted teeth. "Why the fuck are *you* sorry?"

"I shouldn't have taken you to the wedding. They're *my* family. I should have just dealt with it by myself."

"Rest assured, Vicky," I said with absolute conviction. "You are never, under any circumstance, dealing with any of your family alone, ever again. Understand me?"

"Oh… okay."

I'd then had to sit through Vicky's interview at the police station where she recounted what rapey Darrell had done to her two years ago, and what he did today. I'd told the detectives that she was Autistic, and they were actually really good with her, but it had been a long bloody process.

It was now ten at night, and Vicky looked completely exhausted.

"Where are we going?" she asked, and I realised I'd been too consumed with fury and worry that I hadn't even bothered to tell her what was happening.

Forcing myself to ease my grip on the steering wheel and start behaving like a rational, caring human, I glanced over at Vicky, and my chest felt tight. I cleared my throat and tried to soften my voice when I spoke.

"We're going to the cabin."

"Oh."

I'd expected some sort of objection, but then again, Vicky seemed a little out of it—she probably didn't have it in her to object.

Half an hour later when we arrived at the cabin, I noticed Vicky's tense body relax as we drove up the driveway, and I breathed a sigh of relief that maybe I'd done the right thing. But when we pulled up outside, she tensed again as she looked at the front door.

"Why is your mum here?" she whispered, staring at Mum, who was now bustling towards the car with a smile on her face.

I rubbed my forehead.

"Vicky, I'm sorry, but I had to call Mum."

I'd rung her whilst Vicky had been in with the detective for the last bit of paperwork. To be honest, I was just so worried about Vicky, and I knew Mum would know what to do.

"I knew you wouldn't have eaten, and Mum, she just... she makes everything better. I know she'll help me make you feel better."

"Hello, lovie," Mum said as she pulled the passenger door open.

Vicky looked at her warily then jumped when I unclipped her seatbelt.

"You coming out of there, sweetheart?" Mum asked as I opened my door and jumped down, coming round to their side to see Vicky slowly lower herself out of the Land Rover.

"Mikey told me what happened," Mum said softly. "I'm so sorry you were hurt."

Vicky looked between me and Mum before wrapping her arms around herself. "It wasn't your fault, Mrs. Mayweather," she whispered.

"I know that, sweetheart," Mum said, her voice even softer now. "Doesn't mean I'm not sorry. I'm even sorrier I wasn't there with my rolling pin to crack some heads open."

Vicky's eyebrows went up, and her lips twitched. She might think Mum was joking, but I knew for a fact that Hetty Mayweather could be hell on wheels when she was angry.

"Now, I know what makes my kids feel better when scary stuff happens."

Kids? I was a thirty-four-year-old man. "Hugs," Mum explained. "Now it's okay to say no. But, can I hug you?"

Vicky hesitated then nodded slowly.

Mum pulled her in and enveloped her in a classic Hetty Mayweather hug—warm and all-encompassing.

Vicky's arms were limp by her sides for a few seconds, but then she hugged Mum back, letting out a very small sob into Mum's jumper.

"Okay, lovie," Mum said softly as she swayed Vicky gently from side to side. "You've been a brave, brave girl for a long time, but you're safe now. Nobody's going to hurt you here. My son won't let anything happen to you."

Mum's voice was shaking slightly, and when she looked up at me over Vicky's shoulder, I could see her eyes were glassy with tears as well.

It was a good few minutes until Vicky pulled away. When she did, Mum swept the mascara from under her eyes and wiped away the rest of her tears.

"There we are," Mum said gently. "Pretty as a picture. Now, in we go, and we'll have some grilled cheese toasties and tomato soup."

As Mum bustled us into the cabin, I talked low in her ear, "You remember that Vicky likes—"

"I know what she likes, love," Mum said. "Always easy to please as a child weren't you, Vicky? Never seen anyone so happy with a cheese sandwich. Now, off you go and have a shower whilst I get this ready. I've put Mike's softest shirt out for you on the bed and those pyjamas I got you last year for Christmas, Mike. The ones that were too small. No labels or anything, okay?"

"Er... okay," Vicky said slowly, eyeing my Mum as if she was an alien from another planet.

An hour later, I was completely reassured that ringing my mother had been the best plan I could have had.

Vicky was tucked into my side on the sofa with a blanket over her, having eaten a cheese sandwich and even a small amount of soup, her hair back in a plait which she'd let Mum do for her.

Before Mum left, she'd gathered Vicky in for another hug.

"Men like that, they try to take a piece of you," Mum said softly. "You stay whole though. Don't let him steal *anything* from you." Her voice became fierce then. "It's not his to take. Understand me?"

"Yes," Vicky whispered.

"Good girl," Mum said as she pulled back and hitched her handbag up on her shoulder. Then she turned to me. "You'll sort out those people, won't you, Michael?"

It was a command Mum expected to be followed.

"Oh yes," I said firmly. "I'm going to be sorting them right out."

Vicky and I went back inside and watched the rest of *Britain's Secret Hedgerows*. About five minutes in, she'd fallen asleep on my chest. I carried her upstairs to my bed, and she curled into a tiny protective little ball, so small, you could barely notice she was even under the duvet.

I lay awake for the next few hours, staring at the ceiling and silently seething.

When I finally did fall asleep, I was less than impressed when, what felt like only moments later, even though it was in fact the next morning, there was a series of loud, incessant bangs on my door.

Vicky was still out of it in her small ball on the bed, and I didn't want to wake her, so I moved my big carcass off the mattress with as little disturbance to her as possible and hurried downstairs to tell whoever it was to shut the fuck up.

What greeted me when I pulled open the door was a very pissed-off Ollie, flanked by a worried-looking Lottie and a visibly upset Margot.

"Where is she?" Ollie growled, attempting to push past me to get into the cabin.

I stopped him with a hand to his chest, pushing him out onto the porch.

"She's sleeping, arsehole," I clipped. "What the fuck are you doing here?"

"That awful woman rang me," Margot said, her voice shaking slightly. "She was ranting and raving about the police and something to do with Vicky, and how I had to stop her pressing charges. Honestly, she sounded certifiable. Did something happen?"

I crossed my arms over my chest and let out a long breath. "Listen, why don't you lot come back later. I'll talk to Vics, and if she's up to it, then—"

"That's my sister in there, mate," Ollie said in his bloody Duke of Fuckingham voice, the aristocratic one he liked to wheel out to make lesser mortals do his bidding. "If she's been hurt, then I want to see her right fucking now."

"Oh yeah?" I felt my temper rising. "If she's your sister, then where the hell have you been for the last two decades?"

Ollie blinked. "What are you talking about? I've protected Vicky her whole—"

"Bullshit."

"What?"

"Bull. *Shit.* If you've always protected her, then why did her mother tell me yesterday that, and I quote, 'She's always bruised easily'?"

I heard Margot suck in a shocked breath, but they had to hear the truth they've clearly always ignored.

"Why was she never assessed for Autism as a child? And why *the fuck* didn't any of you know about the wedding yesterday? She was going to go on her own, for fuck's sake. God knows what would have happened to her if I hadn't pulled that fucker off her."

"What?" barked Ollie, his face losing colour. "Who did you pull off her?"

"The goddamn groom, that's who. And apparently, it wasn't the first time this bastard had assaulted her. Where were you when he did it to her two years ago?"

"Christ," breathed Ollie. "Two years ago… that was when she went totally into herself for weeks, remember, Mum? She kept working, but beyond that, she was a complete ghost. She never told us what the matter was."

"You must have had some idea about how her mum and sister treat her?" I said in disbelief.

"That woman! She..." Margot shrugged helplessly. "She was so awful. I always thought it was best to just avoid her. And when Hugh told me I had to look after his love child in the summer holidays, I wasn't best pleased. It took me a while to..." Margot swallowed. "It took me longer than it should have to get to know Vicky."

I sighed. "She thinks she's a burden to all of you. She overheard a lot of your arguments with her dad when he brought her to Buckingham Manor. I'm not saying you weren't right to be angry, but—"

"But she was just a child," Margot finished for me, openly crying now. "Don't you think I know that? I realised after a couple of weeks how badly I buggered it up when she first came to the Manor, how much she needed me. But by that stage, she was so withdrawn. She didn't speak. At all. And when I tried to get her assessed, that woman hit the roof."

"If you know how bad her family is, why do you let her see them?"

"I didn't know," Ollie defended.

"But, did you ever ask her, Ollie?" Lottie asked quietly. "I didn't know about Vicky's other family, and that they were... problematic. But I've known something was wrong."

"We're getting off-topic here," Ollie said through gritted teeth. "I want to know what the fuck is going to be done about this bloke who assaulted my sister."

"We're not off-topic, you prick!" I shouted because quite frankly, I'd had enough. "She's been emotionally and physically abused by her family since she was a child, and you lot have done your very best to bloody well ignore it. This is just the latest in a long line of shit that's happened to her, which you haven't bothered yourself with. I punched that bloke in the face, and the police have hopefully arrested him by now, if that bitch's phone call to Margot is anything to go by. There's not much more we can do about him. And you're not all barging in here and upsetting Vicky. She's mine today. I want to watch shit about hedgehogs and de-cluttering programmes with her on telly, make her poached eggs on toast *exactly* the way she likes them, and then show her how to weld. So you can all bugger off."

"You'll show me how to weld?" Vicky's voice sounded from behind me, and I closed my eyes slowly as I moved back from the door. She was standing a few paces back, totally swamped in my flannel shirt with the pyjama bottoms dragging along the ground.

"Hey, Vics," Ollie said softly.

She gave him a small wave but made no move to go to him.

"Darling, I—" Margot said, but then her face crumpled, and she started openly crying.

Vicky moved then, squeezing past me at the door to go to Margot's side. After a moment's hesitation, she patted Margot on the arm awkwardly. "Er… Margot," she said quietly. "Are you quite alright?"

Margot sobbed even louder. "You're asking me if *I'm* alright?"

"Yeah," I grunted. "She tends to do that. Welcome to my world."

Lottie moved forward to Vicky, paused for a moment for Vicky to give her a small nod, then pulled her in for a tight hug. "I'm so sorry," Lottie said into Vicky's hair, her voice sounding a little choked as well.

"How do you know—?" Vicky started to ask after receiving more hugs from Ollie and Margot.

"Your mum, love," I told her, and she nodded.

"I expect Mum's very angry. Actually, I'm surprised she hasn't rung me or—"

"I blocked her, Vicky," I told her.

Vicky blinked at me. "You… blocked her?"

"Yes, love."

"I-I-I don't understand. She's my mother. I can't just—"

"You're never to speak to that woman, ever again," Margot snapped.

Vicky turned back to her with a confused expression on her face.

"But, Margot, you told me I shouldn't turn my back on my family. That they were the only family I had, and I should accept that."

"What?" Margot said in a horrified whisper.

Vicky shrugged. "When I was nine, and I didn't want to go back to Mum, I hid in the cellar."

"Oh darling." Margot's voice was pained now, seeming to anticipate what Vicky was going to say.

"When the staff found me, you were really angry."

"I was *worried* about you and—"

"You told me I had to go back to my real family. That I belonged with them."

Margot's eyes were wide. "Oh my God, Vicky," she breathed. "I..." She broke off and more tears filled her eyes.

I hadn't even been aware that Lady Margot Harding was capable of this level of emotion.

"Darling, I was very worried, so I got angry, and I didn't handle it very well. I didn't mean any of that."

"I'm not very good at telling the difference," Vicky said simply. "So I took you at your word."

"And at my word too," another voice came from behind Margot, Ollie, and Lottie. Margot moved to the side to reveal Claire standing with Hayley and Florrie. "Sorry, the girls wanted to come and see Vicky," Claire explained in a tight voice. "They were worried. They could tell something was up."

Both girls sprinted up the steps of the deck when they spotted Vicky, screeching to a stop in front of her to pause for her nod before they hugged her.

Vicky had already crouched down anticipating this move.

Florrie told her about a family of voles at Buckingham Manor whilst Claire stood frozen, watching Vicky with a pale face.

"Girls," Margot said gently. "Why don't you go and look at Mike's workshop for a minute?"

"Can I use your axe?" Florrie asked me.

This girl never missed an opportunity to bargain.

"No."

"Can I use your blow torch?"

"Right," Lottie cut in with an eye roll. "Come on, you two. Clearly, unsupervised workshop access is a bad idea. Let's go."

"I'm sorry, Vicky," Claire said once the kids were out of earshot.

"Sorry for what?" Vicky asked with genuine confusion.

"Sorry for being a bitch to you when you were just a kid. Sorry for carrying all this resentment around. Sorry for not being a better sister."

"Half-sister," Vicky corrected, as if it was a reflex.

Claire closed her eyes as if in actual pain. "I started that too, didn't I?"

"Started what?"

"The half-sister, half-brother thing. I used to correct you. Christ, I'm so sorry, Vicky. I was pissed off that Dad had an affair; then I was sad that he died and I never made up with him, and then I was jealous of the attention Ollie paid to you. *Then* I was angry that you avoided my shitty husband."

Vicky shrugged. "Claire, you don't like me," she said simply. "That's okay. You don't have to apologise for not liking someone. I'm not all that likeable."

"I *do* like you."

Silence met that statement.

Vicky rolled her lips between her teeth as if to stop herself saying anything.

Margot was still crying.

Vicky did the awkward arm pat thing again.

"Listen, I'm not really sure what you're all apologising for," Vicky said. "It's very kind that you are concerned, but it's not your fault that I was assaulted. And, as a child, I was very grateful that I was allowed to spend some time here every summer. You were always much, much nicer to me than my family was."

"Nicer than your emotionally and physically abusive mother and sister?" Ollie said sharply. "I'm not sure that's much of an endorsement."

"I'm still grateful that you tolerate me being involved in your family now."

"Tolerate you?" Ollie sounded horrified. "Vicky, we don't just tolerate you."

There was a pause before Vicky spoke again. "Okay."

It wasn't agreement, and it was said in that resigned, slightly defeated tone Vicky used when she was retreating from a confrontation that she didn't understand. She stepped back toward me, and I pulled her into my side. When she sagged slightly in my hold, indicating just how exhausted she was, I decided I'd had enough.

"Right, well, you can all fuck off."

"Mikey!" Florrie shouted from my workshop. "There are minors present!"

"She's got bat ears when it comes to swearing," Ollie muttered.

Florrie and Hayley ran around the house to face us all then.

"Can you teach us to weld too today, Mikey?" Hayley said in a small voice, and despite the tension in the air, all eyes went to her.

Hayley was still finding her feet with speech after being silent for so long, and she hardly ever spoke with this large an audience.

"Vicky's been through a lot, love," I started to say gently. "I think–"

But Vicky gave me a squeeze and cut me off.

"Of course he can," she said. "He promised to teach me as well."

I looked down at her face, and her hopeful eyes looked back up at me. And there you go. This woman who'd been assaulted yesterday, who'd just had an emotionally draining family confrontation, who by all rights should still be in bed—she wanted to learn to weld.

How I had ever thought her a rich, snobby ice princess was totally beyond me.

"Fine," I said. "I'll teach the three of you."

That prompted squeals from both the girls and an excited smile from Vicky.

"But the rest of you can bugger off."

CHAPTER 26

Are you trying to kill me?

Vicky

I stared at my phone.

To be honest, I couldn't quite believe it. In the immediate aftermath of what Darrell had done to me, one of my first thoughts was how my mother and sister would make me pay. I imagined the barrages of texts and phone calls.

When it happened two years ago, they'd made threat after threat—so many, that eventually, I'd flinched every time my phone even vibrated. But now… nothing.

Because Mike had simply tapped a few keys and blocked them. And then when my aunt rang me a few days ago and went off on a rant about how I'd betrayed the family and upset my sister, how she knew I was *mentally deficient,* but that that was no excuse, Mike had simply plucked the phone out of my hands, hung up the call, and then blocked her too.

But I was on edge. I wasn't ready to believe that it could be as simple as that. Or that I was allowed to disconnect from my family.

It had been drummed into me for so many years how lucky I was to have a family that tolerated me at all. So blocking them was anxiety-inducing, but I knew that actual contact with them would be worse.

And anyway, I was happy at the cabin.

Mike had shown me and the girls how to weld. This involved Mike swearing excessively and commiserating about how he wished he had a girlfriend and nieces who wanted to go shopping on a Sunday instead of burning his workshop down—an unfair assessment in my opinion, as we were all very careful with the blow torch, and only set something on fire that *one time*.

Then when the girls went home, he phoned Felix.

Apparently, I wasn't working for the next week, and I was staying with Mike at the cabin.

The thought of not working had never occurred to me. I hardly ever took time off. I told Mike in a very matter-of-fact way that I'd carried on working after the last assault despite my silent panic attacks.

This did not seem to reassure Mike; in fact, judging by the slashes of colour that appeared high on his cheekbones and the angry scowl he directed my way, it may have inflamed the situation.

"Well, you're not bloody well working next week," he'd told me, followed by a stream of curse words of different varieties.

Seeing as it seemed very important to Mike, and I did feel a lot safer at the cabin, I agreed.

And, despite the trauma of the weekend, this last week was the best week I had ever had in my whole life. Better than the week I made my first million. Better than the first week I moved into my own house where I could keep my space safe and free from clutter.

Better than anything.

We'd had an argument the second night, though. Mike had promised to teach me fellatio after six more dates—and I'd been counting.

I told him that I counted the welding as a date, even though it involved two eight-year-old girls, and that we should proceed.

He looked horrified and told me I was traumatized, and that I didn't need to force myself to do anything with him. That he was happy to carry on cuddling on the sofa and watch decluttering programmes.

Well, I'd been looking forward to learning fellatio, and Mike had been quite high-handed enough.

I hadn't actually objected because blocking my family and staying at the cabin were things I really *wanted* to do. But him being arrogant and bossy about *this* caused me to have a rare flash of anger. I actually raised my voice, something I barely ever did, and I called him a *liar* and a *purveyor of fake promises*—something that made his lips twitch in a very ill-advised smile, which spiked my anger even higher.

Eventually, he threw his arms up in defeat, crying, "Okay, okay. You can give me a blow job. Christ. So much for being a goddamn nice guy."

The anger drained out of me immediately, and I smiled at getting my way, then slid to my knees in front of him where he sat on the sofa.

"Right," I said. "I've read a great deal of background information, but we might have to go over some of the logistics before we start. I would have watched pornography in preparation, but I'm afraid seeing other people naked makes me feel physically ill."

"Logistics?" Mike's voice was pitched higher than normal, and his eyes were wide. "W-what sort of logistics?"

"Well, I may have a problem with the ejaculate element."

"What?" he said faintly, as I started to grapple with the buttons on his jeans.

"I'm not too good with mess, and if my dislike of sauces is anything to go by, I probably won't like semen in my mouth."

Mike rubbed his eyes then stalled my hands on his fly with his own. "You don't have to swallow, Vicky," he said in a hoarse voice.

I smiled. "Oh good. Because that is the only aspect I don't think I could manage. I'm happy about the penis in my mouth element, even if yours is a bit on the large side. I'm sure I can work around it. I'm very task-orientated and a perfectionist, so I want to get this right."

"Right, okay," he said, his voice now hoarse, "Vicky, whatever you do will be perfect, I promise."

I think I did a passable job.

I mean, I kept having to stop and ask questions… a lot of questions, but he didn't seem too annoyed at having to teach me.

In fact, when I was done, he hauled me up onto his body and cuddled me to him, muttering on and on about how perfect I was, how beautiful. All sorts.

So it can't have been *that* bad.

Anyway, I'd do better next time. Although, when I told him that he said in that high-pitched voice, "Holy shit, are you trying to kill me?"

The rest of the week had just gotten better and better.

In the daytime, I still did some remote meetings from the cabin after I had my stuff couriered up from London, including my laptop.

Lottie had stayed at Buckingham Manor with Hayley as it was half term, so she came over and sat with me, giving me the signals as if we were in the conference room together. Her ability to read people wasn't quite so sharp when she worked remotely like this, but she still managed to identify lies in a couple of the negotiations.

Mike let me watch him sand, varnish, weld and carve in his workshop.

I'd always been told that my staring was a terrible habit. It disconcerted a lot of people, but Mike didn't seem to mind me staring at him. Every so often, he'd look up and smile at me, or ask me something, or he'd drop his tools and come over to kiss me.

A couple of times he did more than kiss me. Once he even demonstrated his superior upper body strength by lifting me up against the wall and holding me there whilst he took me, whispering all sorts of dirty praise into my ear about being *his good girl*.

I wasn't sure what I was doing that was so good, seeing as I wasn't the one putting any of the effort in, but I accepted the praise anyway. Another time he bent me over the smooth wood of his workbench. Afterwards, I informed him that I actually ranked that position at a firm number two, just after the holding me up against the wall thing, and that I liked how he held me down and when he fisted my hair.

He'd muttered, "I'm not going to survive you," in a choked voice.

In fact, the more he held me down, the more secure I felt. Just like the tight hugs, it made me feel safe.

So, from my point of view, the sex was great. I wasn't sure Mike thought the same. He certainly said he did, but I was extremely inexperienced, whereas I knew Mike had had *loads* of sex.

I'd heard girls talking about him at The Badger's Sett in the past, and I'd seen his girlfriends before, both in London and Little Buckingham. They didn't look like the types to have to pause mid-fellatio to ask whether a hand should be employed over the area that the mouth doesn't cover, then wondering aloud if you have the required coordination for that to be possible, and then finding out that no, you really do not.

I mean, Mike hadn't seemed to mind at the time, but I knew people didn't always say what they meant, not like I did.

He'd taken me to his mum's on Monday night, which I'd been worried about.

Hetty had always been nice to me, and she was very kind the day of the wedding, but I didn't really know her very well. Then when I got there, I was shocked to see Lucy and Felix sitting in Hetty's kitchen waiting for us, as if Felix being in Little Buckingham mid-week wasn't a never event.

"But who's running the company?" I asked a valid question, seeing as we were both here.

"Don't worry, Vics," Felix told me, giving me a firm side hug. "I've been there today. We came down for the evening."

"Why?"

Felix had frowned at me then as if I'd grown another head.

"What do you mean 'why'? Vicky, we wanted to see you. We were worried about you."

"Oh."

As far as I was concerned, Felix's interest in me did not go further than our business partnership. I made Felix a lot of money, end of story.

"Are you okay, hun?" asked Lucy, giving me her own tight hug after a brief pause and a nod from me.

"I'm fine," I said, bewildered by all the attention.

"You wanna see some of my new maps?" Lucy asked, and I smiled.

"Yes, please."

Lucy was a successful author of epic fantasy. She knew I loved how she structured her worlds, and the intricacies of the maps her illustrator created for her.

And then the dogs ran in and bombarded me.

Hetty had two massive golden retrievers. I'd only ever seen them from a distance before, and I always thought they were beautiful. The younger one, Samwise, was so excited to see me, that he jumped up on my chest and licked my face.

Mike pulled him off, shouting at him to get down, but I just dropped into a crouch so that both dogs could get at me, throwing my arms around their furry necks in turn.

Samwise got over-excited again and toppled me over, then decided to sit with his front paws on my chest, his weight pinning me down whilst the older dog, Frodo, licked my face.

"Oh my God!" shouted Lucy. "Bloody hell, Mum. You need to train those dogs. This is getting ridiculous."

Mike pushed the dogs back so I could get to my feet.

When I looked up, Lucy and Felix were trying to push a fat pony out of the kitchen.

The dogs were still rubbing up against my legs, and I sank my hands into their thick fur.

"Sorry, love," Hetty said, not really looking that sorry at all. "My fur babies can be a little much. It just means they like you."

"Mum," Mike snapped. "Vicky doesn't want to be—"

"I don't mind," I said, smiling down at Hetty's "fur babies". There used to be a black Labrador at Buckingham Manor. I loved him more than anything.

I found touch more difficult as a child, but not with animals.

When we were halfway through supper, the fat pony pushed his way in through the double doors and ate my salad with its velvety nose.

It was one of the best meals I'd ever been to. I hadn't laughed that much in years.

The next day, we ate at The Badger's Sett again, but instead of heading straight home, Mike walked us over to Pete and Emily's house, so we could watch the hedgehogs.

Margot came over twice. She didn't cry the second time, which I thought was progress.

For some reason though, Mike didn't seem totally comfortable around Margot. In fact, he seemed to watch her like she was some sort of unexploded bomb when she was near me.

And her visits seemed to provoke some sort of anxiety from him. Like he was worried about something. As she was leaving the second time, I saw them through the window, having what looked like a heated conversation by her car.

I couldn't hear what was being said, but Mike looked agitated and was frowning down at her whilst he spoke. I'd asked him about it afterwards, but he just shrugged it off. Then, thinking he was trying to be protective again, I reassured him that Margot was always kind to me, and that he had no cause to worry about her around me.

"I know that, love," he'd said softly, still with that worry in his eyes. "She loves you something fierce. Believe me, I know."

And Mike's reaction to my offer to buy him a new van after it broke down for the second time was also strange. He was vehemently against it, to the point of being ridiculous.

I honestly could not understand his attitude. It was totally nonsensical that he didn't have a working vehicle.

"I invest in businesses all the time," I told him when he'd tried to kiss me into silence, which to be fair, had been working well for him thus far.

He'd stiffened and pulled away when I mentioned investing.

"I don't need your money, Vics," he told me. "I'm not with you because of that. Understand me? I want you for you."

I frowned at him. "Of course I know that, Mike. I would never have such a low opinion of you. You've got more integrity than any other human I know."

Something had flashed across his expression when I said that. I wasn't very good at reading emotions. If I had to guess, I would have said it looked a lot like fear, but that couldn't be right.

What did Mike have to be afraid of?

But before I had a chance to ask him, he'd grabbed me to him in a bear hug so tight I had trouble breathing.

"I mean it Vicky," he said into my hair, his voice gruff. "I only want you. Right?"

My reply in the affirmative was muffled by his shirt, but it did seem to settle him down enough that his arms loosened, and I could take in some much-needed oxygen.

Mike was *really* cagey when it came to anything to do with the business finances. I mean, finance was *my jam,* as Lottie would say. If anyone could help him balance the books it was me. It was also clear to me that Mike needed to expand. He couldn't cope with all the orders coming in. He needed to expand his workforce, and he needed a delivery driver. But he was stubborn.

I was stubborn too, so I wasn't giving up.

But meanwhile, I was something I hadn't been in a long time, if ever.

I was happy.

So happy, I let my guard down.

I forgot who I was, who Mike was, and that someone like him was unlikely to be with someone like me without a reason.

CHAPTER 27

Vicky has no idea

Vicky

"Vicky?" Claire's soft voice sounded from the end of the yard, and I turned to face her as she walked towards me. "Er… hey, do you need a hand? Florrie's off at Hetty's with Legolas, so I'm free to help muck out."

I'd come here to stroke the horses' velvety noses and see if Tony, the yard manager, would let me take some work off his hands. Tony had been the yard manager at Buckingham Manor for decades. He was a quiet, stoic man, more at peace with animals than humans.

As a child, I'd loved that, finding someone almost as silent as me, someone who didn't ask relentless questions.

Tony was a man of action rather than words. When I'd arrived today, he handed me a wheelbarrow and a fork and nodded towards one of the stables.

I'd done one stall and was moving onto Margot's horse, Bertie.

"You want to help muck out?" I asked with no small amount of curiosity.

Claire loved horses, but whilst I was more into the caretaking aspects, she tended to just ride them, and even then, only when they were groomed and tacked up and ready for her.

I didn't ride horses. The two week stints I spent at Buckingham Manor over those summers were too brief to learn properly, and then with the few lessons that were offered to me, I'd always been too scared about the lack of control. I preferred to keep my feet on the ground. The last thing a horse needed was me having a meltdown on its back.

She shrugged. "Don't look so shocked. I can muck out a stall. Plus, it's good exercise."

"Oh, okay," I agreed, handing her a spare fork.

We worked alongside one another for a few minutes before she spoke again.

"I know you have Lottie to help you read people and situations," she said, and I nodded. "But I think you're a better judge of character than you realise. You were right about Blake."

I shrugged again. "I am observant about physical changes and patterns of behaviour. That was how I knew Blake had an alcohol problem. He was also very mean to me. People like Blake are particularly mean to people like me—people they consider vulnerable."

"Vicky, why didn't you ever tell me how mean he was?" Claire asked.

"You were not receptive to my opinions on your husband."

"Ex-husband," she said firmly.

"Ex-husband," I repeated. "Any attempts to impart my misgivings regarding Blake to you were firmly rebuffed."

There was silence for a moment, during which Claire stood very still with her rake in her hand, staring out of the stall door. "Bloody hell, you're right," she muttered. "I'm a shit sister. Aren't I?"

I frowned. "Claire, I'm only your half-sis–"

"Don't say it!" Claire snapped, and I flinched. "Sorry, Vicky." Her voice was softer now. "I didn't mean to startle you, but please don't say anymore bollocks about only being my half-anything. I was a total dick when I said all that as a shitty teen. I'm your sister. End of."

"Er… okay," I replied, not quite sure what to make of this new, full-sister-wanting Claire.

Now, mucking out a stable is hard work. After the second trip to the manure pile, I was boiling. So, without thinking, I took my jumper off, leaving my arms exposed.

"Oh my God, Vicky!" Claire said in a shocked voice. I knew what she was seeing. It was the same thing that made Mike's jaw go tight and his eyes flash.

"Your arms. Are those all from that man at the wedding?"

"Um… well, some of them are from Mum," I said with a shrug.

Claire sucked in another shocked breath.

"What?"

"The ones on my upper arm here are from Mum. She grabbed me after the ceremony. The ones on my wrists and lower arms are from Darrell."

"Your *mother* did that?"

"Well, some of it."

"Ollie says that…" Claire trailed off before she swallowed and squared her shoulders. "He says that your mum hurt you when you were a kid."

I shrugged. "I annoyed Mum and Rebecca. I wasn't an easy child. You must remember? I annoyed you too."

Claire's face was very pale now as she stared at me. "I didn't know that…" She took a step towards me but then stopped and rubbed her hands down her face before crossing her arms. "Listen, Vicky, I was a real bitch to you back when we were kids, and I—"

"You weren't a bitch to me," I said, my forehead creasing in confusion.

Claire sighed. "Vicky, I think you have a pretty low bar for what constitutes someone being a bitch. I ignored you. I-I-I've always ignored you."

"Well, ignoring me isn't being a bitch. You never hurt me."

"But I did, didn't I? I hurt your feelings."

I blinked as I turned to Bertie who was tied up next to his stable. He nuzzled my face, and I stroked his velvety nose in return. I thought back to arriving at Buckingham Manor when I was six, how imposing the building and grounds were, how scared I was when Mum shoved me out of the car and drove off, how frustrated everyone seemed that I wouldn't speak, how embarrassed I was that first night when I sat for the family meal, but there was nothing on my plate that I could eat. Ollie hadn't returned from boarding school at that point, so it had just been me, Claire and Margot sitting at the table. I'd never met anyone as posh or as glamorous as either of them.

Even fourteen-year-old Claire looked like something out of a magazine.

I'd snuck out of my room that night, unable to sleep as I was so hungry, but stopped on the stairs when I overheard Claire shouting.

"Why do we have to put up with Dad's attention-seeking little bastard? It's weird, Mum. How am I going to explain her to my friends? Oh yeah sorry guys, this is just my illegitimate little sister. My dad not only likes to shag around, but he also expects us to take care of the consequences for him."

"I'm not any happier than you, believe me," snapped Margot. "But I'm sure she'll stay out of your way. It won't affect your summer too much, darling."

"She had better stay out of my way."

I'd scampered back up the stairs then, too worried about being caught to risk going to the kitchen to find something I might be able to eat. After that, I made a concerted effort to stay out of Claire's way.

By the time Ollie came home, I'd perfected the art of staying out of *everyone's* way. But one morning after he'd been home for a week, when I hadn't eaten any breakfast, yet again, he took me to the kitchen and pulled out nearly everything in the fridge and cupboards, then held up each item, one at a time, until I nodded. And okay, he didn't make my breakfast himself, he was a future duke after all, but he did instruct the cook to do it.

Then, one day, he even sought me out in my room, saying, "Ah, this is where you've been hiding," and took me out with him to the stables. So, not *everyone* ignored me completely, but Claire certainly had as much as possible.

Then as the years passed, and after Dad died, I sensed the open animosity from Claire lessen. The birth of her daughter, Florrie, definitely helped play a part in this, as even when she was a baby, Florrie always gravitated to me at the family functions I was invited to.

I found Florries's unexpected devotion to me incredibly special—she was one of the first humans to give me a spontaneous hug. But despite her daughter's likely misguided affection for me, Claire maintained her distance. Florrie's dad was never really in the picture, and then Claire married Blake, which didn't help my relationship with her at all.

I absolutely *hated* Blake. He was the first one to start the ice princess nickname, and he always smelt of stale alcohol. I have a very overdeveloped sense of smell, and that man made me want to gag if he was within five feet of me. Luckily, he was out of the picture now.

I sighed. "It's fine, I was invading your space here. Invading your home."

Claire scoffed. "You were hardly invading anything, Vicky. I barely saw you. Listen, I had no idea what your family was like at home. But even before all this happened and everything came out, I was feeling terrible. I know I've been a bad sister to you, but—"

"Half-sister," I corrected automatically.

Claire sighed, and I heard her feet on the cobbles as she came nearer.

"*Sister*, Vicky, remember?" she said softly. "You're my sister. My daughter calls you her auntie. You're family."

"Oh." I didn't know what else to say to that.

"I should have done this a long time ago but… can I hug you? I know there's a certain way you like to be hugged. Ollie practised it with me, so that I would get it right."

"You practised hugging me?" I turned to her. My chest felt tight, and my throat was burning now.

When I looked at Claire, there were tears in her eyes.

"Well, yeah. I didn't want to fuck up my first hug with my sister." There were two beats of silence as I stared into her tear-filled eyes. Then on instinct, I launched forward into her arms.

"Oh, okay," she said, surprised, as she hugged me back tightly. "Well, that was easier than I thought." Her voice dropped to a whisper. "Do you forgive me, darling?"

I pulled away and stepped back to frown at her. "There's nothing to forgive, Claire. You weren't cruel or mean to me."

"Yes, I was," she said fiercely. "You just think that if someone's not hurling insults at you or hurting you, that's a win. You've been taught to have low expectations of people. And I'm a big part of the problem, but I'm going to do better. I promise. Look, I came down to fetch you. We're going to play croquet, and that man of yours is looking grumpy that you're not up at the house."

"Mike's here?" I smiled.

It was Saturday, and Mike had deliveries in London, so I said I'd wait for him at the cabin. However, after he left, I was invaded by all the Hardings en masse, plus, Lottie and Hayley. They said they wanted me at Buckingham Manor for a family day, and now that my *jailer* was away, they'd come to steal me back. Ollie was the one to describe Mike as my jailer. Apparently, he wasn't overly impressed that Mike had been *hogging me all week*.

I'd actually had a good day with them all.

Hetty came over too, with Felix's mother, Bianca, and the Buckingham staff had made us all afternoon tea with scones and small sandwiches, including the plain cheese ones that I could eat.

Florrie, Hayley, and I had spent over an hour looking at the hedgerow to watch for the family of voles Florrie had spotted.

But I missed Mike.

I turned to Claire as we walked up the big lawn towards the house.

"Honestly, Claire." I shielded my eyes from the sun so I could look at her. "It really is totally illogical for you to carry guilt. I'm very grateful to have been allowed in Buckingham Manor at all and—"

My words cut off when I realised Claire had stopped in the middle of the lawn, her arms straight down by her sides, and her hands bunched into fists. "Vicky, if you *ever* refer to yourself as being *grateful* to be in the home that you, by blood, are entitled to, I genuinely will lose my shit. You are Dad's daughter, you are my *sister*, and you fucking well deserve to be here as much as anyone else. Understand me?"

"Are you angry?" I asked in a small voice.

Claire closed her eyes as her jaw clenched.

"Yes, Vicky," she said, and I flinched, but then she opened her eyes, and her expression softened. "I'm very fucking angry, but mostly, at myself. Not at you. And I would feel a lot better if you would get angry with me too, okay?"

I chewed my bottom lip. "Um… maybe I could come up with something to be angry with you about. Do you *always* recycle?"

Vicky's frown faded into a smile at my question. "I don't like rinsing out the plastic containers that raw chicken comes in. Sometimes I'll just chuck them in the normal bin dirty."

I narrowed my eyes. "Okay, well, I *am* angry with you now."

"Good," she said, starting off again towards the house.

"Seriously, Claire," I said, jogging after her to catch up. "Maybe you could put the containers in the dishwasher? Then you wouldn't have to be involved with the chicken gunk and—"

Claire laughed as we came into the boot room. "Vics, I promise, I will clean out the chicken gunk from now on, or at least, I'll ask the staff to do it. Happy?"

I blew out a relieved sigh, and she laughed again. Then I heard Mike's voice through the wall. He was talking to Margot.

"Go on then," said Claire, and I pushed out of the boot room to the main hallway. But just as I was about to open the door to the kitchen, I paused when I heard my name.

"Vicky has no idea about your sham investment company," Mike said, his voice clipped and annoyed. "And you won't be telling her, either."

"We've gone over this, Mike. Of course I won't tell her that I'm behind Highcliffe Investments. That's the whole point. She has to think your relationship with her was completely organic, and that you came to your senses on your own. I don't want her to know that a little incentive was required from me. Just remember, don't hurt her. Without my money, your business would be on its knees by now. If you keep making her happy, I'm sure there'll be more capital available from Highcliffe Investments on the horizon. You could do with a new van, for example."

My hand dropped to my side from where it was hovering over the door handle, and I took a step back, bumping into Claire, who was just behind me.

The ringing in my ears was too loud to hear anything more as my vision went blurry.

Mike at the gala dinner when he'd never gone to one before.

Mike looking after me when I had a meltdown.

Mike's look of disgust when he'd delivered my coffee table all those weeks ago. How he told me he wouldn't touch me with a barge pole.

I nodded my head a couple of times, muttering, "Okay, okay. Alright. Yes." Because honestly, it made perfect sense. And it tracked with the rest of my relationships.

Either people were there under familial obligation or pecuniary interest—and Mike Mayweather was no different.

Claire touched my shoulder, and I flinched away. I could see her lips moving fast, but the buzzing in my ears meant I couldn't hear the words she was saying.

I stumbled back a few steps, and the kitchen door flew open. Mike's huge frame filled the doorway, his face pale as he stared at me with horror-stricken eyes. His lips were moving too, and although I could feel the room vibrating with the timbre of his low voice, I couldn't make out his words either.

Then he moved towards me, and I did hear a high-pitched sound of distress.

Mike flinched, and I realised it was coming from me.

I held my hand up in front of me to ward him off, and he stopped his approach, hands up in surrender as if I was a wild animal he didn't want to spook. At the back of my mind, I knew I needed to get control of myself. This situation was embarrassing enough without going into a full-blown meltdown. I didn't think my pride would *ever* recover if a being-paid-to-be-with-me Mike had to carry me out of the Manor.

So I swallowed, squared my shoulders, and stood my ground. I thought back to the techniques Abdul had taught me, taking deep, slow breaths in through my nose and out through my mouth.

"M-Margot," I started to say, then broke off when I realised how shaky my voice sounded. I swallowed and cleared my throat before I spoke again. "I've just realised that I have to be back in London to prepare for the meeting tomorrow."

"Vicky, baby, please." I could hear Mike's voice now. He sounded panicked, desperate almost. But his guilt simply didn't interest me. He'd seen an opportunity, and he'd taken it. God knows, I'd been stalking him for long enough—he probably thought he could kill two birds with one stone: get paid and eventually get me out of his life permanently. "You don't understand. It was never about the money. I didn't even know that Margot—"

"What wasn't about the goddamn money?" Ollie clipped as he strode into the house. I closed my eyes, my humiliation now complete. "What the fuck are you talking about, Mayweather?"

"This is all a misunderstanding," cried Margot, her face

paling, "I invested in Mike's company, and well... I may have encouraged Mike to—"

"Fucking hell, Mum," snapped Ollie, completely furious now. "What on earth have you done now?"

"I'm with Vicky because I want to be with her," said Mike to Ollie before turning back to me. "I'm with you because I want to be, sweetheart. Please. I love you. Please, Vicky, you *have* to believe me."

I wanted to believe him, I really, really did. But too many negative voices lived in my head:

Ice princess.

Freak.

Empty inside.

Why can't you just be normal?

Why do you ruin everything?

Are you her carer or something?

Of course, he'd want to be paid. Carers were paid, lovers were not.

"I would have given you the money," I whispered. "If you'd have asked, I would have given you anything."

"You piece of shit," Ollie roared as he launched himself at Mike, taking them both down to the floor.

"What the fuck is going on?" shouted Felix as he ran in through the door, followed by Lucy, Lottie, Hayley and Florrie.

I edged away as Felix started trying to pull Ollie off Mike, who didn't seem to be punching back. Years of practice, of trying to be invisible in this house finally paid off as I darted into the space behind the pantry and through a corridor that I knew led outside to the driveway.

Now what? My car and driver were in London.

Then a spray of gravel showered my feet, and I took a startled step back. I blinked at Ollie's Aston Martin in front of me. The window went down, and Claire looked up at me from the driver's seat, sunglasses and a determined expression on her face.

"Let's get *the fuck* out of here."

CHAPTER 28

All I've ever wanted

Mike

"Look, mate," said Felix as he strode down the corridor towards me. "You need to fuck off now, understand me?"

I tried to look beyond him at the conference room where I'd glimpsed Vicky sitting between a concerned-looking Lottie and Tabitha. When I'd caught Lottie's eye, she'd frowned at me and gave a sharp head shake. Then, when Felix had seen me, he'd taken action.

"I need to see her," I said. "You don't understand. I can't—"

"This is her place of business, you dickhead. She's busy."

"At least tell me if she's okay. I'm driving myself crazy here. She had that other meeting with the police, but they wouldn't let me in the station when I went. She won't return my calls. I don't think she even reads my messages."

Felix's hand went to the back of his neck, and he sighed. He looked just as much at a loss as I felt. "I'm sorry, Mike. I can't tell you how she is because I don't actually know."

I frowned. "What do you mean? You work with her every day."

"I've come to realise that Vicky is pretty fucking adept at hiding in plain sight. Over the last three years, there've been times when she's retreated into her shell. I just accepted it as part of her quirks. But the more I think about it, the more I think that it was the result of some sort of trigger each time: the assault two years ago, that thing with you and the coffee table, her family the other times probably. Now is no different. She does her job, and if anything, she's *more* dedicated to it. But she doesn't engage with anyone, not really. That's what she's like now. Not engaging. The lights are on but nobody's home. So, no, I don't know whether she's okay. She won't talk to me or Lucy, or even Lottie. She comes to work, speaks when she absolutely has to, goes home and won't see anyone outside work hours."

"Shit, shit, shit," I chanted as I scrubbed my hands down my face.

"Mike?" I lowered my hands at the sound of Vicky's clear voice and looked up to see her coming towards me from the conference room. She stopped next to Felix then looked between us with a blank expression. "Felix, they need you back in the meeting," she said in that monotone I hated so much. "I'll deal with Mike."

Felix hesitated. "Vics, I can—"

"This is unprofessional," she said, still in that monotone.

This was killing me.

She'd lost weight again; there were dark circles under her eyes that I could see despite the make-up. And that light that I'd seen there more and more over the weeks we were together was totally out now. Her eyes were dull and lifeless. It was as if someone had simply switched her off, and now she was acting on some sort of autopilot.

"Go back. They need you for the final stage."

"Okay, Vics," said Felix softly. "If you're sure?"

Vicky gave a sharp nod, and Felix blew out a breath, giving me a strong bit of side-eye, communicating an unspoken *watch yourself* warning before striding away from us.

"Vicky, I—"

"I realise that you likely feel a great deal of guilt for what transpired between us," Vicky said in that *fucking* monotone.

My hands itched to grab her into a tight hug, to kiss the light back into her eyes, but I forced them to stay at my sides by bunching them into tight fists.

"But I want to reassure you that your guilt is misplaced. Margot's investment in your company was very sound. If anything, you need *more* money to expand. You were right not to jeopardise that. I would have preferred that you explained the nature of our relationship prior to embarking on it, but the fact remains that even if I had known you were being paid, I would still have entered into it. I simply wanted you that much."

"God, Vicky, please listen. The money had nothing to do with why—"

"Did you attend that gala after Margot had threatened to pull her investment?" Vicky asked, her eyebrows raised.

"Yes," I said through gritted teeth. "But I wanted you way before, even before that kiss in the Orangery. I would have come for you with or without Margot. And from the first time I held you in my arms, it wasn't about the money. I swear, you were mine from that moment, whatever Margot did with her investment, I wasn't letting you go. Holding you again at the fireworks only solidified that."

Vicky's eyes flared for a second, and I thought I saw a spark of something, but then the dull look was back. "I find it hard to believe that an adult woman having a breakdown over fireworks was that attractive, Mike."

"You don't—"

"But I want to reassure you that even though I would have preferred to know about the arrangement, I am still grateful to you for so much of your time."

"What the fuck?" I said very slowly.

Grateful for my time? Was she serious?

"I never thought I would be able to have a physical relationship with anyone, let alone one like the one we shared, which, from my point of view, was absolutely wonderful. I realise you likely have a different perspective on this, given my lack of experience and need for guidance, which must have been… tedious. So, if you feel that you have not been adequately compensated for your time, given that when you entered into this deal with Margot you did not know I was a virgin and would need significant work put in for the required relationship, I'd be happy to compensate you for any additional underpayment."

Tedious? She thought I found taking her virginity, taking *all* her firsts, in a series of the most mind-blowingly incredible experiences of my life, tedious?

Christ, I was almost insane with my need for her. She was like a fever in my blood, yet she thought I found any of that *tedious*?

What the *actual fuck* was going on?

"Vicky," I growled. "Let me make this very fucking clear. Being with you was the absolute and complete opposite of tedious. If you think I faked *any* of the attraction I felt for you, you're dead wrong. Everything with you was on another level from anything I'd ever experienced with any other woman. Maybe it makes me a caveman, but I was fucking thrilled and completely humbled by the fact I was your only lover. Every time I close my eyes, all I can see is you naked on my bed, all I can hear is those small sounds you make when you come. I can almost taste you on my tongue now if I concentrate hard enough. I dream about you at night. I'm distracted with this yearning for you during the day. If you don't believe anything else, then please, *please* at least believe that."

Her eyes were wide as she stared at me, her mouth open in shock.

Good.

Finally, I'd cracked that blank expression.

Okay, so maybe talking to her in her office about seeing her naked and how she tastes wasn't totally appropriate, but I was not going to let her believe for a minute longer that any of what happened between us was some sort of fucking chore for me.

"I… well, I—" her monotone was gone now, her voice shaky and real. She clamped her mouth shut and swallowed as she stared up at me. Her pupils were dilated, and she was breathing fast.

I was getting somewhere.

"Vicky, baby, please. I love you. If you just—"

"Stop!" she snapped, and I swallowed down an angry curse. Her expression had shuttered again, but not before I saw real pain flash across her features. "Don't say that you love me."

"I *will* say it, Vicky." My voice was shaking with frustration now. "I will *keep* saying it until you believe it."

"It's cruel, Mike," Vicky whispered, and to my shock, her eyes filled with tears. "Margot's not going to pull her investment. You don't have to do this. And—"

"Fuck Margot and fuck her investment!" I snapped. "I don't care about that. All I care about is *you*."

She closed her eyes, and when one of her tears fell down her cheek she flinched and scrubbed it away quickly as if surprised to find it there.

"All I've ever wanted is someone to love me for me. Just for me. Not for something I can give them. Not because they're under any obligation. Just because they chose me. So for you to say that to me now is *cruel*."

She backed away from me then, her face morphing back into that blank mask, and her eyes dulling as she scrubbed away another tear, blinking until her eyes were back to dry and lifeless.

"You're not a cruel man. I know you're not. So please, *please* don't say that to me again. And please don't try to see me. If I'd known about the arrangement, then I would have been able to keep myself more detached, but I didn't. And once I'm fixated on something, it's very difficult for me to pull my focus back. So you need to stay away from me."

"Vicky, please, I—"

"You broke me, Mike," she whispered. "I'm not strong. I can't take seeing you without breaking more, and I have to have a chance to put the pieces back together."

She turned then and walked away, back to the conference room.

I watched her go, my fists still clenched at my sides to stop myself from reaching for her.

All I've ever wanted is someone to love me for me.

My chest was so tight I could barely breathe.

Well, I wasn't going to get anywhere with her now, but I wasn't giving up.

I was never going to give up.

CHAPTER 29

I don't make threats

Vicky

I wasn't sure what I was waiting for.

Sitting in my car for twenty minutes, staring into the middle distance was not productive behaviour. I needed to get up and make myself go into that house.

Cutting off my mother and Rebecca hadn't been as easy as just blocking their numbers. Okay, so I hadn't answered the door to them when they came to my house, but the incessant banging wasn't ideal as I lived in a quiet neighbourhood.

Then there had been the messages left at the reception of my work for me.

I really, really couldn't have them interfering in my professional life.

All I had was my professional life.

So here I was, sitting in my car outside their house, an entire twenty-one minutes and thirty-two seconds late for the planned meeting. I'd been promised no Darrell and a de-escalation in their harassment if I met with them today. I wasn't too sure whether to believe them or not, but Darrell's car wasn't here, and I'd checked all the streets nearby as well.

"It's safe," I whispered to myself as I closed my eyes. "You're safe. You can do this."

I startled at the loud banging on my window, and my eyes flew open to see Mum frowning at me.

"Are you coming in or what?" she said, taking a step back from the car and crossing her arms over her chest defensively.

I took a deep breath in and let it out slowly before I forced myself to open my car door.

Eat the frog, Margot would say. *Get the bad stuff done early, don't put it off.*

As I followed Mum to the house, I kept doing the breathing exercises Abdul had taught me. Abdul would not be happy that I was here today. He wholeheartedly agreed with Mike and the others that I should *not* have contact with my family.

"I rarely recommend ongoing estrangement, Vicky," he'd said last week. "But I've also rarely come across people as despicable as your mother and sister."

So no, Abdul wouldn't think this was a good idea. And if I was insisting on going, he definitely would want me to take Ollie or Felix or somebody with me. Prior to the Margot investment revelation, he would have also suggested Mike, but now, he seemed almost as disappointed in Mike as I was. He even called him a *fucking idiot* in one of his rare breaks of professionalism.

But, whilst I believed Ollie, Claire and Margot when they insisted that they thought of me as family, I still knew that whatever they said, I needed to be a low-maintenance member of that family. I'd already created an unacceptable amount of drama this month; I didn't need to add to it by dragging them more into my mess.

I felt my heart sink as we walked through all the clutter into the kitchen.

"Hey," Rebecca said in a low voice from her position sitting at the kitchen table with all the dirty cups and plates stacked in front of her.

"Hey," I said cautiously.

Rebecca was not in her standard designer outfit. In fact, she wasn't even wearing make-up, and there were dark circles under her eyes. "Where's your dad?" I asked her.

Mum narrowed her eyes at me. "Gareth's none of your bloody business," she snapped. "You're not *Gareth's* daughter."

I shrugged. That was factually accurate, after all.

"Okay, well what do you want?" I said, keeping my tone neutral.

"Drop the charges against Darrell," Mum said, her voice rising in anger.

I really wanted to reach up and cover my ears, but I knew they'd call me a freak for doing it.

"I can't do that," I told her the truth. "I've already made my statements to the police."

"He was just joking around, Vicky," Mum said. "Who the hell goes to the police after a simple prank?"

I tilted my head to the side as I stared at Mum. "He hurt me," I said quietly.

Mum rolled her eyes as Rebecca seemed to sink down further into her chair. I was surprised that she didn't want to shout at me as well. "You were always too bloody sensitive. Just drop this. It's your word against his anyway."

I shook my head. "There were witnesses."

"One witness," spat Mum. "And you're fucking him, so he should be pretty easy to silence."

"Mum," Rebecca cut in, standing up from her seat at the kitchen table. "Can you please stop saying—"

"I'm not fucking him," I said simply, cutting Rebecca off.

"Bored with you already, is he?" sneered Mum. "I *knew* he was being paid to be with you." My face drained of colour, and I took a step back.

How could she *possibly* know that?

My head started spinning, and my throat closed over.

Mum watched with a smug smile on her face, as if reveling in how much she was upsetting me.

"How utterly ridiculous."

I startled at Margot's loud, crisp voice, and turned to see her swan into the kitchen, her boots clipping loudly across the tiles.

"Janet, Rebecca, as always, *not* a pleasure. I see your housekeeping skills haven't improved over the years."

Mum's back snapped straight as she glared across the kitchen.

Rebecca was eyeing Margot warily as Margot drew up by my side.

"Vicky, darling," Margot said. "What on earth are you doing here with these people?"

"I-I had to—"

"No, you did not *have to*. I'm sorry that I ever implied that you should maintain contact with your biological mother."

"You've no bloody right to be here!" Mum shouted. "Get out of my house!"

Margot turned to Mum, drawing herself up to her full height and readjusting her handbag on her shoulder. The temperature in the room seemed to drop a few degrees.

"*Your* house?" Margot asked, and I watched with fascination as Mum's face paled. "This is your house, is it?"

There was a beat of silence. Margot's icy glare was focused on Mum, who broke first and looked away.

"This house is part of the Buckingham Estate, as is the land surrounding it. It has been part of the Buckingham Estate for over five hundred years. My *son* owns this house."

"You fucking aristocrats own this whole bloody country," snapped Mum, her face reddening with fury.

Margot smiled and nodded her agreement. "I agree. At least seventy-five per cent of it, so yes, the vast majority." Her voice lowered then, and her smile fell. "Do you think a family that's kept hold of a fortune as huge as ours has done so without a certain degree of ruthlessness?" Her voice dropped again to a low, lethal whisper. "Do you think a family like that lets people like you fuck with its members? Lets people put their hands on them?"

Mum looked like she was going to throw up. "Are you threatening me?" she asked in a shaky voice.

Margot flashed a smile that was more like a baring of teeth, and Mum flinched.

"Absolutely not. I don't make threats: I state facts. You will be out of this house by the end of the month. You will *never* speak to Vicky again or attempt any form of contact. I've already spoken to your soon-to-be *ex*-husband, who was never at peace with this arrangement anyway, and he is in full agreement about finding alternative living arrangements. Although I expect that his will be separate from yours, given how disgusted he is at your treatment of Vicky, and how angry he is to find out how badly you've been physically, emotionally, and financially abusing your daughter for all these years."

"Y-y-you can't do this," Mum stuttered.

"My family has been doing whatever the hell it wants for over five hundred years. Rest assured, I can and will do this. Rightly or wrongly, I have the support of the courts, the local police, and the judiciary. I have an army of lawyers at my disposal, and a team of very good private investigators who have already dug up enough dirt on you and your daughter to bury you."

"This isn't your fight, Margot," Mum hissed. "She's not even your daughter. She's your husband's *bastard*—the result of him shagging me when he got bored with you. Why do you care?"

"My husband was an unfeeling shit. You're a disgusting excuse for a human being. But Vicky is, and always has been, absolutely wonderful. She's a sister to my children by blood, and I claim her as my daughter by choice."

"That doesn't make any sense!" Mum said, her voice rising. "You should hate Vicky. You should—"

"If you think I should hate your daughter, why did you drop her off when she was six years old at my house?"

"Vicky was a bloody nightmare," snapped Mum.

"She didn't seem like a nightmare to me," Margot returned. "In fact, I think Vicky may have been the lowest maintenance child that I had ever encountered. Why on earth would you bring her to us without warning? Why didn't you try to look after your own child? What kind of unfeeling monster would—"

"She wouldn't stop bloody screaming, okay!" Mum shouted, and I took a step back.

"What are you—?" Margot started, but Mum cut her off.

"Your bloody husband told her that she was a mistake, and as soon as he said that, she started screaming, and she wouldn't stop. She was just screaming, screaming, *screaming*."

"What did you do to her?" Margot whispered.

I glanced at Rebecca.

She was looking at Mum, her face now pale.

"What was I supposed to do? She wouldn't shut up. Dickhead Duke took off, and I was left with this crazy freak. Nothing worked—I shook her, smacked her, but she just carried on screaming. I had to do something."

"You shook her and smacked her?" Margot's voice was rising now. "Did it ever occur to you to hug her?"

"*Hug her*? Are you joking? Reward that mental behaviour? No way." Colour had risen in Mum's face now, and her hands were balled into fists at her sides. "The neighbours could hear. It was horrendous. I did the only thing I could think of."

My chest tightened as my throat closed over. It was like I was back there again. The cold walls, the spiders, the terror of being left alone, of not knowing when Mum would come back.

"What did you do?" Margot repeated, almost in a whisper.

"I locked her in the basement," Mum said through gritted teeth. "And I let her out when she—"

"When I stopped screaming," I managed to say around my tight throat.

The room was frozen in horrified silence.

"You let me out when I stopped screaming. But it wasn't you that let me out, Mum."

"It was my idea to send Vicky to stay with you, Margot," Gareth's voice sounded from the front door, and we all turned to him.

He walked in and closed it behind him, dropping his keys onto a side table before he turned back to the kitchen. He looked older than when I last saw him, defeated.

"When I came home and saw what Janet had…" His voice broke at the end of that sentence as he shook his head and then looked at Mum. "I made excuses for you. You hid the worst of it from me, but I made excuses for how you treated that girl. But when I came home that day… and I asked where she was. The house was silent, and you wouldn't tell me. When I finally found her and let her out, the silence was *deafening*."

"That's when you stopped speaking," Margot said as she turned to me.

To my shock, I could see that her eyes were filled with tears, which she quickly swiped away before turning to my mother and Gareth.

"You sent me that traumatised little girl with no warning."

"Vicky was a shell of herself when I found her in that basement. Her eyes had this unfocused look of terror in them, and there were bruises on her arms," Gareth said in a low voice. "I thought it was a one-off. I thought that Janet must be under too much stress and just snapped; that she needed a break. I thought with some time out of this house, Vicky would recover, and… and the truth is, I couldn't bear her silence." He turned to me. "I let you down, cariad. I'm so sorry."

He dropped his head in shame then, and I made myself move to him, putting my hand on his arm, just like Lottie would do for me.

"You were always kind to me," I told him. "That's not letting me down. That was important to me."

He shook his head. "I should have protected you, love."

"Protected her from what?" Mum snapped. "From *me*? For goodness sake. She was only locked down there for a few hours. And so what if she had a few bruises? I had to restrain her—she was like a wild animal."

"I'm sorry too, Victoria," muttered Rebecca.

My shocked gaze flew to her.

Rebecca never apologised.

She darted me an uncomfortable look. Her pale cheeks had reddened now, and she was shifting uncomfortably on her feet.

"I was a bitch to you. I didn't know about the basement thing but—"

"You were a year younger than me, Rebecca," I told her. "None of that is your fault."

She shrugged. "I knew Mum picked on you, I saw her grabbing you too hard when we were growing up, and I was still a little shit. Then what I did in that nightclub was horrendous. I actually did feel ashamed after that, but I was too proud to admit it."

"What the hell are you talking about, Becky?" Gareth asked in a now weary voice.

"I invited Victoria out with us, took her to this nightclub, and left her in the crush, knowing it would stress her out. But I didn't realise…"

"You didn't realise how full-on my meltdown would be," I put in. "You didn't know I'd collapse on the dance floor. That I'd have to be carried out."

"My God, Becky," Gareth breathed as he scrubbed his hands down his face. "As if this family hadn't done enough to her."

"I'm so sorry, Vicky," Rebecca said in a small voice, using my preferred name for the first time in years. There were actual tears in her eyes now. "I was jealous of you."

"Jealous?" I frowned at her. "What was there to be jealous of?"

"You were successful, beautiful. You had a whole other family that were way posher than mine."

My eyebrows went up. "It never occurred to me that you could possibly be jealous of me."

Rebecca shook her head. "You've never seen yourself clearly. I was a jealous, bitter shrew when I should have been grateful for the financial support you still offered me and Mum that we didn't deserve. And there's no excuse for Darrell."

"Rebecca!" snapped Mum. "What are you saying? Darrell is—"

"Darrell is a rapey dickhead is what he is." Rebecca cut her off then looked at me. "Loads of my mates have come forward, actually. Seems he's been super gross for ages now, but they didn't want to say anything. Some of them want to go to the coppers to back you up, Vicky. I'm going to tell them to do it."

"Rebecca!" Mum shouted.

"I've dumped him, Mum," she told her. "It doesn't matter how much money he's got, or any of that bullshit now. We're getting the marriage annulled. I'm not staying with someone who assaulted my sister, and frankly, you're a psycho for encouraging me to. But then again, you're a psycho all the way around. I only agreed to meet Vicky with you today to apologise."

"But what will everyone think?" Mum said in horror.

"Who the fuck cares what any of your stuck-up friends think?" roared Gareth. "If you weren't so wrapped up in what everyone else thinks, maybe you wouldn't have abused your own daughter for being a bit different and then extorted money from her to put on that ridiculous wedding. Right, come on, Becky, love, we're leaving."

"Leaving?" Mum screeched. "What do you mean?"

"I'm moving out, and Becky's coming with me, Janet. She's already been exposed to way too much of your toxicity. Hopefully, it's not too late for her to turn her life around."

Rebecca was at her father's side now. They paused in front of me on their way out while Mum screamed obscenities in the background.

"Take care of yourself, cariad," said Gareth. "Uh... is this okay?" He held his arms out.

I nodded, and he pulled me in for a very brief, firm hug.

"I'm always here, you know," he said into my hair. "You probably won't ever want my help, but I'm always here if you need me. Wish I had been from the beginning, but that's a mark on my soul that I'll just have to live with."

He set me back and moved to the door, then Rebecca was in front of me, too. "Sorry again," she whispered, tucking her hair behind her ears.

I gave her a nod, and thankfully, she didn't attempt a hug, but instead, moved out of the house with her father.

"Right," said Margot smartly. "We've wasted enough time in this hovel, Vicky. Let's be off. Janet, it's been an absolute *dis*pleasure. I'll be in touch about your eviction." Then she simply guided me out and shut the door on my mother's ranting and raving.

Half an hour later, I was in the drawing room of Buckingham Manor with a fancy china cup of tea in front of me, and a cat sitting in my lap. I could have argued with Margot, but I didn't think it would have been productive. She had asked my driver to take my car to the Manor, while I was hustled into her car. Apparently, we needed to have a "little chat," and she wasn't taking no for an answer.

"How did you know I was at Mum's house?" I asked Margot.

"Oh, that," Margot said dismissively as she lifted her teacup from its saucer to take a small sip.

We were sitting opposite each other on the ancient but very comfortable armchairs, overlooking the grounds. Somehow, the staff had already rustled up a multi-tiered tray of small cakes and cucumber sandwiches on the table next to us.

"When it became clear to me that I had neglected my duty regarding your welfare, and that I could not fully trust you to act in your own best interests, I decided to have a discreet team of private security follow you. They knew to inform me of any unusual activity, *especially* in the event of your mother or sister approaching you, or indeed, if you should go to them."

I stared at Margot for a long moment.

"You never neglected your duty," I told her.

I didn't address the surveillance stuff – I wouldn't have been able to stop her doing what she wanted anyway. Logically, I should be outraged. But I knew that when it came to people she cared about, Margot was *very* invasive. To be on the receiving end of her overbearing attention and her bossiness was actually... nice. It was one of the reasons that I forgave her for what she did with Mike.

At least she'd cared enough to blackmail someone into dating me.

Wow. I was coming to realise that feeling like I was a burden on everyone my entire life may have messed me up, just a little.

Margot put her teacup back on its saucer, and then gracefully set the cup and saucer on the small table next to her, before she reached across to me, pausing until I nodded, and her hand enclosed mine. Her grip was firm, and her hand dry, so I could tolerate it better than I expected.

"Yes, I did," she said softly. "And it won't happen again. You're a part of this family, and that means me being... now, what is it the young people say? Ah yes, *right up in your grill*."

I wasn't much into slang, but I was quite sure that the young people of Margot's acquaintance said no such thing.

"Now," she continued, releasing my hand and leaning back in her chair. "We need to discuss Mike."

I stiffened. "Margot—"

"Firstly, I'm going to say sorry. I'm an interfering old bat, and it always backfires on me. Just ask your brother."

"You meant well. And, had you not intervened, Mike would never have—"

"Absolute rubbish!" she cut me off. "That boy couldn't take his eyes off you long before I gave him a little push."

I blinked, then shook my head. "You're remembering it wrong. I was the one stalking Mike, not the other way around."

Margot started laughing. "Mike Mayweather has always watched you, Vicky. Even as children, he could never look away. Back then, the more you ignored him, the grumpier he got."

"I didn't ignore him."

"No, I know you didn't, but Mike didn't understand why you wouldn't speak to him. Your mother…" Margot broke off to clench her jaw.

She'd picked her teacup back up, and her knuckles were white from how hard she was holding the handle. She cleared her throat, closed her eyes briefly and then continued.

"Your bloody mother didn't agree to any assessments or in 'labelling you', as she put it, so there was no good explanation we could give to people like Mike. I'm sorry I didn't do something, Vicky. You should have been supported at school. You should have had access to specialist services. I let you down."

"It wasn't your responsib—"

"You were a child under my care. Okay, so maybe that was only for two weeks a year, and maybe I didn't have parental responsibility, but I could have done more."

"I'm not your daughter," I said in a small voice, and her expression softened.

"You're a sister to my children, darling. That makes you my daughter by default. Back then, I'm afraid my pride was hurt by your father. But quite frankly, fuck your father. Who cares if he was shagging around? I was well rid of him anyway by the time you came to stay with us. My pride and your father were never the important things. You kids were important, and in those first precious two weeks after you arrived as a tiny six-year-old, I let Ollie look after you when I should have been the one doing it."

"Honestly, I—"

"No. I won't hear any more on the subject. I was wrong, and that's that. And what I did with Mike was wrong too, but you're just going to have to get over that, because there's no time to waste now. If we don't act quickly, Mike's going to make a huge mistake, and I'll *never* be able to forgive myself."

I'd promised myself that I wouldn't ask about Mike, that I wouldn't let myself go back down that road. I knew it wasn't healthy for me, but…

"What's Mike done?"

CHAPTER 30

Your grovel game needs some serious work

Mike

"Wow," Lucy said, her nose wrinkling as she stood over me where I was sprawled on my sofa. "This is super pathetic."

"Bloody hell, Mayweather," Lottie called from the kitchen as she walked in my direction, picking up beer cans as she went. "You're sinking pretty low right now. How long is it since you showered?"

"Doesn't matter if I shower," I mumbled. "It's just me here. It's always going to be just me."

After going to her office and being turned away, I'd tried the whole walking her home tactic that Ollie had employed with Lottie—it seemed to get him somewhere, so why not me?

But the difference was that Vicky's walk home was all of two steps from her car to her house, not really long enough to convince her to forgive me and that I loved her, especially when she completed those two steps at a run, and most of the time she was wearing noise-cancelling headphones.

Since then, I'd gone into a downward spiral, spending most of the time either working, drinking whisky, or hugging the pillow that just about still smelled of her hair.

That's how my sister and Lottie had found me on the second Sunday of my self-absorbed pity party.

"Oh my God, *the drama*," Lucy said, and I frowned up at her from my position on the sofa. "Get off your arse, Mikey."

"I'm heartbroken," I slurred.

"You're drunk," said Lottie, her nose wrinkling, no doubt at the stale fug of spirits in the air. She was starting to look a little green, and that really made me feel guilty.

Lottie's mum had been an alcoholic, and I knew the smell made Lottie feel sick.

"Sorry, Lots," I croaked, and then my vision filled with my sister, who was squatting down in front of me.

"Get up and have a shower," she said in a clipped tone, so unlike Lucy that I found it hard to believe it was my sister speaking. Lottie tried grabbing away my pillow, but I wouldn't let it go. It was like some sort of security blanket now.

"Why are you being so mean to me?" I mumbled.

"Fraggle Rock," Lottie said, "I really thought Ollie was exaggerating, but you, my friend, *are* a massive wussbag."

"My heart hurts," I told them both, and Lucy sighed.

"Mikey, you need to sober up if you're going to get Vicky back."

"She told me to go away, repeatedly."

"And you're just giving up?" Lottie said in complete disbelief. "Your grovel game needs some serious work, my friend. Haven't you ever heard of the grand gesture? Something to prove that she means the world to you."

I blinked at that, my drunk brain trying to process what she was saying. I started to sit up but then just collapsed back onto the sofa with a huff.

"I was never good enough for her anyway," I answered eventually, my voice despondent.

"Agreed," my sister put in, and I frowned at her. "But guess what? Vicky loves you."

"She could have anyone she wants."

"But she wants you."

"I broke her trust."

"Then fix it!" Lucy yelled in frustration, "Gah! You're ridiculous!"

A sharp pain jolted through my leg.

"You kicked me!" I cried out in disbelief.

My previously sweet and non-violent sister actually kicked me in the shin.

The last time she'd been physically violent was when I stole one of her millions of notebooks when she was eight, but then, I'd been able to hold her back effortlessly with my hand to her forehead as her little fists whirled at me.

"I'm trying to get you to listen," she replied impatiently. "You need to prove yourself to Vicky again. You need to make her see that you love her, and that it had nothing to do with Margot's money."

"How am I going to do that?"

"Figure it out, you big idiot," Lottie snapped.

Ugh, I had harpies attacking me on all sides now. Why weren't my two best friends keeping their women occupied and out of my bloody business?

"She needs you, Mikey," Lottie said softly.

And, in the end, it was that that got me. Despite my dizziness I finally pushed up to sitting.

"What?" I croaked.

"She needs you. Did you know that Janet and Rebecca are harassing her?"

"What?" I was shouting now, but when I tried to surge to my feet, a wave of dizziness forced me back down. Ugh. The harpies were right—I was pathetic. "But I blocked them from her phone."

Lucy snorted. "They've been using Vicky for years. Did you think blocking them would stop them? They've been going to her house and even turning up at work."

"Is she okay?"

"Do you deserve to know that?" Lottie asked in a soft but accusatory voice.

I groaned and put my head in my hands. "No," I muttered. "No, I don't, but I need to know anyway. And I know I don't deserve her, but I want her anyway."

"Were you only with her to hang on to Margot's investment?" Lottie asked, her eyes narrowing on me.

"No!"

Ah, Christ. My shouting made my head hurt so badly I felt like I might throw up. "No," I said in a quieter voice. "It was never about that. I agreed to go to the gala, but as soon as I held Vicky, it was never about the money. I bloody love her, okay?"

I looked up at Lottie. She was studying me with narrowed eyes, then her head tilted to the side, and she smiled.

"Well, prove it then."

*

I hadn't touched a drop of alcohol since Lucy and Lottie's visit two weeks ago.

It had taken me a few days to work it out, but finally, I came up with the solution. Yes, the cabin was my dream, but I didn't want that dream anymore without her.

I didn't want anything without Vicky.

"Are we leaving all the furniture?" Pete asked, and I nodded.

I knew I should be happy the buyer wanted everything, but as I ran my fingers over my hand-finished kitchen table, the one I'd spent two days sanding, the one with the driftwood legs that took weeks to dry and treat properly before they were ready to use, I was struggling to be grateful.

Pete shook his head. "Fucking hell, mate. I can't believe you're giving this up. This is your dream."

I shrugged. "Dreams change."

"Do you even know who bought it?"

"Some London high roller who wants a second home is what the agent said."

Everyone had been pissed off when they heard I was putting the cabin on the market.

Ollie and Felix offered to buy it, of course. In fact, they offered to simply give me the money. But I told them all to bugger off. They were missing the bloody point.

I needed to pay back Margot's investment myself. It was the only hope I had of winning back Vicky's trust. So when the agent told me about the offer, I jumped at it.

Not only was the buyer willing to pay a full twenty per cent above the asking price, but they also wanted the furniture… all of it, right down to my bed, and even the sofa that had seen better days.

Seeing as I would now be living in the small flat above my old workshop at Mum's house, I didn't actually need much stuff, so I thought that was fair enough—especially after I was told about the additional lump sum the buyer was willing to pay to keep the place furnished.

So, I wasn't just getting enough to pay back Margot's investment—I had over double that amount now. Enough to expand the business, enough for a new van, even enough to pay a delivery driver. It seemed that just as my personal life had fallen apart, my professional life was looking up. Not that it helped. Nothing helped.

I missed Vicky with a fierceness that was almost overwhelming.

So here I was, standing in my living room, with Pete helping me move out of the cabin I'd built with my own hands.

"Well, I hope you don't regret giving up this place," Pete said as he lugged the last of my boxes over the threshold.

"I know what I'm doing," I told him.

"You poured your heart and soul into building this," Pete argued, and I turned to face him.

"My heart and soul aren't here," I said, gesturing to the cabin. "They're currently in London, with the most beautiful woman inside and out I've ever known, and I need to get them back."

CHAPTER 31

You need someone strong

Vicky

The fog lifted slowly, but it did lift. By the time Margot and I had finished our tea, I was starting to feel more alive.

After numbing everything for nearly a month, it was almost painful to have all of those emotions back again, like when you've slept on your arm overnight, and you get those awful prickles as the sensation comes back.

I was feeling *everything.* And I was missing Mike. I missed him so much, it was almost scary. I'd been alone and afraid way too much already. I decided it was time for me to be brave.

"I have to go," I said, putting my teacup down on the saucer with a clatter and jumping to my feet.

"I thought you might say that," she said through a smile.

Then, as my car drove out of the Manor, I saw Mike's van parked outside the cottage on the estate that Claire used as her country home. Next to it, was a low-slung sports car. Maybe Ollie was there too?

Focused on my mission, I asked my driver to pull up outside the driveway and jogged towards the house. All I could think was that Mike was there, and after what Margot told me, I *had* to see him.

But I froze in the entryway when I heard Blake's voice.

What was he doing here?

"This is my bloody home." Blake was shouting. He sounded absolutely furious. "I'm not being thrown out by some fucking employee. Bugger off, Mayweather."

"I'm *not* an employee," Mike said. "And you *are* getting thrown out. This is still Claire and Florrie's home, even if they live at Buckingham House now. Claire had to ask me to come and chuck you out when she heard you were here, because I was closest, and she doesn't want her sixty-five-year-old mum to have to act as a bouncer for her. Although, I've gotta say man, I think Margot could take you."

"Fuck off, you smug git," spat Blake. "You think you're sorted just because you've got a sweet gig as that blonde freak's carer with benefits?" Blake laughed as ice trickled down my spine.

Carer with benefits?

"That's if the frigid weirdo lets you fuck her—I'm guessing unlikely when she can't even shake hands without losing her shit. Well, good luck with that, and I hope they're paying you enough."

There was a scuffle then. I heard a chair being turned over and shouting, but the ringing in my ears meant I couldn't quite make out the words. All I seemed to be able to focus on was Blake's voice on repeat, saying *carer with benefits*.

The shame I'd felt when I'd heard almost exactly the same comment at Rebecca's wedding from a member of my own family came flooding back.

I knew Blake was a horrible human being, but was what he said actually that inaccurate?

All my quirks, all the restrictions on what I could do, and what I could tolerate. That time in The Badger's Sett when I couldn't even look his friends in the eye or greet them like a normal person.

And Mike was a good man. He would do it; I knew that. He would care for me. But wouldn't he eventually resent the fact he didn't have an equal partner? Resent that I wasn't normal?

I blinked and took a few stumbling steps back, away from the commotion inside, then I turned and ran back to my car. I sat in the back passenger seat, staring at the house for a long moment, trying to make my decision.

"Shall we go now, Vicky, love?" my driver Richard asked gently.

I cleared my throat. "Yes, please," I said in a small voice.

Just then, Blake came flying out of the front door, which was slammed after him. Blake's nose was bleeding, but he got to his feet and kicked some of the stones on the driveway before stomping to his car. But before he opened the door, he caught sight of me watching him. He tilted his head to the side as a nasty expression came over his face.

"Freak," I saw him mouth at me before he flung open his car door and sped away from the house.

*

A week later, I blinked at the figure waiting on the pavement as we pulled up outside my house. He was so beautiful, my heart actually hurt, and I was finding it a struggle to take a breath in. I thought that Mike had given up with the whole walking me from my car to the door thing. You couldn't really blame him—I'd totally ignored him every time he did it, and more often than not, I had my headphones on anyway. But when he stopped showing up, there was a small part of me I wouldn't admit to that was disappointed.

"You okay, love?" Richard asked, eyeing Mike with suspicion. I knew Richard had been worried about me, and I knew he blamed Mike for breaking my heart, so seeing a larger-than-life Mike in all his glory outside my house again wasn't going to go down well. "Want me to hang around?"

"I'm fine, Richard."

"You always say that," Richard snapped, surprising me as I reached for the door handle. "And I *know* it's not the truth. I *know* you're not fine. I've been your driver for ten years. I care about you."

"Oh, right. Sorry, I didn't think that—"

"I know you didn't think. You don't think that I notice how much time off I get? You don't think I notice when you buy my wife an entire nursery full of furniture after you overheard her crying on the phone to me because she didn't think we were prepared for the baby?"

"Um… I tend to see problems and try to fix them. I don't mean to—"

"Yes, well, you're good with *other people's* problems. Not so much with your own. If I need to get out of the car and punch that big bastard in the face, I will."

My eyebrows went up in shock. Mike was at least double Richard's size. "It's okay, Richard," I said softly. "And thank you for… er, thank you for caring about me." I reached over and gave Richard a very awkward pat on the shoulder.

When I opened the door, Richard shouted, "Watch yourself!" at Mike, who didn't even flinch. He just gave my driver a small salute, which looked like a gesture of respect.

"Er… hi," I said to Mike as I climbed out of the car, and Richard pulled away. "What are you…? I mean, what are you doing here?"

Mike took a deep breath and crossed his arms over his chest, looking extremely uncomfortable. "I know you said to stay away, and I was going to give you more time, but then I found out that you went to your family's house, and I…" He swallowed, uncrossed his arms, and shoved his hands into his pockets. "I'm just worried. I don't want you around those people, Vicky."

He was *caring* for me again. Worrying about me. I suppressed a deep sigh. He looked wretched. His bloodshot eyes had dark circles under them, and his face was drawn and stressed.

"I won't see them again, Mike," I told him in a firm voice. Mike needed to stop worrying about me and get on with his own life. "Margot's seen to that."

I took a step towards him, and his whole body went on alert. My voice was soft when I spoke again.

"You don't have to worry about me anymore." I reached up and put my hand on his chest simply because he was there, he was so big and strong, and his woodsy scent was all around me.

I felt the muscles bunch under my hand as he stared down at me.

His eyes flashed, and his jaw clenched tight.

"Vicky," he breathed, hesitating for only a moment before those huge arms closed around me, and suddenly, I was surrounded by everything Mike.

I let myself have those few seconds. A few more moments I could file away and bring out, over and over again, when I was alone, just like I'd done for the last week since Margot told me what he'd done, and since the fog had lifted.

I breathed in his shirt as I melted into him.

"God, baby, I've missed you," Mike said as he kissed the hair on the top of my head. "I've been out of my mind with worry for you. I couldn't believe you went to those people again. And I know you're not eating right. Ollie told me that—"

I pulled away in a sudden movement, taking a few steps back.

There he was, worrying about me again. Wanting to look after me, to *care for me.*

I shook my head.

"I-I shouldn't have done that," I whispered, and Mike frowned down at me.

"Please, love," he said, a desperate quality to his voice now. He lifted a hand towards me, but I flinched away, causing what looked like actual pain to cross his expression.

"We won't work," I said in my firmest voice, annoyed that I couldn't quite keep the shaky element out of it.

"We bloody well will," Mike growled in a stubborn tone. "I'm *not* giving up either."

I have to admit, this surprised me. When I'd informed Mike that our relationship wasn't going to work, I had expected him to back off, like he had before—this time, guilt-free because he'd made some effort, but secretly relieved that he wouldn't have to be someone's carer. Then we'd go our separate ways.

I had not anticipated him growling at me and not accepting my very reasonable arguments.

He tried again. "If this is about Margot and the money, then—"

"No," I snapped. "This is about the fact that you need to be with someone who you don't have to look after. You need someone strong." My throat closed over, and I had to blink rapidly so that my eyes wouldn't well up.

Judging from Mike's expression, I wasn't all that successful.

"Vicky, baby, please. You're talking rubbish." Mike's voice was softer now, but no less bossy. "If that's the only problem, then—"

"I love you," I whispered, and he froze in shock for a moment before the tension drained from his expression, and his face broke into a huge smile as he reached for me again, only for it to drop when I stepped back out of his reach.

"Vicky, you know I love you too. We can—"

"I love you *too much* to burden you with someone like me."

He was far from smiling now. In fact, he looked absolutely furious.

"What the bollocks are you on about now?"

"Goodbye, Mike," I told him as I backed up to my door.

Mike glowered at me. "This is *not* over, love," he said in that stubborn voice.

"I'm not going to change my mind, Mike."

"We'll see."

CHAPTER 32

Love it. Love you

Mike

"What the fuck?" I muttered as Ollie, Felix, and I walked into The Badger's Sett.

"Thank Christ you're here," said Jimbo. "I can't bloody well deal with this. Look at the state of them! And there's that bloody pony, *in my pub*! The fat bastard's done a shit by the bar. I know we're not classy like those posh joints you kids go to in London, but we don't want actual horse shit on the floor."

"Bloody hell," said Felix as he rubbed his hands down his face. "This escalated quickly."

"My husband!" shouted my sister. "My big, beautiful soon-to-be-husband! He's here!" She stood up as if to go to him, but then swayed on her feet. "Ooh, head rush." She collapsed back down into her seat like a ragdoll. "He'll probably need to carry me," she told the rest of the table of women. "He does that sometimes, you know." She lowered her voice to a stage whisper, which was almost louder than her speaking voice. "It's *very* sexy."

"I like it when they do that," said Lottie, who was staring at Ollie with a dreamy expression on her face.

Lottie didn't even have alcohol as an excuse, as she didn't drink.

"I really, really like it too," said Vicky, which was a surprise, seeing as she looked like she was asleep on Claire's shoulder. Her eyes were closed, and there was a small smile on her face. "It feels warm and safe. It might be my favourite."

"Ugh, barf," snapped Claire, before grabbing a shot from in front of her. "You guys are gross. It should be a hard no on the carrying you around thing. You're not bloody toddlers. Now, do your shots."

"Yes, darlings," slurred Margot, who had her arm around my mother. "You mustn't let them carry you around. Bad form."

"I wouldn't mind it," said Mum, who then, to my horror, gave Jimbo a slow wink.

"My little boy!" cried Bianca when she caught sight of Felix.

Felix was well over six foot; little, he was not. But then her smile dropped as she squinted up at us all. "But you're naughty boys. This is only girls tonight. Only for hens. No cockerels."

Lucy giggled into her shot glass. "Yeah, no *cock*erels, boys." She then turned to Felix and winked sloppily. "Until later," she said in another loud stage whisper.

"Barf again," said Claire. "Right then, one, two, three..."

"Alla salute!" shouted Bianca. All three of us rushed forward as they lifted their full shot glasses—other than Lottie who lifted her can of coke instead—repeating Bianca's words, but we were too late to stop them downing the lot, except thankfully for Vicky, who was still asleep on Claire's shoulder.

"I think I'm gonna throw up," Claire said after a moment, her face going an unnatural shade of green as she bolted away from the table.

Vicky started to topple over when her human pillow disappeared, but I shot into the booth to hold her up before she could face plant onto the chair beside her.

Then I had her soft weight in my arms; her lavender scent mixed with tequila around me. I heard her let out a small sigh as she snuggled further into my chest. Her small hand fell into my crotch, and I gritted my teeth. I did not want to be hard, sitting at a table with my mother and sister.

"I need to get you home, love," I muttered into the hair at the top of her head.

"I love the cabin," she whispered, and I froze.

The others were trying to get the rest of the women up.

Mum was arguing with Felix about what time it was.

"Hetty," Felix said with extreme patience. "It's three in the bloody morning. Jimbo wants you and that pony out of here. Why on earth did you bring Legolas anyway?"

"Weirdest hen party I've ever seen," said Ollie as he and Lottie tried to extract Margot from her chair.

Lottie was giggling too hard to be of much use.

I knew I should probably help Felix, who was dealing with both my mum, his mum, and my sister, but I ignored them all to focus on what Vicky had just said.

"You like the cabin, love?" I asked in a soft voice.

"Love it," she told me, her voice fading as she relaxed more into my side. "Love you."

My heart felt like it was beating outside of my chest. I had to swallow against the lump in my throat before I could speak again. "I love you too, sweetheart."

Then, to my horror, I felt wet through my shirt.

Vicky was crying.

"Hey," I said, gathering her closer. "Why are you sad?"

"I miss you," she whispered.

"Christ, I miss you too, love. So much."

"Not for me."

"What's isn't?"

"You're not."

"Mayweather," snapped Ollie, who was dragging his mum out of her chair with Lottie still giggling too much to help. "We're going, mate. Jimbo's about to lose his shit."

So I stood up with Vicky in my arms, dead asleep now. "Bullshit, I'm not for you," I muttered in a firm voice.

When we made it outside the pub, the cold air hit us like a brick wall, and it was enough to wake Vicky up.

When her eyelids fluttered open, the cold must have sobered her up a little, and she stiffened.

"Put me down," she said.

"Vicky, I—"

"Put me *down*." Her voice rose enough that the motley crew around us fell silent to look at us. "I mean it, Mike."

I had no choice but to lower her to her feet.

She swayed for a moment, and I reached out for her elbow to steady her, but she flinched away.

"No," she semi-shouted.

I put up both my hands in a gesture of surrender. "Okay, love. I won't touch you."

"It hurts too much," she said in a broken voice, and I felt that chest tightness again. She shook her head.

"I'm hurting too, baby. I miss you too. If you'd just…"

"No!" she was nearly screaming now. She staggered back and nearly fell, but that small fat pony was behind her. Her hand went into his fur, and then she sank down, wrapping her arms around the pony's neck and shoving her face into the deep fur.

Legolas snorted softly and nuzzled her with his nose.

"Mike," Ollie said, stepping in front of me to block my view of Vicky wrapped around Legolas. "Leave it for tonight, mate. I'll see her back to the Manor. She's in no state for this now. And anyway, you need to help Felix."

I glanced over at Felix, who was struggling to guide both his mother and mine to his car whilst Lucy happily hung off his neck. I sighed in frustration as I acknowledged the truth of his words.

Love it. Love you.

"Look." Ollie cut into my thoughts. "I'm no stranger to a good grovel. But you've got to pick your moments. This is the first time Vicky's ever been drunk in her life. Now is not the time to pick her up caveman style and take her home with you."

"She's miserable, Ollie," I said in a pained voice. "She's making herself miserable, and I know I can make her happy. I *know* I can. She's lost weight again. I don't think she's sleeping. I'm worried."

"She's fine. We've—"

"She's not fine," I snapped. "Look, I've been doing my research, and intelligent Autistic women are eight more times likely to-to …" I broke off and blinked as my eyes started to sting. I couldn't bring myself to repeat the terrifying statistics I'd found. "If I lost her, I—"

"Mike," Ollie said firmly, one of his hands going to the back of my neck, and the other, to my shoulder. "We're looking after her, I promise. When she's not with Mum at the Manor, she's under twenty-four-hour surveillance in London. And we're not letting her hide away when she's hurt anymore. We've let her down as a family, but that's over now. So she's not alone."

"Okay," I said in a broken voice.

"You'll get your chance," Ollie told me before he gave my back a slap and moved away. "But it won't be tonight."

I sniffed, took a deep breath in and out, and squared my shoulders. It took all I had to walk away from Vicky, letting Ollie untangle her from the pony.

"Come on, Jimbo," I heard Mum slur at Jimbo as he emerged from the pub, glowering at her and everyone around her. "How's about it, love?"

Then my mother threw her arms around the pub landlord and kissed him on the cheek.

What I could see of Jimbo's face under his thick beard went bright pink, and his eyes flew wide.

"Er… Hetty," he said, his arms going out to the side. "I think you might be a bit worse for wear. Maybe when you're sober and *ponyless,* we could—"

"I love your beard!" she shouted, and I decided that was enough.

I extracted my mum from a terrified Jimbo, and then Felix and I herded them all into our cars.

Ollie had picked Vicky up now and was striding over to his car where he'd already deposited his mum and Lottie. As they went past my windshield, Vicky looked straight at me, and I almost surged out of the car to get to her.

The sadness and longing in her eyes were painful to witness.

I gritted my teeth as I started the car and then shook my head to clear it, but I couldn't get her voice out of my mind.

Love it. Love you.

CHAPTER 33

Carpenter-boy

Vicky

"What are you doing?"

I looked up to see a furious Lucy standing in front of me with her arms crossed, and I frowned.

"I'm watching you rehearse for your wedding."

What was I supposed to be doing?

"From the very back of the church?"

I glanced up to the altar where Felix, Lottie, Ollie, Mike, Margot, Hetty, Claire, Emily, Hayley and Florrie were all gathered.

"Lucy, I think you'd better get back to the wedding party."

She blinked at me.

"Vicky," she said slowly. "Why do you think I asked you to come here today?"

I bit my lip and then blew out a breath. "To be honest, I'm not sure. I've never been to a wedding rehearsal before."

"Didn't you go to Claire's?" Lucy asked with a frown.

I looked down at my feet.

"I…"

"No, she didn't, because I'm an over-sensitive cow." Claire had walked over to us now and was standing next to Lucy.

I shrugged. "I said your wedding dress looked itchy. It was the incorrect response."

"I still should have asked you to the rehearsal." Claire shifted uncomfortably then. "I let you sit at the back of the church on the day, too."

"It doesn't mat—"

"Yes, it does," she said fiercely. "I told myself that you'd probably be happier there anyway, but if I'm honest, I was still being a petty bitch, angry that Dad had left Mum and had another kid; angry at you for being there. Angry that I knew you'd be the most beautiful woman in the room, and nobody would be able to take their eyes off you when it was supposed to be my day. But I shouldn't have excluded you. You're my sister. It was wrong, and it *did* matter. Okay?"

She was so fired up, her face and her eyes were flashing. I thought it best to agree with a small, "okay."

It didn't seem to make her any less angry.

Lucy's impatient expression had softened. "Vics, you're part of the wedding party, you silly goose. So you can't sit at the back of the church."

I blinked at her. "I-I don't understand."

I knew Ollie was Felix's best man, and Mike was doubling up as his other best man and walking Lucy down the aisle. I wasn't sure where I fit in.

"Emily, Lottie, Claire, Hayley, Florrie and *you* are my bridesmaids," Lucy said patiently. "So, you need to get up off your butt and come stand at the front of the church. You agreed to it at the hen party. Remember?"

I blinked at her.

Lucy's hen party had been the first time I'd really drank to excess. But I'd been sad about the carer thing and confused about Mike after Margot's revelation—and, for the first time, I'd felt like I could trust the people around me enough to lose some control.

I had a vague memory of Ollie, Felix and Mike turning up towards the end, despite the fact it was meant to be just girls. But I wasn't sure what exactly happened after that. All I knew was that I woke up in Buckingham Manor the next morning with a very sore head.

And I didn't actually remember agreeing to be a bridesmaid, which was very disconcerting, because I always had almost perfect recall of everything I experienced. But, then again, I never usually drank that many shots of tequila.

What else didn't I remember?

"Are you sure?" I asked, then lowered my voice to a whisper so that the others couldn't hear me. "You don't have to ask me."

Lucy was frowning at me. "Why do you think I wouldn't want to have you as a bridesmaid? You're one of my best friends!"

I blinked at her. "I am?"

"Wow," Lucy said. "Vics, I'm trying *really* hard not to take offence here. But yes, I think you're one of my best friends."

"Oh..."

"So you need to come up to the front of the church."

I nodded and then followed her up to where everyone else was standing.

When the vicar started going through the ceremony and where we'd be positioned, I pulled my phone out and put it on the altar, switching it to record.

"Vics?" Lottie asked softly in my ear. "What are you doing?"

"Oh, I'm recording the information so that I can reference it later, and run through it in my mind with the audio queue. I'll be able to recall the words correctly without the recording, but there may be nuances I miss, which I can ask Abdul to interpret when I play it for him. I'll probably make a PowerPoint at home."

"Why?"

I shrugged. "I don't want to get overwhelmed on the day. If I know what to expect, I won't be startled. I don't want to embarrass Lucy and Felix."

"Okay, honey," she said softly, giving my hand a very quick squeeze, which wasn't one of our signals—I had come to understand it was how Lottie communicated affection. Why me recording a vicar speaking should inspire her to feel affectionate towards me was a mystery. But then, there were often aspects of human behaviour that I didn't understand.

"It's not an exam, hun," said Lucy, frowning over at me. "You don't have to stress out about it, okay?"

I shifted on my feet, feeling uncomfortable with everyone's attention on me. I was ruining this already. "I know... I just—"

"Leave her be," snapped Mike. "Let's get on with this horse-and-pony show."

Lucy glowered at her brother, her hands going to her hips. "This is my wedding, you big oaf. Not a horse-and-pony-show."

Mike rolled his eyes as Hayley said quietly, "Can we have ponies?"

"Oh yes!" shouted Florrie. "Legolas would make a great ring bearer!"

"That pony is not becoming a part of my wedding," Felix said through gritted teeth, and honestly, I felt the man's pain. He'd taken a lot of abuse from the Mayweather animals during his courtship of Lucy.

When I looked at Mike, he gave me a small smile and a wink.

We weren't even together anymore, and he was still looking after me. He'd taken the focus away from me when he could see I was uncomfortable, and he did it without even thinking.

I blinked and looked away.

He looked particularly amazing today. His long-sleeved shirt was rolled up to reveal his muscular forearms, his hair just a little too long, so that it brushed his collar, and his beard was a few days past needing a trim.

My hands itched from the need to sink my fingers into his hair. I clenched them into fists and squared my shoulders. It didn't matter how delicious Mike looked; I wasn't going to drag him back into the role of carer. So I spent the rest of the rehearsal ignoring him. I assumed that once we'd finished, I could just shoot off back to London.

What I didn't factor into the equation was my interfering stepmother.

"Right, darlings," Margot said as we walked out of the church. "As we're all here, we can sort out the outfits in one fell swoop. So I've arranged for us all to have the fittings now."

Before I knew it, all the cars had filled up with people, and the only space left for me was with Mike, who looked unreasonably smug about this turn of events. It was only when he noticed my hands shaking as we drove away from the church that his smile dropped.

"Vicky, love," he said softly, his voice full of concern. "If it's too much for you, I can drop you at Buckingham Manor. You don't have to—"

"S-stop looking after me, Mike Mayweather," I snapped.

He let out an actual growl of frustration as his jaw clenched and his knuckles turned white on the steering wheel.

"What if I *want* to look after you?"

I shook my head. "You should find an appropriate woman who does not require that," I told him.

"I could bloody well murder that mother and sister of yours," Mike said in a furious voice, and I frowned in confusion.

"What have they got to do with this?"

"Everything," he said. "They've got everything to do with it, and you're too brainwashed to see it."

"I am not brainwashed," I said, totally affronted. "I always approach everything with rationality and reason."

"Not us, you don't," he said darkly. "When it comes to us, you're the most illogical woman I've ever known."

With that cryptic statement, Mike parallel-parked us outside the shop, stormed around to my side to open my door, and then ushered me inside with his hand on the base of my spine whilst I tried not to cry at how much I'd missed that.

To my relief, the men were sent to one section of the shop, and the women to another.

When Lucy tried her dress on for us, I kept my mouth firmly shut. I did not want a repeat of what happened at Claire's wedding dress fitting, when the only thing I could come up with about the dress was that it looked itchy.

But it had looked itchy! It was pure lace. I hadn't been able to see anything else about the dress other than the itchy factor.

But, to my surprise, this time, it was very different. This time, when I saw the lace trim on Lucy's dress and could think of nothing else, Claire had come up to me and given me a firm side hug.

Lucy noticed and got off the pedestal arrangement they'd set up for her to stand on to come over to me.

"I know it looks itchy, but the lace is actually really soft." She paused. "Want to try feeling it?"

Slowly, bracing for the scratchiness, I ran my finger over her collar and blinked. It *was* surprisingly soft. I smiled at Lucy.

"You do look beautiful," I said in a quiet voice. "And you know that's the truth, because I never lie."

"Thanks, hun." She beamed at me. "Now it's your turn."

When the shop assistant wheeled in a rack of bridesmaid's dresses, I started to feel sick. They all had labels, there was tulle and lace, and all manner of scratchy materials.

I took a step back but ran into what felt like a brick wall.

"No lace, no seams, no labels, none of that floaty stuff," snapped Mike from behind me, and my eyebrows went up as I jumped forward, away from him.

"What are you doing here?" I snapped at him.

"I won't have you being uncomfortable," Mike told me, then his gaze went over my head to the shop assistant. "She's not trying on anything that makes her feel uncomfortable."

"Stand down, big guy," Lottie said with a smile.

In fact, they were all smiling.

I didn't know what was funny about Mike barging into his sister's bridesmaid's dress fitting to bark out orders, but clearly, everyone had lost their minds.

"I know way more about Vicky's clothing preferences than you. Do you think for one minute I'd let her feel uncomfortable?" Lottie said.

"Run along, love," Hetty said with a dismissive wave to her son. "You're in the way here."

Mike harrumphed but did as his mum said.

"I'm really sorry, Lucy," I muttered, my face feeling like it was on fire.

"No, don't apologise for my brother." Lucy's smile was wide now and she was bouncing on her toes with excitement. "I know first-hand how protective he can be. I'm just so happy you guys are finally working things out."

I didn't have a chance to correct her. In fact, I didn't really have a chance to do much of anything other than try on dresses.

We settled on a soft satin dress with hidden seams, and magically, no labels. It wasn't too dissimilar to the nighties I already wore, so I knew I'd be able to tolerate it—I'd probably even be able to sleep in it, it was so comfortable.

With outfits sorted, everyone decided to go to The Badger's Sett for a post-fitting drink, and despite me feeling like I was at the end of my tolerance for Mike exposure, it was made clear that I was coming too.

Now, I blame what happened at the pub on my being slightly overwhelmed by the general situation. This included hearing Lucy calling me one of her best friends, having Mike touch me when I'd been dreaming about him every night and longing to touch him so much I'd felt like I was coming out of my skin, and the glass of champagne I'd already had at the dress fitting.

The low-level fury I felt when Mike was cornered on his way to the bar almost scared me.

I recognised Olivia—she was a family friend of the Hardings, equally posh, very beautiful and extremely charming. Her family lived on an estate in a neighbouring village, so it wasn't that unusual for her to be in the pub.

When she turned her considerable charm on Mike, I froze, bracing for him to smile at her, for him to see the possibility of an actual functioning partner for him, rather than someone who needed a *carer.*

"Ugh." Lucy huffed when she saw me glowering at them from our table. "She's been after Mike for a while. Just ignore her, Vics."

But I couldn't ignore her. I couldn't look away.

But instead of leaning into her and smiling at her, Mike stiffened.

When she put her hand on his chest, the expression that crossed his face was one I actually recognised.

I'm not that good with facial expressions—a lot of them are tricky for me to interpret—but I could almost feel the emotion behind this one. Maybe because I'd felt it so often myself when someone I didn't want near me touched me. It was a feeling of horror mixed with disgust and claustrophobia.

I stood up from my seat so suddenly that it scraped back behind me with a sharp sound.

"Vics?" Lottie asked, looking between me and Mike with some growing alarm. "I don't think..."

I didn't stay to hear the rest of what she had to say. I was weaving my way to the bar. My only plan was to get that woman's hands *off* Mike. I had to brace myself to squeeze through the crowd, not wanting to be so near these people, but I couldn't get his expression out of my head.

"Olivia, I'm sorry," I heard him say as I got closer. "I've tried to be nice about this, but I'm not interested."

"Come on, carpenter-boy," Olivia purred, and I stiffened.

Carpenter-boy? Who the hell did she think she was?

"What's the problem?" Her hand was moving from his chest down to his crotch, and I was done.

"Stop touching him!" I shouted, and the low-level noise of the pub quietened around us. "He... he doesn't want you touching him."

Olivia gave me a withering look, but she did take her hands off Mike.

I let out a sharp breath of relief.

"Bloody hell. Chill, would you?" she said, holding her hands up in surrender. "Didn't know you were still slumming it."

I narrowed my eyes at her. "Slumming it?"

She shrugged. "I thought you dumped him. If you don't want your bit of rough long term, you should let the rest of us have a go."

"He's not a bit of rough," I said. "He's kind, honourable, beautiful, loyal, and intelligent. He makes me laugh, which is not always an easy thing to do. He's the best man I've ever met *in my life*. And he doesn't deserve the way you've put your hands on him without his consent." I shook my head jerkily from side to side. "He doesn't deserve being called *carpenter-boy* when he's a skilled artist."

"Woah." Olivia backed off with her hands in the air. "Calm the fuck down. Keep your blue-collar bit of stuff."

"You shouldn't call him—"

"Hey, hey." Mike's soft, amused voice cut me off, and suddenly, my view of Olivia was blocked by his big body.

I blinked up at him. Why was he smiling?

"I think she gets the message, love."

"She shouldn't speak to you that way," I said, my voice tight as Olivia stalked off to the other side of the bar.

"Okay," he said, still smiling.

I shook my head. "And she shouldn't touch you if you don't want her to touch you."

"I know," he said. "I'm okay, I promise." He stepped into my space and reached for my hands, which I realised were clenched into tight fists. "You can stand down, love."

I let out a breath in a huff, still not ready to let go of my anger completely.

"Let's go back to the table, okay?" He steered me back to the others with that hand on my lower back again.

"Why are you all smiling?" I asked.

CHAPTER 34

Our cabin

Mike

Vicky was still bristling with anger on my behalf. She was like a little ball of indignant fury, and I felt better than I had in weeks.

This Vicky—the Vicky shaking with rage next to me—was infinitely better than the blank Vicky from before, the one who'd displayed nothing.

This Vicky, I could work with.

"Well, you definitely told *her,* Vics," Ollie said with amusement.

Felix stifled a laugh. "Yeah, you saved poor little Mikey from the big bad supermodel before she could compromise him."

Vicky's rage ebbed, and doubt entered her expression when Felix said supermodel.

I frowned at him.

"Shut up, Moretti," I snapped. "Who says I didn't need saving?"

Vicky bit her lip. "Maybe you could have handled it yourself," she whispered. "It's just, she was pawing at you, and—"

"I'm very glad you sorted her out, love," I said softly.

"I didn't like her touching you," she whispered.

"I didn't like it either," I whispered back.

"I think what you said was lovely, sweetheart," Mum put in softly to Vicky.

"So do I," said Lucy.

Vicky blushed and ducked her head.

"I shouldn't have done it," she muttered.

The shutters were coming down again. I could feel her retreating behind her walls. The good-natured teasing directed at me had gotten to her.

I could punch those posh bastards right in their smiling faces.

"She's probably a more appropriate partner for you anyway."

That last sentence pushed me over the edge. All these weeks of patience, of longing for her, of worrying about her, caused me to snap.

I turned to Vicky and frowned down at her.

"No, she is not," I said slowly, through gritted teeth.

"Mike, I'm not—"

"I am fucking sick of hearing about what you're not, Vicky," I said, my voice rising, not caring who we were with, or who could overhear us. "All I've heard from you in the last two weeks is how you're *not* normal, how you're *not* what I need, how you're *not* good enough. When are we going to start talking about what you *are*? Because you *are* beautiful."

Vicky flinched slightly at that statement. She knew she was beautiful, so to her, it probably didn't feel like much of a compliment. After all, she hated the ice princess nickname, and the perception most men had that she was untouchable.

But I wasn't finished, not by a long way.

"You *are* kind, you *are* a straight-up genius, you *are* a great sister, a great step-daughter, a great friend. You are the most selfless person I know. You are the reason my sister managed to feel settled when she moved to London."

"I'm not," she cried, tears filling her eyes. "I let Lucy down."

"You made *one* mistake."

Bloody hell, I knew this shit was still eating away at her.

Felix was the main bastard of the situation, and my sister was marrying that particular bastard, but Vicky still couldn't forgive herself.

"But before that, you looked after my sister, and you've been doing it ever since."

"I don't—"

"If it wasn't for you, Lottie and Ollie would never have found each other again. Lottie might not even have custody of her sister anymore if you hadn't insisted she work for you. Why the hell you think that you're a burden and that people have to look after you, I've no idea."

Vicky's eyes went wide at that. Her mouth opened and closed a couple of times, but nothing came out.

That was good; I had more to say.

"So you *are* a good friend. You are the best time I've ever had—I've never laughed with a woman as much as I have with you. I've never found any woman as interesting."

"Interesting?" Vicky said in shock. "What? Even when I'm banging on about my stupid obsessions?"

"Hey, hedgehogs are not stupid!" I protested. "I love knowing more about them. And we should all care more about the environment."

"You're making fun of me," Vicky whispered, and my heart clenched in my chest. She looked so unsure and so sad, but just underneath, there was this little thread of hope in her voice.

"I'm not making fun of you, love," I said softly.

And then I did what I should have done weeks ago—I gathered her in my arms and pushed the hair back from her face, keeping it tilted up towards me so that I could look into her eyes as I said the rest.

"You are all of those things, Victoria Harding. But most of all, you are the woman I am madly in love with."

There was a long pause. It felt like the entire pub was collectively holding its breath.

Vicky blinked up at me: fear, anxiety and hope all warring behind her eyes.

"You love me?" she whispered.

"From the moment you told me that being in my house feels like being hugged all the time."

"I loved you the first moment I saw you," she said.

I laughed. "Vicky, baby, you were six."

She nodded. "I know. You came into Buckingham Manor carrying an injured hedgehog. Your hands were bleeding from the spikes, but you didn't care. You'd walked two miles holding that hedgehog."

Jesus, I'd forgotten that Vicky had even been there. How could I have forgotten her? But then, I barely acknowledged her the few times I'd seen her as a child.

"I'm sorry I ignored you back then," I told her.

"It's fine. I was—"

"It's not fine. I was an insecure piece of shit with a chip on his shoulder, and I took it out on you then, and again, a few months ago, when you first made your move. But now that we've straightened everything out, now that you're mine, you're never going to accept that type of behaviour from anyone ever again. Got me?"

"I'm yours?" she whispered, hope overcoming fear as her features became more animated than I'd seen in weeks, and that was it for me.

No more waiting to claim her. No more tiptoeing around.

Both my hands went into her hair, and I kissed her.

She jolted in shock for a moment, but that was all it took for her to melt into me, and her mouth to open under mine.

But then, the first cheers started, and she stiffened.

Affection as a whole was new for Vicky; public displays of affection would need to be eased into.

Plus, there was the fact that *my mother* was sitting a few feet away. So I pulled back to tuck Vicky under my arm.

"We're leaving," I said to the table, all of whom were smiling up at us.

"About time, Mayweather," muttered Felix.

"I may have to bleach my eyeballs, but I'm still so happy," my sister said, bouncing on her seat.

"You look after her now, love," Mum said in a soft voice.

"Yes," said Margot. "Don't fuck it up, Michael. I've gone to a lot of trouble to sort this out."

I rolled my eyes and pointed at Margot. "No more interfering."

"Well, of all the ungrateful..."

"Margot," said Lottie, amusement in her voice, "I think Mike might have a point."

Margot huffed. "Nobody appreciates my efforts."

"Right, come on, love," I muttered, steering Vicky away from the crazies that made up our family and friends.

I'd anticipated at least a small amount of resistance from Vicky as I led her out to my Land Rover, but if anything, she melted further into me.

When we got to the passenger door, I turned her towards me, so I could search her face. She looked a little dazed, but to my relief, there was definitely no blankness in her expression.

"You okay, sweetheart?" I asked softly.

"D-did you mean what you said in there?" she asked. "I'm not like Lottie. I can't tell if people are lying."

"I will never lie to you, Vicky," I told her. "Ever."

Her voice dropped so low that I had to strain to hear her next words. "You really think all those things... about me?"

"We all do, love."

"You really love me?" she whispered, and my chest clenched painfully at the hope and longing I could hear in her voice.

"I love you so much I can't breathe when you're not there," I said, pulling her into me. "I haven't been able to take a full breath for over a month."

Her small hands were resting on my chest as she stared up at me, searching my face. Whatever she saw there must have done something, because to my shock, she went up on her tiptoes and kissed me.

It took me a moment to recover, but once I did, I wasn't wasting any time. One of my hands went into her hair, and the other lifted her up against me.

"Good girl," I muttered against her mouth as she wrapped her legs around my hips and let out one of those small moans I loved so much.

"I missed you," she whispered in between kisses. "I love you."

I groaned. The sound of the pub door swinging open brought me back to the present, and I stopped kissing her to rest my forehead on hers.

"You're coming home with me," I growled.

"Yes," she breathed, nodding her head with enthusiasm at that proposition. "Yes, Mike. Take me home."

But when we were in the truck, and I was driving towards my workshop, Vicky shook her head.

"No," she said firmly. "Take me *home*."

I frowned over at her. "Vics, I live above the workshop at Moonreach now, love. Didn't Margot tell you? I sold the cabin, so I could pay back her investment."

"Why did you do that?" Vicky asked in a soft voice.

"You must know why I did it," I said tightly. "I needed to prove to you that I only wanted you for you. I fucked up by not telling you about Margot's investment. I'm sorry I hurt you, love. It was never about the money. You know that, right?"

"I know," she said simply, and I let out a relieved sigh. "Take me to the cabin."

"Vicky, don't you understand? I sold it, love." I felt the familiar ache of loss as I spoke the words but then I shook my head to clear it.

Yes, I built the cabin with my bare hands. Yes, it had been my dream since I was a child, but it was just a building.

It didn't matter.

Having Vicky's trust was all that mattered. And anyway, there was no dream without her.

"Take me there," she said in a stubborn voice, and I sighed. Maybe she needed to see the cabin occupied by someone else to let the reality of it sink in.

"Okay, love," I said in a resigned voice. "We can go and look at it, I guess."

But I didn't *want* to see the cabin with someone else there. I wanted to go there and open *my* fucking front door that *I* carved myself. I wanted to take Vicky up to the mezzanine and fuck her on the bed *I* made.

I gripped the steering wheel too tight, my driving jerky as we turned down the long gravel drive.

When I pulled up outside, there was a large van in front of the house. It was the exact make that I'd looked at last week to buy. As I was frowning at the van, Vicky took the opportunity to fling open the passenger door of my Land Rover and jump down onto the gravel.

"Vicky!" I said as she walked straight up to the front door. "What the hell are you doing? You can't—"

I broke off as I watched her unlock the door and push it open, then disappear inside.

"Shit," I muttered, stalking from the Land Rover to the open door.

When I made it inside the house, Vicky was standing in the middle of the large space, watching me with cautious eyes.

"Baby," I said, striding over to her as I checked for the likely irate new owners, but there was nobody else there. "I don't know how you got hold of a key, but you can't just barge in here. It's not—"

When I was right in front of her, Vicky reached out and grabbed my hand, lifting it up, turning it over and then dropping a set of keys into it before she closed my fingers over them.

"I was *very* cross with you when I heard you were selling this house," she said.

I was blinking down at the keys in my hand, frozen to the spot in shock.

"This is *your* cabin, Mike. I won't let anyone else set foot inside the house you built."

"Our cabin," I said, looking up from the keys to Vicky's face.

"What?"

"Our cabin," I repeated in a firm voice as I tightened my grip around the keys.

"Our cabin," Vicky whispered, her eyes filling with tears as a tremulous smile formed on her lips.

I dropped the keys and shot forward to sweep her up in my arms. I was not wasting any more time without this woman.

One of her tears fell, but her smile grew as she threw her arms around my neck.

I kissed her once, closed-mouthed, hard and brief, and then I strode over to the staircase. When we made it to the bed, we landed with me on top of her.

Two more tears made their way into the hair at her temples as she smiled up at me.

I kissed one then the other as I brought my hands up to frame her face.

"You bought our house back for us, baby," I said in a low voice.

She nodded.

"You're going to live here with me," I told her, frowning at the thought of her returning to London. "You can commute. I mean, we can stay in your house in London sometimes, but mostly we should—"

"I'll live here with you," Vicky said, and the tension in my body I hadn't even realised I'd been carrying relaxed.

"You'll marry me," I told her.

"Okay," she said simply.

"You'll have my babies," I bossed some more.

"Okay, Mike." Her voice was soft now as her hand came up to stroke the side of my face.

I let out a relieved sigh. After so long thinking I'd lost her, I was feeling like I needed to lock her down in every way possible.

Oh bollocks, that might not have been the most romantic way to propose.

Most women wanted flowers and diamonds, and maybe Paris, not being pinned to a bed in a wood cabin in the middle of the forest by some big lout and *told* they were going to get married, not asked.

"I'll do this properly," I muttered, kissing the corner of her mouth.

"Properly?" she breathed, moving against me as her legs fell open on either side of my hips.

"Propose," I said against her neck as I kissed my way to her collarbone. "I'll propose properly."

"Mike," she called, and I lifted my head to look up at her. "That was the best possible way you could have proposed to me. Clear, concise, with no room for interpretation."

"Vicky, I—"

"Am I yours?"

"Damn right, you are," I growled.

"And you're mine?"

"Always."

"Well, that's all I need," she said through a smile.

*

Vicky

I woke up with the sun streaming in from between the wooden beams. When I stretched out on the bed, I felt aches everywhere, and I smiled.

The first time last night with Mike had been hard and fast, as if both of us were too desperate to take it slow, both too scarred from our time apart.

Mike pinned me down, taking me with an urgency that met my own. We went over the edge together, stars exploding behind my eyes as Mike roared with his release.

Then Mike made us sandwiches from the ingredients I'd stocked the fridge with yesterday, and we ate them in bed. It was the first time I'd ever eaten *anything* in bed. I still wasn't quite at peace with the crumb aspect. This was before he chucked the plates on the floor and made love to me, slowly and excruciatingly gently until we both lost control again.

He gathered me into his arms afterwards and spoke into my hair.

"Christ, I missed you so much it scared me." His voice cracked at the end of that sentence, and I was shocked to see actual tears in his eyes when I pushed up on his chest to look at his face.

"You're my favourite human being," I told him firmly, the best compliment I could think of.

He scanned my face for a long moment, then levered us both up and carried me to the shower. Once under the warm water, he made me put my hands on the tiles and told me not to move them, then called me his *good girl* when I did as he asked.

Shower sex was amazing. It combined cleanliness, being told I was a good girl and no fewer than two orgasms—three of my favourite things.

When I felt for Mike, his side of the bed was cold, and my eyes flew open. I pushed up to sit and turned to look at the kitchen from over the balcony, breathing a sigh of relief when I saw a gloriously muscled, bare-chested Mike putting some bread in the toaster.

When I saw him set his timer on his phone, I smiled.

Of course, he was going to make me my breakfast just the way I wanted.

His gaze met mine when I made it down the spiral staircase, a possessive look coming over his expression when he saw I was wearing his shirt from yesterday and nothing else. He opened his arms, and I went straight into them, pushing up onto my tiptoes to give him a kiss.

"Hi," I whispered when I broke the kiss.

"Hi," he said back, his arms giving me a squeeze. "Vicky, is that a new van in the drive?"

I looked to the side and out of the window to where the van was parked. "Yes."

Mike scowled at me. "Why did you buy a van?"

I shrugged. "You needed a van."

"Right. Boundaries, okay?"

I nodded.

"No more buying me stuff."

"Hmm." I bit my lip, thinking that the new industrial circular saw in his workshop might be a problem.

"I mean it, Vicky," Mike told me, his voice intense as his hand came up to my jaw to lift my face and look into my eyes. "I want to look after you. Not the other way around."

I frowned at him before I lowered my head to his bare chest, loving the feel of his skin under my cheek.

"You do look after me," I whispered, listening to the strong beat of his heart under my ear. With perfect timing, the alarm on his phone went off. "You make me eggs just the way I like them."

His low, rumbling laugh vibrated under my face. "Making eggs is not buying a van and a whole bloody house."

"No, it's more. It's everything. It's love."

EPILOGUE

An overbearing, interfering pain in the arse?

Vicky

"Did I do something incorrect?" I asked Lottie as I stared at the typed letter she'd just handed me.

"Of course not, hun," she said gently. "It's just time for me to move on. You know I've completed my psychology degree now, and the next step whilst I train to work with children is going to take up far more of my time."

I frowned. "I will double your income. Effective immediately."

Lottie laughed. Clearly, she was not in tune with the grave seriousness of this situation. "Vics, babe, you've already doubled my income over the last two years. It's not about the money."

I shook my head in denial. "Well, I need you, so you simply cannot leave. I will not accept it."

"You were fine when I was on maternity leave."

"That was different. I knew it was a temporary arrangement."

Lottie sighed. "Vics, you want me to be happy, don't you?"

"Of course I do. You're happy working for me."

"I love working for you, hun. But I want to work with children. Help them overcome trauma, in the same way those counsellors helped Hayley. It's my calling."

"*I* need your help," I grumbled.

"Victoria Mayweather," Lottie said sharply, and I looked up from the letter to make eye contact with her. Lottie rarely used a sharp tone with me as she was well aware that I was sensitive to it, and she knew I disliked the formality of my full name. "You do *not* need me."

My eyebrows went up. "That is a lie, and I am extremely disappointed that you would attempt to deceive me."

Lottie tilted her head to the side. "Why do you think you need me?"

I frowned at her. "To stop me going into hyperfocus mode, to stop me insulting people, to read the room for me, to help me discern if people are lying."

"Okay, okay, the lying thing I get. That *is* my superpower. And Felix needs me as much as you do in that regard. I've promised that I'll sit in on the occasional meeting where necessary, as being able to read the room does give you guys an advantage in business. But as for me stopping Vicky from being Vicky, quite frankly, that's bullshit."

"You swore."

Lottie smiled at me. "I'm aware."

"You never swear."

"Well, about this, I bloody well will." Her voice was fierce now. "I don't agree with the idea that you need to tone yourself down to suit other people all the time. Your directness can give you a huge advantage, and if people can't accept you for who you are then why would you want to do business with them anyway?"

I opened my mouth to reply then realised I didn't actually *have* a logical reply to what Lottie had said. That was extremely irritating. However, despite my irritation her words did spark a small kernel of warmth in my chest.

"You don't think I need..." I trailed off, not sure what I was asking. "You think it's okay if I'm just... me."

"Vics, can I give you a side hug?" Lottie asked. I nodded, and she moved to where I was sitting on the chair, put her arm around me and gave me a tight squeeze with firm, consistent pressure, exactly the way I preferred. "You should *always* be you, hun. You're enough all by yourself. I'm sorry if people have made you feel like you weren't. Me included"

I cleared my throat after Lottie moved away, willing the stinging in my eyes to subside. This was an office environment, after all, and not the appropriate place for emotional interactions. So I sniffed and blinked a few times. When I was sure that everything was back under my control, I spoke again.

"I will miss you," I blurted out. "You know I don't like change. You not being in the office is unacceptable."

Lottie smiled at me. "I'll miss you too, love. But we'll be seeing each other on the reg, won't we? Are you forgetting the fact that I'm married to your brother? Or that we both mostly live in the same village? You'll see me all the time."

"I'll see you less, and that is still an unacceptable change."

"Now Vics, remember how you want me to be happy?"

"Of course."

"Well, working with kids will make me happy."

Ugh. Other people's autonomy was such a bother. But yes, of course I wanted Lottie to be happy. I cared very much for Lottie and her happiness. I crossed my arms over my chest.

"I'm still not convinced that being *me* is in the company's best interests. It's far better if—"

"What the chuffing heck are you on about now?" Mike's deep voice cut me off, and I sprang out of my chair. Well, I would have sprung out of my chair if it wasn't for the huge Mike-sized baby that he'd impregnated me with. So, instead of any springing, it was more of a slow clamber where I had to use the desk and the arm of the chair for leverage.

By the time I'd made it up, Mike had walked into my office

so I didn't have to waddle far to get to him. When I did, I laid both my hands on his chest as his arms came around me, bump and all, and I went up on tiptoes to kiss him. This was still the Standard Mike Greeting, even now that we were married and I was pregnant with his daughter.

I had asked him if he wanted to revise this policy a few months ago, after it invoked a substantial amount of teasing from his friends at The Badger's Sett. This turned out to be an ill-advised query as it made Mike extremely cross. He told his friends to "bugger off" and said that he'd "kiss my missus whenever I bloody well like" and that "you bastards shouldn't make her feel uncomfortable," which I felt was extremely rude but which they seemed to take with very little animosity if their smiles and profuse apologies to me were anything to go by.

"Hi," I said as I smiled up at him. Sometimes smiling at Mike could distract him successfully. I had learnt to use this to my advantage. His arms gave me a squeeze, and he frowned down at me. Clearly, this time, my technique was not working.

"Why are you asking if it's okay to be you? Did somebody say something?"

"Stand down, big guy," Lottie said through a laugh. "Nobody's said a word to Vics." Her voice softened before she spoke again, "We've just been talking about my resignation, and Vics isn't overly on board."

"Ah, I see," said Mike. I laid my head on Mike's chest so that I could feel his deep voice rumble there. It was one of the best ways I knew of to feel calmer if something upset me. "And you think you need Lottie here, love?"

I shrugged. "Lottie is being illogical."

"How so, sweetheart?"

"She says I don't need her to help me alter my behaviour. Apparently, I should just be me."

"Why is that illogical? I happen to *love* you."

I very reluctantly lifted my head from his chest to frown up at him. "You, Mike Mayweather, are an exception to the rule.

Only last week I insulted a group of contractors enough for them to storm out of the office."

"Oh yeah," Felix said from my doorway. "You should have seen it, man. It was beautiful."

"It was not beautiful, Felix," I told him. "It could very well impact the development's progress and—"

"Honestly, Vics," Felix cut in. "It's best we find out they're dickheads early on rather than a few weeks down the line when they're a nightmare to replace. All you did was ask them a few questions. It's not your fault that you apparently know more about structural engineering than they do. That's a red flag right there anyway. If they were worth their salt, they could have held their own with you."

I pulled away from Mike to an office-appropriate distance. Office-appropriate didn't last very long though, as he immediately put his arm around me and tucked me into his side.

"Well, if you're happy with me going around being all… *unfiltered Vicky,* then look forward to a lot more disgruntled clients and contractors."

Felix sighed. "Vics, don't you think it's better for you to be a little less filtered?" he said softly, and I blinked at him. "So what if we lose clients? Like I said – who wants to work with them anyway?"

"Hiding who you are every minute of the day isn't good for you, love," Mike rumbled next to me and pulled me tighter into his side.

"Oh," I said in a small voice, my eyes stinging again. I'd been told too many times to hide who I was. It was going to take some significant adjustment to change this mindset now.

"I want you to be full-power, unfiltered Vicky here," Felix said decisively, and the stinging got worse as my throat closed over. His expression softened as a tear slipped down my cheek. "Can I give you a hug?" Felix asked and I nodded. "Er… Mike, mate, you're gonna have to actually let her go a sec. I don't want to hug your hairy arse."

"Fine," Mike grumbled, letting his arm drop so that Felix could give me a very brief, tight hug. Mike pulled me back into his side.

"I apologise for this totally unprofessional display of emotion in the workplace," I said stiffly.

"The twins brought a piglet into this office yesterday, Vics," Felix said in a dry tone. "As far as professionalism goes, I think you're good."

"Yes, that was... unusual for a Thursday morning."

Felix shrugged. "Bea's into pigs at the moment and Lucy thought a piglet would cheer everyone up."

"It *was* entertaining," Lottie put in. "We could have done without the squealing though."

"And that was just from Felix," Tabitha said as she came up next to Felix and patted his arm.

I smiled. The piglet *had* been entertaining, if not totally conducive to a professional environment. A wave of tiredness swept over me then as I leaned more heavily into Mike and stifled a yawn.

"Right, I'm taking my wife out of this madhouse," Mike said. "She's dead on her feet."

"It's only three in the afternoon, Mike."

"And you're thirty weeks pregnant, sweetheart," Mike said.

"*And* you fell asleep sitting up in the conference room earlier," Lottie said helpfully.

I narrowed my eyes at her. "You rang him, didn't you?"

She bit her lip. "Maybe?"

"Pregnancy is a natural, physiological state," I told her. "It does not require special treatment. Just because my feet are sore due to the large nature of my baby does not mean..." I broke off as Mike simply picked me up. "What are you doing?"

He frowned down at me. "Getting you off your feet."

Then he turned around and walked out of the office with me in his arms as if I weighed nothing at all, which was very much not the case.

"You are extremely bossy," I said without heat as I settled my face into his neck and inhaled his woodsy Mike smell.

"I know, baby," he muttered as he leaned around to call the lift. I really was tired, though, so as ridiculous as it was to be carried around when you were a grown woman growing another human inside you, I decided to let it go. "Let's get you to the Land Rover, and you can sleep on the way home to the cabin."

I smiled against his neck as he walked us into the lift and the doors shut behind us. "I love the cabin," I said sleepily.

His arms gave me a squeeze. "I know you do, love."

"Mike?"

"Yes?"

"Do you really think I should just be me?"

"Of course I do, love."

"What if unfiltered me is too much?" I voiced my fear in a small voice.

"We love you, Vicky," Mike said firmly. "The real you is never going to be too much for us. So what if some people don't understand you? Fuck em. Best to be yourself, love. Everyone else is taken."

2 years later...

Mike

"Harding, there's a small child on a pony in my front garden... again," I said into the phone as I stared out of my window.

"Thank Christ for that," Ollie said in relief. "We've been looking everywhere."

"She's three years old, mate," I told him as I watched said three-year-old trot up to my back door. "How does she keep giving you the slip?"

"She's no normal three-year-old," Ollie muttered darkly as a small fist started pounding at my door.

At the sudden noise, a load of barking erupted from the sofa, and I glanced over just in time to see Bilbo struggling his way out of Vicky's arms, where moments ago he'd been peacefully lying.

Laughing, Vicky negotiated around her huge stomach to gently put the fat, golden retriever puppy on the floor, and he shot off towards the door.

I sighed into the phone.

"Your daughter has woken up my pregnant wife." I was not happy to have my Sunday, or Vicky's much needed nap with our new puppy interrupted.

Vicky rolled her eyes at me.

"I'm fine," she said, then, "Hello, Ollie," as she passed me to the door.

Bilbo had already collided with the wood and was scratching to get to the little girl on the other side.

Margot junior was waiting with open arms to receive the excited puppy as soon as Vicky opened the door. The fat pony with her pushed past the child and dog bundle before strutting right into my bloody kitchen.

"Hello, Margot," Vicky said with a smile, as if a pony and small child making themselves at home in our house was perfectly normal. Which, in our crazy life, was a pretty accurate assessment.

There were advantages and disadvantages to living this close to your friends and family. They all commuted now. Felix and Vicky's company was so successful that they could call the shots with their investors anyway. This included no more business wear for Vicky. If she did have to go up to London, she'd be in leggings and soft jumpers, and nobody said a word.

Vicky had become much better at advocating for herself. She had confidence now that she never had before. And she no longer shied away from labels.

She didn't mind being different, being an outlier.

Often, she even leaned into it when it gave her an edge in business.

"Okay, Legolas," she said to the pony, who was shoving her leg with his nose.

"Hey!" I shouted at the furry little bastard. "Stop shoving my wife."

Vicky just grabbed an apple from the fruit basket and gave it to Legolas, who snorted again before trotting away to flop down on the rug we had in front of the sofa.

"Get this pony out of here!" I said to Ollie through gritted teeth.

"I'm on my way to get Margot. If you want Legolas removed, you'll have to speak to your sister. You know that little shit hates me."

He hung up on me, and I growled as I shoved my phone into my back pocket.

Vicky waddled over to the door and shut it behind Margot, who was now standing with the squirming puppy in her arms.

"Margot Harding," I said sternly, and she scowled at me. "You ran away again."

"I needs to see the puppy," she said in a stubborn voice. "I only had one cuddle with him yesterday. Henry, Bea and Theo got loads more cuddles than me."

I rubbed my hands down my face.

"Well, that sounds perfectly reasonable to me," said Vicky.

"Vics, she ran away."

"Whilst that's not ideal, the disparity of the puppy cuddle situation *does* sound unfair."

Vicky moved over to the sofa and then sat down with Margot and Bilbo.

Legolas moved over to rest his head on her lap, and Bilbo lay across both Vicky and Margot's laps with his paws in the air, accepting tummy scratches.

I sighed. "You're not going anywhere, are you Margot?"

"No, Uncle Mike," Margot said seriously. "I has to be with the puppy."

"Fine," I said in a resigned voice, pulling my phone out.

Within minutes of me posting my grumpy WhatApp message on the family group for someone to come and claim one pony and one small child, arrangements had apparently been made for a Sunday roast at my house, followed by croquet on Buckingham Manor's lawn.

Then I heard a small cry from the monitor.

I looked over to Vicky, who still had the dog and little girl snuggled into her side on the sofa.

"I'll get her," I muttered, moving across the space to the ground-floor extension I'd built two years ago.

"Hey, gorgeous," I said with a smile at my daughter.

She was standing in her cot, her blonde hair all over the place, her big blue eyes blinking at me, and a big gummy smile on her face. "Finished your nap?"

"Go-Go!" she shouted, and I rolled my eyes.

Of course that was what had woken her up.

Harriet *loved* Margot.

"Come on then, you," I said softly, picking her up and kissing her hair as she snuggled into my neck, just like her mother.

As I carried her out to the living area, I glanced at my phone—as predicted, the WhatsApp was going crazy.

"Ugh! What if I wanted a quiet Sunday with my family?" I grumbled, frowning over at Margot, who was in my rightful spot.

"Go-Go!" shouted Harriet, stretching out her arms for Vicky and Margot.

"You'd think that those buggers would take a hint seeing as we live in the middle of a bloody forest." I stomped over to the sofa and raised my eyebrows. "Come on then, shift up, you lot."

The three of them moved up the sofa, and I slipped in next to Vicky and pulled her into my side.

Harriet clambered over her mum, allowing a quick kiss and a cuddle before tucking herself between Vicky, Margot and Bilbo.

I kissed the top of Vicky's head, and she let out a sigh.

The girls giggled together, alternating between playing with the squirming puppy and "listening to the baby" with their ears pressed against Vicky's stomach.

"Your mum is just worried that I'm not eating enough."

I grunted. "You've been much better for the last month. That's just an excuse."

The first trimester of Vicky's pregnancy had been just horrendous, which was a shock, as she hadn't had morning sickness with Harriet. It had been a struggle for her to keep anything down, and she nearly had to go into hospital.

As always, when I was overwhelmed, I called Mum, and, as always, she turned things around. Mum's homemade ginger biscuits and peppermint tea were often the only things Vicky could tolerate.

Margot senior was furious that Hetty had succeeded where she had failed, and so once Vicky was better, she turned up at the house with Bilbo, and so the game of trumping each other in terms of best grandmother continued.

Even on the WhatsApp now, war was breaking out over who was going to bring the roast potatoes, and whether Lucy's Yorkshire puddings were better than Lottie's. Personally, I hope Mum took over the Yorkshires—neither my sister nor Lottie made them soggy enough for my liking.

I huffed. "She doesn't think I look after you properly."

Vicky laughed. "You know she does, she's just…"

"An overbearing, interfering pain in the arse?"

"She's just wonderful," whispered Vicky, and I let out a long sigh.

Okay, so maybe having overly involved family and friends who weren't too hot on boundaries wasn't that bad.

Not if it made my wife smile like that.

The End.

Read on for Claire & Callum's story.
Exclusive paperback content.

CLAIRE AND CALLUM

Can I help you, Lady Harding?

Claire

"It's just so bloody unfair!" wailed Florrie.

"Darling, please don't swear," I said under my breath as I led Florrie and Hayley through the courtyard of the school, flashing polite smiles at the other parents. As normal, Florrie was drawing way too much attention. "I didn't think you even liked hockey that much?"

"I *love* hockey," she said dramatically, coming to an abrupt stop in the middle of the quad. "It's my *life*. And he's taking it away from me."

"Florrie," I muttered through a smile. "Honestly, sometimes you are such a drama queen. Is this really so important that—?"

I broke off when I looked down at Florrie's face. Her cornflower blue eyes were filled with tears. My smile dropped as my overdeveloped protective instincts surfaced. Nobody made my little girl cry. She'd had a tough enough time over the last few years as it was thanks to *my* stupid decisions. Thankfully my ex-husband, Blake, had been sent packing over a year ago now, but the guilt of having allowed that abusive arsehole anywhere near my daughter still lingered.

I crouched down to her level and took her shoulders in my hands. "Darling, tell Mummy – who's upset you like this?"

She sniffed and looked down at her feet, scuffing a small stone with her toe. "I really shouldn't say," she said as a tear made it down her cheek which I swiped away, my chest filling with real rage now.

"Hayley, do you know what's going on?"

Hayley looked at Florrie then me before pulling her lips in between her teeth. Florrie shot her a quick look that I couldn't quite decipher, and then it seemed as though Hayley held back a very subtle eye roll. The girls were so close now that they often appeared as though they could communicate without words. I had no idea what that little convo was about, but I felt a snap of irritation towards Hayley. She was usually such an empathic child. Florrie was crying for goodness sake!

Hayley cleared her throat. "I think it's Mr Hargreaves who's upset Florrie, Auntie Claire."

Callum Hargreaves.

I suppressed a shiver. The school's head of sport was a huge, well-built god of a man with a rough Scottish accent and an abrasive manner. He'd retired from professional rugby last year after a glittering career, surprising everyone given that he was arguably one of the best players on the Scottish squad – the same squad that had won the World Cup for the first time in its history last summer. Callum Hargreaves was a household name, and I was objectively terrified of him. I did not need to be around large men with attitude problems.

My body, however, didn't seem to have received that memo, if my fevered dreams about him were anything to go by. But after everything I'd been through, I'd vowed that if I ever let another man near me and Florrie again, he would be a kind, short, homely-looking chap, definitely not a beast who looked like he could lift his entire rugby team above his head without breaking a sweat.

I willed away the heat I felt rising in my cheeks at the mention of his name so that I could manage an encouraging smile for Hayley. Her voice was still extremely quiet compared to my daughter's (well, compared to most people's really), but I could hear her clearly even with the noise of the quad surrounding us, which was a huge step forward for her.

"Thank you, darling," I said, giving her shoulder a squeeze and straightening up from my crouch.

"Just because he's head of sport, he thinks he can push everyone around," Florrie put in, her tear-streaked face now screwed up with anger. "It's all about stupid rugby all the time. He doesn't care about hockey or netball. And now he's taken our pitches! We have barely any practice time. He said that it wasn't worth the cost of electricity for the floodlights we'd need for our practices once the days got shorter. I don't think he thinks girls' sport is worth the effort."

What fuckery was this? That bastard!

Hayley snorted. When I flashed her an irritated look, she pressed her lips together as if trying to suppress a smile. I frowned at her, and she ducked her head. What had got into Hayley? Honestly, there was nothing funny about this.

"Right," I said, smoothing down my skirt. "I'm going to bloody well sort this out. Come along, girls. We'll go straight to the headmistress with this nonsense."

A flash of panic crossed Florrie's face, her tears receding as she grabbed my arm to stop me when I turned in the direction of the headmistress' office.

"Mum, you don't need to go to Mrs Bramell," she hurried to say, her voice pitched high now.

"Why ever not? Honestly, Florrie, this should be dealt with, and I—"

"Yes, exactly, that's why you should go straight to *him*," Florrie said, blocking my path.

"Straight to him?"

"Straight to Mr Hargreaves."

"Oh… I…" I cleared my throat and looked to the side.

Marching up to the headmistress was one thing, but going to confront a six-foot-four rugby-playing man with hands the size of dinner plates was not something I felt comfortable with.

At all.

"I don't think that I should be—"

"You always tell us to be direct, Mum," Florrie said, tilting her head to the side as she looked up at me.

"It's okay if you're a bit scared of him, Auntie Claire," Hayley added.

"I am not scared of that man," I snapped, heat hitting my cheeks again.

Florrie shrugged. "If you say so."

"I'm not!"

Hayley was biting her lips again. I narrowed my eyes at her and she looked away quickly.

"He's only just over there on the rugby pitch," Florrie said helpfully. Her tears seemed to have dried suspiciously quickly. "You could talk to him now. If you're not too scared, that is."

I huffed. "F-fine," I said in an unsteady voice. A vision of my daughter's blue eyes, glassy with tears, firmed my resolve. "I may as well give the man a piece of my mind directly. Follow me, girls."

I turned sharply and marched back across the quad to the rugby pitches, determined to show the girls a good example of a strong independent woman who took no shit.

"Bollocks," I muttered as one of my heels stuck in the thick mud when I rounded the sports hall and stepped out onto the side of the pitch.

Christ, it was an absolute mud bath out here. The rain over the last few days had turned the ground into a veritable swamp. Not that the mud stopped Mr Hargreaves and his rugby team – at least twenty boys were running drills out there, covered from head to toe in the stuff.

I flinched at a sharp whistle, and my gaze flew from the mud-covered boys to the large man who was now issuing sharp commands to them. All the boys stopped what they were doing to look up at him like he was some kind of god. I knew he was a popular teacher, but this kind of hero worship was ridiculous. After a few more commands in his deep voice, the boys fanned out into two lines, one side drop-kicking the ball to the other to catch.

"That's it, boys!" Mr Hargreaves shouted, his deep voice shooting right through me and making my stomach clench. "It's all about the timing. Much better, Jack! Good lad."

I picked my way across the uneven ground, ruining my beautiful four-inch heels in the process while trying to stay upright. When I was a few feet away from him and close enough to see the way his biceps strained under his mud-splattered t-shirt, I very nearly lost my nerve. But then his head turned towards me, gorgeous dark brown eyes locking with mine, and I froze.

He blinked a couple of times in shock, then proceeded to do a full body scan before his gaze came back to mine, and he smiled. My breath left me in a sudden whoosh. For the life of me I couldn't remember why I was there. That gorgeous smile, the white teeth in his bearded, tanned face short-circuited my brain.

"Lady Harding," he said as he turned towards me, tilting his head to the side. "Can I help you?"

"I-I…"

His smile widened as he took a step towards me, but it dimmed somewhat when I took a corresponding one back, almost toppling over when my heel dug into the soft ground again.

"Careful, love," he said, his low voice soft now. "Not sure those shoes are built for these pitches. Did you need something?"

"Yes, I…" Oh God, come on Claire! Why wasn't my brain cooperating? I cleared my throat, trying to draw up the vision of my daughter's tear-streaked face. I was there for Florrie and the rest of the girls. I needed to give this man a piece of my mind. "Mr Hargreaves, I—"

"Callum."

"What?"

"Call me Callum." He wasn't asking, he was demanding, and for some reason it sent a shiver up my spine.

I shook my head. "It would be inappropriate for me to address a teacher in such a way in front of the children and I—"

"There's no kids in earshot, love," he told me as he took another couple of steps towards me. I would have moved back again, but my legs were shaking now and I didn't quite trust myself to manage it without falling on my arse. "You can call me Callum."

"Of course there are…" I trailed off as I checked behind me to see no sign of Florrie or Hayley. I gritted my teeth. Where the bloody hell had those girls gone?

"Now, why have you trekked out here over to me? You're stunning in that get-up, but it won't hold up long out here."

My face flooded with heat. Stunning? I was wearing a cream sheath dress with a fitted jacket over the top as we'd had a board meeting for the Buckingham Estate that afternoon. It was hardly stunning.

"I don't think that's appropriate either," I whispered.

"Sorry, sweetheart," he said through a grin, not sounding sorry at all.

"Heads up!" I heard a shout from the pitch and turned just in time to see a rugby ball sailing towards my head. With a high-pitched squeal and fully expecting to be slammed right in the face, I flinched backwards, immediately losing my balance as my heel dug into the soft mud. I braced for impact, but instead of hitting the ground, Callum's arm shot out around my back, drawing me up against his hard chest. His other free hand snatched the ball from mid-air before it could connect with my face. He threw the ball back towards the boys, not breaking eye contact with me for a moment.

I could feel his muscles flexing underneath my hands on his chest. The smell of his aftershave mixed with fresh mud and clean man made me feel lightheaded.

My gaze fell to his mouth and for a mad moment I really thought I was going to kiss him, right there in front of his entire rugby team. His arm flexed on my back, his biceps bunching, and I was reminded of how powerful a man he was. My ex was half Callum's size, and he had done enough damage to me when we were together. This man could crush me like a bug.

I cleared my throat and pushed against his chest. He scanned my face for a long moment before his eyes flashed and he reluctantly pulled back, using both his large hands to steady me on my upper arms and make sure I wasn't going to fall before he stepped back.

"Boys!" he shouted, and all twenty of them looked over to him. "Clear up the balls now and off to the changing rooms. Good session today."

All the boys started picking up the balls and returning them to the bag in the centre of the pitch. I waited as Callum went out to help. He ruffled one of the smaller lad's hair and said something to him which made him break into a huge smile, then slapped a couple of the other boys on the back as he passed them. All of them were smiling at him, none of them seemed to mind the fact that they were completely covered in mud.

"Right then," he said to me as he strode back over. "As I asked before, Lady Harding. How can I help?"

He stood in front of me with his arms crossed over his broad chest and I swallowed, the sheer bulk of him making me feel intimidated again. Just then a gust of bitter wind swept across the exposed pitch, and I shivered. He frowned down at me before turning around abruptly, reaching into the bag beside him and pulling out a huge long-sleeved rugby jersey.

"Arms up," he said, and I blinked up at him.

"W-what?"

"Lift your arms, sweetheart."

I'm not sure whether it was the soft but firm delivery of that command, or how unbelievably attracted I was to him, but I lifted both arms immediately.

"Good girl," he muttered as he pulled the rugby jersey over my head.

The head rush I felt at that growly voice giving me those two words of praise was so strong I almost wobbled on my feet again. The jersey smelt deliciously of him and it fell almost to my knees. I had to push the sleeves up a ridiculous amount to even find my hands. He smiled at me again.

"You alive in there, love?"

Oh my God. I was just standing there, staring up at the man like I'd had some sort of stroke, and I'd let him dress me like a child. I was a thirty-six-year-old mother, for Christ's sake.

"Mr Hargreaves." My voice came out a little strangled, and I swallowed before continuing. "It had been brought to my attention that as the head of sport you are not prioritising the girls' games appropriately. My daughter and my niece deserve just as much school resources as your rugby players. They have just as much right to train under floodlights as any other sports team, and I—"

"What exactly did that little shit-stirrer tell you now?" he asked.

"How dare you call my daughter a shit-stirrer?" I snapped, my hands going to my hips, although the effect was slightly ruined by the fact my sleeves had fallen down. The man was smiling! How dare he? Here I was giving him a thorough dressing down and he had the gall to smile in my face. "She's raised some serious concerns, and I—"

I broke off when I realised he was looking over my shoulder, not focusing on what I was saying any more. He pointed two of his fingers of one hand to his eyes then pointed one of them at something behind me. I turned just in time to catch a glimpse of Florrie and Hayley scurrying away around the corner.

"What are you—?"

"You've been played, lass," he told me as his eyes went back to mine. "That little shit-stirrer daughter of yours has played you."

"Sh-she what?"

"I'm the one *advocating* for floodlights to be installed over the netball courts. I've been pushing for the girls to have access to rugby and football as well, if they want to. It's ridiculous to restrict them to netball and hockey. They should be able to play whatever bloody sport they like. I've even taken it to the board of governors."

I shook my head. "I don't understand. Florrie wouldn't—"

He snorted. "Are we talking about the same girl here?"

I narrowed my eyes at him. "She was crying, for God's sake. She was totally distraught, and I... oh, bollocks." I remembered the consent form I'd signed last term. "Bloody speech and drama. That shitbag."

He laughed. The rich sound so glorious that I almost leaned into him. When he looked down at me his eyes were dancing.

"Well, I'm very sorry for wasting your time," I said, taking a couple of stumbling steps back. "I've no idea why she would have—"

"I think you do," he told me in a low voice, stalking closer.

I shook my head in shaky jerks. "No. I can't imagine why—"

"*I* think you *can* imagine plenty of things when it comes to me."

I blinked in shock. "I-I have no idea what you're talking about. Th-this entire conversation is completely inappropriate and I... gah!"

One of my heels sank far into the ground again, and I nearly fell for the third bloody time, but, of course, his hand shot out to my elbow to steady me. Then, before I knew it, I was practically lifted off my feet and propelled across the uneven ground with Callum's arm supporting me under my ribs. He didn't break stride as he rounded the corner into the sports hall and then through a door which led to a large office. He shut the door behind us and I stumbled away from him.

"W-what are you doing?" I breathed, looking around him to the exit which he was blocking. That uneasy, unsafe feeling that I bloody hated started bubbling to the surface and I swallowed.

I never used to feel like this. Before I was married to Blake nothing scared me. But it was like the scales had been ripped away from my eyes as far as men were concerned now. Their superior physical strength and their capacity to hurt me weren't ever considerations before, but now they were always at the forefront of my mind. So when Callum reached for me, I did the one thing I hated doing above all else. I flinched.

"Shit!" he swore in a horrified voice. "Claire, I'm sorry. I'm not going to hurt you, lass."

"Of c-course," I stuttered, tucking my hair behind my ears in an attempt to cover my movement, but it was already too late.

"Listen. I'm going to move away from the door, okay?" His voice was so gentle now that it almost brought tears to my eyes. "I'm not trapping you here. I don't want to hurt you. I just wanted to speak to you for a minute. I'm sorry, love. I shouldn't have scared you like that."

"I-I-I'm not scared."

"Okay, you're not scared." His voice was still gentle as he moved back with his hands up in surrender as if I was a wild animal he didn't want to spook.

Once he'd moved out of the way, I walked to the door, but something stopped me from reaching for the handle. Now that I didn't feel trapped, I could take a deep breath and start to calm down.

"I'm sorry for having a go at you out there," I said. "My daughter can be… a handful. God knows what she's trying to achieve with this, though, other than embarrassing the hell out of me."

"Your daughter wants you to be happy."

I turned to look up at him and frowned.

"What on earth are you talking about?"

He tilted his head to the side. "You're attracted to me."

"Don't be absurd!" I snapped.

"You're attracted to me, and it scares you shitless."

"That's insane," I whispered, and he shook his head slowly.

"I didn't understand it before," he said as he took a slow step towards me, giving me a chance to escape if I wanted to. "The parents' evenings when you wouldn't meet my eye, the matches where you ran off before I could talk to you about Florrie."

I scoffed. "As if you would have had a chance to talk to me from under the pile of desperate housewives throwing themselves at you."

I wasn't the only mum at the school with a Callum fixation, but the others made their interest much more obvious. To be honest, it made my blood boil when they crowded round him, laughing and touching his chest, complimenting his coaching, bringing him cakes. I told myself that it was because of how vulgar they were being in front of the children, but really I knew that…

"Jealous, Lady Harding?" Callum said in a low voice as he stalked closer.

I swallowed. "No, of course not."

He was so close now that I could smell that delicious earthy but clean scent again, and my head started to swim.

"You know I don't want any of those women, right?"

"Y-you don't?"

He shook his head. "Nope. You see, there's this one woman I can't stop thinking about. I catch her looking at me, but she won't let herself come close. Every time I think I'm getting somewhere she runs away."

"I don't run away."

"You ran away last weekend."

He'd moved even closer then, towering over me as my back pressed up against the door, his electric masculine energy all around me.

I waited for the fear, but as his eyes looked into mine, my body started to relax, as if I could see straight through to his soul, see that he wasn't going to harm me, that he would *never* harm me. It was quite uncanny.

Last weekend had been the fundraising ball for the school, and I'd put more effort into looking perfect than I would have done for even the highest society party. If I was honest with myself, I'd done it for him. And it had been worth it when he saw me and an almost fierce look crossed his expression.

"Lady Harding," he'd breathed as he scanned my outfit after he'd stalked over to me. I'd swayed towards him, but a glass breaking next to us startled me out of my trance, and I blinked before stepping back into the crowd to find Ollie and Lottie, who I stuck with for the rest of the night. Unfortunately, Callum got on with Ollie like a house on fire, so there was still no avoiding him. But with my brother right there I wasn't so scared. I could let myself listen to Callum's deep Scottish voice and stare at him surreptitiously to my heart's content.

But Ollie wasn't here now.

"I did not run away," I said, trying for an indignant tone, but it came out more breathless than put out. Callum was simply too close for me to process anything properly. He smiled that gorgeous smile again, and I stopped breathing altogether. This close up, he was so beautiful it was almost unreal.

"Yes, you did, love. And then you hid behind your brother all night."

"Don't be absurd. Of course I—"

"But that's okay," he cut me off in a soft voice. "Because I know why now, don't I?"

"I-I don't know what you're—"

"You've been hurt."

I shook my head, panic building in my chest. "I—"

"Don't lie to me, sweetheart," he said in that low rumbly voice. His hand came up very slowly towards my face. "Is this okay?" he whispered.

I hesitated for a moment but then let out a long breath and nodded. The need for his touch overriding the fear. His huge hand moved to my jawline then, his calloused fingers brushing my cheek, spanning along my jawline into my hair.

"Let's try this again," he murmured, his lips almost touching mine now. "You've been hurt, haven't you?"

I nodded once against his hand and his eyes flashed with fury briefly before he tamped it down.

"I'm sorry, love." The gentleness in his voice made my eyes sting. I had to blink to try and push back the tears, but one spilled over onto my cheek. His thumb came up to sweep it away. "How could anyone hurt something so beautiful?"

It was all too much. His heartbreaking gentleness, his intoxicating smell, the feel of being surrounded by his big body and the irony of how safe that made me feel, all combined to push me over the edge.

My hands came up and slid into his hair as I went up on tiptoes and sealed my mouth over his. He started in shock for a moment, but just as I was about to pull away, his other hand shot around my back, lifting me up and against his hard body as he deepened the kiss, his tongue sweeping into my mouth. He then lifted me up higher and my legs came up to circle his hips before he turned to walk us back towards the desk in the centre of the room. Without breaking the kiss, he swept all manner of rugby and sports paraphernalia onto the floor before pulling his rugby jersey off me in a sudden movement and lying me back onto the wood surface. His mouth broke with mine to kiss across to my jaw and I moved against him almost desperately.

"Callum," I breathed, and he smiled against my neck.

"That's it, baby," he rumbled. "I knew you'd say my name eventually."

I smiled as his mouth moved back to mine, then moaned when his hardness moved against my core. Just as I felt I might tip over the edge (it had been an extremely long time since I'd been anywhere near a man, and I'd never been with one quite so bloody gorgeous before), Callum broke the kiss and froze. I blinked up at him.

"W-what?" As reality filtered back in, I registered the boys' voices beyond the door of his office. "Shit."

He smiled down at me. "Probably better the lads don't catch me pinning one of the mums to my desk."

"Probably," I squeaked.

He pulled back and I immediately missed his incredible warmth. As I struggled up to sitting, still in a bit of a daze, he helped me with his large hand under my elbow then lifted me off the desk onto my unsteady feet.

"Sorry, love," he said, not sounding sorry at all. "I've messed up that pretty little outfit with my big muddy paws."

I looked down at my cream suit. There were dark handprints all over my sides and likely on my back. Good God, why was that so bloody sexy? My face flushed.

"Not to worry," I said in a choked voice, wondering how I was going to explain this to the girls. A sense of almost crippling loss washed over me then when I realised we were going to have to leave the office and go back to the real world, where big, sexy Scotsmen didn't routinely pin me down to desks and almost make me come with just a kiss. I swallowed down my disappointment as I slipped my shoe back on, which had fallen off during the desk antics.

"Mum?" I stiffened when I heard Florrie's voice from the corridor.

"Bugger," I muttered under my breath, smoothing my hair down and trying to brush off the mud from my jacket, but it was a losing battle. Callum strode over to the door and pulled it open, totally unbothered.

"Florrie, Hayley," he called and the girls both appeared in the doorway. Florrie looked between me and Callum. Colour rose in my cheeks as her gaze dropped to my ruined jacket. Her eyes twinkled, and a wide smile broke across her face as she elbowed Hayley.

"I told you!" she said to her in an excited whisper and Hayley rolled her eyes but still smiled just as big as Florrie. I looked between the girls, reaching for a stern expression, but with my lips still stinging from Callum's kiss, I knew I wasn't quite managing it.

"You girls lied to me," I said, still trying to be stern and still missing the mark.

"Ugh! Mum, honestly," Florrie said. "We had to do *something.* You fancy the pants off the man, and Mr Hargreaves is cool."

"You can both call me Callum outside of school hours," Callum said as he ruffled Florrie's hair. "Now, if you wee tinkers are quite finished with your meddling, you can get Lady Harding home."

"Sorry, Claire," Hayley's soft voice put in, and I looked over to where she was standing with an unsure expression. I smiled at her.

"Darling, I'm quite sure this was all my daughter's idea," I said as I walked over to her and stroked the side of her head. "Don't you worry about it."

I straightened and then looked up at Callum, getting lost in his warm brown eyes for a moment before I blinked and shook my head to clear it.

"R-right, best be off."

He'd all but dismissed us by telling the girls to take me home, hadn't he? He'd probably had enough of the Harding family antics. I really needed to rein Florrie in. She was getting out of—

"You'd better nip home and change first," he said, then put in casually, "I'll meet you lot there."

"Meet us? Er… what do you…?"

Then my view of the girls was cut off by his big body. I blinked up at his smiling face before he leaned down and, right there in front of the girls, brushed his lips against mine. I wobbled on my heels, and his hands came up to steady me before he turned me towards the exit. "Off you go then, beautiful," he told me.

"Florrie," I said as I walked on unsteady feet across the courtyard towards the car. "Where is that man meeting us?"

"Oh, we're all going out for dinner. Uncle Ollie, Auntie Lottie and Hails as well."

I shook my head as I opened the door for the girls.

"Florrie, honestly, what are you trying to achieve here?"

"Mum, just go with it," she cried.

"I'm still not very pleased about the lies, young lady."

Florrie rolled her eyes and climbed into the car. I thought Hayley was going to climb in after her but she closed the door instead and turned to me, laying her small hand on my arm.

"She just wants you to be happy, Auntie Claire," Hayley said in a soft voice.

"Oh, darling," I said as I gave her a side hug. "I'm already happy with you lot."

Hayley shook her head. "She wants more for you. We all do. And to be honest, today is actually my fault. Lottie and I, we could see how you watched him."

My cheeks flooded with heat. Christ, had I been that obvious?

"We notice things others might miss," Hayley went on as if reading my mind, which was actually quite normal for her. Lottie and Hayley could read people with almost unnatural precision. "So I'm the one that planted the idea. I didn't quite agree with Florrie's method but..." she trailed off, then her gaze dropped to the muddy handprints on my sides, then back to my face. "It seems to have worked."

I laughed. "Yes, I suppose it has."

Her smile dimmed as she reached out and took my hand in hers.

"He's safe, Auntie Claire," she told me. "We can sense that too. You'll be safe with him."

I cleared my throat as I felt my eyes sting. "Thank you, lovely girl," I whispered. She gave me a nod and then pulled the car door open to climb in.

I stared down at my ruined, muddy heels for a moment, letting all the memories of the last half hour flood through me, and I smiled.

ACKNOWLEDGEMENTS

I will start by thanking my wonderful sensitivity readers who helped me so much with the manuscript, and huge thanks to the readers from my ARC team with lived experience of Autism who were kind enough to read very early copies and give up their time to send me invaluable feedback on *Outlier.*

Of course, thanks also to all my readers. I never dreamt that people would take the time to read the stories I have thought up in my quirky brain, and I am honoured beyond words. I am eternally grateful to the reviewers who have taken a chance on me – your feedback has made all the difference to the books and is the reason I've been able to make writing not just a passion, but a career.

Susie's Book Badgers – you are wonderful humans, and your support means the world.

My fantastic alpha readers – Jane, Jess, Small Suse, Aurelia, Carly, Jane, Ruth, Katie and Andy – your feedback was essential and much appreciated.

Thank you to my agent, Lorella Belli, for your support and encouragement.

To Jo Edwards, my brilliant editor and dear friend – thank you, thank you, and I'm so sorry about all the semicolons!

Thanks also to my publisher, Keeperton. I've been chuffed to bits with your excitement for the Daydreamer series and for *Outlier.*

Last but not least, thanks to my very own romantic hero. I love you and the boys to the moon and back.

ABOUT THE AUTHOR

Susie Tate is a #1 Amazon bestselling author of addictive, feel-good contemporary romance. She can be counted on to deliver uplifting but also heart-wrenching stories that make her readers laugh and cry in equal measure. Her charismatic but flawed heroes have to work hard to earn their heroine's forgiveness but always manage to redeem themselves in the end.

The real and raw themes that underpin Susie's books are often inspired by her experiences working as a doctor in the NHS for the last twenty years. Susie worked in a range of hospital specialities before becoming a GP, during which time she looked after a women's refuge for victims of domestic violence as well as being child safeguarding lead for her practice. Susie's medical career gives her a unique insight and understanding of the social, psychological and physical issues some of her characters face, lending authenticity to her writing.

Susie lives in beautiful Dorset with her wonderful husband, three gorgeous boys and even more wonderful dog. Her very own romantic hero and husband, Andy, suffers from Motor Neurone Disease (aka ALS). Susie's career as an author has allowed her to spend more crucial time with Andy and their boys after this devastating diagnosis. Susie and Andy work to raise awareness about MND/ALS and support charities like the MNDA and My Name5 Doddie, who are searching for a cure and supporting sufferers.

Connect with Arndell

Love this book? Discover your next romance book obsession and stay up to date with the latest releases, exclusive content, and behind-the-scenes news!

Explore More Books

Visit our homepage: keeperton.com/arndell

Follow Us on Social Media

Instagram: @arndellbooks
Facebook: Arndell
TikTok: @arndellbooks

Stay in the Loop

Join our newsletter: keeperton.com/subscribe

Join the Conversation

Use **#Arndell** or **#ArndellBooks** to share your thoughts and connect with fellow romance readers!

Thank you for being part of our book-loving community. We can't wait to share more unforgettable stories with you!